THE GIRL
IN TWO WORLDS

Time travel to Ancient Athens

by

J M Newsome

The Connection Trilogy
The Boy in Two Minds
The Girl in Two Worlds
An Ancient Connection

Birkby Books

Praise for 'The Boy in Two Minds'
(originally titled *The Boy with Two Heads*)
Prequel to 'The Girl in Two Worlds'

"A very clever concept for time travel. … I'm loving it … !" *Caroline Lawrence*, author of *The Roman Mysteries* series and the *Time Travel Diaries*, on Twitter.

"This book transported me effortlessly back to ancient Greece, vividly evoking its exotic sights, sounds and even smells. And it seems that young people's issues have hardly changed in 2,400 years!" *Marion Clarke*, fiction editor.

"A wonderful story which brings the ancient Olympics to vibrant life. You can almost smell Greece from its pages … I was so engrossed by the story and the dramatic climax that I did not realise how much I had learnt until it was all over." *Philippa Harrison*, former Managing Director of Macmillan and Little Brown UK.

"… extremely well written, highly believable and engaging … I would love to see this book used in schools, because the aspects of every day life in Ancient Greece are so cleverly and easily portrayed here." *Fiona Robson* on Goodreads.

"This was a very engaging read. Lovers of the Grecian era will find it interesting, and the blog is a good twist." *Prudence* on Amazon.

" … a story on different levels, from different points of view. It brings ancient Greece to life, … excellent … well-researched … well-written story." *Sally Katherine Bracher* on Amazon.

" … well written with plenty smells (*sic*), intrigue and pace to keep the reader wanting to turn the next page …" *Anne Bryson* on Goodreads.

" … enthralling read, I did not want to put the book down." *Bill* on Amazon Kindle.

Also by J M Newsome

Fiction:

Maria's Dilemma (Richmond Readers, level 1)
Saturday Storm (Richmond Readers, level 2)
Nelson's Dream (CUP, Cambridge English Readers, level 6)
Winner of 2009 Language Learner Literature Award
Dragons' Eggs (CUP, Cambridge English Readers, level 5)
Winner of 2011 Language Learner Literature Award
Better Late Than Never (CUP, Cambridge English Readers, level 5)
The Connection Trilogy (Birkby Books)
1. The Boy in Two Minds
2. The Girl in Two Worlds
3. An Ancient Connection

Translation:

Europa
(Ammos Editions, Athens)
(Modern Greek to English)
Vergina: Treasures, Myths and History of Ancient Macedonia
(Ammos Editions, Athens)
(Modern Greek to English)

Contents

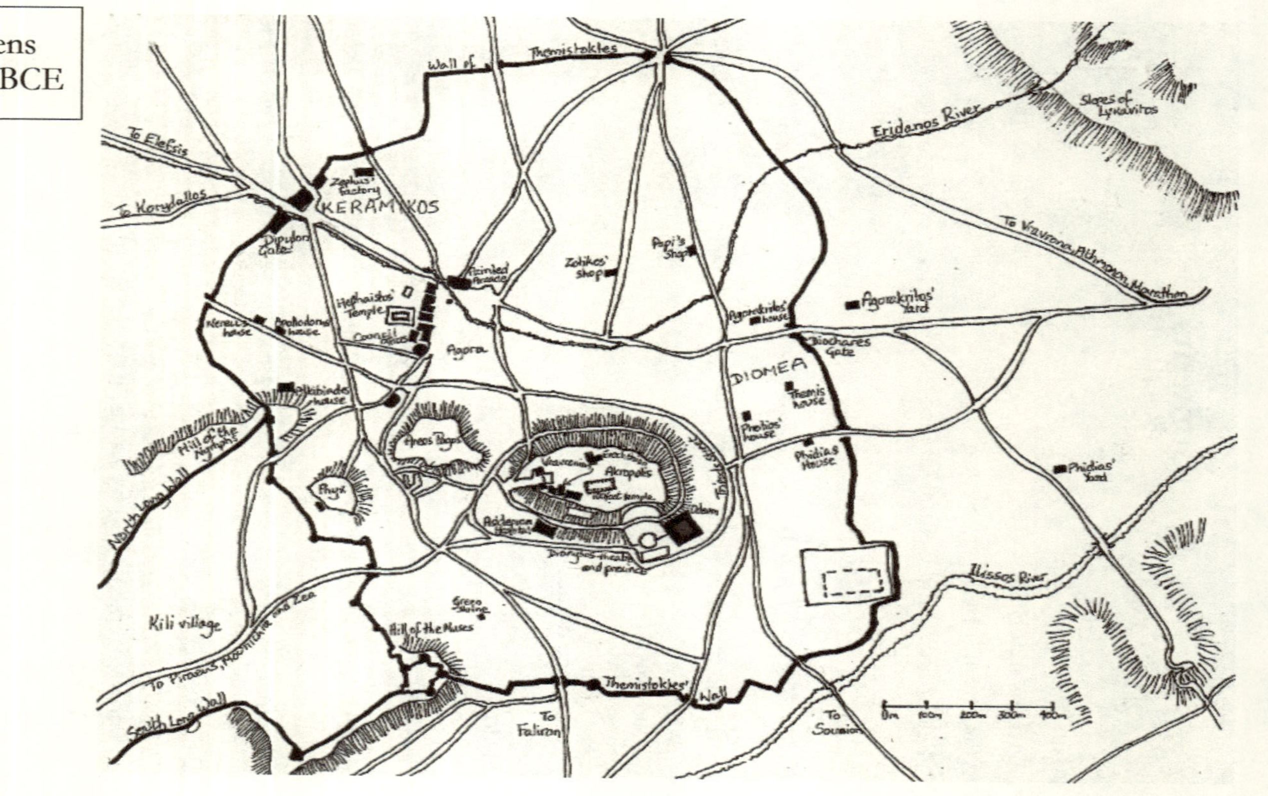

Athens
420 BCE
Wall of Themistokles
To Elefsis
To Korydallos
Eridanos River
Slopes of Lykavitos
KERAMIKOS
Zophus' Factory
Dipylon Gate
Painted Arcade
Papi's Shop
Zotikos' shop
To Vavrona, Athmonon, Marathon
Hephaistos' Temple
Nereus' house
Apollodoros' house
Council House
Agora
Agorakritos' house
Agorakritos' Yard
Diochares Gate
DIOMEA
Themis' house
Alkibiades house
Areos Pagos
Phidias' house
Phidias' House
Phidias' Yard
Hill of the Nymphs
North Long Wall
Pnyx
Vravronia
Enclosure
Akropolis
Nike temple
Asklepion Hospital
Dionysos theatre and precinct
Odeon
Ilissos River
Grave Shrine
Kili village
Hill of the Muses
To Piraeus, Mounichia and Zea
South Long Wall
Themistokles' Wall
To Faliron
To Sounion
0m 100m 200m 300m 400m

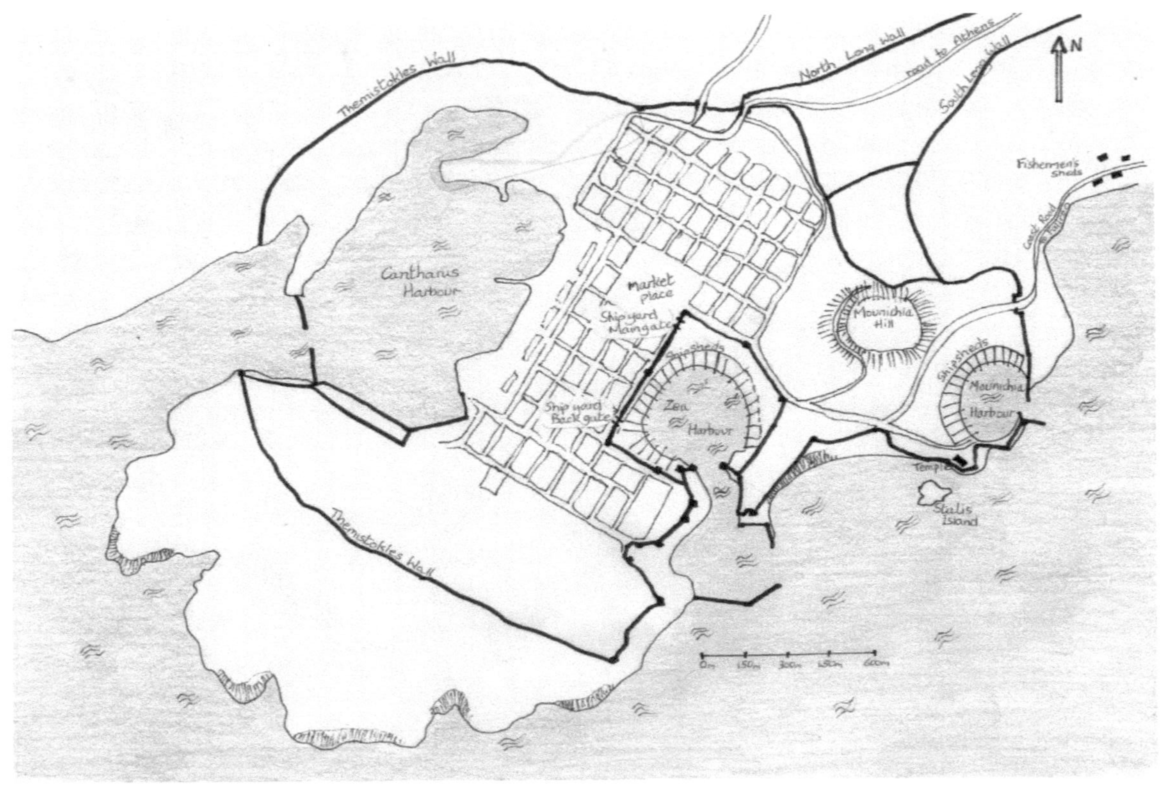

Piraeus
420 BCE

Central
Greece
420 BCE
EVIA/EUBOEA
Halchis
DELPHI
Kirrha
VIOTIA/
BOEOTIA
THIVAI/THEBES
Marathon
Athmonon
ATHENS
Piraeus
Vravrona/
Brauron
ATTICA
Lavrion
PATRA
Heraion
Akraia
Isthmus
Diolkos
KORINTHOS
ELIS
Nemea
Tenea
Fleves Is
Orchomenos
Mykines
Egina/
Aegina Is
Olympia
Mantinea
Argive
Heraion
Epidavrus
Sounion
Pheia
ARGOS
Kios
Nafplia
Methana
Tegea
Ydra Is
N
Farai
SPARTA
LAKONIA/LACEDAEMONIA
10km 0 10 20 30 40km

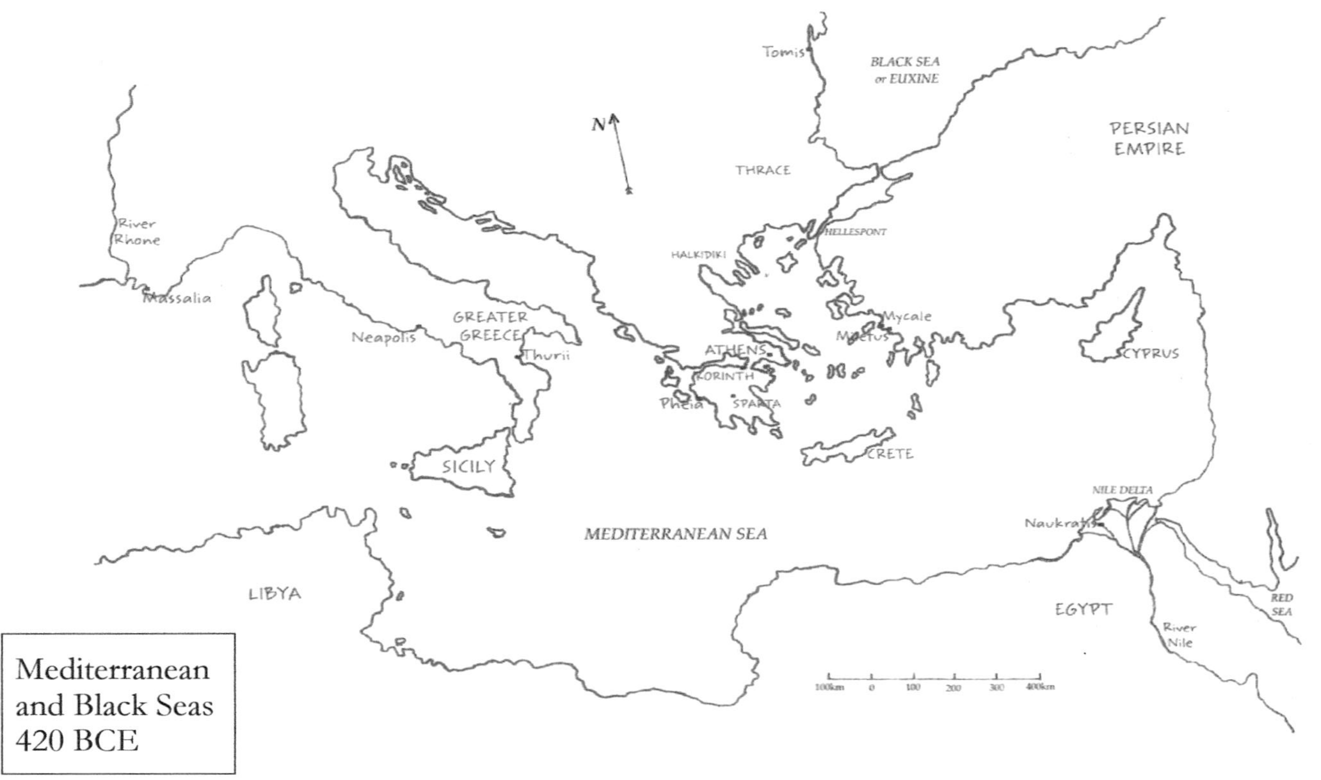

Mediterranean
and Black Seas
420 BCE

Characters

The spellings used here are almost all based on Modern, not Ancient, Greek pronunciation. The debate as to what the Ancients sounded like continues. So, rather than try to resolve a centuries' old academic controversy, I've used modern versions of the ancient names except for the few most well-known. People who really existed are marked with an asterisk (*).

Ancient Greek gods and mythical figures are in a separate list after the mortals. The name Themis can be either male or female, referring to someone called Themistokles (male), or to the goddess of justice and natural law (female).

Athens and the Peloponnese 418 BC

Adrasteia, Anthoussa's personal slave
*Agis, King of Sparta
*Agorakritos, sculptor, student/colleague of Phidias
*Alkamenes, sculptor, student/colleague of Phidias
*Alkibiades, Athenian celebrity and politician, intermittently general
Androklos, Athenian healer, army friend of Themistokles
Anthoussa, Agorakritos' wife, Melissa's mother
*Antiphon, chief Athenian Archon 418 to 417 BCE
Apollodorus of Melite, Commander, Athens City Watch 419 to 418 BCE
*Archias, chief Athenian Archon 419 to 418 BCE
Arianos, former physical training tutor, now farm steward
Ariphron, Photios' cousin, now living in Miletus
Asterodia, priestess of Athena and Demeter, mother of Xenovia
Astrapi, Diodotos' cavalry mare
Belos, Athenian cheese-maker and rower
Benefactor (the), anonymous instigator of possible treason
*Brasidas, Spartan general
Canthus, Chloe's eldest son
Chilon, defence engineer of Argos
Chloe, Themistokles' younger sister
Damianos, superintendent of Naval Shipyards, Piraeus
Damon, Scythian archer
*Demosthenes, Athenian general, deceased
Diodotos, Themistokles' older brother
Efthalia, Leokratis' wife, Themistokles' aunt in Massalia
Eirini, Themistokles' mother
Epifanios of Kephisia, neighbouring farmer at Athmonon
Eryx, Athens Planning Department civil servant
Esperos of Massalia, boy boxer, Themistokles' opponent at 87th Olympiad
Eteokles son of Adrastos, member of Diodotos' supper club

Evanthi, Diodotos lover in Argos
Evrisakes, Athenian sculptor in wood
Frog, Themistokles' personal slave and friend
Glykon, in Themistokles' supper club
Gulkishar, former scribe to Phidias
Hermione, Agorakritos' sister from Paros
Hipparchos, Chloe's husband
Hyllos, an Athens Planning Department boss
Ilarion, member of Diodotos' supper club
Inaros, waiter at the Leather Sleeve tavern, Piraeus
Iole, paid female companion or hetaira
Ismini, Eirini's friend, wife of Phidias
Judge Iasos, Anthoussa's father, living in Elis
Kallias, erascible Athenian politician
Kallias, playwright, cousin of other Kallias
Kallikrates, Athenian sculptor and architect of parts of the Akropolis
*Kallimachos, Athenian sculptor
Kalliope, female slave in Themistokles' country household
Kallistos of the Diomea, Themistokles' father, deceased
*Kleomachos of Magnesia, victor at 89th Olympiad in men's boxing
*Laches, Athenian general, commander of Themis' unit
Leila, Melissa's personal slave
Leokratis, Zephyros' and Eirini's brother, Themistokles' uncle in Massalia
Leontis, Photios' father, trierarch
Lidha, sex worker at Zotikos' massage parlour
Linas, fisherman from Piraeus
Lukos, fisherman from Piraeus
Lysikles, Commander of Athens City Watch 418 to 417 BCE
*Lysimache, contemporary priestess of Athena in Athens
Lythaia, acolyte of Hera at the Heraion of Argos
Madam Magda, Egyptian sex educator
Melanas, male slave in Themis' country household
Menelaus, Themis' brother in law, deceased
Menestratus of Milesia, suspected criminal
Melissa, daughter of Themistokles' friend Agorakritos, artist and clerk
Melissus, son of Themistokles' friend Agorakritos, artist, apprentice sculptor
Mika, female slave in Themistokles' city household
Mikro, young male slave in Themistokles' country household
Mistress Karina, pharmacist
Myrto, Themistokles' older sister, deceased
Nereus, Athenian general, trader
*Nikias, important Athenian general and peace-maker
Nikodemos, owner of the Wings of Victory tavern, Piraeus

*Nikostratos, Athenian general in Peloponnesian campaign
Niovi, Diodotos' first choice for wife
Numa, slave in Photios' household
Nurse (Old) employed intermittently by Anthoussa
Old Yellow, dog Themistokles' acquired in Olympia in 432 BCE, deceased
Orcus, Photios' shield slave, Numa's son
*Panainos, Themis' uncle, Eirini's cousin, Phidias' brother, master painter
*Pantarkes, Phidias' companion
Parilios, Themistokles' gelding horse
Persian (the), mercenary
*Phidias, Themistokles' uncle, Eirini's cousin, famous sculptor and architect
Philomena, sister of Adrasteia, slave in Agorakritos' household
Photios, Themistokles' classmate and friend
*Polykleitos, sculptor from Argos, Phidias' rival
Popi, shopkeeper and apothicary, ex slave
Portheus, priest of Eros in Athens
Protos, boy slave, son of Melanas, in Themistokles' country household
Rizos, student of Sokrates
Scythian Archers, the security forces of the City of Athens
Skionian (the), slave in Themistokles' city household
Skopas, Melissa's younger brother
Sokrates, Athenian philosopher and one-time mason
Straton, Themis' school-days enemy
Sunny, a black horse
Talaos, new superintendent of Naval Shipyards, Piraeus
Tanu, groom slave in Themistokles' city household
Terpsichore, marriageable girl who interests Photios
Themis/Themistokles, son of Kallistos
*Themistokles, son of Neokles, Athenian general, long deceased
*Timanthes of Kythnos, artist and painter
Timnes, door slave at Photios' and Leontis' house
Tryfonos, merchant
Tydeus, a hooded man
Tyro, prospective wife for Diodotos
Warden of Athens prison
Xenovia, one-time priestess of Athena, daughter of Asterodia
Yellow, Themistokles' dog
Zephus, Master potter, factory owner
Zephyros, Eirini's brother, Themistokles' uncle from the far West
Zotikos, owner of the 'Corner of Paradise', herb shop and massage parlour

England, 2017

Bernie, friend of Suzanne's from school
Cassie, Suzanne's previous athletics trainer in Carlisle
David, athlete at the French training camp
Grandad, Suzanne's grandfather in Florida
Jenkins, Mrs, Suzanne's mother
Keir, athletics coach at Mid Lancashire Athletics Club
Lawson, Dr, professor of Sport and Exercise Dept, Lancaster University
Natasha, Suzanne's second year flatmate
Penny, Suzanne's third year artistic housemate
Ron, Suzanne's boyfriend
Sears, Mr, neurosurgeon in Durham
Short, Mr, Dan, Suzanne's father
Suzanne Short, sometimes called Suzz, 2nd yr student at Lancaster University
Theo, Natasha's boyfriend

Ancient Greek gods and mythical figures

Agamemnon, mythological King of Mykines, brother of Menelaos, as told in
The Iliad
Aphrodite, goddess of love, married to Hephaistos, daughter (or sister) of
Zeus
Apollo, god of the sun, the arts, living souls, son of Zeus
Arion, famous wealthy musician
Artemis, goddess of virginity, the hunt, the moon, twin of Apollo
Asklepios, god of healing
Athena, goddess of wisdom, guardian of Athens, daughter of Zeus
Circe, mythological enchantress of great beauty
Demeter, goddess of agriculture, harvest, the seasons, fertility, sister of Zeus
Dionysos, god of wine, madness, and theatre
Hades, god of the dead and the Underworld, brother of Zeus
Helen, wife of Menelaos, King of Sparta, the Trojan War was fought over
her
Hephaistos, god of crafts and metalworking, son of Zeus
Hera, goddess of marriage, patroness of women, wife of Zeus
Herakles, mythical hero, demi-god, one of the Argonauts
Hermes, messenger of the gods, conductor of souls to Hades, son of Zeus, a
bit of a rogue
Homer, ancient poet
Menelaos, mythological King of Sparta as told in *The Iliad*
Nike, goddess of victory
Odysseus, mythological King of Ithaca, hero of *The Odyssey*
Pan, god of the countryside

Persephone, daughter of Demeter, abducted by Hades to the Underworld for the winter months each year
Poseidon, god of the sea, brother of Zeus
Zeus, father of the gods

Greek words used in the story

Agora: open space in a city used for a market and other municipal functions.
Amphora: large, earthenware storage jar, some were larger than a man.
Andron: room used only by men for eating and socializing and as a study.
Archon: magistrate/city official. In Athens, one of nine chosen by lot each summer. Generals, and a small number of other officials dealing with security and the treasury, were elected.
Chiton: pronounced 'kite-on' in English(but *hitona* in modern Greek). This is the main garment or robe worn by men and women. It fell from the shoulders almost to the ground, hitched over a belt or sash tied round the waist or hips. Slaves and children and men working, hunting or riding, wore shorter versions.
Drachma: unit of currency, worth six obols which were originally bars of iron before coins were made. The word drachma comes from the Ancient Greek for hold or grab. An average man could hold six of the bar obols in his hand.
Hellas: The name for Greece in Ancient Greek. The modern Greek for Greece is Elladha, a different form of the same name. **Hellenic** is the adjective, and **Hellenes** are the people.
Hetaira: paid female companion for cultured company and possibly sex.
Himation: outer garment or cloak usually fastened round the neck or on the shoulder, sometimes long, sometimes shorter, often with a hood.
Hoplite: citizen foot-soldier, usually armed with a spear and shield.
Hundred-foot temple: (in Greek Ekatopedon) later called the Parthenon, it was known by this name at the time it was built.
Kithara: stringed musical instrument similar to a lyre.
Klepsydra: timer using measured volumes of water.
Kylix: drinking cup, usually for wine.
Median: Persian.
Megaron: large, high room, usually with a circular hearth in the middle.
Metic: welcome immigrant without citizen's rights.
Nike: Victory. The abstract quality, and the goddess believed to crown victors
Obol: one sixth of a Drachma.
Oinochoi: wine-mixing bowl or jar.
Paean: song or hymn of triumph or thanksgiving.
Peplos: full-length garment worn by women, hanging from the shoulders, with a deep outer layer to the belted waist.

Stade, stades: measure of length, 1 stade was approximately 200 yards or metres, the length of a stadium. It varied. Five stades were approximately equivalent to our kilometre, 8.8 to our mile.

Strophion: a band of fabric tied tightly over their breasts by women.

Symposium: a drinking party for men, usually involving an evening meal and discussion of serious topics, at least to start with.

Thalamios, thalamites: rower, rowers in the bottom tier.

Thranitis, thranites: rower, rowers in the upper tier of a trireme.

Trierarch: donator and/or commander of a trireme.

Trireme: war ship powered by three tiers of rowers and sail.

Xestis: measure of volume, liquid or solid, about half a litre.

Zygios, zygites: rower, rowers in the middle tier of a trireme.

Ancient Greek place names
as they often appear, and as they appear here:

Aegina	Egina
Eleusis	Elefsis
Euboea	Evia
Corinth	Korinthos
Lacedaemonia	Lakonia
Laurion	Lavrion
Lycabettus	Lykavitos
Mycenae	Mykines
Boiotia	Viotia
Brauron	Vravrona
Hydra	Ydra (island)
Hymettus	Ymittos (mountain)

Some place names have changed altogether. These appear in the story.

Athmonon: now Maroussi

Mounichia: now Kastella (in Piraeus)

Mounichia Harbour: now Tourkolimano

Stalis Island: now Koumoundourou Island

Zea Harbour: now Pasalimani

Beauty forgotten yet is beauty still,

For nothing lovely ever upon earth,

Not Helen's face, nor Alexander's will,

Passing to death, but comes again to birth.

In some new brain the sleeping dust will waken …

From "Amaranth" by John Drinkwater

For

Alexandra and Dimitris

Andrew and Kanella

PROLOGUE

Saronic Gulf close to Piraeus, Greece, Spring, 418 BCE

The dead man in the bottom of the boat groaned.

'Shit!' hissed the oarsman. 'You said he was dead.'

'He should be,' whispered the man from Miletus. 'He had enough to kill a bull.'

The oarsman stepped down into the body of the boat. 'You row. I'll finish him off,' he said, his eyes reflecting the starlight as he drew his dagger.

'No!' snapped the Milesian. 'It's got to look like he drowned. No wounds.'

The dead man groaned again and moved his head.

'So what *do* we do?' The oarsman stroked a finger along his blade.

The Milesian stepped up onto the stern and took the oar. He sculled towards the land, looking up at the great walls, pale above the dark cliffs. No guards were visible.

'Unload him here,' he murmured. 'See? Three boat lengths from that rock like an acorn.' He shipped the oar and stepped down. 'Come on! Help me!'

The two men checked the knots in the ropes. The not-quite dead man's feet were bound to a net filled with rocks. The Milesian checked the rope around the man's wrists.

'Right,' he whispered. 'All tight. Ready? Heave!'

They slid the body and the weighted net into the water. There was hardly a splash. The oarsman leapt back onto the stern of the boat and sculled it silently away from the rocks.

The Milesian sat on the main thwart. 'You sure you know where it is when you come back later?'

The oarsman grunted 'Yeah'.

The man from Miletus smiled. 'That's when you can use your knife,' he murmured, 'but only on the ropes, or we won't get our money.'

The other grinned. 'There won't be a mark on him,' he whispered.

The Agora, central Athens, Greece, Spring 418 BCE

The first rays of the sun lit up a notice on the wall of the Council buildings. It said, 'Poseidon, great God of the Sea, has seen fit to take from us Damianos, superintendent of the Naval Shipyards in Piraeus.

Fisherman Lukos found his corpse floating in the shallow waters off Faliron last evening. There were no wounds or marks on him. The god was kind. His body will be cremated with full military honours tomorrow in the Municipal Cemetery.'

'Impossible!' murmured Themistokles, son of Kallistos.

'What's impossible, young Themis?' asked the Assistant Council Treasurer, who was standing next to him in the crowd.

'Damianos can't have drowned,' Themis said, turning to him. 'There must be some mistake. Damianos can swim better than I can.'

'And that's yet another thing you can do better than most, eh, young Themistokles?' The Treasurer's chuckle was tinged with spite.

A horrified man in the crowd exclaimed, 'But Damianos knew everything about the Yards! Who'll keep the navy equipped and at the ready now?'

'Hmm. Important men often attract what you might call bad luck. Kind of Poseidon to drown him without assaulting him first,' added the Treasurer with heavy irony.

A lugubrious voice said, 'Poseidon isn't always on our side. He often favours the Spartans.'

'But he hasn't stopped Athens ruling the seas,' said a younger man.

The crowd began to drift along the tree-lined road past the army headquarters and up towards the Pnyx, where the Assembly was gathering.

Themis raised his voice a little. 'Does no one else feel it's odd, when a man who can swim like a fish, drowns in his home waters?'

No one answered. The shadows of the trees flickered over the men as they walked off, apparently in earnest debate.

>>>

PART ONE

Chapter 1: friends?

Sport City, Manchester, June 2017

Suzanne's feet thudded on the track. Her eyes were on the box, the pole was upright. She lowered it as she ran. Everything balanced. She thrust the pole into the corner of the box and smiled as it flexed, forcing her upwards, feet first, rocketing into the sky. The bar came level with her chest. She bent at the waist. For that long, perfect moment she was looking down on the track, the blue cushioning in the pit, the whole world. Flying.

Then she pushed the pole away from her and relaxed into the fall. As she came down for the bounce, her eyes were on the bar, still in its place at four metres thirty-five centimetres. And it stayed there.

She'd done it! She'd qualified in the B category! She had a chance of going to the Commonwealth Games in Australia!

She bounced on her back on the cushioning, and again to land on her feet, arms in the air. 'Yeah! This is who I am. This time I got it right!'

She jumped down off the padding, waving to Cassie, her home trainer. Her dad and Cassie and her student mates were all leaping up and down. She ran over to them.

'Fantastic!' her dad was shouting. 'You flew over that!'

He put his smart phone away, leant over and wrapped her tight in his arms for a second. Then he held her away from him, looking at her with wonder. 'Suzanne Short, you are amazing,' he whispered.

'Where's Ron?' she asked, looking round for her boyfriend. 'He said he'd be here.'

'Haven't seen him,' said Cassie, her grin so wide she could hardly speak. She gestured to Suzanne's belongings. 'Come on. We need to make sure you're registered properly.'

Suzanne laughed and turned back to the track. As she collected her things, she scanned the crowd. Ron hadn't qualified in his hammer event the day before, and she knew how that felt. She'd failed to qualify for the 2014 Commonwealth Games in Glasgow and the 2016 Olympics in Rio. But Cassie had had faith in her and she'd kept trying. She took a deep, happy breath.

Behind her she heard Ron's voice. She turned and ran towards him.

He was leaning over the barrier, his face mottled and contorted. She couldn't hear what he was saying at first. When she did, she stopped dead.

'And isn't that just miraculous?' he was shouting, his voice crackling with irony. 'Now I get it. I got no thanks for listening like an idiot when you were depressed. No thanks for waiting for you while you buggered off to university. No thanks for sympathy when you failed for Glasgow and Rio. And now? Now you'll be away winning medals all over You Tube. Millions of followers. Well, I won't be one of them! I'm not coming second any more. I just hope you break your fucking neck.'

'What …?' Suzanne stared at him, mouth open. She took a step towards him.

'Stay away from me!' he yelled, turning into the crowd behind him and shouting over his shoulder. 'You're the last person I want to see just now. Better if we'd never met! Fuck you, Little Miss Perfect! Stay out of my life!'

Ron pushed through the stunned crowd, sprinted to the exit, and disappeared.

Part of Suzanne's mind knew that she was standing alone, beyond the barrier, with her mouth open. But the rest of her mind was blank. She couldn't move, couldn't breathe, couldn't control her shaking legs. She felt like something had stabbed her in the belly. She doubled over. Everything went dark.

<<<

Athens, Spring, 418 BCE.

(Breeds of Sheep 01)

Everything was dark. The half-moon came and went above thick, racing clouds. The breeze smelled of wood smoke and incense, with a seasoning of sewage. Themis was running along the street that skirted the Hill of the Muses. After a stimulating evening, he had sprinted to the guard post at the top of the Hill to inhale the view to Piraeus, with the rippling sea and distant islands beyond, before setting off home to sleep.

Ahead, light and music were flooding the street from a big house on a corner. 'Yet another wedding,' he thought.

The moon came out. A man coming up the road towards him ran into a pool of its light. Themis stopped dead.

'Hey Photios, you're a dark horse, aren't you?' he said with a chuckle. 'We missed you at the gym today. Someone said you were away, spying on the Spartans.'

Photios stepped back, looking at Themis in furious alarm, eyes wide, brow furrowed. 'What are *you* doing here?' he asked.

'I'm just on my way – '

'Stay away from me!' Photios hissed. 'You're the last person I want to see just now. Better if we'd never met! Curse you, Themistokles!' He looked from side to side in panic. 'You never saw me!' he rasped and dived into the blackness of the alleyway to Themis' left.

Themis looked after him in astonishment, shock stabbing painfully through his belly. Photios and he had been close since they were boys. There had been a time when everyone in Themis' life was lying to him except Photios. But now? What was this?

He stood for a moment, rigid with disbelief in the middle of the road.

Then he ran into the blackness of the alley. Shadows shifted in the moonlight. 'Photios!' he called. 'What in Hades is wrong? Where the fuck are you?'

He called again, but there was silence. Was that basement door closing? He could hear rats and smell rubbish laced with the wild spearmint growing on the wall.

He ran to the door and shook it. It was shut now, and locked. He beat on it. 'Open up!' he called. 'Are you there? Photios, open up!'

No answer. He called Photios' name again.

The wedding was making a lot of noise, perhaps too much for anyone inside to hear him. He examined the end of the alley. The houses had been cut into a low cliff. He swarmed up the rocks till he could look into the windows. They were small, filled with stone lattice. A slight glimmer of light grew in the room he could see. He ducked and the light passed on. He moved along till he could see into the next window. A woman carried a small lamp as she shuffled past the next doorway. She was stooped and hooded. Before he could call out to her she was gone.

Should he call in the official city guards? And say what? 'My friend is behaving oddly and has disappeared into the house of an old woman'? Perhaps not.

He scrambled down and ran home. There, he woke his dog, Yellow, and his slave, Frog. They returned to the alleyway at a run.

'This is where I'll be with Yellow,' he said to Frog, stroking the sitting dog's head almost on a level with his hip.

The wedding was so noisy there was no need to whisper. 'You go home now. If I'm not back by dawn, bring me some food.'

'Weapon?' asked Frog, dark eyes thoughtful.

Themis patted his waist.

When Frog had loped off, Themis sat down under the old olive tree opposite the alley and the house. He wrapped himself in his cloak. Yellow lay down beside him, stretching out almost as long as a man, and immediately fell asleep.

If Photios appeared, he would surely be visible from here. In his mind, Themis went through all the times he'd seen his friend lately. What could have made Photios behave like that?

'No arguments, eh, Yellow?' he whispered as he rested his head on the smooth, warm stomach. 'No fights over girls or boys. No debts. I even kept my worries about his new job to myself. And for once we agree about politics. He can't be upset about the Phidias rumours, can he? Or be having an affair with that old woman?' Themis grinned at the thought. Yellow's stomach gurgled and he twitched as he dreamed.

'But I'm pretty sure something's going on … They found Photios' old boss dead in the sea at Faliron three days ago. Did you know that, Yellow?' The dog's muzzle twitched. 'He'd drowned, they said – Damianos, superintendent of the naval yards, who could swim better than a dolphin, had drowned. And now Photios is superintendent in his place. And you know I love Photios, Yellow, but I just feel he's not really right for a job as tough as that…'

Yellow snorted and shifted in his sleep, reminding Themis of the girl he'd been with earlier. She may have been poor, but at least she was clean.

Which led Themis to another thought. Perhaps Photios didn't want to see him any more because he, Themistokles, son of Kallistos, was too poor. Photios had suddenly become such an important and wealthy employee of the City, and was from an important and wealthy family.

Yes, Themis had been the boy boxing champion at the 87th Olympiad and later worked with the cream of celebrity painters and sculptors at his uncle Panainos' painting studio and school. But two years after Panainos died leaving Themis to manage the school, the City had commandeered the buildings for the army. Since then, Themis had been a jobbing artist.

His family did have land and his brother was in the cavalry, but Themis himself was just a foot soldier. 'With dreams of making beautiful things to please the gods, and perhaps even my father in Hades,' he said wryly to the dog's twitching flank. Then he laughed at himself and wriggled into the curve of Yellow's warm belly. '*But no,*' he thought. '*Photios doesn't think like that. He hasn't got a pretentious bone in his body.*'

The wind died down as he sat thinking and watching…

He took a breath through the cloth over his face. The stench was unbearable. He looked between the dark pine trees at the shining sea below, beyond the gaping rock hole at his feet. Down in the darkness of that closed-off cave, scores of bodies must be piling up. He bent again to his work. They were pitching another wagonload of the dead men of Skioni into the cave-pit, one by one. Flies hovered and settled all over the men on the ridge, alive and dead. But they rose in clouds to escape from that black maw.

Yellow stood up, dislodging his master's head from its pillow. Themis shuddered and took a deep, sweet breath. No stench, no sweat, no flies. The dream was gone. And the wedding music had finally stopped. The guests were leaving, hushing each other noisily.

The sky was lightening. 'No Photios, Yellow?' Themis whispered. The dog licked his hand. 'Did I miss him by dashing home, or just now by dropping off?'

He looked carefully at the front of the two-storey house where Photios had disappeared. Large like other houses in this once-wealthy part of the City, it was built against the next house on one side and the cliff at the back. There could be no doors but onto this street, or the one in the alley.

A female slave came out of the main street door carrying the night soil bucket. She ran off before he could attract her attention.

When she came back, he asked, 'Who lives here?'

'Mistress Karina,' she said.

'Did you have any visitors last night?'

'None, sir,' she said. Her eyes held a challenge. 'But you can come any time, I'm sure.' The door opened and she went in.

Themis shook his head. 'Yellow, you should have told me this was pointless,' he said. 'I'm cold and uncomfortable and it's time I was at the gym.'

>>>

'She's been so focused…' murmured Cassie's voice.

'Is this a result of that accident back in 2010?' asked Suzanne's father.

'No. She's been over that for years. I know she thinks it changed her, but believe me, it had no effect on her abilities – or her school work. No, this is Ron's fault – and her tendency to train too hard.'

Suzanne opened her eyes. She was lying on the back seat of her dad's parked car. She sat up. 'I thought we were going back in the team bus,' she said to Cassie, who took her hand and laughed with relief.

'Of course,' she said, and smiled an 'I told you so' smile at Dan Short.

Cassie had insisted that Suzanne saw a doctor at the university campus health centre as soon as they got out of the bus in Lancaster. The doctor had said, 'This often happens to athletes, and the time of the month doesn't help. Go home and rest.'

So Cassie had brought Suzanne back to her student lodgings in a tall, narrow terraced house, and left her alone in her room with the curtains drawn against the afternoon sun. Then Cassie had left to catch her train back home to Carlisle.

Now Suzanne could revel in the thought that she was through to the next round of the selection process. And carefully avoid remembering the poison in Ron's eyes.

In the minibus on the way back, someone had shown round a phone with a picture on Snapchat of her going over the bar. They'd added angel's wings. That's what she would remember.

And in the quiet and dark of her room she gradually relaxed, lying on her back with her eyes closed. She focused on her breath coming and going, and the pulse in her neck. She could feel herself drifting towards sleep.

Behind her closed eyelids, a shadowy street on a windy night appeared. A long-forgotten feeling was seeping into her mind... Someone else's heartbeat was running parallel to hers. Someone else's thoughts were reaching her from far away... It was unnerving, beyond her control, irresistible, and wonderfully familiar. Themis was back.

<<<

The session in the palaistra at Themis' local gymnasium had indeed begun. The trainer beckoned to Themis to join the exercises. He slipped into the back row.

'Two hundred!' called the trainer. 'Change legs!'

Themis began working his left leg and its attached weight in time to the flute and drum. He heard someone else come into the practice yard and turned his head to see.

It was Photios! He looked fresh and rested, and lifted a hand in greeting with a smile. He had stripped and was in his usual place near the corner in moments. Themis couldn't believe his eyes.

'You OK?' he grunted.

'Never better,' whispered Photios.

Themis shook his head in relieved confusion, offered up a brief prayer of thanks, and focused on the training.

When they were scraping off, he asked Photios, 'Where did you go when you left me last night?'

'Left you last night?' echoed Photios. 'But I didn't see you at all yesterday.'

'Not at the gym, no,' said Themis. He looked quizzically into his friend's cheerful face. 'But on my way home in the evening, I was passing Mistress Karina's house, under the Hill of the Muses, and I met you in the street.' He smiled a knowing smile. 'You weren't exactly pleased to see me. What had you been up to? Something you don't want me to know about, obviously.'

'Really, Themis, I wasn't in that part of the city,' Photios said seriously, 'and I certainly didn't see you in the street. I didn't even go out, the wind was strong and the moon fitful.' He seemed confused and alarmed.

'Must have been a mirage in the moonlight,' Themis said with a laugh. Could it be that Photios didn't want to discuss whatever it was in front of the gym crowd? 'Look, I have to paint all day once I've eaten,' he said, 'but if you're free we could meet up after dark at my place.'

'Good idea,' said Photios with a slight frown.

Yellow ran ahead into the house as Themis pushed open the street door. Frog appeared and Themis said, 'Seems Photios is fine after all.' He kicked the door closed behind him. He paused at the shrine to Zeus-of-the-House to drop a handful of walnuts into the dish below the idol, then came over to the table by the water trough. A strong smell of savoury baking hung in the sunny courtyard. 'What do you think of marriage, Frog?'

'That's good about Photios,' said Frog. 'What d'you mean — marriage?' Frog put down the dish of curds he had brought out as part of Themis' breakfast.

'Is it time I started looking for a bride?'

'What brought that on?' asked Frog, amused.

'Ah. Well, you see, Straton is boasting at the gym about how his matchmaker has come up with four luscious young women for him to choose from, all beautiful and all pining for him.' Themis emptied the rest of the walnuts from the pouch on his belt onto the table. 'Sounds tempting, of course, but what is really going on is that his father feels it's time he took on some family responsibilities. It's only a year until he can be nominated for public office.'

Frog sighed, and chanted in his charming tenor, 'We're all getting older/ and some of us bolder./ It's hard to decide/ on taking a bride,/ but there's no other way/ for me to stay/ known on this earth/ once I'm gone.'

'That last doesn't rhyme,' said Themis, collecting up the rolling nuts. 'Did you eat yet?' he asked.

'Mika won't let me "loiter in the kitchen" till the pies are ready, so no.' Frog began cracking the nuts with a nut hammer.

Themis sat and dropped some pieces into the curds. The dog lay down on his feet. 'Never mind. I'm starving. It was a … busy night and we did extra weights at the palaistra.' He took a spoonful and said with his mouth full, 'Photios says he wasn't out last night, that the man I saw must be someone else …' An unwelcome thought suddenly came into his mind.

Frog shrugged. 'Not many people in town with that blond hair,' he said.

Themis looked up at him, his mind now full of foreboding.

>>>

A knock sounded on Suzanne's door. She stretched and sat up. Her housemate, Natasha, was saying, 'Are you ok? Hey! Suzanne!'

'Mmm. Just a minute!' Suzanne leapt out of bed, then stopped dead on her way to the door. The smells of baking pies, sour milk and distant fetid drains faded away. She wasn't there: she was here.

She looked round her room. Here was Lancaster, 2017, not Ancient Athens. She was a second year university student of Sports and Exercise Science, not a totally cool, naked-exercising ex-boxer. She was a modern English woman, not an ancient Hellenic man.

She grinned as she reminded herself that she was also a Lancashire County athlete, one of two pole-vaulters in the team. And now she was on the GB selection list for the Commonwealth Games in Brisbane, Australia! Yay!

And Bernie, *her* best friend, was studying comparative religion at Durham, not doing iffy things in darkened streets or getting mixed up in a murder. No. 21st Century England was much more comfortable – it had streetlights and even smelled quite nice most of the time.

She breathed deeply, squared her shoulders and opened the door.

'You ok?' asked Natasha again, her sharp-boned face creased with concern.

'Yes,' said Suzanne. 'I'm absolutely fine. I must have been asleep – dreaming – and you woke me. Come on in.' She stood back.

10

'Sorry!' said Natasha, with an exaggerated hangdog expression. 'But everyone's celebrating. Except Ron, of course. No one's seen him again. Did you see what I put on Snapchat just now?'

Suzanne picked up her smart phone. 'Where?' She laughed suddenly. 'Why don't I feel bad about Ron, Natasha?'

''Cause he turned into a jerk. Found it?'

Natasha had posted an old photo of Ron, tinted a jealous green.

'Clever,' Suzanne said with a grin. 'Let's go out! I have celebrating to do!'

<<<

Chapter 2: proposition

A knock sounded on the street door.

Frog went to open it. 'Forgot to tell you,' he said over his shoulder to Themis. 'There was a slave at the door when I came in from the market. He said he was from your uncle, but I didn't recognize him. This may be him again.' He lifted the latch and looked out.

'Has my nephew returned?' asked a loud, unfamiliar voice.

Frog squared his shoulders. 'Who is asking for him, sir?'

'Zephyros of Massalia, brother of Eirini of this house.'

'My apologies, sir,' said Frog with respect, 'but is there someone who can vouch for you?'

'Ach, Athens has become so suspicious since this … disagreement with Sparta,' said the voice. 'I assume Diodotos is away from home? And there was a tall Nubian slave … ?'

Mika had come out of the kitchen at the sound of the loud voice. She approached Frog from behind saying, 'I remember that voice, Frog.' She spoke to the visitor. 'Master Zephyros, how is your brother, Master Leokratis?'

'Ah,' boomed the voice, echoing off the houses in the street. 'Mika, you haven't changed one iota.'

Frog stood back from the door and a stout, untidy man shambled into the courtyard like a bear eager for honey. He was followed by a slave of medium height but as thin as a river reed.

Themis enjoyed this contrast as he bent down to push Yellow off his feet. He stood up and met his uncle in the centre of the courtyard. 'Uncle Zephyros! You were away in the west when I was staying in Massalia all those years ago. I haven't seen you since I was a small boy.' In Themis' mind a memory of Zephyros' brother, Leokratis, also made him smile. Leokratis was tall and wiry with moods that changed like quicksilver.

Zephyros took a step back and lifted his head enough to look into Themis' face with a comical expression of surprise. 'Not just an Olympic champion, I see,' he said. 'But a true column of the household, it seems.'

Themis turned to Mika and Frog. 'Prepare food for Uncle Zephyros and his man,' he said. 'We'll be in the andron for a few minutes.'

He led the way into the chilly andron and motioned to Zephyros to sit on the couch opposite the window. 'Have you come straight from the port?' he asked. He couldn't help thinking, '*The port where Photios must be now, having taken over Damianos' position …* ' He put aside his suspicions, sat down and looked up at his uncle.

Zephyros did not sit. He walked around the room, picking up a scroll here, a piece of coloured rock there. Now he turned from examining a bronze belt buckle that Themis had found in the sea off Methana and said, 'Got in last night. Came up from Phaliron this morning but missed you. So I went to the Agora to hear the gossip. It seems that two Scythian Archers accused of taking bribes will be tried today.' He looked pointedly at Themis. 'You rise early, young Themis – or was it that you were out late?'

'Habit,' Themis said from his couch under the window, his jaw clenched but his smile polite. 'Please sit down Uncle, and tell me what brings you to Athens.'

'All in good time,' said Zephyros. 'How is my sister?' He picked up a delicate antique drinking cup that had been Themis' father's favourite and turned it over in his large hands. The cup was by Makron, a painter Themis aspired to emulate. 'Good piece,' said Zephyros.

Themis forced himself not to leap to the cup's rescue. His stomach growled. 'Mama was well when I last saw her. She is very happy still, out in eastern Attica, helping to teach her young charges how to be perfect wives.'

Zephyros put the kylix down with a clatter and sat at last, sprawling across the cushions. 'Ah. How convenient. Will you be choosing one for yourself soon? Or perhaps for your brother? Time the family expanded!'

'Diodotos is on the farm at this time of year,' said Themis, ignoring that. 'The Spartans haven't raided Attica for some years and we've been officially at peace with them for three years now. The new olive groves even had a few fruit – first time for twelve years.'

'From what I remember of him, he will be missing the excitement of the city,' said Zephyros. His laugh frightened the finches in the courtyard vine into a great twittering.

Themis nodded. Was the food still not ready? He couldn't remember the name of Zephyros' wife to ask after her, so he said, 'And your brother, Uncle Zephyros, my Uncle Leokratis? He and Mrs Efthalia were so kind to me and my slave when we lived with them. It was the beginning of the war and you were in Iberia. Are they well?'

Zephyros looked over at him with a tilt of his head. 'Didn't you know?' he boomed. 'Leokratis died last summer. I thought your mother would have told you.'

Themis' eyes prickled with involuntary tears. Leokratis had been a tough master, but he had taught Themis all he knew about the art and commerce of vase painting. And he'd been a distant but kind father figure when Themis returned to Athens three years later. He'd sent letters and small professional gifts every so often. 'I'm so sorry, Uncle,' said Themis. 'No, I had no idea. And I'm not sure that Mama does either. Her own brother … Have you seen her yet?'

'Not on this trip, no,' said Zephyros abruptly. 'But I wrote to her a month or so after he passed on. Now I come to think of it, I didn't get an answer.'

'Perhaps she never received your message. I know it will upset her deeply. She talked of you and him last time I saw her.'

'Did she now?' Zephyros sat forward. 'And what about our dear relative in Egypt, now known as Evdaemon? Do you also not know the news from there?'

Themis felt a shiver across his shoulders. 'I heard he is ill, but still insisting that his whereabouts be kept secret from the City.'

'Was,' said Zephyros shortly. 'Was ill. He's gone now.' He sighed. 'My generation seems determined lately to add to the population of Hades.'

Themis looked down, feeling suddenly separated from his own hands. He promised himself some quiet time later to remember his Uncle Phidias-Evdaemon. He wiped tears from his stubbled cheeks with the corner of his chiton.

'Sad news,' he said. 'But not unexpected. He'd had a few extra years at least. Was it marsh fever?' Zephyros shrugged and shook his head. Themis went on, 'And your brother, too? Mama was worried because we'd heard there was fever in Massalia. But she believed you and he, as wealthy merchants, would have the best healers.'

'Well, that all is – or was – true.' Zephyros sighed dramatically. 'We did. But Leokratis died of the fever anyway, and his wife not long after. His daughters are married to local men. I am an important merchant still, but no longer in Massalia. I couldn't find anyone to take Leokratis' place. But our name is a big asset, so I'm moving business and wife to Thurii.' He paused as though expecting a round of applause from Themis. The quiet settled like dust.

After a moment, Themis focused his thoughts and said, 'Thurii in Greater Greece?'

'Twenty-five years since it was founded and Spartans and Athenians there are still working together peacefully,' said Zephyros, nodding enthusiastically. 'That's what lucrative trading will do.'

'So moving there for you will be more … conducive to trade?' This had been Leokratis' favourite phrase.

'Should be.' Zephyros stood up and paced the room again. 'I've found the very place – stopped off on my way here. Brand new house beside an open space perfect for a workshop … Did you do these frescos?'

Themis stood up too and moved towards the door. Was he going to be asked for money? 'They were painted for my father by … Evdaemon, but I refreshed them a few years ago. Food must be ready by now, Uncle. I prefer to eat in the courtyard. It's warmer in the sun. Will you join me?' he said, and walked out into the light.

Couches had been moved out of the shade. Low tables were laid with bread rolls and fruit on large platters. Mika came out with another, piled with steaming pies. The smell made Themis' stomach ache.

He went over to the water trough and rinsed his hands and face. Zephyros watched him.

'Frog will bring water and cordial immediately,' said Mika and left them.

After the libations, they ate in silence for a while.

Then Zephyros began. 'The market for ceramics in the many cities around our sea is growing, you know, young Themis. Although, of course, it's shrinking in Attica and Sparta, so you may soon be out of a job here. This war, or whatever it is, may be ridiculous, but it's being fought on more fronts than is obvious. Trading partners are changing. Athens may soon become irrelevant to east-west trade. Her ceramics and other goods are getting too expensive.' Crumbs sprayed from his mouth as he spoke and his voice seemed to flatten the emerging vine leaves against the columns.

Themis took advantage of the pause to say, 'But you don't deal in ceramics, Uncle.'

'Didn't use to,' agreed his uncle. 'But I've decided to go that way now, concentrate on my brother's side of the business. P'raps we'll be able to branch out again if that goes as well as I expect.'

'Mmm,' said Themis into his duck pie. In his preoccupation with Photios and the family deaths, he'd forgotten the shelves of pots he'd agreed to paint by evening. He would have to free himself from his uncle soon if he was going to keep his word.

'So I have a proposition for you,' said Zephyros, sitting back. He let out a large, satisfied burp. 'That was delicious, Mika,' he added as Mika came out with damp towels.

Themis thought, *'Here it comes. And what can I say? I'll just have to send him on to Diodotos.'* He relaxed a little and asked out loud, 'And what proposition would that be, Uncle?'

'As you are already involved in ceramics, I thought I would ask you to come and be my potter and painter,' said Zephyros, with a grin.

Themis was still for a moment. Then he chewed his mouthful slowly and swallowed. 'But Uncle,' he replied, trying to keep his voice calm and reasonable, 'I am committed here – to my work – I don't just paint ceramics, you know – and as a soldier and engineer in the army. And I have my family responsibilities. So I can't possibly leave Athens.'

'Surely that's the job of your older brother. This is a time in your life when you can be bold and inventive, not just rest on your laurels. I would make you an equal partner in the business. You could work for yourself entirely,' said Zephyros. 'You'd be a boss again and, as soon as you knew enough about the export market, you'd be rich!'

'Uncle Zephyros,' said Themis as politely as he knew how. 'I thank you for even considering me, but I am needed here to keep my own family fortunes together. I couldn't possibly walk out on them!'

Zephyros sighed and put on a pathetic face. 'My wife said you probably wouldn't want to, but you see, we have no sons and I'm not getting any younger. With my brother and my cousins dead and no other men in the family (except sons-in-law, both useless except for their money), how else am I to sustain us in our old age?'

Themis stood up. 'Uncle, we all have similar problems. If you go and visit my mother, perhaps you and she will come up with a different solution.' He stepped away from the table. 'Now I'm afraid I have to go. You are welcome to stay if you wish, but the weather is changing and travelling may be difficult later.'

Zephyros stood too, sucking his teeth. 'Not this time, young Themis.

As you say, I should visit my sister. I've a hired cart waiting in the street.'

'Then please give Mama my affectionate greetings. I hope you have a pleasant and safe journey.' Themis took his uncle's hand, embraced him gently and stepped back. He trod on Yellow's paw and there was a quiet growl. Themis fondled the dog's ears by way of apology.

Zephyros said, 'Think about what I said though, nephew. I'll be in Attica for a month or so, Spartans willing. I have business in Piraeus in a few days. Good pies!' he said, gesturing at his crumb-scattered table. He called his slave and left, shouting goodbyes from the street.

Frog was collecting dishes and cups. 'Exit the bear and the stick insect,' he murmured in the welcome peace. 'The bear's name is almost the same as your present boss, Master Zephus. Odd that.'

Themis turned to him and said quietly, 'Imagine having to work with Zephyros, though. It would be like working on a pig farm.'

'No lack of funds, though,' said Frog. 'Families need to stick together these days, and the world beyond Athens is not all pig farms.'

Themis laughed. 'Massalia certainly wasn't, was it? If I was offered a place there, I might well be tempted. But by all accounts, Thurii is not like Massalia – it's new and chaotic, full of inexperienced merchants and second rate artists.'

'The stick insect told me that's where Herodotus went to finish his Histories. Can't be that bad. Even a one-armed man is king among the armless,' said Frog over his shoulder, as he carried a tottering heap of dishes to the scullery on one arm.

Themis made a rude gesture and called after him, 'Meanwhile in Athens, this two-armed man is doing just fine! … But,' he muttered to himself as he prepared to leave for work, 'At least he didn't ask for money.'

Chapter 3: buns and a boy

'Herakles isn't looking good,' said Frog when he joined Themis later. He had to raise his voice above the rain that was thundering on the roof of the ceramics workshop. 'His nose had a strange bulge … '

'And the feet of his lionskin look like bread buns,' added Themis. 'I know. But I'm cold and whichever hand I use, it shakes.' He put down his paintbrush and leaned back with an explosive sigh. The bench wobbled and the tall jug he was painting teetered.

He steadied it with his right hand. 'You learn anything from Timnes at Photios' house?' He kept his voice steady.

'He says a man called for Photios very late that night. Photios went out to meet him on the street. Timnes stayed behind the door and heard the man whispering to Photios to go to a certain house near the green shrine to meet someone very important about the deal.'

Themis looked at Frog in confusion. 'Deal? What deal?'

'No idea.'

'And in the middle of the night?'

'Yup,' said Frog with a deliberate wink. 'And Photios was to tell no one, not family, not slaves, not friends, especially not his boxer friend!'

'That's ridiculous!' Themis felt slightly sick. His hand shook. 'And Photios says he remembers nothing … Can Timnes describe the man?'

'He said not,' said Frog. 'He hardly saw him. The only thing was that, at the end, the man kind of squeaked "No one!".'

'Squeaked? Could Timnes imitate him?'

'Well, he's not really a mimic, is he?'

'Not like you, you mean,' said Themis, looking up from under his brows.

'Exactly,' said Frog. 'Oh, and there's a customer outside. Wants to talk to Master Zephus about making an order.'

'Good,' said Themis, loading his brush again with white. His hand was steadier. 'He must be mad coming out in this rain. He can talk to the boss.'

'The Master is out, but should be back soon. He'll get a soaking, too.'

'Who's the customer?'

'That merchant, Tryfonos. The one who sponsored the play about the dung beetle going to Olympus. No shit on him, though. Seems ready to spend a lot of money.' Frog hefted a closed fist as if it was full of coins.

Themis put his brush down on the mixing palette and stood up.

The bustle in the partly-roofed workshop and the lack of consistent light had driven Themis to work alone in a north-facing back room. The painters usually worked outside, though now they were sitting quietly under a roofed section near the street entrance. Further back the potters and kiln slaves existed in constant pandemonium, with their wheels and shovels, exhortations and curses, heat and smoke.

Tryfonos stood just inside the door of the main storeroom. He was about ten years older than Themis, an Athenian who had spent a lot of his life in the East.

He had taken off his wet cloak and was wiping his hands on a towel offered by one of the kiln slaves. Themis shook hands with him. 'Themistokles, son of Kallistos,' he said. 'And you are Tryfonos, the well-known merchant.'

Tryfonos said, 'Ah, yes. Themistokles. I keep hearing your name as a one-time boxer and now as the painter of fine pots.' His yellow hair was streaked almost white in places and his fleshy lips were unusually red. His light brown eyes were teasing as he went on, 'Of course, that's not to say they're any good, just that you're in fashion this season.'

Themis inclined his head with a smile. 'And the East loves to follow Western fashion.'

Tryfonos picked up an elegant, long-stemmed cup. 'At present? Yes, Athenian fashion.'

'The last man to buy a set of those,' said Themis, 'was Damianos, superintendent of the Naval Shipyards in Piraeus.'

Tryfonos turned his head away for a moment. 'I knew him of course,' he said. 'The Navy is my customer. I was at his funeral two days ago.'

'I saw you there.' Photios had been there, too. Themis had thought, *'Checking up that Damianos was really dead?* Now he added, 'Bad business.'

Tryfonos nodded sadly, then looked Themis in the eye again. 'Back to the matter in hand,' he said. 'The perception is that the quality of Athenian ceramics is not what it was before the Spartan war. What d'you think? Are you and Master Zephus still turning out the goods? Is this one of yours?'

Themis shook his head. 'No. It's by Onias. His style is more like Polygnotos than Panainos.'

'Ah, Panainos, your late uncle and employer, I seem to remember?'

Themis nodded. 'Yes. I ran his school for a while after his death.'

'Very sad.' Tryfonos looked at Themis' face and then his hands as if measuring him for something. 'Don't waste yourself with mass production,' he said. 'For those with the energy and knowledge, there's a very lucrative market for unique or commissioned works.'

Themis raised an eyebrow and smiled. 'Thanks for the advice,' he said. 'It seems to be my day for it.'

Tryfonos nodded thoughtfully, then made a wry face and looked around the large workshop as if for the master potter.

'Master Zephus will be back shortly. Can I show you some further samples?' Themis said, suddenly remembering his worry about Photios.

They walked along the aisle between the drying racks and the shelves of finished pots.

'You know, I have customers for many commodities,' said Tryfonos as they stopped to examine some wine-mixing jars. 'You'll have heard of the forests of the Istros? The men there are happy to trade their timber for such items.' Tryfonos winked. 'Beautiful women, those northerners.'

Themis made an effort and laughed. 'I must visit one day,' he said. He could hear Zephus' voice deploring the weather. 'Please, come and meet Master Zephus. He'll be able to help you better than I can.'

Tryfonos stopped at a shelf of perfume bottles and picked up one that was in fact painted by Themis. The figure was Aphrodite pouring a drop of scent onto her hand from a similar-shaped bottle. Themis had used Anthoussa, his teenage crush, as his model – Anthoussa as she was before she married Agorakritos, lissom as a yearling doe.

'Exquisite,' said Tryfonos as he replaced it on the shelf. 'As I said, there may well be commissions for you and your master potter.'

A few minutes later, with Zephus and Tryfonos deep in conversation, Themis returned to his workroom. Frog came in with a cup of soup and two buns exactly like the lionskin's feet. The soup steamed.

'That smells good,' said Themis. And yet he wasn't hungry.

'All this wind and rain – Zeus must be in a snit about something,' said Frog. 'It's too cold here for painting today, and you had no sleep. Can't you work on something at home and do these tomorrow?'

Themis gestured with his chin at the ten or so tall slim jugs waiting for their final details by his workbench. 'Got to finish them today so they can be fired ready to ship when the weather improves.'

'Where're they going?'

'West on the first sailing, I heard. Some market in Iberia, I imagine.' Themis picked up a tool. 'I'll incise some details while the soup cools.'

Frog fed the brazier, and Themis lifted the vase onto his knee. He always used his left hand to draw in the fine lines. This time they were the rippling muscles of red figure Herakles vanquishing the many-headed, scaly Hydra.

'That young Melissus, Agorakritos' kid, is waiting to see you,' said Frog. 'He's helping load number three kiln, getting warm after a wetting.'

'Enough soup for him too?' asked Themis.

'Plenty,' said Frog. 'I'll get some for him and bring him in, shall I?'

'Mmmm,' Themis grunted nodding, the incising tool in his mouth and a paintbrush in his hand.

Over the soup and paw-shaped buns, Themis looked at Melissus carefully. Dark curls of wet hair escaped from the drying bonnet and the smooth cheeks were flushed with the heat of the factory. The lines of the face were that perfect balance between strong and soft. Themis often used Melissus' features when painting young figures.

But today the expression was tense, and the hard, dirty hands were twisting together. Themis remembered how battered his own hands had been when he was the same age, working at a bronze foundry *and* training as a boy boxer. Melissus, however, spent his time in his father's sculpture yard, running errands and drawing the preparatory sketches for his father's statues. He'd inherited Agorakritos' talent and Anthoussa's beauty. Themis thought, *'Is he here on an errand or to spy on Zephus' designs? Nah. Enough cynicism! The boy's a decent kid …'* He smiled, handing Melissus a bun.

Melissus noticed the smile and said through a mouthful of bread, 'Glad you're feeling pleased with life.' He swallowed, his full, sculpted lips pressing into the attractive pout that was so similar to his mother's. 'Because I have to tell you about something a bit … er … disturbing.' He looked pointedly towards Frog, who was standing near the door.

'Frog, could you take that wine jug through to Master Zephus. Check that he's happy with all the details. Take your time,' said Themis with a steady look.

'Fine,' said Frog, taking the jug in both hands. 'If you need any more food, poke your head out and call.' He ghosted a wink at Themis as he left, shutting the storeroom door.

Themis drank the dregs of his soup straight from the bowl. He wiped his hands on one of his work rags and looked again at Melissus, his head on one side. 'This isn't like you, Melissus. What's going on?'

Melissus wiped round his bowl with his last piece of bread. Holding this dramatically in his hand, he looked straight up at Themis and, raising his voice over the drumming of the rain, said, 'My father – who is finding fault with everything these days – seems to think you have been … er … spending too much time … with my mother.' Then he popped the piece of bread in his mouth with a flourish.

'What?' exclaimed Themis. 'I thought you were going to accuse me of not spending *enough* time at your dad's yard, painting his latest statue!'

Melissus swallowed. 'My mother asked my dad last night if you'd been doing just that, and then they had this huge argument. Of course, I know, he thinks his citizenship is being delayed by an invisible someone on purpose.' Melissus looked at Themis with tragic eyes and a false smile. 'It makes him paranoid about everyone's motives.'

Themis sighed. 'There has never been anything for him to be jealous of between me and your mother,' he said. 'True, when I was about your age I was a bit obsessed with her. She's lovely and she made me laugh. But I've hardly seen her since you were born. You all went to live out near Rhamnous. But now he's brought you into the City, I've been looking forward to seeing more of you all.'

Melissus nodded ironically. 'You are such a good liar, Uncle Themis.'

Themis laughed. 'It's no lie! And even if it were,' he added quietly, '*you* have no right to criticize a liar, with your leather apron and boots and the way you swagger around. Even though there's no sign of a moustache, anyone would think you were a boy!'

'Shhhh!' Melissus hissed, standing up in genuine alarm. 'You promised not to give that away!'

'I haven't given it away,' Themis said calmly. 'I'm teasing you. No one here has any idea. Nor anywhere else, as far as I know, except your parents. Though how you get away with it, I can't imagine. You are safe to go wherever you please dressed like that – at least,' he teased, 'until you have to go to Vravrona for your wife-training as the daughter of an Athenian citizen.'

'Don't remind me!' Melissus paced back and forth. 'Once Dad's citizenship is granted, I can't see how to escape it.' He stood still and stared dramatically at Themis. 'The thought of being a girl full time … it's worse than Hades! There's only one thing that might make it tolerable. Oh!' He clapped a hand over his mouth.

'Really?' asked Themis. 'And what's that?'

Melissus looked around desperately for a moment, then turned to Themis. 'Knowing I could go on being a boy sometimes,' he said, his eyes fiercely green. 'Oh, Uncle Themis, what am I going to do?'

Themis ignored the histrionics. He stood up and put his hands on Melissus' shoulders. Melissus looked up at him. The damp lashes almost reached the dark brows. Themis had to pause a moment. Then he said seriously, 'Tell me what happened last night.' He gently guided the 'boy' to his stool. 'Does your dad truly believe I'm fu…fornicating with your mum in secret?' He spoke lightly but his stomach churned.

Melissus said, 'Well, he didn't quite say it like that. But you know Dad. He has a temper like the fire in a kiln.'

'Unlike his … er … son?' said Themis, raising an eyebrow. Then more grimly, he said, 'I think I need to pay a visit to Master Sculptor Agorakritos. When will he actually be at home?'

'Better meet him at the yard. Then you won't upset Mum.' Melissus suddenly grinned wickedly. '*And* there'll be someone there to stop him trying to strangle you.'

When Melissus was gone, a little warmer and certainly less hungry than when he came, Themis called to Frog to take the bowls away.

'He looked a bit happier,' said the slave, as he picked them up.

'He's working on a new statue at his dad's yard,' said Themis with his back to Frog as he began painting another Herakles.

'He's permanent now, as a boy apprentice, is he?' said Frog innocently.

'Whatever you think you know about him,' said Themis, turning to look Frog in the eye, 'you don't. OK?'

Frog opened his eyes wide in mock despair and chanted, 'But he'd be the perfect lover/ brighten up your days/ even please your mother/ with his pretty winning ways.' He was shaking his head sadly.

Themis snorted. 'I know that's fine for some, but you know it's not *my* way. I had my fill of being patronized and manipulated by older men when I got back from Olympia that first time. I wouldn't wish that on anyone.'

'But there are others who would court him if they could,' said Frog, serious now. 'And the gossip that keeps them at bay is that everyone believes he's yours.'

Themis took a deep breath and declared in a pompous, orator's voice, 'It is quite extraordinary how discerning the mass of the people can be.' Frog laughed. Themis went on in his own voice, which sounded annoyingly shaky. 'It seems I have a bone to pick with his father. And while I'm at it, I'll warn him that Melissus doesn't realize his own attractions. Any more lead white? I've nearly used this lot up.'

Themis finished the last vase in time to call in at Agorakritos' yard before meeting up with Photios. The rain had cleared away to the south and east and there were intermittent sunbeams.

He was told the Master had gone home already and he didn't think to ask for Melissus.

The frontage of Agorakritos' new house, granted to him by the City as thanks for sculptures and public works, was impressive. There were no windows to the street but it was painted with elegant designs and its doorway was between two slim pillars. When Themis knocked, the door slave, who knew him, let him in without question. He was already in the courtyard when he heard voices in Anthoussa's salon.

'I can count, wife!' came Agorakritos' angry voice. 'I was in Egypt five months ago.'

'You may be able to count, husband.' Anthoussa's voice was quiet and calm. 'But you seem to have a bad memory – particularly of a certain night just before you left when you came back from a symposium full of the joy of living and spirit of the vine, noisily grateful for your wonderful family and beautiful wife.'

Themis knocked loudly on the door, opened it, and looked in. 'Anyone here?' he asked. 'Couldn't find you at the yard, Agorakritos.'

Agorakritos turned from his wife to his friend and back, like a wolf at bay. His greying beard jutted and his eyes were furious. 'You're taking a liberty, knocking on that door unannounced,' he said.

'Oh, come on, my friend. If you'll permit, Anthoussa?' said Themis, stepping forward into the room. 'Do I really need announcing? Haven't you always said that I'm part of the family?' Anthoussa's wide eyes were both exasperated and apprehensive.

Agorakritos almost choked, his handsome face dark with anger. 'Part of the family?! So much a part of the family, are you, that you've sown your seed in my wife's belly?'

Themis stepped backwards, accidentally shutting the door with a bang. 'You don't really believe that!' he exclaimed.

Agorakritos jumped towards him and lashed out with his fists. Forewarned by Melissus, Themis shouted, 'Hey! No need …!' and put a hand on Agorakritos' chest. He pushed him back, then spun him round, pinning his arms to his sides in a wrestler's hold.

Anthoussa said loudly, 'Stop it, or I'll call the slaves!'

'Stop now,' Themis whispered in Agorakritos' ear. 'Stop and consider.'

Agorakritos stopped fighting but stood rigid in the circle of Themis' arms. Themis thought, *How do I get us out of this?* Out loud, he said to Anthoussa, 'When is your baby due?'

'In four months,' she said. Her voice shook slightly.

Themis let Agorakritos go, and stepped round to look him in the eye. They were the same height, although the older man was thinner. 'I don't know why you have this idea,' Themis said. 'It is false.'

Agorakritos said, 'Prove it!'

Themis sighed. 'Surely you know me well enough…' he said slowly. 'If you can't take the word of a friend…'

Anthoussa said quietly, 'There is a solution, Themis. Please stay out of this house and away from Agorakritos until the baby is born. When my husband sees that the child resembles him, he will realize his mistake.'

Themis shook his head in dismay. Agorakritos had been a tutor and a friend, and Anthoussa always made Themis laugh, even now when her looks and sense of mischief had been dimmed by domesticity.

He glanced at her. She was in control, but he saw pleading in her eyes.

'Ha!' shouted Agorakritos. 'Hiding your shame by denying him now!'

With his jaw set, Themis said, 'Of course, you're right, Anthoussa.' He looked away from her and turned to Agorakritos. 'I will stay away until the baby is born. But I'm telling you now, Agorakritos, it is not my child. Some god has made you mad, and when you recover you will understand that. Goodbye to you both.' He turned and went out, leaving the door open.

As the street door closed, he laid a shaking hand on the herm by the door, between fury and tears. 'Help him over this,' he said to the god.

A small, dirty hand appeared and rested on top of his. He looked down into Melissus' quizzical eyes.

'I said he would strangle you,' he said. 'You should go home before he sends someone out after you. He heard about the delay to the citizenship last night and didn't sleep. Mum tried to give him a sleeping draft but he wouldn't take it. Did she tell you to leave?'

Themis nodded, looking sadly at Melissus. 'And yet that doesn't sound like enough to make him this angry ...'

'Nothing to be done just now,' said the 'boy' wisely. 'I'll bring you what news I can.'

>>>

Chapter 4: Photios' double

Suzanne woke up too late next day to go for training. She was glad she had a room to herself. She needed to think.

'Am I really going to go on seeing bits of Themis' life? I wish I knew what set them off?' After her accident, years ago, she'd sometimes made the connection with a particular phrase of music, but this time it was coming without invitation.

'And,' she thought, as she divided her laundry into sport stuff and normal, *'if last time is anything to go by, I'll have to find a way to keep his life separate from mine, so people don't think I'm mad and unreliable. That could matter a lot now I'm older, and supposedly a "responsible adult". What really freaks me out, is that I think I remember kind of "seeing" Damianos being*

murdered. At least, …' She was gathering up the dirty sports clothes in both arms. *'I think that's what it was. It was pretty dark – shadowy. But definitely a boat and a body.'*

She put her face among the clothes and sniffed deeply, then smiled. *'I smell miles better than Themis,'* she thought. And stopped dead. *'And that's exactly the kind of thought I'll have to watch out for, and make sure I don't say out loud.'*

She managed to open the door of her room without putting down the bundle. *'I used to write it all down so that I knew what was him and what was me.'* She sighed. *'But what's going on? It's not quite the same, And is it going to continue? Have I got time to keep a record now?'*

As she watched the water rising up the washing machine window she came to a decision. *'I could use the dictation program on my laptop and record it as it happens, or as I remember it, as soon as I can afterwards – a kind of blog. Other people write blogs on-line,'* she thought, going back to her room. *'I'll write one off-line, just for me.'*

With her door shut, she pulled her laptop onto her knee and set up a folder called 'Breeds of Sheep'. She put what she'd already written down about Themis in it, as a file numbered 01. None of her friends were interested in sheep, even if they managed to guess her password.

'I really can't believe how old Anthoussa and Agorakritos look,' she thought. *'And Photios is at least twenty-five now – he's got a beard – so Themis must be about the same. That's about twice as old as he was before. He was younger than me then, but now he's quite a lot older.'*

She worked out the approximate date – 419, or maybe 418 BCE – and did a search on the internet. "The war between Athens and Sparta, known now as the Peloponnesian War, went on in fits and starts for nearly 30 years." So 418 was twelve years in. And it was going to escalate, with huge numbers of men dying in Sicily in 413.

This frightened her, but excited her, too. Living someone else's life, way back then, even if it was only short, was amazing! But she really hoped Themis wasn't going to be caught up in what sounded like a disastrous campaign. It would be so much better if he took up his uncle's offer and went to what is now Italy. Surely he could see the sense of having a decent job in a thriving economy rather than doing the equivalent of piecework in a war zone? *'If I knew what it is that joins us up, maybe I could warn him,'* she thought.

She took a deep breath. *'Better not to think like that,'* she told herself. *'It may not even be real. Think about the present! Think about now… And now I'm going to need a decent job myself for the summer, unless I get funding as a competing athlete.'*

Would it help to tell Natasha about Themis? Natasha was the only housemate with any empathy – after all, she was doing social studies at the university. '*No,*' thought Suzanne. '*Saying "I have a parallel existence in Ancient Greece" is just too crazy, even for her to accept. I'll stick to what I decided at school – If he ever comes back, I won't tell ANYONE.*'

'*Even BFF Bernie never understood,*' she thought. '*And the specialists just wanted to find a suitable label so they could write papers about my "extraordinary mental landscape" or whatever.*' She looked at her reflection in the screen of her laptop, superimposed on a photo of her vaulting. 'And Mum and Steve, and even Dad and the teachers, just treated me with pity … Pity! It's not me who needs pity,' she whispered to her transparent, grinning face, the 4.35m bar across her eyebrows. 'It's everyone else who doesn't get the same opportunity!'

This time, she'd keep it truly secret – two completely separate worlds.

<<<

(Breeds of Sheep 02)

Themis had to run up and round Lykavitos Hill before he could be still. At last he sat on his favourite rock near the small temple to Apollo, a little back from the lip of a disused quarry. Swallows swooped after flies below him, close to the quarry cliffs. Far away, the low sun picked out ravines and ridges in the three high mountains surrounding the City's plain. Flocks of starlings swirled and danced above the flanks of Ymittos and Pendelikon to the east and north, darkening patches of the still-bright sky.

'*If I hadn't been so obsessed with her all those years ago,*' he thought, '*and if I didn't like Agorakritos so much, I wouldn't be so angry. What an idiot he's being!*' He punched his right palm with his left fist.

Something that had been rustling in a nearby bush went silent. '*Well, I'm not going to beg him to stay friends. I'll do as she says and stay away.*' He stood up. '*I've got enough worries, including Photios the ghost – or criminal – coming to supper. That should be interesting.*'

At home, he changed out of his work tunic into an old red linen chiton. 'Photios will be here soon,' he told Frog. 'I smell food. OK for him, too?'

'You didn't mention it, but I dare say Mika will manage,' said Frog. 'More water to fetch, more dough to stretch,' he added, demonstrating with his hands.

Themis rolled his eyes.

Frog went on, 'I assume Photios will explain who the man with the weird voice was. You'll be unlivable-with if you have another sleepless night. All well at Agorakritos' place?'

'Don't ask!' exclaimed Themis. He was tying an embroidered fillet round his hair and fumbled it. He pulled it off. Frog pushed him to sit down and took the ribbon from him.

'You'll tell me anyway,' he said. 'So what happened?'

Themis exhaled. 'The Spartans have stolen our sanity as well as our peace,' he said, bowing his head so that Frog could tie the fillet. 'In just one day, I find I have a much-loved uncle who's died, a much-unloved uncle who wants me to emigrate, a stranger who thinks I should be more ambitious and dynamic, a friend who doesn't remember insulting me, and another who thinks I screwed his wife. Everyone's gone crazy!'

'Done,' said Frog. 'Dashing and dandified as always.'

Themis stood up. 'Huh,' he grunted and stretched impatiently.

Frog went on, 'Dinner will sort you out. Fish in green sauce, and crispy honey cakes with soft cheese.' He smacked his lips.

There was a knock on the street door.

'The disappearing one reappears. So maybe some of us are still sane,' Frog added cheerfully, going into the kitchen.

'We'll walk to the square and back,' Themis called to him. 'Then we'll eat.'

At the door, Themis took Photios' arm and they set off down the street.

Photios seemed very tense. He unlinked his arm and turned to Themis. 'So where do you think you saw me last night?' he asked.

'On the street under the Hill of the Muses, above the southern Gate.' He was keeping his voice cheerful in spite of his painful suspicions. 'I was going up to look at the open sky before coming home from … well. I'd been at Melpomeni's place. I'd passed the shrine to Poseidon that they painted green last month. You were coming the other way and walked into a patch of moonlight.'

Photios looked sideways at him with a confused frown. 'I did? And did this apparition of me speak to you?' he asked. They moved out of the way of a loaded wagon.

'Yeah, you spoke to me,' Themis answered when it had grumbled past. 'You were pretty mean. You – he – said I was the last person he wanted to see and that it would have been better if we'd never met.'

Photios' frown deepened. 'But … I would never say anything like that. It's not true! What did you do?'

'Well, I was shocked, angry. You – he – cursed me and ran into an alley, so I followed. I called your name, and searched the alley.'

'Nothing?'

'Nothing and no one. Just a locked door. Yellow and I kept watch all night, but no one appeared – no Photios, no one at all.'

Photios relaxed a bit. 'That was good of you!' he said. 'Especially after whoever it was, was so … vicious. Thanks. But all I can think is that it must have been someone who looks like me.'

Themis was thinking that Photios had either suddenly acquired a talent for clever acting, or he was truly as mystified as Themis himself. He said, 'As I sat there in the dark listening to the wild wedding going on in the house opposite, all sorts of nonsense went through my mind. I wondered whether perhaps you'd heard the rumours about when Phidias escaped, and you were angry with me – or afraid.'

Photios stopped dead. 'Phidias' escape? That was ages ago. What rumours?' he said.

Themis leaned closer and spoke quietly. 'There was some murmur in the Agora, about my being involved, as Phidias and I are related. He has now died, I've learned. Perhaps that news set the rumour off. Anyway, because it happened so long ago, everyone just laughed. So did I, and no one mentioned you, but …'

'And you thought I was angry with you for involving me in something illegal when we were kids? You're crazy. I enjoyed it! And I still believe it was right, what we did. Sad he's dead now, though. Still he evaded his jealous enemies that bit longer because of us. Which reminds me that I heard some jealous talk about you at the Cretan sweets stall near the Heroes statues. No mention of Phidias, but it seems you skive off and build walls on campaign instead of facing the enemy directly.' When Themis frowned, Photios went on, 'Anyway, I didn't even know about the Phidias rumour.'

'So … could it be something to do with your new exalted status?' asked Themis.

'I hope you're joking,' said Photios, stopping and looking directly at Themis. 'If not, that's an insult.'

Themis took his friend's arm again. 'There *are* those who think like that, but no, I meant it as a joke … And yet the mystery remains. You really don't remember anything about it?'

'No. Nothing.'

'Not even being called into the street and asked to go and give advice to someone in a specific house up near the green shrine?'

Photios stopped again and pulled his arm away, shaking his head. 'What are you talking about? What advice? And was that in the middle of the night, too?'

'Yes. Someone saw you … near your house. Talking to a man who was giving you instructions.' Themis sighed and smiled. 'But I see you really don't remember.'

'Zeus in heaven, what man?' Photios exclaimed.

'I'm not sure,' Themis said, walking on. 'It's just hearsay. But I have been wondering whether – could it somehow link to Damianos' death?'

Photios' face was genuinely shocked as he shook his head. 'I can't imagine how,' he said. 'All I know is, I wasn't there. You know it would have been a *pleasure* to bump into you. You could have come back to the house with me. I had some rather good sweet wine.'

Themis laughed. He was right. Photios was still Photios – innocent of cunning, hospitable and ferociously honest.

The pigeons were clattering and calling as they settled in the trees by the river. Lamps were being lit in the houses they passed. People were hurrying to get home before dark.

'Well, where were you, then?' asked Themis.

'Last night? At home,' said Photios. 'My father had been sent the wine by a friend of his and I drank a cup with him. When he'd gone to bed, I sat a little longer by the brazier. Oh, and I wrote a love song I want your opinion on. Then I went to bed, too.'

'So you definitely didn't go out for a walk to clear your drunken head?' suggested Themis.

'Not unless I walked in my sleep,' said Photios with a shrug and a smile. 'I must say, I don't actually remember going to bed, but I woke up with the sun, in my own bed, feeling great.' He stopped again and put a hand on Themis' arm. 'Look, I'll keep an ear open for that rumour about Phidias. That was definitely the most dangerous of your madcap schemes. I dare say there are those who would deem it traitorous.' Then he said with a grin, 'Are we walking all the way to Piraeus, or do we get to eat tonight?'

Themis smiled. 'Mika's expecting us at home.' They turned back. 'I gather there's fish and some of those honey cakes you like.'

'Perfect,' said Photios.

'And what about your new job? How is it going? Anyone jealous of *you*?'

Photios laughed and said, 'Also perfect! It's a great feeling when you tell people to do things and they actually do them!'

Themis said with mock seriousness, 'But what do you know about triremes except how to wrap the handle of an oar?'

'Oh, nothing much,' answered his friend. 'Just what you learn from five years sweating and working your way up in the shipyards, repairing the damage done by overzealous rowers and generals.' He elbowed Themis' ribs.

'Will you be at Faliron Harbour the day after tomorrow?' Themis asked. 'My name's on the list in the Agora to be an overzealous rower on exercises at dawn.'

'Possibly. My father will be one of the trierachs that day. Three of the triremes we're fitting out at the shipyard at present are being paid for by him.'

Themis laughed. 'You'll be choosing a wife soon, with all that money you're earning.'

'I'm in no hurry,' said Photios. 'Unlike Straton.'

'What a moron he is,' chuckled Themis. 'If I ever start preening myself in front of my peers like that, just give me a kick up the arse.'

'Likewise,' said Photios seriously. 'I can't imagine being manipulated by a matchmaker. How can he bear to be led by the nose like that?' and he patted the herm outside Themis' front door on its classically straight nose.

'His father's doing,' said Themis as they went in. 'That's the only good thing about having a dead father – he can't interfere in my life, unlike some relatives and even strangers.'

Themis slept deeply that night, but woke with a start next morning. He had dreamed that his dead father had led him to a cliff edge, promising to show him something important. Themis was deeply reluctant close to cliff edges. He'd seen a woman ride off one to her death when he was a boy. But in this dream, when he and his father got there, Photios was being pulled by a rope through his nose towards a huge drop.

Themis sat up, suddenly awake, the sight of Photios teetering still fresh in his mind's eye. It took a while for his heartbeat to slow. 'A message from the gods?' he asked himself ironically, getting up.

As he walked through the crisp dawn to the gym, he realized that it wasn't just Photios' ghost that was disturbing him. There was a faint hum in his chest on and off, a vibration rather than a sound. It was oddly familiar – perhaps the gods really were trying to tell him something …

At the gym, Photios did not appear. Themis joked about the dream with his friends, but felt uneasy all day at the pottery factory. As he worked on the last batch of the Herculean jars, he thought to himself, '*I suppose it's better to be obsessed by that than by Agorakritos' jealousy.*' Hercules had never been so intensely muscled.

Later, towards evening, he set out to walk the few stadia to Photios' house, hoping to ask him more about Damianos. The streets were still busy in the apricot glow of sunset. Above were rags of cloud streaked with fire, and the myriads of sparrows chattered as they began roosting in the plane tree on the corner near Photios' home.

As he came round this corner, Themis saw Photios hurrying away in the opposite direction. Themis followed, hoping to catch him up in spite of the crowds.

Photios turned off the main street and Themis had to run to see where he went next. He stopped on the corner and checked something in a pocket. Then he looked around as if to make sure he wasn't being watched, and dived into the gap between two buildings.

Themis ran to the gap and looked down the alley. It was entirely steps down to a large door in a high, earth-brick wall. The tops of piles of timber showed above the wall. As Themis watched, Photios unlocked the door and slipped inside the timber yard.

Themis heard someone approaching. He leapt down a few steps and wriggled into a niche between two walls. Three men passed him in the gloom of the alley. They walked down silently and purposefully and knocked on the door. It opened and they disappeared inside. Themis approached it quietly and listened for a moment. No voices, no sounds, not even of men working.

He suddenly felt ashamed of spying on his friend and walked slowly back up the steps to the street.

As he did this, he noticed the hum was there again. Suddenly, he was twelve again, just after he'd cracked his head because his pony shied at a lightning strike and threw him. There'd been all kinds of odd visions then. And a similar hum. Perhaps seeing Photios at that crossroads really had been just a dream, a kind of hallucination, like back then.

As he passed it, he patted the old herm outside Photios' house.

'What's going on, old man?' he murmured, and walked home feeling distracted.

'Message from Master Diodotos,' said Frog as Themis came in. 'Says he'll be in the city tomorrow evening and you and he are invited to a symposium.'

'Right.' Themis nodded and yawned. 'Wake me early, though. Naval exercises at Faliron first thing.'

'And an interesting new work appointment when you get back,' said Frog. 'Don't forget that.'

'As if I could,' said Themis with smile and a lifted eyebrow.

>>>

'Shit, I look dire today,' said Suzanne to herself in the mirror.

Her face was puffy and the shadows under her eyes were darker than usual. She hadn't slept well and had got up early to write. She'd learned to type faster this last couple of days.

Dictating, which was much quicker, had turned out to be a problem because her housemates asked her who she was talking to so earnestly. 'One of the signs of madness?' Penny had joked. Penny was an art student who was nearly always out. Suzanne had laughed, but stopped the dictation unless she was alone in the house.

'I wish I knew what had happened to your sister Myrto, Themis, and your mother and everyone,' Suzanne whispered to her reflection. 'Where are they? And what have you been doing all the time since we were connected last time? And how come you're so … comfortable being naked. Is it because there are penises drawn on walls and on those way-marker herms everywhere? I – or rather, you – see people touching them as if for good luck. Bit different to here!

'I've got to say, though, that I like it that you feel me as a hum. You're more like a buzz on the skin at the back of my neck. When I feel it I know, if I close my eyes I'll see and hear what you're seeing and hearing. And you're wrong, you know,' she went on quietly. 'That other Photios was not a dream. I saw him too. Something weird *is* going on.'

'You done in there?' called Natasha from the other side of the door. 'Isn't it time you got up to campus for that Sport Psychology lecture?'

<<<

Chapter 5: trireme

(Breeds of Sheep 03)

Themis lay looking at eyes that were looking at him in the reflected moonlight. But these weren't the grey, tired eyes of his dream. They gleamed dark and liquid. Yellow was standing by his bed, tense and questioning.

'It was the nymph,' Themis murmured to the dog. 'I'm sure …
though I only saw her that once, of course. Her chin, the line of her
hair, both the same, but her eyes are greyer now, her eyebrows thinner.
She's older, and her hair's different. Is that possible? Do nymphs age?'

He reached out a sweating hand and stroked Yellow between the
ears.

'Seeing a nymph can be a bad omen,' he said to the dog. 'But she
doesn't seem to wish me harm – more just interested in what I'm
doing. Strange kind of nymph … but better than some of my other
dreams.' He turned over. The dog got onto the bed and lay down
beside him. Themis drifted off to sleep again, without his usual gruff
'Get off, Yellow!'

Later that morning on the quay, hundreds of men were milling
around, laying their offerings of tiny twists of salt or dried fish on
Poseidon's altar or getting water bags filled. Themis turned from adding
his own offering and saw Melissus standing near the boarding ladder of
the Loyalty, Themis' assigned trireme.

'What in Hades are *you* doing here, Melissus!' Themis called out as he
ran over to where the ship was moored, stern first to the quay. It was a
cold morning, with a light wind, and a calm sea. The sun was about to
rise.

'Why?' asked the Row Master from the foot of the ladder. 'He's here
on my orders. What's your problem, Themistokles?'

Themis didn't have time to speak before Melissus said, 'I have
something for you. Something you'll like,' and his eyes gleamed.

'Uh ho, young Melissus,' said the Row Master with a grin. 'I'd better
leave you two alone, it seems.' And he turned to the gathering crew of
rowers. 'Get in line, there!'

'What sort of something?' asked Themis quietly as he marched
Melissus towards a bench. 'And why does the Row Master want you
here?' The other rowers were queuing to fill their drinking water skins.
'I'm holding them all up. What have you got?' He turned his back to
the quay so no one would see what Melissus gave him.

Melissus laughed. 'I'm here because I'm coming with you this time,'
he said with glee. 'I'm to make portraits of a series of rowers as a
cartoon for a frieze we are working on at the yard.' He fished a thin
package wrapped in linen out of his satchel. His hand shook as he
handed it to Themis. 'This is for you.'

Themis took the package and put it in his rower's bag. It weighed
nothing and was sealed. Melissus laughed a little too loudly. 'It won't

bite you or pee on you or anything,' he said.

Themis couldn't help smiling too. 'Thanks,' he said. 'You be careful on the ship. Don't do anything silly.'

Melissus' expression changed abruptly and he exclaimed angrily, 'What d'you mean, silly!' Then he relaxed. 'Sorry. Of course, I know what you mean, and I'm learning that once you've jumped into the sewer you have to live with the smell for a long time. I'm avoiding other sewers.' He smiled ruefully.

Themis looked at the boy and shook his head. 'What have you been up to, I wonder,' he said. 'No. I don't want to know! I just meant … Well. You know they all think we're lovers?'

Melissus' smile broadened into a wicked grin and he nodded knowingly. 'Better than their knowing the truth,' he said.

'You're impossible,' said Themis. 'Come on. We have work to do. I'll look at this later.'

'Mind it doesn't fly away,' said Melissus.

The Trierarch was arranging a cushion for behind the head of his seat, high up on the stern. Themis was amused to see that it was Photios' father, Leontis. He was an ex-general who had fought the Spartans in the northern campaigns years earlier. As Trierarch, he was paying for the maintenance and provisioning of the whole ship. Everyone, including Themis, greeted him quietly as they came on board with a nod and a brief 'Sir!', while the Row Master ticked each man off on his list. There were four passenger soldiers. In a battle there could be dozens, so they had to learn how to stay out of the way of the rowers.

Themis slipped into his place half way along on the starboard side, facing the stern. His seat was in the extended deck-space that jutted out all along the side of the ship – more pleasant but harder work than those below, where he'd been until a year or so before. From here he could see behind and out to the side of the trireme. There was fresh air all round and the sea under his feet. It was good to be a 'thranitis'.

He strapped his cushion to his bench, stowed his water skin and bag underneath it, put his feet into the sandal-shaped sheaths and laced them up. He checked his tholepin and oar loop, then the oar itself for cracks or lumps that could create blisters. He lowered the oar into the water to get the feel of the angle.

No one spoke. To his left, and on a level with his feet, the man with the oar immediately under his was spitting on his hands. And below him in the rank-smelling depths of the ship, the rowers in the lowest tier were already in place, quietly waiting. Themis took a series of deep breaths as he sat looking along the quay. Other ships were preparing to go out with their crews, but this wasn't like a commercial harbour. The men worked in silence. It was birds that made the most noise, greeting the new day.

Melissus had disappeared onto the deck somewhere above. Everyone was still now, and ready. The Row Master was standing to attention below the high stern.

'Quiet, now!' he called, with a grin. The rowers rolled their eyes and nodded silently. 'Listen up! Today some of you are going to be models.' All through the crowded ship, shoulders shrugged and hands questioned. 'Yes. We have an artist on board who is looking for models for a sculpture. He'll be allowed on the central gangway as soon as we're underway and he'll make quick sketches of some of you at your oars. So make sure you look beautiful.' The men looked at each other and made exasperated faces. 'And don't sweat!!' shouted the Row Master.

Everyone laughed out loud, putting up a pair of egrets from the rigging.

As they quietened down, he began his high-pitched rhythmic call to set the pace, slowly at first, but picking up speed once they were away from the quay.

'OoopAH! OoopAH!' The drummer and flute player adjusted to his rhythm.

Out on the water, the familiar feeling of power and excitement took hold of the men. They were flying. The oars were their beating wings. Themis grinned at his neighbour who grinned back.

Those in the bottom row, the thalamians, couldn't see anything but they could feel the ship slicing through the water, leaping forward with each stroke. Within minutes, Themis could see headland beyond headland, stretching all the way to Sounion, where Poseidon's temple on its cliff stood tiny but clear against the dawn sky.

After the usual manoeuvres to practise turning, accelerating and backwatering, they made for the islet of Fleves to practise ramming. Themis hands were pleasingly hard now, so the only blisters he could feel rising were from the foot straps.

The Row Master recited them a rhythmic, bloodthirsty poem about an expedition he'd been on to subdue Samos, back when the men 'were mere babes'. Themis' father had lost part of a leg in that campaign, so he knew the stories by heart and joined in while he still had breath.

Melissus moved along the central planks, drawing heads, hands, bent and straining bodies.

As they neared the island, the Row Master, his story completed, shouted 'Prepare to ram!!' He increased the stroke speed by taking the drummer's mallet himself. The Helmsman steadied the ship on a straight course and called out the distance still to go every few moments. Themis couldn't see what they were going to hit, only the wake they were making in the water.

The Row Master was shouting now in time to the rising rhythm of the drum. 'She's flying now, flapping her wings! Faster, faster! Stab that Persian! Faster, faster! Split 'er scull! Crack 'er nut! Faster, faster! Spill 'er crew, lice in the water!'

And the Helmsman bawled, 'Two, One, Now!!!'

There was a great crash and the ship shuddered from end to end. All the rowers shot first backwards on their benches, then forwards. The Trierarch lurched forwards then back, saved by his cushion. Melissus fell off the deck, landing on the walkway below. No one else noticed and Themis couldn't see him now. He'd tease him later.

'Reverse! Reverse!' shouted the Helmsman. The Row Master thumped his mallet and called, 'Back one. Back two. Back three,' his piercing voice clear above the creaks and thuds of the ship's movement.

The Loyalty seemed to stretch and thrum like a live thing. She began to make way backwards. Themis strained and sweated, pushing his oar away from him with all his strength each time the mallet fell. He looked down into the water and could see the dark shapes of rocks on the seabed. *'Would Damianos have been visible from above like this?'* he wondered. *'Is that how they found him? … And how's Melissus?'*

'Keep in rhythm,!' shouted Leontis from the stern. 'Keep together!'

Themis noticed the lowest oar under him was trailing in the water. It would snarl those on either side of it at any moment. 'Pull in that oar,' he shouted down to the thalamians.

The rower had knocked himself out on the beam behind him when they'd hit with the ram. The men around him, unable to stop rowing, were calling for help. Themis pulled in his oar, unlaced his feet and stood up. He could see Melissus now, lying winded on his back. One of the passenger soldiers was kneeling beside him, loosening his belt.

Themis shouted to him, 'Get that oar first!' The soldier leapt up and pulled the oar in. Meanwhile, Melissus stirred and sat up, looking surprised. He noticed his loose belt and tied it back tight. Then he jumped up and offered to help the soldier with the unconscious rower.

Themis sat down again with a wry smile.

The Trierach called out, 'Veer to starboard!'

The Row Master ordered Themis' side of the ship to 'go half' while the other side 'went full'. The ship came round. Leontis stood up.

'Stop the ship, Row Master,' he called. 'Let's see the damage we did.'

The old hull they'd rammed was now in two pieces, one floating, one almost submerged. A cheer rose from two hundred throats.

'Better than last time!' called Leontis. 'Back to the benches! Eat and drink now. And when you're done, we'll race the Piety back to Piraeus.'

'Heave! Rest. Heave! Rest,' called the Row Master later. The crew had manned the ropes and were dragging the Loyalty from the water up the slipway into one of the scores of shipsheds in the naval harbour. She was to dry out during the night and be checked over next day.

The Row Master came up to Themis as he hauled on the rope. 'Can you take the signing off list today, Themistokles? I'm on duty in the Council from noon.'

'Of course,' panted Themis. He'd done this before. 'How many exactly?'

'A hundred and ninety-seven. Here's the tablet,' said the Row Master.

Themis had ticked off a hundred and ninety six, including himself and Melissus, who waved a hand and disappeared at a run towards Athens. Themis was in a hurry to leave, too. He had an appointment and this one missing man was delaying him.

He called out the man's name, 'Belos!' but got no answer. There was a lot of noise from the shipsheds on either side where the same exodus was going on. So he climbed on board to check that Belos wasn't the one who'd knocked himself out, although he was pretty sure Belos rowed in the mid-tier. From up there he could see down to the front of the shed where all the storage bins for oars and ropes and sails were. Belos, a cheese-maker, was walking away from them, dusting his hands together. *What business could Belos have at the storage bins?* Themis thought as he ran down the plank.

'Nothing wrong with the bins, Belos?'

'No. All fine,' said the cheese-maker with a shrug and a smile. 'See you next time.' And he ran off to the exit gate of the shipyard.

Themis turned to the Loyalty's shipwright. 'All yours,' he said, handing him the tablet. 'She took a battering today. She split the wreck and knocked a rower unconscious!'

'She's a tough old bird,' said the shipwright with a laugh. 'But she flies better than most.'

'Is Yard Master Photios around?'

'Entertaining some oak merchants from Illyria, last I saw of him. On the other side of the harbour.'

'Never mind. Just tell him I was asking after him,' said Themis. 'And say the real him, not his double,' he called over his shoulder as he ran off. He was late and needed a quick visit to the baths before his appointment.

Suzanne opened her eyes. The lecture was over. Everyone was standing up and sidling along between the rows of desks towards the exit. Natasha and Theo sat on either side of her. They looked at each other over her head and then laughed. Theo pushed his iPad into the front pocket of his bag. 'Well, at least you didn't snore,' he said. 'I'll send you the notes you missed. You coming for a sandwich?'

'Thanks,' said Suzanne. 'Yes. Look, I'll meet you both in the canteen. I just need the loo.'

They set off towards the Café Republic.

Suzanne stared sightlessly at the graffiti on the loo door. She couldn't believe it. Themis had heard her and seen her face! She'd looked in a mirror and talked to him and he'd woken up and heard her! And then gone back to sleep.

This was new. They'd never communicated directly in those far away days after the accident. What was going on? Would she be able to influence him, after all? She was as breathless as if she'd sprinted two hundred metres.

She splashed water on her face and did a mental calming exercise from training. She'd try contacting Themis again later while the others were out drinking. She'd say she had a headache and go home alone.

<<<

Chapter 6: symposium

(Breeds of Sheep 04)

Themis returned home at dusk to find Yellow lying across the door of the andron. He stepped carefully over the dog, but Yellow stood up and sniffed at his master. Themis' brother, Diodotos, was by the window, a slim, wiry silhouette examining a cut on his hand in the fading light.

He turned towards Themis. 'Where have you been? You said you'd be back before dark.'

'Just made it,' said Themis with a gesture at the darkening window. 'Good journey?' He fondled Yellow's ears.

'Fine.' Diodotos came towards him. 'But what have you been up to?'

'Research,' said Themis shortly. They embraced. Themis couldn't keep his smile from widening as he saw Diodotos register what he smelled of.

'Funny kind of research, from the smell of you. Research for what?' Diodotos threw himself down on a couch.

'I have a commission,' said Themis, sitting down opposite his brother. The dog lay down, placing a heavy paw on his foot. 'I'm going to paint the walls of a couple of therapy rooms with suitably erotic scenes for a dealer in natural remedies.'

'Remedies? What for?' asked Diodotos. Then he nodded knowingly. 'Oh, I see. For the older clientele. So,' he added with a chuckle, '… what was she like?'

'Oh, there was more than one.'

'Hah!' Diodotos exclaimed. 'And you didn't think to invite your brother along too? Even after I got you an invitation to the symposium tonight?'

Themis looked down at his hands. There were traces of the sweet smelling ointment the girls had rubbed on him under his nails. No, he'd enjoyed it more alone. He said, 'The opportunity arose a bit … unexpectedly.'

'You could have sent Frog for me.'

'He was busy,' said Themis with a shrug and a grin.

'You spoil him,' said his older brother. 'He'll turn on you one day.'

Themis looked Diodotos in the eyes. 'I owe him my life,' he said quietly. 'And anyway,' he teased. 'Why would you be interested? Have you fallen out with Iole?'

Diodotos stood up wearily. 'Iole will never make any promises, you know that. She's so popular, *she* chooses who … and when.'

He looked so dejected Themis had to smile. '*And* how much,' he said.

Diodotos looked at Themis with a smirk. 'Not always,' he said.

Themis laughed out loud. 'She must really like you, then.'

'Maybe,' said Diodotos, grinning now. 'I'm thinking you'd better have a good wash and put on clean clothes. We're going to be late.'

'Why exactly am I going?' Themis asked as he stood up. 'It's your supper club, not mine.'

'The host, Eteokles, specifically wanted to meet you. He told me it was with an eye to your possible future participation. But I think he he's related somehow to Photios' dad. The others are probably older than us, but then they're richer, too.'

'Ah! Our Olympic champion and super-oarsman,' gabbled Eteokles, standing up from his plain couch to welcome Themis and Diodotos as they came into his andron. They'd washed their hands in the courtyard and were adjusting their sweet smelling garlands.

'Welcome, welcome, gentlemen … Please make yourselves comfortable.' He spoke in spurts, gesturing towards a long, empty couch without cushions. The room was well lit, the walls frescoed with seascapes of islands and ships. It was longer than it was wide and the green-covered couches were arranged as three sides of a rectangle. But there was no other decoration, unlike at other supper club parties.

The brothers stood by the couch Eteokles indicated as he kneaded his hands together. He went on, 'You both know Nereus, the general?'

A distinguished man with a grey streak on either side of his dark curling beard inclined his head. His hands lay motionless on his wine-coloured himation. His garland was white iris and narcissus, his belt of gold threads.

'And I'm not sure … if you know Ilarion?' Eteokles went on, his bulging eyes intense. He emphasized the last word of each phrase he spoke.

The man on the end couch raised a hand and bowed his head. His back was humped, and he was the only person in the room with the comfort of a cushion. He said, 'You trained with Arianos, didn't you, Themistokles? He's an old acquaintance of mine.' Themis bowed and smiled. 'And this is your brother?'

'Diodotos, son of Kallistos, my first invitation as a member of this club in my father's place,' said Diodotos, with a bow to Ilarion and Nereus. 'Greetings, gentlemen.'

'Sadly, my other young guest, Photios, is unable to come this evening,' said Eteokles. 'He's busy with his new job… His father is my cousin.' He indicated the fifth couch. 'This is for Tryfonos, assuming he comes.'

Nereus the general nodded. 'Hmm. He's usually punctual,' he said. 'Unlike our other blond friend, Alkibiades. Something important must have kept him.' His voice was deep, his accent crisply Athenian, his manner pompous. Themis knew Nereus from his army service, a bold soldier, but a cold man. The only thing they had in common was athletic success. Two years before Themis won the boys' boxing at Olympia, Nereus had won the pentathlon at the Isthmian Games. He was perhaps ten years older than Diodotos.

Diodotos' head came up. 'Alkibiades has saved a few lives, though,' he said pleasantly. 'I saw him myself protect Sokrates in the rout at Delium.'

Eteokles tut-tutted. 'Once Alkibiades enters … the conversation, all other subjects are forgotten,' he said with a short laugh. He clapped his hands at the slaves, and went on, 'Let us keep him till later … and talk now of other interests. Ilarion, I see you are much improved in your health … To what do you attribute this?'

Themis turned to Diodotos. He made a 'why are we here?' face. He didn't fancy four or five hours with these men if there was to be no younger, more lively company. Diodotos nodded meaningfully towards the conversation.

'Ah,' sighed Ilarion happily. He had a pleasing, musical voice. 'I have been taking a powder that has strange and wonderful properties. It has cured my aches and the tightening of my tendons.'

A pair of twin slaves brought in platters of food and put them on the low tables in front of the couches. Another slave mixed wine and water in the great mixing bowl with splashy panache. Beside him a musician played on a kithara. Themis was intrigued by the wine-slave working to the music. Ripples on the kithara echoed splashes in the oinochoi.

'However,' Ilarion was saying, 'I find I have to be careful to take this powder only when I am at home and can be prevented from leaving the house. Not long after I take it I lose my awareness of where I am and remember nothing for perhaps a day. But when I return to myself, I feel as though my whole body and mind has been cleansed and renewed and I have almost no pain for two or three days.'

'Do you think that's what Sokrates takes?' asked Diodotos. 'There were times when he stood quite still and didn't speak for hours. Then, when he did, he would be even more cheerful than usual.'

'And where do you get this magical potion,' asked Nereus with irony.

'It's available in the Street of the Winds, on the corner with the Old Way,' said Ilarion. 'Have you not heard the street criers calling "Come to the Corner to forget your ills"?'

'Really?' said Themis, suddenly focusing. 'Are you sure?'

'Of course,' said Ilarion. 'It is quite a trek for me to go there, and they wouldn't serve my slave the first time I bought it, in case it got into "untutored hands", they said. Why do you ask?'

Diodotos looked his own question at Themis who said, 'I ask because I have a commission to do some frescoes for that shop.'

Eteocles stood up and signaled to the wine-slave. 'Let us pour our libations now. As you have probably noted, … we are drinking half wine and half water tonight instead of my usual one third to two thirds … The flavour of this vintage is … a little thin to my taste.'

After the short ceremony, they began to eat. The musician filled the quiet with a lyrical song of far mountains and the dangerous naiads who live there. Themis thought of his own naiad or nymph and noted the presence of his hum. *Is she with me even here?* he thought.

Nereus tasted the wine and nodded to Eteocles. 'You were right, honoured host. The wine is a little sour, though strong.' He turned with a patronizing smile to Themis and said, 'And so, Themistokles, perhaps I will need to ply you with less than I expected.'

Themis stopped with the leg of a pigeon half way to his mouth. 'I … don't understand, sir?' he said. The challenge in his voice sounded more aggressive than he'd meant.

Nereus smiled calmly. 'It is my intention, you see – knowing of your prowess as an athlete and swimmer – to offer you the leadership of a new aquatic army unit I am setting up. It would entail extra training and free travel, often separately from the main army cohorts.'

This seemed such a crazy idea to Themis (and the pigeon was tough and hard to chew) that he merely shook his head with a polite downward glance.

'No?' asked Nereus. 'Is that, I wonder, perhaps because you cannot bear to leave your young beloved alone for so long at a time?'

Themis was taken aback by such rudeness. His mouth now empty, he looked at Nereus with wide eyes. 'Which beloved is that?' he asked. Diodotos leant forward to take some food, trying not to smile.

Nereus said, 'That delicious little scamp, Melissus. I gather he follows you everywhere.'

Chapter 7: temptations

Themis sucked in his cheeks so as not to laugh. 'Melissus. Of course. I have known him since he was born, though we see more of him now that his family has moved into the City.'

'He is, I gather, Agorakritos' eldest child?' Nereus had a tendency to stare without blinking when he spoke to someone. He was staring at Themis. Eteokles was obviously not going to do his duty as host and divert the conversation, so Themis decided on a little rudeness of his own.

'Would you not be able to lead the aquatic unit yourself?' he asked.

Eteokles had the grace to look at his feet.

'At my age, that's no longer a possibility,' said Nereus, taken aback.

'You are much too modest,' said Themis insincerely.

'But you, now,' said Nereus with feigned courtesy, 'are at the height of your powers.'

Themis might have been tempted by the excitement of serving in such a special force, but the thought of being at the beck and call of General Nereus at all times made it easy to resist. 'It's a pity Damianos died,' he said. Nereus blinked. Themis went on, 'He would have been the perfect man for you. Whereas I am not in a position to take on something like that. I have commitments both at home and to my usual unit that I cannot ignore.' He inclined his head politely. 'Though I am aware of the honour you do me with your suggestion.'

Diodotos choked.

'I know of course about your home commitments,' said Nereus, ignoring this, '*and* of how little they help with the family finances. If you were to join this unit ...' He leant forwards, eyes intent. '... you would be highly paid. As a further inducement, I could arrange for you to take part in the competition for a whole wall in the Painted Arcade in the Agora. You would be younger than your uncle Panainos was when he painted his Battle of Marathon. Would that not be of interest to you?'

Themis looked at Nereus. That was of course exactly what he dreamed of. But he'd never spoken of it in public. And why was Nereus offering it as bait? 'I would be interested if the commission were offered to all as usual in the Agora. Why is it so important that *I* take part?' he asked.

Nereus took a sip of wine. 'Athens needs a special force to protect herself against all kinds of attack. It is true that we already have volunteer swimmers on each trireme. You are one, I hear. But I believe that we need a more organized, better-trained, paid division. There has been a spate of deaths, men either drowning (while on duty, not like Damianos) or being attacked when they do repairs during campaigns against our enemies. But of course, if you feel it would be too dangerous ...'

'I would imagine,' said Diodotos, 'that such a unit would cost the City a good deal of money. I don't recall it coming up at the Assembly.'

Nereus smiled. 'Not yet, of course. The costs are not all counted yet.'

Ilarion cleared his throat and said, 'Would you re-direct funds for this? The extra money the Assembly voted to the Scythian Archers to stop them accepting bribes, for instance? Surely not. What about asking that golden friend of yours, Kallias? He inherited enough to gild a temple not long ago. Or would it be better to use slaves? That's an area where Kallias' expertise is even greater than your own, is it not, Nereus?'

Nereus looked startled. 'As far as I know, Kallias is not involved with slaves with such skills!' he said, turning his unblinking eyes on Ilarion. 'And I certainly am not. And we couldn't rely on slaves, however skilled. Rather than help the repairers of our ships, they could be a danger to them.'

Ilarion seemed unmoved by Nereus' stare and said thoughtfully, 'Not long ago I was at the official slave market, looking for a strong young male to help me get around. I thought I heard your voice in the er ... "informal" enclosure, so I looked in. You were arguing the versatility of a group of wretched-looking females, presumably gathered up from the streets.'

Nereus smiled and shrugged. 'I remember that well,' he said smoothly. 'I was standing in for a man I know who was ill that day but needed to augment the workforce of his weaving factory. Normally I have nothing to do with that trade.' His voice and eyes never wavered.

'I hope he paid you commission,' said Ilarion.

'Hardly,' scoffed Nereus. 'It was just the once.' Before Eteokles could change the subject, he went on, 'But Themistokles, you must consider this offer with care. It is one that won't be repeated. You – and your family – will be disappointed if you turn it down and then hear of one of your colleagues being paid a large, dependable salary instead of you. And I can't believe you want to feel disappointed again. Surely the eighty-ninth Olympics, when the gods deserted you, was enough disappointment for a life time?'

Themis kept his face in his wine cup to cover his anger.

Even Eteokles thought this was too much. 'We have all felt that the gods ... were on our side in one endeavor or another ... and then discovered they weren't,' he prattled.

'Ah, the gods,' sighed Ilarion.

Themis looked up now at the humorous tone of Ilarion's voice.

'We use them to build illusions of our popularity and grandeur, don't we Nereus?' Ilarion asked sweetly. 'Then we hear them laughing on Olympus when the Assembly saddles us with the job of sewage disposal instead of general of an army campaign.'

Everyone laughed except Nereus, who was studying the design on his cup. His previous official job had been cleaning up the open drain that the Eridanos River had become.

Ilarion went on, 'And, as for me? My dear god, Asklepion, briefly deprives me of my consciousness in return for a few days without pain. Here I am, like one of Phidias' stone heroes up there on the temple, my back side rigid as rock and my front busy with hero-ing – though not quite to Nereus' standard, of course. But perhaps my new "medicine" will restore my back to me. Or then again it might make me fall from the temple and fracture. Then my manslave would have to pick up the pieces. It's all a matter of "to my slave I'm a god, but to the gods I'm a slave",' he finished, with a comical expression on his face.

Everyone laughed, and even Nereus smiled wryly.

Themis surprised himself by saying, 'Does this "medicine" taste good, Master Ilarion?'

'Are you thinking of putting it in your beloved's bread? Bad Themistokles!' Ilarion wagged a finger at Themis with a broad grin.

Themis nodded mock seriously. 'That was where I was taking the conversation, I must admit,' he said.

Ilarion laughed. 'No, it has no flavour – or at least nothing you couldn't mask with a little honey or some cheese.'

'So … sweet wine would do it, would it?' Themis said.

'Ah, is that his weakness?' said Ilarion.

With an adoring expression, Themis said, 'He has no weaknesses in my eyes.' But he caught Diodotos' glance and they both exploded with laughter.

Diodotos said as he recovered, 'Gentlemen, the boy and Themis are just old friends. Themis' interests in that field lie … elsewhere.'

Just then a slave came and whispered to Eteokles. He excused himself and left the room.

Nereus immediately turned to Ilarion and said, 'What do you think of Alkibiades provoking trouble and insisting that the Spartans have not kept faith with the peace treaty? How much mud will that young pup stir up before he falls on his face?'

Ilarion laughed. 'In a way he's right, you know …'

Eteokles came back with another visitor, but it was not Tryfonos.

'Dear Friends,' gushed Eteokles, 'Please welcome Glykon ... to our little party.'

Glykon was young and handsome. Themis took particular note of his perfectly straight nose and neat ears. He was too muscular for an Apollo but would have made a good model for a Jason or an Achilles. Themis felt he knew him, but wasn't sure from where. After the greetings, Glykon sat on the couch reserved for Tryfonos.

Eteokles turned to him. 'So Tryfonos won't ... be coming tonight?'

'No,' replied Glykon. 'He sends his apologies and hopes that I will be a worthy stand-in.' He smiled confidently around the room.

'Ah. Now I remember,' said Themis. 'You were a rower on the Piety. I saw you disembarking from her at midday.'

'So you were on the ... ?'

'The Loyalty. To your starboard side. How was your ramming practice?'

'We took on the broken hull you had failed to overcome. It fought back bravely, but we managed to stove it in and kill all the crew,' said Glykon with a straight face.

'The weather was clear and bright, but did you find the oars had shrunk with the cold?' Themis was looking at Glykon's neck. His beard hid a slackness that would later become a double chin.

'We destroyed a few oar-loops today. Maybe that was why. And I doubt we'll get them replaced immediately.'

The older men were waiting politely to start a more general conversation, but Themis went on, 'What do you mean?' Perhaps Photios hadn't ordered enough loops and he could be teased about it.

'As I was leaving,' said Glykon, 'I heard the shipwright bawling out one of the other rowers for interfering with the storage bins in the shipshed. It seems the rower had managed to spill a whole basket of loops in the mud and they'd need cleaning before the next time out.'

'What was a rower doing among the storage bins?' asked Themis.

'Not sure.' Glykon shrugged. 'Never go near them myself.'

'Nor do I. Not our responsibility.'

Eteokles made an impatient gesture and the wine slave and the musician began their mixing dance again. 'Gentlemen, let us give our thanks ... to Dionysos, then charge our wine cups ... for the next part of the evening.'

The twin slaves took away the tables of food and swept the floor. After they'd sung the prayer, the musician was joined by a flute player.

Her chiton was so fine that the curves of her body were obvious.

As the six men made themselves comfortable on the couches, three more female figures came into the room, dancing to the new rhythm. They were all unrecognizable, dressed in many layers of multi coloured tunics and veils. As they enacted a story of the nymphs who taught Dryope to dance and sing, one by one the veils came adrift and floated to the floor or over one of the watching men. Diodotos moaned slightly a couple of times as he watched.

The last of the three to show her face was also the tallest. Themis saw that it was Iole. *'Poor Diodotos,'* he thought mischievously.

The music changed and the three women began to sing a different song. The words were in fact a call to bid for their favours. Themis had been in this position many times and usually enjoyed the bidding – and the aftermath – but he'd had a busy afternoon, and anyway, he wanted to get away and have a word with Photios as soon as possible, to warn him about that sweet wine.

It was clear who was offering the most and who expected to win Iole. Nereus laid coin after coin on the arm of his couch as the girls sang and twirled to the rising rhythm. Diodotos laid his only three coins in a line on the arm and then watched with slumped shoulders.

The rhythm grew faster and came to a climax followed by silence and stillness. The two shorter women turned to Iole to make her choice. She made one stately turn on her toes, her one remaining garment drifting around her. Then she walked over to Diodotos to pick up his three coins. Themis laughed out loud at the look on his face.

One of the others took Nereus' coins and the third went and sat beside Glykon, taking the one large silver coin he held out on his hand.

Nereus stood up and left without a word. The girl who had chosen him lifted an eyebrow at Themis.

He grinned but shook his head and also stood up. He said his thanks and goodbyes, and left.

But when he got to Leontis and Photios' house, it was dark and silent. 'Tomorrow,' he thought, and loped home.

There he took out the little package Melissus had given him. He unwrapped the linen and found a folded piece of much-used papyrus.

'I think I now understand what has happened to make my husband so jealous,' it said, *'but I need to be sure before I explain. It has nothing to do with you, so please be patient and do not lose your love for him.'*

It was signed Anthoussa.

>>>

Chapter 8: disguise

(Breeds of Sheep 05 – Trying to contact Themis doesn't work – seriously hit and miss. Also, I've been spelling names as they sounded to me. Could Alkibiades be someone important? Looked him up and find that a man often spelled Alcibiades was totally a star. Hope that's him and Themis meets him! Otherwise, I could live without symposiums. All that talk! And sniping at each other. I thought that was supposed to be a female thing! I *have* tried to remember it all but I'm sure I missed bits. Themis wasn't focused some of the time, and anyway, I don't think I catch *all* his thoughts.)

<<<

'Time for a run to warm up?' asked Diodotos. He was shivering. They were walking down from the Pnyx with the hundreds of other citizens after a long session of the general Assembly. The wind had been cold up there in spite of the close-packed crowd.

'Race you to the house?' Themis suggested.

'I was thinking more of round the base of Lykavitos Hill,' said Diodotos.

'No time,' said Themis. 'I need to drop by the Street of the Winds.'

The crowd of men on the steps forced them apart for a moment. Diodotos shouted over the men's' heads, 'Needing a f…fix, eh?'

Themis made a rude sign at his brother.

They hitched up their warm cloaks and set off together at a jog. Themis peeled off north towards the Street of the Winds not far from home.

At the shop on the corner with the Old Way, labeled The Corner of Paradise, he went round the front to the herbalist department. This opened onto the main street. The rooms he would be painting were off the side street, entered by their own highly ornate door.

'Can I help you?' asked a youth he didn't know behind the counter.

'I think so,' said Themis. 'I heard from a friend last night that you stock a powder that can make you forget who you are for a short time, but when you come to yourself again you feel refreshed and full of vigour.'

'Ah, yes. Perhaps you would come this way?' And the youth led Themis through a curtained doorway, down a corridor, and into a room off a secluded courtyard. This was where Themis was going to paint the walls! It seemed there was a special buying procedure for this drug.

'Master Zotikos!' called the youth. A man came in from the courtyard.

'Themistokles!' Zotikos' dark eyes widened in surprise. 'What brings you here today?'

'Good day, Zotikos. Nothing to do with our work,' said Themis. 'I heard about one of your miracle powders last night at a symposium and wanted to ask you a couple of things about it.' The youth left.

'Who did you hear it from?' asked Zotikos.

'The customer I know about is Ilarion. He lives near the – '

'With the hump back? Yes, I know Ilarion. And I know the powder you mean. We call it "Lethe's Ladder to Heaven". It gives you a very happy day or two after a short time "elsewhere".'

'That's sounds like it,' said Themis. 'Can you tell me what happens during the "elsewhere" time, and how long it lasts?'

'Most men just seem to daydream, but some carry on as usual. That stage can last two or three hours, or more sometimes. They don't remember anything at all later – temporary amnesia, you see.'

'Could they be persuaded to do things they would not normally do in that time?' asked Themis.

'Perhaps.' Zotikos' wry grin showed white teeth in his dark face. 'I heard of a man who made love to his wife under the influence.'

Themis shook his head and laughed. 'And can anyone buy it?'

'It's not cheap.'

'I don't want to buy any myself,' said Themis. 'It's just I think I know someone else who was given it without his knowing, and I wanted to try and stop that happening again.'

'Ah, Master Themistokles. I'm sure you realize, I can't tell you who my other customers are. I suggest you just tell the unknowing person about it, and to be on his guard ...'

'Surely, to prevent a crime, you could let me know who was buying your Ladder to Heaven?' Themis smiled his sweetest smile.

'I'm sorry,' said Zotikos sincerely. 'That's just not possible. I could be arrested. And anyway, my whole business depends on my discretion ...'

'I see,' said Themis. 'Of course, some of your clients must be truly influential. Do you sell it in large quantities?'

'No more than five doses at a time. They have to be carefully measured and they are sold in little jars with wax stoppers. Two doses together could kill a man.'

'In that case,' said Themis, his smile still sweet, 'and in your place, I would only sell one at a time.' He turned to go. 'Thank you anyway. That's been very helpful. And I'll be here in three days to start on the walls.'

The sun was low as Themis arrived at Photios' house. He knocked on the door and the slave told him that Leontis was out and Photios had left a few minutes earlier with some friends.

'Which friends were these?' Themis asked.

'Not sure of their names,' said the door slave. 'They've only come by once before. But I could tell they were going to have a fine evening out.' Themis knew this old man. His name was Numa and he was not the brightest of Photios' family slaves.

Themis sighed. 'Did they say where they were going?'

'No, but I overheard them say they might meet another man in Zea.'

'Were they on horseback?'

'No, sir. Went off on foot, but I reckon they had horses waiting. They were dressed for riding.'

'What were these men like?'

'I didn't like them, sir. They looked a bit … you know … Spartan.'

Themis had to smile. 'Did you give him the note I sent this morning?'

'I told him it was by the courtyard shrine. He said he'd read it later.'

'And did he?'

'I'll look,' said Numa. He went in, but reappeared almost immediately. 'It's here,' he said. 'I don't think he read it.'

Themis' heart sank.

'Is Mister Leontis in?'

'No, sir.'

'When he left, did Photios look well? Did he look lost, or … strange?'

'Can't say he did, sir,' said the old slave, shaking his head.

'Thank you, Numa.'

Themis dashed up through the darkening streets past the Akropolis and along the road to Piraeus between the hills of the Pnyx on his right and the Muses on his left. A livery stable was still open in the village of Kili outside the city walls. He hired a spirited horse for a day and a night, and set off at a canter for Piraeus. There was no time to let anyone know where he was going. He had to catch Photios and friends before they disappeared into the grid of streets round the harbours. But as he left the cemetery on the outskirts of Kili behind, he saw a familiar figure running towards him.

'Melissus?' he called. 'Is that you?' His horse skidded to a stop on the stony road.

Melissus stopped in surprise. 'Uncle Themis! What ..?'

'Are you going home?' he asked, trying to control the horse as it danced.

'Yes. I've been out too long already…'

'Could you drop by my house and tell Frog I'm on my way to Zea Harbour? It's very important. Ask him to meet me there as soon as he can. He'll give you one of Mika's pies if you ask,' he added with a grin, 'in case you're punished with no supper at home.'

'OK,' agreed Melissus with a laugh. 'Zea Harbour.'

'Thanks,' called Themis, getting the horse under control. 'Oh, and tell him to bring some money!' he called as he set off again.

Melissus raised a hand and ran on towards the city.

Themis came within sight of Photios and his two companions a little before they dismounted and set off through the market square of Piraeus. They turned into a street that ran parallel to the wall of the navy shipyards. Behind that wall would be scores of navy triremes in their open-sided shipsheds, hauled out of the water by their crews. Themis reckoned most of the navy ships would be in the harbour as there was no major campaign going on. The maintenance stores and the armory were housed there, too.

In this side street, there was a back gate into the shipyard, smaller than the imposing main gate from the market square. But all the gates would be locked for the night by now.

Themis watched the three men hand their horses to a slave at a tavern almost opposite that back gate, and rode straight past, his head down. He went round a corner and dismounted at a chandler's store. He threw a coin to the horse boy there. 'He's a lively one,' he said. 'Keep the saddle on.' He ran back to the corner.

The two men and Photios were just going into the tavern. There was no sign of a third man.

Themis pulled the hood of his cloak over his head and bent his back into a hump like Ilarios'. He rubbed his sandals and the hem of his cloak in a heap of horse manure. Then he went around to the back door of the tavern in the alley. A young cook was taking a breath of cool air.

'Any stale bread for a veteran of Potidaea?' he croaked.

The cook looked at him with resigned irritation. 'Oh, alright,' he said. 'You're the third today. Come in and I'll find you something.'

Themis looked into the kitchen. There were huge pots set in firepits in the floor, and others that steamed and hissed on the charcoal fires in a long, waist-high trough. Herbs and a kid's carcass hung from hooks. Loaves cooled on the shelves nearest the door. Heat poured almost visibly into the street, and there was no view of the diners from the kitchen.

'May the gods bless you,' said Themis. 'Just bring anything you have to me here and I won't bother you further.'

With his broken piece of cheese-and-nut pie and a chunk of dry bread he returned to the street and settled himself in an angle in the high, navy precinct wall. He was in fact very hungry. He sat huddled under his stinking cloak and ate. *'Perhaps they chose to eat with Photios to be sure that he took his powder,'* he thought.

'Then again,' he went on, *'maybe this is a perfectly ordinary commercial meeting and I'm being an idiot.' 'Possibly,'* he answered himself. *'But even my nymph thinks there's something really odd about Photios these days. Can it be linked to Damianos' death? Anyway, I've nothing more important to do…'*

But by the time he'd finished his food, he'd convinced himself he was overreacting. Just then, the three men come out of the tavern. They were still just three. They stopped to talk quietly in the rising wind which blew their voices towards Themis. He pulled his hood further over his head.

'With the Assembly in the city today, there was no training and the ships didn't go out.' The voice was urgent, persuasive, and not Photios'.

'Well, the weather *is* ideal – nice strong wind,' said the other stranger with a Spartan crispness. Themis thought, *'The old slave wasn't wrong …'*

Then Photios' voice was clear. 'Well, if you want to see what needs doing, then let's get to it.' He strode away from the two men and approached the gate. Themis saw one of the men walk to the other side of the tavern and raise a hand as if signaling along the alleyway there.

But Photios was oblivious. 'Guards!' he commanded, as three tall men in armour stood to attention in front of the gate. 'As you know, I am Yard Master here and I need to make a tour of the triremes in this harbour tonight. These gentlemen are going to supply us with skilled men to repair our hulls more rapidly. I want them to see what's needed.'

One guard held a torch close to Photios' face. He nodded to the others, who unlocked the chains and lifted the bars.

'Thank you,' said Photios as he walked in. His two companions followed and the guards were pulling the gate shut after them when Themis saw three large men in dark cloaks step silently up to the backs of the guards, grab their throats from behind and push them through the gates. Three other men, in armour and guards' colours, appeared from the alley. They pulled the gate shut from the street side, and stood to attention outside it.

Themis could hardly believe his eyes, the men had been so quick and quiet. Who were they? Was Photios this very moment being stabbed to death? There were no sounds from beyond gates.

Under the eyes of the false guards, he had two choices: run to the next watch tower and raise the alarm, or go the other way to the Scythian Archers in the main square. Whichever he did, he would find himself impaled on a spear if he showed any signs of haste.

He gathered up his cloak to go and summon the Scythians, but saw Frog jogging towards him, obviously on the lookout.

He stumbled out into Frog's path.

'Watch where you're going, young Toad,' he croaked as they collided.

'What the … !' said Frog.

Themis used his shuffling gait to mask his pushing Frog along the street. 'It's me!' he whispered.

'Of course,' said Frog. 'I should have known by the smell.'

Themis whispered urgently, 'Listen! Photios has gone inside the naval yard with five strangers. They overcame the real guards and those men now on the gate are part of the gang. I think they're planning some kind of sabotage of the fleet tonight.'

Frog understood immediately. 'I'll run for the Scythians.'

'I've a better idea,' said Themis. 'Come with me a minute.' And he shambled into the tavern. Once inside he straightened up and threw back his cloak. 'Who's the boss here?' he called out.

A tough looking man with a long scar down his chin and neck came forward. 'That'll be me,' he said in a pure Piraeus accent.

'You see anything odd at the shipyard gates just now?' asked Themis.

'Can't say I was watching,' said the tavern boss. 'What sort of thing?'

One of the servers was listening to this conversation. He said, 'I saw the guards go into the yard and then three more guards came and close the gates. Seemed a bit strange – not the usual way it's done.'

The boss shrugged. 'So what do you want from me?' he asked Themis.

'I think there are some men bent on sabotage in the shipyards. If you could send someone to get the Scythians – they will need at least twelve men – I'll try and see what's going on inside.'

'Good enough,' said the boss. He signaled to the server who had spoken before. 'Inaros! Get along to the Scythians and tell them something really bad's up in the shipyards.'

Inaros was stripping off his apron before the boss finished speaking.

He disappeared through the kitchen.

Themis and Frog nodded thanks and set off to find a way to get over the wall without the false guards seeing them. It was fully dark by now.

Chapter 9: ship sheds

Once out of sight of the gate, they ran along with the wall on their right to the first guard tower. Beyond it the wall reached out into the sea.

'It's no good. I can't see any weakness in the walls,' whispered Themis. 'Nowhere to get a foothold. And the wind's too gusty to hear anything.'

'Why don't you tell the guard in the tower?' suggested Frog. 'He could help us get in and perhaps stop whatever is going on inside.'

'We don't know whether this guard is genuine or one of them,' said Themis.

Frog looked at him from under his lashes – and began to sing in falsetto. 'Every time you have to row / The ships of war to fight, / And even when it's just to train, / You're rubbish by the night. / So please don't go to train today, / Stay home and polish up your sword.'

Other people on the road alongside the wall turned to look at him as the subject of his song became clear. One or two laughed and even joined in.

'It's time you got it out to play. / Four nights I've sizzled while you snored.'

The guard in the tower looked out and shouted, 'Stop that caterwauling there! Can't keep an ear open for miscreants with all that noise.'

Frog saluted drunkenly to the guard and fell into step beside Themis. 'See,' he said. 'Genuine guard. No "miscreant" would react like that.'

Themis stood at the bottom of the tower and called up quietly. 'Seen anything odd in the yards tonight, officer?'

'Don't often get visits from the Yard Master at this hour,' said the guard. 'But he's showing some VIPs round, by the look of it.'

'Those VIPs are not what they seem, officer,' said Themis carefully. 'Is there some way we could talk quietly?'

'And who are you, sir, if I may ask? You don't seem to have much control over your slave.'

'I am Themistokles of Diomea. I'm a painter and engineer. I serve in the rowing crews and as a hoplite. We were trying to see if you were a genuine guard. The ones on the back gate at present are not.'

The guard looked along the wall for a moment, then back at Themis. He bent behind his parapet, then threw a rope ladder down to the street.

'We'll both come up,' said Themis. 'My man is not really drunk.'

The ladder shifted in the wind until he put his weight on it.

'I can't leave my post,' said the guard as they stepped onto his platform. 'They've been economizing on us to pay more Scythians. I don't have a partner to send for help.'

'Someone's gone from the tavern for the Scythians,' said Themis. 'But I'm not sure what these men are planning. There are now five of them inside with Master Photios, as well as the three outside the gate. But Photios has been drugged and doesn't know what he's doing. I heard him speak at the gate, and he didn't sound at all like his normal self.'

'That's as maybe,' said the guard, pointing at the gate, his voice suddenly thick with shock. 'I believe you but not because of that. Look there! We don't normally have three of our men lying on the ground, not moving.'

Themis looked at the three dark bodies in the shadows. They were wearing the uniform of the guards and lay with their feet to the inside of the precinct wall. 'Can you see where the VIPs have gone?' he asked.

'Can't say I was looking in that direction before,' said the guard. 'My job is to keep people out, not see what the ones inside are doing.'

'Of course,' said Themis impatiently.

He was only too familiar with this place as a rower, but from up here on the tower he had a much wider view. He could make out the whole of the almost circular harbour in the starlight, protected behind the high, curving wall. Scores of ship sheds, each with a roof held up by plain pillars but no walls, lay in a parallel curve to his right and all the way round to the opposite, western, side. The gentle slope between the sheds and the water was striped with slipways. From each shed protruded a bronze ram attached to the prow of a trireme, each prow painted with a large eye. The circle of great eyes stared malevolently at the wind-rippled water gleaming dark in the centre of the harbour.

Immediately across the sea entrance from this tower was another. These two towers guarded the way in from the Saronic Gulf. Lights burned on the thick buttresses either side. There were other towers at intervals along the line of the wall, standing out dark against the lights and buildings of the town. Themis could look down into the paved space between the backs of the ship sheds and the inner side of the wall. The top of the main gate from the market square was just visible above the roofs of the sheds diagonally opposite. The back gate, nearby to his right, was hardly discernible in the gloom.

Themis saw no sign of movement. Where had the intruders all gone? Why had none of the other guard towers noticed anything?

'So, Master Themistokles,' said the guard, opening the door at the top of the spiral stair. 'You'll be wanting to see what's happening down there?'

Themis nodded.

'You know I can't help if you get yourself in trouble? I can't give you a weapon. All I can do is raise a big noise.' He tapped a metal horn hanging on the wall.

'Right,' said Themis. 'But not unless we shout. Come on, Frog.'

He and Frog ran silently down the spiral stairs of the wooden tower and stood in its shadow, listening. The sea hissed on the pebbles between the slipways and the wind whined around the pillars of the ship sheds. 'You get as near as you can to the back gate,' whispered Themis. 'See if those men are still alive. I'll see if I can find anyone else.'

'I should have brought your sword. Watch your back!' Frog whispered, and set off along by the wall.

Themis moved silently across the paved space and looked into the inland end of the nearest ship shed. Looking along the side of the trireme there, he saw nothing but the oar-blades sticking out in their three rows like bristles on a balding hedgehog. Spare oars stood in a tall rack beside him. The storage bins were closed and the area tidy.

He ran silently to the next shed and saw the same scene, except that it was even darker there, the starlight doused briefly by running clouds. He'd gone round the stern before he noticed a heap of what looked like rubbish half way along the hull. He stepped back to look down the other side of the ship and saw a similar heap on that side.

In the next shed there were heaps on both sides, too. He went to examine one and before he even reached it he could smell the reek of pitch and sulphur. He lifted some of the 'rubbish' and found it was wadding, mixed with charcoal, pitch and sulphur, soaked in oil and piled up against the wooden hull. One tiny spark, and the whole ship would be alight.

He ran along behind the sheds to the back gate. Frog was bending down by one of the three prone men.

'Dead?' asked Themis.

Frog stood up, nodding.

Themis whispered urgently, 'They're going to set fire to the triremes! Go back to the tower and get out. Get the Scythians here fast.'

As Frog turned to go, he hissed, 'But don't raise a general alarm yet. I think they're still preparing. Go! Now!'

Frog nodded and ran off. Themis took a quick look at the dead men. He couldn't help them and they couldn't help him. He turned back to the ship sheds and slipped silently from one to another, searching for the fire setters. *'Does Photios know what they're doing?'* he thought. Then with dread, *'Or is he doing it, too?'* 'Of course not!' he whispered outloud.

The sea was lapping noisily at the waterline, but he heard the first man before he saw him. The oil jar he was taking out of the storage bin made a 'clunk' as he lifted it. He was very tall, one of the three who had murdered the gate guards. Themis undid his girdle. He came up behind the man as he stood taking the stopper out. Themis threw the girdle over the man's head and pulled it tight round his throat as he struggled. Holding it with his right hand, Themis found the soft spot at the temple. He pushed hard, and the man collapsed in silence. Themis caught the jar before it fell.

He went on to the next shed, knowing now what to look for, but knowing too that he had no hope of getting round all two hundred before the first fires were lit. He found another with the fireheaps, then a gap, then another. He picked up a short piece of timber as he searched. Under the roof of the next shed he found a man piling wadding against the hull. He crept towards him but the man heard something and stood up, turning towards Themis. Themis swung the wood before the man could take a breath to shout. He fell sideways, hitting his head against the hull with a thud. Themis checked that he was unconscious and ran on.

He guessed the intruders wouldn't try setting fires near the main gate in case they were seen. So he ran past it in its shadow. A few sheds beyond, he found fireheaps in five sheds and then a gap of ten or so, but no men.

Then he heard the sounds of a fight.

Chapter 10: arrested

Creeping round the high stern of a ship, Themis saw two men struggling to hold a third down. The man on the ground was Photios. One of the other men was quite small. He must have been the persuader at the tavern. Themis ran up behind him, put a hand between his legs and another round his throat and lifted him up. He threw him at the big man still trying to subdue Photios. 'Roll away, Photios!' he gasped. 'Get out and get help!'

Photios rolled out from under the shed and stood leaning against one of the pillars that held up the ship shed roof, shaking his head.

Meanwhile, Themis was trying to keep his hands free while the little man hung onto his legs and the big man raised an oar he had pulled out from the ship to hit him with. But the oar was too long and caught on a pillar. Themis hit the man on the ground across the face with both hands and on the upward swing caught the oar-wielder under the chin. His head snapped back and he fell. Themis' legs were free now. He knelt over the second man, lifted his torso by his garments and launched a short punch with his left fist to the man's jaw. He fell back as though dead.

Photios hadn't moved. 'Come with me,' Themis said urgently. 'They're going to try and light all these firebombs and burn the fleet!'

'Impossible!' said Photios, shaking his head violently. He slid down to a sitting position. 'Impossible!'

Themis left him there and ran to find the other man. But he was too late. Flames were already licking the roofs of four or five of the sheds on the east side of the harbour, near the back gate. He dashed towards the fire. The wind was from the south-east, blowing the flames towards the unlit ships in their sheds.

Men were streaming in via the main gate now. Some were already dealing with the fires. Themis heard a dreadful cry and ran towards it. The last arsonist had thrust his torch into the face of an attacker as he was caught.

There was a man in Scythian Archer officer's uniform in the group arresting him. Themis said, 'There are four other men in various ship sheds who are injured and perhaps dead. They were building the tinder heaps beside the ships. There is also the Yard Master, Photios, son of Leontis, in a terrible state – drugged and confused.'

'Right,' said the officer. 'And you are?'

Themis gave him his name and the officer ran off towards the other side of the harbour, calling his men to him.

Meanwhile, some of the men who had appeared through the market gate had made a bucket line. The ship shed nearest to the fire was being soaked with seawater as a firebreak. Themis thought of joining the line, but then remembered Frog. He ran back towards the tower and met Frog half way.

'You alright?'

Frog nodded.

'Let's see how Photios is,' Themis said. 'He's between those two sheds.

Photios was still sitting on the ground. Three Archers were standing round him.

'I'll take him home,' Themis said. 'He's been drugged and he doesn't know what he's doing.'

Photios looked up imperiously. 'I know perfectly well what I'm doing,' he said. He stood up energetically and walked towards the sea. 'I'm the Yard Master here. What are *you* men doing?'

'More importantly, why are you here, sir?' said the leader of the Archers, keeping close formation around Photios.

'I'm overseeing the activities of my visitors,' said Photios clearly. He turned to look back at the sheds. 'They are here to calculate exactly how many …' His voice trailed away as he realized there were flames leaping up from the boats at the end of the curved line.

'What in the name of all the gods is that?' His face was a mask of horror.

'Your visitors have been busy,' said the Archer officer.

Themis stepped over to Photios. 'Photios, who were these men you came with? What was it you were all calculating?'

Photios swayed. His eyes rolled in his head and he staggered sideways. Themis caught him before he fell.

'Time to get him home,' he said. 'He's not well.'

'Sorry sir, you can't do that, I'm afraid,' said the Archer officer. 'I'll have to take him with me and ask him some questions when he comes round.'

'But you can see he's ill!'

'Not too ill to be able to throw some light on how and why this crime was committed – once he's better, of course,' said the Archer with irony.

'Look,' Themis said, 'I'll take him home till he comes round, and then we'll come to your headquarters.'

'Not now, sir,' said the Archer. He signed to his two men to pick Photios up. 'We'll be taking him with us for now. You come to the guardhouse in the City in the morning and I'm sure he'll be pleased to see you.'

Themis stepped forward to stop them..

'Now, now, sir,' said the Archer again, laying a flat hand on Themis' chest. 'Don't spoil your evening's work by trying to defend a possible traitor. You've just about single-handedly stopped this attempt to destroy most of our fleet. Enjoy the glory and don't worry about this man.'

Themis felt the old fighting tension building. His whole body began to vibrate like a lute string.

Frog stepped in front of him and said quietly, 'Let's go. Melissus said you'd hired a frisky horse.'

Themis stood breathing heavily, looking at the three men as they took Photios away. 'It's at the chandler's,' he managed to say. 'But I want to see those men I … dealt with earlier.'

He turned and ran to the back gate. There was now a line of five men lying by the wall – the three guards, the first man Themis had attacked, and the oar-wielder. A healer was bending over them.

Themis skidded to a stop. 'What state are they in?' he asked.

The healer looked up at him. 'The three guards have been stabbed in the back very efficiently and are dead,' he said without emotion. 'These other two are both dead, one by strangling and the other with a dislocated neck and broken face.' The healer prodded the man's temple and it wobbled like a wineskin. 'He probably died of blood filling his head.'

Themis suddenly felt sick. He ran to the wall further along and vomited.

Frog came up behind him and waited.

Themis wiped his mouth on the edge of his tunic. 'I'd better report to the guard post,' he said.

'And then we'll go to the Temple on the point and get you purified,' said Frog. 'You can't go running around with blood and vomit all over you.'

Later, on the road to the city under the waning moon, Themis began to tremble violently. The horse slowed to a walk. Frog had one arm round Themis' waist. He was holding onto the saddle with the other to keep them on the horse.

'Hey, you alright?' he asked. They were both still wearing damp tunics from the purification, though they had been lent dry cloaks.

'N-n-never k-k-killed a man who wasn't trying to kill me until t-t-tonight,' Themis said through clenched teeth.

There was a pause as the horse walked on. Then Frog said calmly, 'Like the priest said, they'd both killed tonight. You did the work of the gods.'

Themis grunted.

Frog went on, 'Imagine if you'd not been there tonight.' He sang quietly, 'Flames blooming, ships consuming. / No one lingers to be cinders. / Running, choking, harbour smoking. / Blazing sky fires, worse than plague pyres, / Blotting out the moon. / You stopped the plot and killed the rot, / You hero of the town!'

Themis wasn't listening, so Frog said in his ear, 'Not my best ever effort, it's true. But if that fire had taken hold, the Spartans would have been at the gates of Athens within a month, treaty or no treaty.'

Themis slumped forward and murmured, 'But they think Photios was one of the gang.'

'Give me the reins,' said Frog. 'We need to get you home,' and he kicked the horse into a canter.

>>>

(Breeds of Sheep 06. This is getting scary, and I feel totally useless. Photios may be condemned to death, then whoever that was who murdered Damianos would be able to take over the naval yards. It'd be much easier for the traitors if they had one of their own as an inside man. I've said all this to Themis in the mirror but I doubt I got through to him again. Anyway, no chance he hasn't thought of it himself, he's so desperate to get Photios off. Can't find anything like this in the historical sources on-line.)

<<<

Photios jumped up from his bench with a sunny smile when Themis and Leontis were let into his cell next morning. He said, 'Good morning Father, Themis! Good of you to come.'

Themis was not as confused as Leontis by this, having seen the effects of the drug before.

Leontis, bewildered but still authoritarian, demanded, 'What *is* all this about, Photios? No one seems to be able to tell me why you are in prison.'

'I don't know, either, Father. I don't remember anything after having

61

a meal with some merchants from Kyrene. We were going to make a deal about some skilled workers they said they could supply.'

'And now you're being accused of trying to burn the fleet,' said Themis. 'This is very serious, Photios. You may be tried for treason. What did you eat at that tavern?'

'And you are a hero I hear, Themis,' said Photios, shaking his head with a wondering smile. 'Again! My closest friend is a hero! The gods are smiling on me.'

Leontis took his son by the shoulders and shook him a little. 'What's the matter with you, son? Why don't you remember yesterday evening? Have they told you what happened?'

'Yes, Father.' Photios' eyes were pools of delighted blackness in the gloom of the cell. He was almost dancing with pent up energy. 'They say five men got into the shipyards because I told the guards to let them in. They say that these five men started to set light to the fleet. They say that Themis stopped them before more than a few ships could be fired, and that he rescued me from two of them who were trying to murder me. It seems he killed two and injured two others. They say all that, but I don't believe it as I can't remember any of it!' said Photios with a shrug and a smile. 'Although I must say I have some bruises today that I didn't have yesterday ...' and he touched his neck and swollen cheek.

Leontis turned to Themis. 'So you say this is the effect of a special powder. Can you prove that Photios took this powder?'

'Not at the moment,' said Themis. 'But if it turns out I need to, I'm sure I'll find a way. I know someone else who takes it as a medicine and the shop that sells it.'

'Is he going to be this kind of stupid happy for long?'

Themis shook his head. 'As far as I know, it will just be for a day or so.'

'Let's hope so,' said Leontis. 'He may have to defend himself in the Assembly tomorrow if an official accusation is confirmed.'

Photios was restless but smiling. Themis turned to his friend. ' Sit down, Photios, and try to remember,' he said, holding his friend down on the bare bench. 'What did you eat with those two false merchants?'

Photios batted Themis' hands away and jumped up again. 'I don't remember eating anything,' he said. 'But I could eat a horse now. Have you got anything hidden in your pocket?'

'I'll have someone bring you something,' said Themis. He turned to Leontis. 'We'd better see the Warden. Has an official charge been made?'

'As far as I know he's here to answer to the officer of the Archers.' Leontis suddenly looked drained. 'A son of mine …' he murmured.

'I'll see the Warden,' said Themis. 'Surely they can see that Photios himself was injured during the incident. How can they accuse him?'

A guard came in. 'You must leave now,' he said. 'The prisoner is to be shackled.' Two of prison guards came in with shackles and a hammer.

'No!' shouted Leontis. 'This is ridiculous! Take us to the governor.'

The head Warden marched across the courtyard towards them as they came out into the sunshine. 'Are you Photios' father?' he asked Leontis.

'Yes, of course I am,' answered Leontis. 'You know me, Evmenes.'

'I do, Leontis. But I have been ordered to detain him until the Assembly decide whether there is a case against him,' said the Warden. 'He is being accused of aiding the arsonists in Zea Harbour last night.'

'But everyone knows he is one of Athens' most loyal citizens!' cried Leontis. 'His appointment was passed by the Assemby just days ago. I am a trierarch myself. It is inconceivable that my son would be a traitor. Who could possibly accuse him?'

'The citizen Kallias says he has proof that Photios aided the five traitors in their plans over a long period of time, including this attempt to burn the fleet. He has asked for an emergency meeting of the Assembly tomorrow to decide whether there should be a trial for treason.'

A cold, calm anger was rising in Themis. 'What motive does Kallias say Photios had?' Themis asked.

'That will appear in the official agenda item,' said the governor.

'And when can any proof that this accusation is false be presented?' asked Themis.

'Anyone who wishes to speak against trying Photios for treason will have the opportunity at the Assembly. If you please, gentlemen, I must ask you now to leave the prison.'

Themis took Leontis' arm. They looked back at Photios, who waved to them, then sat down to be shackled with a shrug. They walked stiffly out into the street.

They stood in the shadow of the jail, looking up to the rocky hill of Areos Pagos, stern above the noisy, colourful stalls along the road at its foot. If the Assembly accepted the accusation of treason, Photios might have to defend himself up there, in the highest court of the City.

Themis turned to Leontis and said earnestly, 'Believe me, sir, these charges will not stick. Kallias may feel he is rich enough to achieve anything, but I doubt the Assembly can be convened so soon after the last time. I know there was a conspiracy to destroy the fleet and I'll make it my business to find out who was behind it. Photios may know himself, without realizing. He will probably not even stand trial.'

Leontis looked kindly at Themis. 'You are your father's son,' he said. 'Always the energetic optimist. How I miss him.'

'You were good friends?' asked Themis.

'We are from the same Deme but not the same brotherhood. Of course, you won't know about the escapades we got up to before we married.' Leontis eyes had lit up for a moment at his memories. Now their light died again. He looked back at the prison. 'Call my slave, Themistokles. I'm going home,' he said.

As soon as the older man had gone, Themis ran home to find Diodotos.

His brother was in the stable helping Tanu, the horse slave, groom Astrapi, his bay mare. 'So what's the verdict?' he asked.

'I need your help,' said Themis. 'We've got to prove there's no point in bringing Photios to trial at the Assembly. I need you to help find out who told the rowers to leave their cushion stuffing in the storage bins.'

Diodotos stared at Themis over the back of the horse. 'What?'

'The fires were set,' said Themis slowly, 'by piling wadding from rowers' cushions against the hulls of the triremes, soaking it in pitch, oil and sulphur and combining that with charcoal. I need to know who gave the orders for that to be prepared.'

'And how will *I* find that out?' asked Diodotos with a shrug. 'And why don't you do it yourself, come to that?'

'The rowers know me and they won't talk to me. But you haven't served as a rower for years and they probably don't even know who you are. You'd have a much better chance of getting them to relax in a tavern or somewhere – and perhaps even boast to you about it. You're good at relaxing in taverns.'

Diodotos twisted his mouth. 'I'm not sure how to take that, little brother,' he said. 'This is something to do with that conversation you had with Glykon at the symposium, isn't it?'

Diodotos was hooked! Themis said, 'You'll need to find Glykon and ask him who he saw at the storage bins. The man I saw is called Belos. It said on the list he's from Korydallos. Good place for taverns, Korydallos ...'

Chapter 11: on the trail

Once he was sure Diodotos would look for the rowers, Themis set off for Piraeus on his own horse. There was a local festival and a market in Kili, so he took the track up the Hill of the Muses to get round the village.

From the hill, he could see carts and people all along the road between the parallel Long Walls down to the harbours of Piraeus. There were villages and small fields on either side of the road within the walls. To his left, the more distant third wall, built from the city to the sea to include the harbour at Faliron further east, was obscured in many places by replanted olive groves and the few remaining taller plane trees in village squares. The sun shone in his eyes and the sea was almost white. The far away horizon of islands and mountains came and went as clouds built and unraveled in the brisk wind. He sent up a quiet prayer of thanks to Zeus, promised him half his next goblet of wine, and set off at a canter.

The tavern was only just opening, but was already full inside, away from the chilly wind.

'Is Inaros here?' Themis asked.

The slave he asked disappeared inside without a word. Themis followed. The tavern boss came towards him from the kitchens.

'Ah, it's you,' he said. 'Congratulations on last night. So you were an Olympic boy champion? Good thing you haven't forgotten your skills!'

Themis shook his head. 'Thanks,' he said, 'But I wanted to thank Inaros for getting the Archers so quickly.'

'We're used to having to "invite" them to our tavern,' said the boss with a wink. 'What can we do for you today? A seat by the window so you can speak to your admirers?' He gestured towards his crowd of customers.

'No, no. Thank you,' said Themis. 'I actually need to ask some questions about the meal that the Yard Master had with those two merchants.'

'What sort of questions,' said the boss, suddenly defensive.

'Perhaps I could talk to whoever was serving them? Or anyone who may have been watching them as they ate.'

'Why? Do you think we poisoned them?'

'No. Of course not,' said Themis. 'But did they poison each *other?*'

'Ah. I see. Well, it was actually Inaros who served them.'

He turned and made his way towards the back of the tavern through his boisterous midday clientele. Men waved at Themis and shouted their appreciation. A few came over to slap him on the back and one or two even squeezed his biceps in mock wonder.

He had to laugh but shook his head and said, 'You would have done the same. And the whole thing is far from finished with yet.'

Inaros appeared and Themis led him outside, away from inquisitive ears. 'I want to ask you about the three men who were eating here at sunset last night,' he said. 'The ones who went into the Naval Yard afterwards.'

'Go ahead,' said Inaros.

'Tell me about what they ate and anything … unusual.'

Inaros looked steadily at Themis. 'The Yard Master had a dish of pigeon and leek stew with barley bread. The others had pies. They all had bread as well, and they drank watered wine.'

'Did they bring anything themselves, add anything they'd brought?'

'There *was* a moment,' said Inaros, 'when one of them went to the barrel rack for a refill. I looked over to their table to make sure the cost of the wine went on the right bill – and I saw the smaller man shaking something over the Yard Master's stew. The Yard Master stirred it with a finger, and then licked the finger. He seemed to be saying that it was good.'

'Is that something a lot of people do?'

Inaros shrugged. 'It's not common. I didn't think about it. It could have been silphium or lovage powder. They're expensive and we keep our prices down by not including them. I was just glad he liked the stew.'

'And you're sure of this?'

'Quite sure that I saw them add something, yes.'

So Photios really had been drugged! Themis looked Inaros in the eye. 'This is important,' he said. 'Don't mention any of this to anyone else just now. But I want you tell the Assembly what you saw, if necessary.'

'The Assembly won't listen to me,' Inaros said, looking down. 'I'm just a slave, not even a metic.'

'Evidence from anyone is acceptable when the correct procedures are followed,' said Themis, hoping this was true.

'Then I suppose I am happy to say so,' said Inaros. 'I'd be interested to see the Assembly in session. But what good would it do?'

'It would prove that the Yard Master was *not* a traitor,' said Themis.

'Ah,' said Inaros. 'That's quite important, I suppose. Now, will you come in and have something to eat and drink? The customers will stand you a magnificent meal, I'm sure.'

'Thank you,' said Themis, handing him a coin, 'another time maybe. I have to get back to the city.' He turned to get his horse. 'Remember! Not a word about this to anyone yet.'

Themis went in search of Melissus. At Agorakritos' sculpture workshop, he waited outside to avoid meeting Agorakritos himself. He still didn't know what Anthoussa's note meant, so his own conflict with the sculptor could wait. After a few minutes a man came out.

'Is the Master here?' Themis asked.

'Haven't seen him at all today,' he grunted as he walked away.

Themis went in. He greeted three men he'd worked with in the past. A couple of statues were being finished off in one corner, but the noise and dust were no worse than usual. Themis went up to the foreman.

'Melissus around?' he asked.

The man pointed with his beard. 'In that shed, drawing, as usual.'

Themis stood in the doorway of the shed, blocking the light. Melissus looked up. 'Oh,' he said, with eyes wide and challenging. 'Is that you, Themistokles, son of Kallistos, Hero of the Piraeus fire attack?'

'You know it is,' said Themis with a laugh. 'Why the sarcasm?'

'Because you could have put me up onto that horse with you and I could have helped you stop those traitors!' said Melissus, smooth chin jutting.

'But you did a far greater thing and sent me Frog with money and muscle power,' said Themis mock-seriously.

'Don't you patronize me, Themistokles,' said Melissus. 'I know all you wanted was to be hailed as a hero.'

Themis sighed and sat on a very dusty stool. 'Of course, you're right, Melissus. You know exactly how my mind works.'

'Oh, shut up!' said Melissus. 'I'm just jealous because men get to have all the fun, and today I find I'm really going to have to accept that I'm never going to be a man.'

He looked so deflated that Themis was worried. 'Why? What's wrong?'

'I know I'm not supposed to tell men, but when I got home last night and undressed, there was blood from …' and Melissus gestured to his crotch. He looked up at Themis and sighed deeply. 'So you see, somehow, I have to find a way to live a *real* life, and yet be a woman, too.'

Themis looked at him kindly. 'But you won't bleed all the time,' he said. 'So you can go on being both, just increase the amount of time you're female by – what? – three or four days a month?'

Melissus laughed out loud. 'You always make me feel better, Uncle Themis,' he said. 'Tell me I don't stink and that I still have a brain.'

Themis smiled. 'You don't stink any worse than usual and I have to assume your brain works in much the same confusing way as it always has done. And,' he said with emphasis, 'if your female affliction is under control, I have a job for you.'

'Oh, Mama showed me a system to deal with the affliction, but she still thinks I shouldn't be out of the house. She warned me not to do anything too physical so the system doesn't leak.' He laughed. 'Thank the gods I have *my* mum and not one of the others I know. So. What shall I do?'

'Take your sketching things over to the prison and draw anyone who visits Photios, or the governor, or anyone there, for that matter. Can you do that, or does your "system" force you to stay nearer to home?'

'I'll manage,' said Melissus. 'I gather the second day is usually the worst, so I may have to disappear tomorrow.' He began collecting up his drawing tools. 'How long should I stay there?'

'The best time, I think, would be the last couple of hours of daylight. I'm trying to find out who planned the harbour fires. Whoever it is may want to see that Photios really doesn't remember.'

'I'll tell them I'm making sketches for a painting our Master is going to do,' said Melissus.

'Good,' said Themis and stood up. 'Don't you have pain – or anything?'

'Not now,' said Melissus. 'But last night, after I met you, I thought I'd been poisoned, my guts hurt so. Much better today.'

They went out into the afternoon sunshine. Themis said, 'Then it's better I didn't take you with me to Piraeus, isn't it?' He clapped Melissus on the shoulder. 'By the way, thank your mother for her … message. Tell her I'm looking forward to her news. And thanks for doing this,' he added. 'I'll come by early in the morning and you can tell me what you learned. They say the Assembly will be called tomorrow.'

'I might be confined to barracks,' said Melissus with a rueful smile. 'Try the house first, but go round to the slaves' door!'

He ran off and Themis set off for the Street of the Winds.

At the Corner of Paradise he went to the back door and used the coded knock Zotikos had taught him. Zotikos himself let him in.

'I think I've guessed,' he said, 'who your taker of "Lethe's ladder" is.'

Themis looked at his dark face seriously. 'Perhaps you understand now why I need to know who your customers for it are.'

'Oh, yes, I do understand *your* position,' said Zotikos smoothly, 'but mine is still the same. The whole point of my policy has to be to never give out names. This will not be the only use of this powder by one person to control another. When you're in this business – '

'I realize that,' interrupted Themis. 'Of course you have to be discreet. But this is a matter of a man wrongly accused of treason who could be executed. It isn't some domestic spat or bid to control a business rival.'

Zotikos moved away from the street door into the courtyard. 'However dreadful the use it was put to,' he said, 'I cannot change the rules I base my business on. All my customers are protected by my good name. If I lose that, I lose them. And that's the end of it, Themistokles. I cannot help you with this.' He went through the door behind him and closed it quietly.

A muscular slave who had been sitting in the shadows stood up. Themis looked at him and said, 'All right. I'm going.' He raised his voice. 'But you may regret not making an exception in this case,' he called out as he left.

He ran back up the Street of the Winds, weaving between the mules and carts and people laden with sacks and trays and baskets. His frustration had taken him past the Agora and the Akropolis, out of city and through two villages on the road to Faliron before he was calm enough to consider his next move. He stood by a herm under a plane tree at a crossroads, catching his breath. Across the sea to the south, the pointed Mount Oros on Egina island floated in the evening mist. Far to his right, the mountains of Corinth, the Argolid and Methana made a ragged edge to the western sky. The hill of Mounichia, above Zea Harbour, was dark against them.

He made a decision and started back.

>>>

The Lancaster University fell-running club met once a month. Suzanne had dashed up the fellside from Buttermere lake and stood on the col now, catching her breath. The view in her mind was still the sea, islands and mountains that Themis had been seeing, but she banished it by picking out landmarks in the wide, impressive vista before her.

To her left, across the deep Buttermere valley, was Red Pike. Ahead, at the end of U-shaped Rannerdale, was Crummock Water, with Loweswater further away, reflecting the blue and white sky. Beyond them was a glimpse of misty sea. If the air had been as clear as in Athens, she'd've seen Scotland across the Solway Firth. She could still hear Themis' thought: *'Chloe'll be able to help.'*

'Chloe's his sister, isn't she?' Suzanne asked herself. 'How could *she* help?'

'Whose sister?' asked a voice behind her.

Suzanne jumped and turned sharply. It was Theo, Natasha's boyfriend. He'd caught her up. The others were strung out down the path from the village.

'You gave me a fright!' she said with a laugh.

'You were talking to yourself. You ok?'

Suzanne looked around and threw out her arms. 'How could I not be ok?' she said. 'Look at this view. We're like eagles up here.'

Theo looked at her sideways for a moment then turned to look back. He waved at Natasha, who was in the middle of the group still labouring up the path. The faces turned up to them as they stood on the skyline were all grimacing with the effort. Suzanne got out her phone to take photos to enjoy with them in the pub later.

<<<

Chapter 12: release

(Breeds of Sheep 07)

Themis rode up to the farm where Chloe and Hipparchos lived as the sun was dipping behind Mount Aigaleo far away to his left. He marveled again at the symmetry of the house and storehouses. The walls were all newly whitewashed, the roofs weathered terra cotta tiles. Water flowed in a channel across the neatly paved yard. Sweet narcissus and hyacinth scented the air from planted troughs on either side of a barn entrance, and unlit torches stood in brackets on the columns of the portico of the house. The ceiling of the portico was painted blue with golden suns, one for each child Chloe had given birth to.

Chloe's husband, Hipparchos, was older and difficult, but he had the money and taste consistent with his family's long history. Some years before, he had even commissioned Themis to design a colonnade along the back of the house so that Chloe could rest in the shade when tending her herb garden. She had so far given Hipparchos three sons, so he was pleased with her. The two youngest were chasing chickens in the yard.

Chloe ran out of the front door of the house to meet Themis. Two large dogs barked and the chickens scattered as he dismounted. His two nephews stood still, waiting for their mother's permission to greet him. He swept Chloe up in a brotherly hug.

'Put me down, you great bear!' she cried. 'I can't breathe.'

Themis set her gently back on her feet. 'You're thinner. What's wrong?'

Chloe nodded to the boys, who each grabbed a hand of their uncle's. He threw them up in the air in turn and gave them each a kiss on the forehead. Then Chloe led him into the house as the stable slave took his horse. 'I'm not thinner, I'm just neither pregnant nor nursing,' she said with a happy shrug. 'Come through to my lair.'

In her small salon looking out over her herb garden, she offered him a chair and searched his face with solemn eyes as he sat. 'So. How have you been? You look … tired.'

He told her briefly of the changes in his friendship with Agorakritos about which she rolled her eyes but said nothing. He mentioned their Uncle Zephyros' offer.

'Might be fun,' she said ironically, 'but that's not why you're here, is it?'

'Not this time, no,' he said, sitting forward excitedly. 'There's been an arson attack on the Zea Harbour ship sheds. There were eight attackers, and at least one of them was a Spartan.'

Understanding dawned on Chloe's face, but all she said was, 'Go on.'

'I was there, Chloe – and I nearly killed him. He was attacking Photios. It was easy. I did kill two others. One of them didn't even know I was behind him.' He suddenly slumped, and looked up at her in horror. 'You know, I've never done that before, killed a man without seeing his face.'

She laid a hand on his. 'But you've been purified?'

Themis nodded.

'So the gods have forgiven you,' she went on. 'Can you forgive yourself?'

'Not …' He sighed deeply and said, 'It's something to do with honour. Giving my opponent the chance to defend himself.'

'But he was a killer and you had a good reason,' she said. It was a statement, not a question.

'I know. I was trying to stop them setting light to the ships.'

'So you killed two men and injured two others to save the navy,' she said with a slight smile, her dark eyes thoughtful.

He looked at her but didn't speak. The hairs on his arms rose. 'I didn't tell you about the second man I injured.'

She nodded and said, 'This was last night, wasn't it? Not long after dark?'

'Yes,' he said. He thought, *'How does she do this?'*

'And Photios was there,' said his sister with a slight frown. 'You were … looking for him.'

'Yes. He … I was sure he was drugged by two of the men. I watched him persuade the guards to let them all into the precinct.'

'Ah, so that's what it was,' sighed Chloe. 'I felt your desperation. I couldn't eat … And I felt you find him, and yet not find him. It was … confusing,' she said, looking unseeing at the floor. 'He's been in my mind a lot lately.' She looked at Themis. 'Is that via you? Or is he unwell?'

Themis took a breath. 'I don't know, Chloe. Every time you do this I feel … disoriented. I don't understand the workings of other people's minds – or is it the workings of the gods through people? I don't even understand my own mind,' he said with a rueful smile, seeing a fleeting image of the nymph with the grey eyes. 'But, putting that aside, Photios could go on trial for treason and I want you to help me with something that will prove he was drugged.'

She examined his face. 'What sort of something?' she asked suspiciously.

'I want you to try and find out who ordered him to be drugged. I want you to speak to the herbalist that sells the powder I think was used, and get the names of the customers who've bought it in the last few months. It seems the Spartan put it in Photios' stew.'

'What is it?'

'They call it "Lethe's ladder to heaven" and it makes you have amnesia for a bit, but then you feel absolutely wonderful. Nothing bothers you, your have no pains, the world is a perfect place – just for a day or two.'

'I've heard of it,' said Chloe. 'They say it was what Helen used when Telemachos came looking for news of Odysseus. It's only lately been available here as far as I know, and it's almost impossible to get.' She stood up and paced the floor. She reminded Themis so much of their mother when she was agitated. 'Someone my husband knows got some for his wife. I think Hipparchos thought I might like to take it, but I'm not interested in amnesia, temporary or not. I remember how desperately you were frustrated by it. And anything could happen!' she said, standing still and looking down on him with a wry smile. 'So. How do I go about this little bit of espionage?'

Themis relaxed back into his chair. 'You go to the Corner of Paradise on the Street of the Winds and ask for it. You can only get it in person the first time, until they know that you are who you say you are.'

'Good to spend some money before I start asking questions, I assume?'

'As much as possible. But they probably won't tell you the names of any other customers. They'll ask you who told you about it, but that's as far as they'll go. But I want you to try and find a way to learn more.'

'And is that the only place where you can get it?' Chloe sat down again.

'The only one I know of,' said Themis. 'But they must get it from someone. I don't think they make it there. And the herbalist won't tell me. I know him too well. I'll be painting a couple of his therapy rooms soon.'

Chloe raised an eyebrow.

Themis went on, 'We may not have much time to help Photios, you know. There are men baying for his blood already.'

'I'll go first thing in the morning,' said Chloe. 'And I'll give the name of Hipparchos' friend as the customer I learned about it from. What shall I say I need it for?'

'If you say it's for someone else, someone with old wounds or born with a twisted spine, I think he'd be nicer to you. I think he's only just understood that it can be used for harm as well as good, so he's trying to control its use in case he gets closed down by the market inspectors.'

'Right,' said Chloe. They could hear a commotion at the front of the house. 'Do you want to stay for supper and sleep? That'll be Hipparchos. We won't say another word about this. You came to talk about Uncle Zephyros and his crazy ideas.'

Themis arrived home just before sunrise next morning. Melissus was waiting in the courtyard, pacing up and down.

'You're out early,' said Themis as Frog appeared with a basin of water and a towel. 'Are you well?'

'Fine, fine.' Melissus was excited. 'I just came through the Agora. Two things. There's a call for submissions concerning a public wall painting you might be interested in, and Assembly is called for dawn tomorrow.'

'Ah,' said Themis into the towel. Then he looked up. 'I think I was offered that painting as a bribe the other night. I'd do a lot to get a commission like that, but not take it as a bribe.'

'Me too,' said Melissus, unfolding a tattered piece of papyrus. He handed it to Themis. 'Here's who visited the jail.'

'Tell,' said Themis, taking it.

'Look there,' said Melissus, pointing to the sketch of a face. 'Alkibiades came to the jail yesterday evening!'

'What?! Why him?'

'He came to see the Spartan you injured, it seems. I had to do some climbing on roofs to get to hear what they were saying.'

'Hermes would be proud of you,' said Themis, picturing Melissus climbing onto the roof of the jail. He had done something similar himself once with some friends and Frog, who now winked at him. 'Go on,' said Themis, throwing the towel at him. 'What did Alkibiades say?'

'The Spartan seems to have said something about Photios arranging the arson ... so that a friend could make money selling timber to his father Leontis ... who would then have to build lots more triremes to replace any burned ones.'

'Convoluted,' said Themis, 'and illogical.'

'Exactly,' agreed Melissus. 'Alkibiades said that sounded unlikely. He and the Warden agreed that the Spartans were to be tried today, before tomorrow's Assembly. They may summon you as a witness. Alkibiades asked where he could find you but the Warden didn't know. Then he went in to talk to Photios.'

Melissus suddenly stood still. 'Ach! I think the system may be coming apart,' he said disgustedly.

Themis stood up. 'Shall I call Mika?'

Melissus shook his head and started for the door. 'I'll go home. I just wanted to tell you that Alkibiades thinks Photios isn't likely to be condemned by the Assembly as a traitor, but may be punished for being gullible. It doesn't sound like he was the one who set the whole thing up.'

Melissus was at the street door. Themis said, 'No, it doesn't. Who else was there?'

'No one I knew,' said Melissus, 'but they're all there on the papyrus. Oh, and Alkibiades is still looking for you!' He set off home at a loping walk.

'Thanks!' Themis called after him. 'I'll come and find you this afternoon.' Melissus waved a hand as he turned the corner.

Kallias was arguing with the Warden in the small prison courtyard when Themis got there.

'But he caused the death of the three guards on the gate,' he was shouting. 'He let the criminals in to the ship sheds. He's as guilty as they are. The three false guards got away. He'll be plotting with them again as soon as he's free. Or he'll make a run for it to his friends in Lakonia!'

The Warden read from a piece of parchment. 'Leontis has stood as guarantor that Photios his son will not abscond. The arresting officer says Photios survived an attempt to murder him after he had gained access for the criminals. This makes it likely that he did so under duress. Therefore, there are viable doubts that Photios is guilty of complicity.' The Warden looked up at Kallias. 'In other words, when Photios says he didn't know they were going to try and burn the ships, he's probably telling the truth.'

'Rubbish!' said Kallias. 'This needs proof. You can't allow him …'

'Sir! I have my orders.' The Warden's voice was louder than Kallias' and he did not stop speaking even when Kallias tried to shout him down. 'Leontis is here. Photios is going home. He will be under guard at home until the Assembly has ruled on whether he is to be tried for treason. He is to have time to prepare his defence. He is not allowed near any naval or army precincts. There will be a trial if the evidence against him is proved to be sound.'

'This is a miscarriage of justice,' shouted Kallias, gesticulating. 'It is an insult to our laws. It is pandering to that whelp, Alkibiades, who thinks he can rule the city and the Hellenes and the whole wide world.'

The Warden was ignoring him and speaking quietly to Leontis. Themis couldn't hear what they said while Kallias raved. Photios was brought out. He wasn't shackled but his eyes were tired as he looked at Themis across the yard. Themis avoided Kallias' flailing arms as he went over to him.

'Has your memory come back?' he asked.

'Not really,' said Photios. He was very subdued. 'Now I can remember eating a meal with the two artisans near Zea harbour, but then I woke up here covered in bruises but feeling wonderful. It's worn off now, more's the pity. It's … very strange. Some people tell me one thing about what I did, and others something else. But *I* don't remember doing anything!'

The Warden had managed to quieten Kallias down a bit, but he wouldn't leave. 'I'll go,' Kallias declared loudly, 'when I see this dangerous man locked up and guarded in his house.'

Themis took Photios' elbow. 'Oh, you did things,' he said with emphasis, 'but you were drugged during that meal. Has anyone told you that?' Themis was looking carefully at his friend's eyes. The pupils were now a normal size and the eyes were their usual grey-blue.

'Father said that's what you believe.'

'I don't believe,' said Themis. 'I know.' He spoke to Photios, but so that Kallias would hear. 'Where are the two men who were arrested with you?'

'They're here, but they're in such bad shape that they can't – or won't – talk.' Photios shuddered. 'The Spartan (who is not Spartan by the way, he's from Taras originally – he and I had a chat about that during our meal). Well, he did a lot of talking – mainly about my non-existent friend who would benefit from the burned ships by selling lots of timber to my father to build new ones. But he's stopped talking now. He won't say a word.'

'It seems the Assembly can't be convened until tomorrow,' Leontis said, taking Photios' arm. 'You are now officially my responsibility,' he said. 'So we'd better go home.' He nodded to the Warden and two guards came and stood behind him and Photios, ready to accompany them.

'It'll be like being six years old again,' said Photios bitterly.

'Better than being sentenced to death for something you know nothing about,' said Themis loudly.

Kallias was still there, growling in the corner.

They walked out of the jail and into the Agora. Some people called 'Good day!' to them. Others stared aggressively, or spat and turned away.

Themis could see Photios was almost in tears. 'I think I already have admissible proof that you were drugged and knew nothing of the conspiracy,' he said quietly. 'Just be glad that Alkibiades saw fit to intervene and that he is so popular at the moment. Look everyone straight in the eye. You are not a traitor!'

Photios took a deep breath and straightened his back. They passed out of the Agora into the narrower streets, the soldiers one step behind.

At the door of Leontis' house, a small group of people were waiting. As they approached, one threw an egg at Photios and shouted, 'Traitor! Spartan cocksucker!' Others tried to block the door.

A veiled woman took a few steps back. Themis pushed a couple of snarling men from in front of the door with a firm, 'Excuse us, gentlemen.'

The guards took their positions either side of the doorway. Photios and Leontis managed to get inside but a man spat on the herm. Themis grabbed his hair and bent his head down to rub his nose in the spittle. 'Hermes is not to blame for your sick mind,' he whispered in the man's ear. The crowd began melting away.

The woman tugged at Themis' chiton. 'Allow the poor man to breathe,' she said. It was Chloe, now joined by her woman slave. 'Can we come in?'

The guards held back the two remaining protestors. Themis stood back for Chloe to go in, then followed her. The door slammed shut.

Numa, Leontis' slave, led Chloe and Themis through to the colonnade round the courtyard. The sun was warm now, though the shadows were still chilly. They sat on a bench and Chloe lifted the veil from her face.

'So, what happens now?' she asked.

'Photios is confined to this house,' said Themis, 'until tomorrow's Assembly. He will need to be able to speak there to explain his part in the arson attempt. If he is unconvincing, he will be back in the jail and tried the next day for treason.'

'And sentenced to death if convicted,' said Chloe, deeply concerned.

'Yes,' said Themis. 'But this situation is not as bad as his still being in the hands of the Archers.'

'Well,' said Chloe. 'I came later than you into the city and went to your herbalist. I have here five little pots of Ladder to Heaven. They cost me more than Hipparchos will like, but so be it. I asked the very attractive young man which of my peers were offering the powder as part of their ladies' soirees, so that I could stay ahead of them in the fashion. He was utterly charming, but called in the Master Herbalist. He was, as you said, a man in a cleft stick. If I hadn't known what you told me about the Ladder to Heaven I would have left the shop quite frightened by his warnings. And you know, I don't think he even knows which of his customers it could have been.'

Themis stood up. 'You're possibly right about that. But we have to find out!' He paced the colonnade. 'I'm not sure that the tavern slave's evidence will be accepted. I think we'll have to get an order to close Zotikos down for dealing in poison. Maybe I can blackmail him with that to tell us.'

'Oh, no,' said Chloe. 'Surely there's a better way. If you do that, you'll lose a commission! There's time, before the Assembly tomorrow.' She stood up, too. 'I'll have to go now, but may we spend the night at Mama's house?'

'Of course.'

'And can I leave these little jars with you? I really don't want them at home. Zotikos said the powder has no taste, and, now I come to think of it, Hipparchos did seem very interested in it. So I would never know if it was going to turn up in my food!'

'True. Shall I take them now? I know someone who needs them for medical purposes. I'll sell them to him and maybe get you your money back.'

'Better and better,' said Chloe, and she extracted the jars from her linen bag. 'I really have to go. I said we'd meet the farm slave by mid-morning at the entrance to the Odeon. I'd forgotten how busy the city can be and how long it takes to get around.' She reached up and kissed Themis' bearded cheek. 'Be careful and stay well,' she said as she left with her woman.

Themis went inside to the andron.

Leontis was instructing a slave. 'Tell him to come immediately. I'll pay him double if he's helped us prepare the defence by midday.'

The slave left. Photios and his father sat down on opposite couches. 'I've sent for an orator well versed in defence. Stay and advise us, Themis.'

Themis remained standing. 'I think I can get proof concerning the drug,' he said. 'You will do better with your independent orator than if I try to help. I'm still much too angry.'

Leontis nodded. Photios said, 'But you are coming back?'

'Of course.' Themis turned to go. 'There is nothing to fear. You are not a traitor,' he repeated.

Chapter 13: users

Themis hurried back to the Agora. At the Prytaneion building he applied to the city committee of the day for a warrant demanding Zotikos' customers' names. Even after the long negotiations with the councillor and clerks, this meant waiting for the actual document, so Themis wandered between the stalls listening to the crowd. He had covered his hair with a hood and walked with a limp so he wouldn't be recognized, though he knew he wouldn't fool anyone who knew him personally. He did think he should seek out Alkibiades to see what he wanted with him, but then he might miss the warrant being ready.

As he turned over some votive trinkets on a stall in the shade of a plane tree near the Painted Arcade, a voice behind him was saying, 'Why didn't the Assembly meet today? We need to be quick and send a hundred triremes over to Sparta to teach them a lesson.'

This was greeted with derision. 'Sparta has no port!' said one voice. 'You can't get triremes up the River Evrotas!' said another.

'No,' said a more educated, calculating voice. Themis turned a little to see who it was, but he didn't know the man and he didn't look like any of Melissus' faces. 'We need to make an example of those who help the Spartans. The two foreigners are in court today and I'll wager that we'll see them shackled to the Long Walls by this evening. But the Athenian citizen who let them in – he shouldn't be spared. His crime is worse than theirs. He has betrayed his city.'

Themis turned away as the murmur of agreement grew. Someone said, 'And there are those as are trying to prove he's not a traitor!'

The educated voice said, 'A pointless and perhaps dangerous task.'

Themis returned to the Prytaneion to wait for his warrant.

At last, with the official slip of papyrus in his hand, he arrived at the Corner of Paradise. It was well after midday.

'They told me you'd come with a warrant,' said Zotikos, his usually urbane manner giving way to irritation. 'You'd better come in. I've got the list ready. It's not long.' He led Themis into the business room and closed the door. 'These are the five people who have bought the powder,' he said, handing Themis a small tablet. 'But none of them are the kind of people to use it for such traitorous purposes.'

Themis took the tablet. He had a look at the names. 'Not even Kallias?' he asked. 'The man accusing Photios is Kallias the Rich. Is this the same man?'

'I have no idea. You'd better ask him.'

'I will,' said Themis, his heart beating fast. 'Thank you. These names could make all the difference between life and death to Photios.'

Zotikos shrugged, as though refusing the thanks. Themis changed the subject, saying, 'I'll be here to begin on the frescos as soon as the Assembly finishes tomorrow.'

'Everything stops for a treason trial,' said Zotikos bitterly.

'I doubt it will come to trial, though,' said Themis.

They went out into the courtyard and the slave opened the street door. 'I've decided to stop stocking Lethe's Ladder to Heaven,' Zotikos went on. 'It's more trouble than it's worth.'

'How did you get hold of it?'

'I was receiving the doses ready made up and delivery is done by a different person each time.'

'But you must have made a deal with someone to get them in the first place,' countered Themis. 'Who was that deal with?'

'I understand he's sold up, to someone I don't know. Elusive.'

Themis said, 'Well, thanks again,' and set off at a run.

Kallias lived in Melite where the rich had their airy homes. It was the other side of the Agora. Themis was running past the Royal Arcade when he heard the grating voice he'd last heard in the prison yard. Kallias was arguing the price of silver with a small group of men as they walked towards the Akropolis. One of them was the man with the hooked nose.

Themis ran round in front of them and, walking backwards, said loudly, 'May I have a brief word with you, Master Kallias?'

'You already are,' Kallias said. 'You're that friend of the traitor, Photios, aren't you? I won't answer any questions about him.'

'It's a different thing altogether,' said Themis, turning to walk with them. 'I just wanted to ask you what it is that you buy from The Corner of Paradise shop on the Street of the Winds.'

Kallias stopped, to the confusion of his companions. 'The what? Where are you talking about?' He sounded mystified.

Themis took a breath. 'The Corner of Paradise. They sell … remedies.' He could see that Kallias was genuinely confused.

'Don't know what you're talking about,' he said, starting to walk again. 'Sounds like you need to talk to my sick cousin. His name's Kallias, too. Lives down towards the sea in Daphni. Now get out of the way. I have business to discuss with these men.' He grinned. 'See you in the Assembly for the arraignment.'

Themis ran home.

Frog was in the yard, mending a sandal. 'Diodotos?' Themis asked.

'Still away on your orders to get drunk in a tavern,' said Frog, looking up. 'But he sent word to say he has no news.'

'Hmmm. Well, I have the list of customers for the drug,' Themis said. 'There are five names and we need to follow them up, however unlikely they seem. They're Ilarion (we know him) five doses, Iole (always first to try new fashions) one dose, another woman called Evniki five doses, only too predictably Alkibiades one dose –'

'Alkibiades?' said Frog, straightening up. 'He seems to have fallen in love with you, asking for you everywhere. It could be to cover up that he was behind the attack.'

'I doubt that,' Themis said. 'He's too recognizable – and too ambitious. He wouldn't set up something secret like this. He doesn't do anything without telling the whole world how clever he is. Perhaps he wants to see me to tell me about taking the drug in private. But he can wait.' Themis added. 'Because the last name on the list is Kallias!'

'The accuser?' asked Frog.

'He says not. I met him in the Agora. I need to check with his cousin to see if it was he who bought the Ladder stuff. If not, then we can really knock the wheels off his case against Photios!'

Frog pulled a long face. 'It seems unlikely though. It's obvious you'll check with the cousin. I'd say drugging is more of a feminine thing. What about the woman, Evniki?' Frog was taking his tools into the kitchen. 'You should find out some more about her.'

Themis followed him. 'Is Chloe here?'

'She sent word she'd be back soon for a meal.'

'Come with me now, then. We'll take the horse together to the cousin in Daphni. Then you can go on down to Piraeus this afternoon and bring Inaros back. He can stay the night here and be available tomorrow if necessary. And I'll come home and see Chloe.'

At Daphni, they found Kallias' house with no trouble. They could see him lying outside on a specially shaped couch, under a single almond tree that had just come into pale pink blossom. In the road outside Themis said to Frog, 'You get off to Piraeus. I'll run back from here.'

Frog leapt up onto the horse. 'You won't need me to protect you?'

Themis snorted with derision. Frog shrugged. He said, 'Just don't let anyone flatter you into believing lies.'

'You're talking about Alkibiades, aren't you? Not this poor Kallias.'

'They say you can warm your hands on the glow that man gives off,' said Frog. 'I'll bring Inaros.' He wheeled the horse and set off at a canter.

Themis was shown into the garden. The himation covering Kallias' legs was the same dark green as the oleander bush beside him.

'I'm sorry to disturb you, sir,' said Themis. 'I have come on a rather delicate mission.'

Kallias had surprisingly light brown eyes in his tanned face. 'Please take a seat,' he said. 'You must excuse me …' He struggled to sit more upright on his couch.

Themis sat on the stool indicated. 'No, you must excuse me,' he said.

He was thinking, '*How could I ask this man to come to the city to testify about the effects of the drug? He can hardly move.*'

'My slave told me your name,' said Kallias. 'I served under your father in the Akropolis Guard. You were a child.'

'Yes, I was at that time,' said Themis.

'How can I help you now?' asked Kallias.

'I have to ask you about the powder you take called Lethe's Ladder.'

'Ah, my saviour,' said Kallias with a smile. 'I heard of it from Ilarion and it certainly helps me deal with my pains.'

'Have you ever sold any on to anyone?' asked Themis.

Kallias looked taken aback. 'Why would I do that? It is far too valuable to me to allow it out of my hands.'

'And what is its effect on you, sir?' asked Themis.

'Why do you ask?' said Kallias.

Themis told him briefly about the attack on the triremes, how the drug had been used and the effect on Photios.

'Well,' said Kallias, 'apart from the fact that I can't use my left leg, that sounds exactly like what happens to me, too. Of course, I'm not in a position to be of use to the enemy, but I do lose my awareness for a while in the security of my home, and then have a wonderful day or two feeling almost like my old self.'

'Do you use it often?' asked Themis.

'I promise myself that it will only be every tenth day, but I did use it one very cold day that was not in that schedule. It is rather expensive …' He smiled ruefully in his greying beard.

'And have you ever given any or discussed it with your cousin Kallias, son of Hipponikus?'

'Certainly not. I never see him these days.'

Themis stood up. 'Thank you for your frankness, Master Kallias,' he said. 'My search for a conspirator goes on, it seems. And I would ask you not to mention anything about it in connection with this case as yet.'

'You must have twisted Zotikos' arm to get my name,' said Kallias.

Themis looked down at him. 'Yes. I had to apply to the Council. But the situation is so grave that they were surprisingly helpful. And he seems to regret supplying it. I think he may stop stocking it.'

'Oh, calamity!' said Kallias in mock horror. 'Thanks for letting me know. I must try and persuade him not to.'

'Please let me know if he tells you where else you could source it,' said Themis. 'It may well still lead us to who is behind the attack.' He took his leave and set off back to the city at a run.

Chloe still wasn't back when he arrived home. Themis felt frustrated and powerless. His mind kept wandering to the speech Photios was preparing, and the mystery Anthoussa was unravelling, things he could do nothing about. So he began sketching ideas on his practice wall for the frescos he would paint for Zotikos. He started with a man and a woman undressing each other seen from floor level but decided this was not erotic after all. He washed off the chalks with impatience. Mika came out of the kitchen.

'Got a friend of yours at the back door,' she said. 'Melissus.'

'Again?' said Themis, following Mika. 'What's wrong now?'

In the kitchen, Melissus was drinking from a beaker of water. He was breathless and tense.

'You have to let me stay,' he said. 'I can't go home now.'

'What happened?' asked Themis, wiping his hands on a rag.

'Nereus happened,' spat Melissus. 'Why can't he leave me alone?'

'Why? What's he done to you?' Themis had visions of Nereus' slaves chasing Melissus through the back streets. Meanwhile, he could hear Chloe arriving in the courtyard.

Melissus stood with his hands on his hips. 'First of all, he kept sending presents to Father to accept him as my lover,' he said angrily.

Themis sighed with relief and smiled an I-told-you-so smile.

Melissus took a breath to go on, but Chloe came into the kitchen, hot and tired. 'Is there any chance of food?' she was saying. 'Oh, who's this?'

'Come through to Mama's room,' said Themis. 'Mika, please bring Mrs Chloe something delicious to eat.'

'Me too!' said Melissus quickly, then his face changed. 'But … er … I just need to er … first.' He slipped through the door into the sluice-room.

Themis and Chloe stood at the top of the three steps from their mother's salon down into the yard. It was at least a month since Eirini had visited from Vravrona.

'That boy,' said Themis, 'is not actually a boy.'

'I wondered,' said Chloe. 'I smelt menses, and it didn't seem to be Mika.'

'Melissus is actually Agorakritos' daughter, Melissa. He – I suppose I should say she – has been allowed to live as a boy, at least since they moved into the City. He helps his father because he can draw and use figures so well. Agorakritos didn't seem to grasp the dangers of the situation. But perhaps now he's beginning to. Melissus … er … Melissa runs errands around the city, and studies music and mathematics and poetry with her younger brother. She has two sisters, too, who seem to be quite content to be girls, but of course they are younger than she is and they're not talented in the same way.'

'She'll have trouble denying she's a woman now.' Chloe smiled. 'But I admire her spirit. I had a wonderful time as a child, but I was lucky. If I'd been a girl in some of the families I know, I might have ended it all by jumping off the Akropolis.'

'Oh come on. I can't believe there are women who think like that.'

'Can't you?' said Chloe, surprised. 'Most women would love to live as men, choosing when to do what, and who with, having a say in how the city governs itself. Of course, the disadvantage is that a lot of men get wounded or killed, but then a lot of women die having babies. The best thing I suppose, would be to be a priestess all your life.'

This was something Themis couldn't think about just now. 'Anyway,' he said, 'Melissa's in a difficult situation. Nereus is the kind of man you wouldn't want your son to have anything to do with.' He turned as Mika brought in a small table laden with sweet-smelling buns and cakes and a platter of soft fruits and nuts.

'Oh, wonderful, Mika!' cried Chloe, clapping her hands. 'Your very own doughnuts with honey. My slaves just can't get them right.'

Melissus almost ran into Mika in the doorway. Looking at the brother and sister standing against the light, Melissus stood still for a moment and murmured, 'You two could almost be twins – like Apollo and Artemis.'

'But how are *you*?' asked Chloe. 'I know about your present predicament, by the way. I guessed. Themis didn't tell me.'

Melissus' face clouded over again and he sighed heavily, working his hands in his lap as he sat gingerly on a stool.

The others sat in chairs. Mika came back and they all washed their hands in the basin she brought. When she'd gone, Themis turned to Melissus.

'Look Melissus, I've got a lot to do today to try and save Photios from the shackles. So don't waste time. Out with it!' he said with a wry smile.

Melissus jumped up, then thought better of it and sat down quickly. 'My father wants me to marry Nereus,' he said dramatically.

Themis' mouth fell open. 'What!' he exclaimed, his stomach

clenching in a spasm. He put down the cheese-filled bun he'd chosen and said slowly, 'But you said Nereus had come with presents as a lover.'

'He did. Many times. Of course, Father turned him down. But he was in the house yesterday evening again, and I didn't know. He heard me call out to Mother about my clothes smelling bad because of my bleeding. Nereus was eavesdropping!'

Chloe sighed. 'Oh dear,' she said sympathetically.

'So then he insisted that Father brought me out dressed as a girl so he could see for himself. He was very angry and said Father had been making a fool of him, letting him talk about becoming my lover, even if he hadn't ever accepted any of his gifts.'

'You can see his point,' said Themis.

'No, I can't,' said Melissus. 'Father didn't want to be rude, that's all.'

'Odd that,' said Themis, 'considering how rude he's been to me lately.'

'That's … a bit different,' said Melissus. 'Anyway, Father came through and made me get dressed in a girl's chiton and tie my hair up. I tried to escape but he grabbed me. He's never done that before. So I tried to explain to him how horrible my life would be if anyone else knew I wasn't a boy. But he said I had known for ages this would happen and I'd just have to accept it. He promised to force Nereus to keep quiet about it by threatening to make him look stupid for not noticing himself.' Melissus jumped up and paced the room in fury. 'And of course old Nereus IS stupid,' he went on, 'and he thought I was wonderful and all that rubbish and immediately forgave Father and asked to be allowed to court me as his WIFE! Can you imagine? My whole life is being destroyed and I can't stop it!' Melissus stretched out his hands in frustration as angry tears splashed onto his grubby tunic. 'So I can't possibly go home again.'

Themis and Chloe exchanged looks.

'But you still have to go to Vravrona, don't you?' asked Chloe.

'And a lot can change in the time that will take,' said Themis. His reason told him that Nereus was a good match – rich, and quite a catch for Agorakritos' family who were still not accepted Athenian citizens. They came from Paros and Elis, and had only lived in the City for a few months.

And yet Themis felt sick.

Melissus suddenly stopped dead, shoulders slumped, and said, 'But in the end, I still have to do as my father tells me, don't I, Uncle Themis?

Otherwise I could end up as a prostitute or a slave.'

Chloe stood up and put her arm round Melissus' shoulders. 'We'll see about that,' she said. 'But for now, let's eat. Themis has a lot to do to keep Photios out of court, otherwise *he* could end up *dead*. But you and I will spend the afternoon together, if you like.'

'Just as long as I don't have to meet Nereus again until I've worked out how to put him off me,' said Melissus.

Themis shook his head ruefully. After the libations and offerings, he said, 'Actually, I have a task for you both, if you aren't too busy.'

'Another "something"?' said Chloe.

'Yes. There's a woman on the list from the herbalist whose name is Evniki and who, he says, lives nearby.'

'And you want me to visit her and see if she is capable of persuading foreign mercenaries to burn our navy?' Chloe was teasing him.

'No, I want you to see if she gave or sold on any of her five doses.'

'Ah. I see,' said Chloe.

'Can I come?' asked Melissus. 'I'll be a girly girl, I promise. And I can usually tell if someone's lying.'

Chapter 14: evidence

(Breeds of Sheep 08)

When Themis got to Photios' and Leontis' house, all was quiet. He had half expected there to be a hostile crowd, but there was no one except the two burly guards at the door.

Leontis was sitting in the andron and Photios was standing in front of him, practising his speech for the Assembly.

'The two men I had been introduced to were from Cyrenaica, they said, although one was from Taras as I learned. They had spent some time in Sparta. They had access to a large pool of carpenters and joiners who had worked on ships of many kinds. These two men asked to see how and where our triremes are maintained so that they could make sure they sent me the best artisan slaves for the job. I needed men who could refit and repair pine and oak planking and beams at speed. I had been asked to see whether it was feasible to have a carpenter on each ship instead of one on every third ship, as we do at present.

'When we arrived at the Zea gateway into the shipyard and arsenal, these two men asked me if we could have something to eat before getting down to business as they had not eaten yet that day. I agreed and we had a meal at the tavern called the Leather Sleeve. Afterwards, I led them over to the gate … '

Themis was surprised. Had Photios regained his memory? What a blessing if he had!

'… and asked the guard to let us in to examine a ship to gauge the skills needed by a repairing carpenter. As we were let in, a group of three men I had not seen before raced in after us, slaughtering the guards and slamming the gates shut.'

'Good,' said Leontis. 'Now we just have to make sure we make your story of what happened next believable.'

Themis was bewildered. 'But haven't you got your memory back?' he asked. 'Can't you remember what happened next?'

'No,' said Photios. 'I still can't remember anything. But the orator said it would be better not to mention the use of the drug as that will smack of sorcery and turn a lot of the crowd against me.'

'But – '

Photios held up his hand to Themis. 'The two men were obviously lying to me all along, so there was hardly any need for a drug when I was being so gullible,' he said bitterly. 'If I just say I was tricked, then I will of course lose my job and be a laughing stock, but at least I'll be alive.' He looked at Themis. 'I don't fancy the Samian Shackles, or the hemlock.'

'It won't come to that.' Themis shook his head angrily. 'I've been getting the evidence that shows you were quite clearly drugged!'

Photios came over to him and looked into his face. 'I know,' he said. 'And I appreciate that more than you can imagine. Knowing I was drugged has saved me from madness. It also explains how I could be so … offensive to you that evening. But this way is more feasible to others.'

Themis tried to think logically. 'I suppose so … ' he said, 'but you'll be lucky to ever get another job. And you'll be ridiculed … ' He turned away, gritting his teeth. He paced the room punching his right hand with his left.

Leontis sighed deeply. 'Only the gods know how it will end,' he said. 'We're going to suggest a fine that's equal to the price for repairing or replacing the ships burned and the men lost,' said Leontis.

'No, Father! That will cripple your business,' said Photios, his jaw set. 'I would rather be banished, perhaps for ten years like an ostracism.'

Leontis stood up. 'They won't agree to that. They'll want you here, to keep an eye on you, in case they were wrong and you really are a traitor.'

Themis swung round. 'So,' he said, 'you've been manipulated and hoodwinked. And you're making a pretty good show of remembering things you don't. You'd better be word-perfect with all the details! Don't forget, I saw some of what happened and I've told people about it. What will you say next?'

Photios held his hands tightly together to hide their shaking. 'I'll say I tried to ask them what was going on but they knocked me out and left me lying between two ship sheds,' he said. 'I'll say I guess it was only a few minutes later that I came round and stood up. They saw me and came running to murder me. They'd beaten me to the ground when you appeared and fought them off. But I was half-unconscious again by then.'

'That sounds about right,' said Themis. 'Will you call on me to confirm any of this?'

'If I'm allowed to,' said Photios. 'But I doubt the citizens will let me. So probably not unless they decide I have to be tried.' He threw out his hands in despair. 'Oh, by the gods, Themis,' he said, 'I don't understand how this happened. Without you, it could have been so much worse … '

'It still could be if you lose your nerve,' said Themis, calming down. 'I've learned how it was done, but I've got no further finding out who planned it all.' He stood up. 'Diodotos may have some news from the rowers who left their cushion stuffing in the ship sheds, but … '

'I doubt that,' said Leontis. 'Whoever is behind this is very careful.'

'I'll see what I can learn, anyway,' said Themis. 'Keep practising, and address the Assembly tomorrow as clearly and confidently as you did just now, and you'll be fine.'

Photios smiled wryly at Themis as he left, although none of them really believed him.

On his way back, Themis ran past the steps of a small temple to Artemis. He heard one of the group of men sitting on the steps say, 'But Phidias wasn't the only man to ever escape from the jail. This Photios might never even stand trial.'

Themis stopped to hear more and saw that the group were all looking at the man on the top step. It was Sokrates, a man who took time out from being a stonemason to philosophize about the meaning of life with anyone who would listen. He'd served in the army with Diodotos at Delium and had been a friend of Panainos. The philosopher looked up at that moment and saw Themis. He moved his head as if to say, 'Join us,' while the discussion went on.

'Did Phidias really escape?' asked a youth.

Sokrates shrugged. 'Who knows?' he asked, looking straight at Themis for a moment. Then he turned to the men sitting with him. 'Whatever happened, he was not there the day after his trial. And as you say, Alkaios, more than one man has escaped from that jail. But our discussion here is not about the strength or weakness of the jail, but about the concept of justice in the present situation.'

Themis was tempted to sit down and join the group, but he knew if he did, he would disrupt the conversation. He bowed slightly to Sokrates, and ran on home.

'You're drunk,' said Themis as Diodotos came through the street door and immediately tripped over the dog. Yellow growled good-naturedly and moved to a sunnier patch in the courtyard.

'As a rat in a winepress,' said Diodotos cheerfully. 'You're right. Good place for taverns, Korydallos.'

Themis helped Diodotos wash. 'And what did you learn?' he asked.

Diodotos shook his head, spinning sparkling drops from his hair and beard. 'Belos said he and a couple of other rowers had been told to leave the stuffing of their cushions in the storage bins, like you said.'

Diodotos stumbled into the andron and onto a couch. Mika stood at the door. 'Shall I get the usual?' she asked. Themis nodded to her and said to Diodotos, 'Who was it told the rowers to … '

But Diodotos was still talking, slowly and deliberately. 'The explanation was,' he said, 'that there are some rowers who are too poor to have decent cushions but are too proud to admit it. So Belos and friends were doing the poor ones a favour.'

Themis said, 'That couldn't account for the amount of stuffing I saw.'

'Well, the rower that Glykon mentioned turns out to be less gullible. He asked what it was all about and the man he spoke to said he'd be paid if he didn't ask questions. So he didn't.' Mika returned and held out a cup to him. 'By the gods, this stinks.'

'Always has, always will,' said Themis with a laugh. 'Go on. Drink it!'

Diodotos held his nose with one hand and poured the viscous yellow liquid into his mouth with the other. He gagged, and handed the empty cup back to Mika, who shook her head indulgently.

'Seems he got a few obols out of it,' Diodotos went on, his voice slurring. 'He said he was paid by a different man each time, so no help there. He left the stuffing of about twenty cushions over the months.'

'Months?' exclaimed Themis. 'This has been planned for months?'

'I wouldn't know.' Diodotos sighed. 'I only do the interrogating.' His eyelids drooped and he stretched full length on the couch.

'Thanks a lot,' said Themis as Diodotos started to snore.

Mika was in the doorway. She whispered, 'Mrs Chloe and her ... companion are back. They're in your mother's salon.'

Chloe was re-pinning Melissa's hair. 'Our two ladies were fascinating,' she said. 'You didn't tell me that Iole knows Diodotos so well.'

'Iole knows a lot of men so well,' said Themis.

'So I learned.' Chloe had a strangely amused expression on her face. 'Iole was politeness itself. She said she has only used Lethe's ladder once, and that was upon request from one of her clients.'

'Ah. Which client?' asked Themis excitedly.

'You won't believe it, though it kind of makes sense to me.' Chloe sucked in her cheeks. 'My husband!'

Themis relaxed his shoulders and sat down. 'Dear Zeus on Olympus! Hipparchos and Iole – hard to imagine ...'

'What *do* you mean?' Chloe's indignation was elaborately false and her eyes sparkled with fun. 'He may be older, but he's still ... eminently robust!' Melissa giggled.

'You know that's not what I meant,' said Themis seriously. 'I meant Hipparchos and Iole being behind the Zea Harbour arson. But from your tone, you seem to think she had other clients who used the Ladder?'

'She said not. But I'm sure she'd taken it herself, as she described exactly what it feels like. She said you need to be with people you trust completely when you take it. You become extremely suggestible.' Chloe laughed. 'And Hipparchos has been thinking of using it on me! I was right not to want it in the house. Melissa,' she went on, 'you tell him about the other lady.'

Melissa turned to Themis. 'This lady, Evniki, lives a few houses away. She is not in Iole's business, but arranges ... er ... ceremonies. She'd bought five doses and used them at a special ritual to do with life after death with four other wives of powerful men. She said she was preparing another ceremony but it would be in a secret place, with the same five women, and at a time she couldn't divulge.'

The back door to the kitchen banged shut. Themis stood up. 'That'll be Frog with Inaros,' he said. 'Look,' he went on. 'What you did was helpful, but Photios has been advised not to mention the drug after all.'

Chloe nodded knowingly, but Melissa exclaimed, 'Why not?'

'The orator says that its use suggests witchcraft and that will certainly upset the majority in the Assembly,' said Themis. 'So we're probably chasing the wrong hare with all this. Still, it does no harm to have evidence in reserve. I thought I might be called today to the trial of the men they've arrested. Luckily, I wasn't.'

He went out to meet Frog and Inaros in the courtyard. Frog was alone.

'He refused to come,' said Frog in disgust. 'He said he'd been mistaken. The powder they put on Photios' stew was lovage left on the table.' Frog was washing mud off his hands at the water trough. 'He was lying, of course, sweating and not meeting my eye.'

'Someone had threatened him?' said Themis.

'I'd say so, yes,' said Frog. 'I rode away, but went back on foot and watched for a while. Inaros came out and ran to the market place. I lost him there in the crowd, so I came home.'

'Pity,' said Themis. 'As it turns out, Photios won't be mentioning the drug in his defence. But if we knew who provided it, that might lead to whoever planned the whole thing.' Yellow leant against Themis' legs and he patted his neck. 'At least it explains Photios' odd behaviour. And he said knowing about it had kept him from going mad.'

Chloe and Melissa came out into the sun.

Themis lay sleepless on his bed, obsessed with looking for solutions to Photios' situation. Yellow twitched and snored on the floor beside him. Exasperated with himself, he finally sat up and whispered to the night, 'But the fundamental question is not: how do we prove that Photios isn't guilty? It is: are there are enough men in the City who hate him or his father, to win a vote for a trial? And the answer to that is No. No one hates Photios. He's not important or powerful enough for that kind of vindictiveness.' Themis relaxed and slid down among his blankets again. *So it's not like when Phidias was put on trial by his jealous rivals,* he thought, trailing his hand along Yellow's warm flank. *'No. It's not like that at all.'* And in the stillness, he sensed the hum.

She was keeping him company.

>>>

Chapter 15: divine intervention

(Breeds of Sheep 09 – OMG … that business of Melissa having to marry someone she doesn't like at age 14 or so really sucks. I was 14 when I had that accident that put me in touch with Themis. I can't even imagine being married at that age. I know there are cultures where that's still accepted, but to my mind that's gross. Of course, it's all to do with starting your periods and being able to have babies, and it's not quite The Handmaid's Tale, but I'm just so glad I live where I do and when I do, not there and then.

Moving on, this next bit doesn't seem to follow at all. At first I thought Themis was dreaming and I wasn't going to record it because it felt so weird. But then I got it. It's a memory, definitely in Athens, when Themis wasn't much older than he was at Olympia. Frog looked much the same as then, but it was dark so I couldn't see the others.)

<<<

The city was deathly quiet. The verdict was due by now. Themis paced up and down the street outside his home, waiting for the roar of the crowd that would confirm Phidias as not guilty of blasphemy.

Doves conversed throatily on the roofs and he could smell the smoke of kitchen fires. The reek of the sewers was stronger now that the plague had hit so many in the city.

Phidias had been like a father to Themis and his brother and sisters since they got back from Olympia. Because of his age, Themis wasn't allowed near the courts on this day of the trial. Nor was his mother, in spite of her being the defendant's cousin. People were going about their normal business, but no one spoke.

Themis stopped to listen, his hand on the herm. Frog was running along the street from the Akropolis. There had been no roar of triumph.

The worst had happened.

Phidias was now a prisoner. He would probably be sentenced to death for blasphemy, a charge everyone knew was brought by those jealous of the success and celebrity the great sculptor and architect enjoyed.

Frog stopped in front of Themis, his eyes full of tears, a sheen of sweat in the dark down on his upper lip.

Themis breathed out and squared his shoulders. 'So,' he said quietly. 'We have work to do.'

Frog stopped wiping his face on the corner of his tunic. 'We do?'

'I'll tell Mama we'll meet her at Uncle Phidias' house,' said Themis.

Eirini sat in the shade of the courtyard vine and just nodded her head at the news. 'Will you be all right, Mama?' Themis asked.

'I'm not surprised, of course,' sighed Eirini, her shoulders drooping with despair. 'He is too successful, and – too proud of himself!' Suddenly she was angry, spitting out words as she stood up. 'But to destroy the best sculptor the world has ever seen purely out of spite and jealousy! The gods have gone mad! I must go to Ismini.' And she called to Mika to help her put some gifts together from the kitchen for Phidias' wife and daughters.

Themis ran out, joined Frog on the street, and got to Phidias' house before the crowds arrived.

Inside the house, Themis found his Aunt Ismini helping the slaves and Gulkishar, Phidias' scribe, to pack up Phidias' belongings from his andron.

'Aunty,' said Themis. 'I heard, but I don't know the sentence.'

'How could you *not* know?' said Ismini fiercely. 'It's death! It was always going to be death or liberty. At last we know which we are dealing with.'

'I'm so sorry,' said Themis. 'When will the sentence be carried out?'

A great clamour arose at the street door. Ismini called out, 'Keep the door shut! We're nearly ready!' She turned to Themis. 'They say in two days, at the dark of the moon,' she said bitterly, and went back to packing pots and containers, tools and scrolls into sacks with furious energy.

Themis had to stop himself from smiling. He and Frog joined in to help with the frenzied collection of this tiny portion of Phidias' works. His workshops and sculpture yards had been officially seized and locked on the day of his arrest. With Gulkishar, they loaded the sacks and baskets into a cart in the stable. They scattered a thick layer of straw over them. 'I'll get the cart out of the city now,' promised the driver, 'while you have company and before the court officials arrive.'

'Take it to the sanctuary of Hephaistos in Holargos,' Ismini whispered. 'And stay with it till I come in a day or two.'

Then Ismini ran into the courtyard and stood for a moment at the shrine of the god. Themis watched her wash her face and hands at the basin and tidy her hair. She took a deep breath and closed her eyes for a moment as she touched the small but exquisite Zeus her husband had carved from a piece of marble from her native Paros.

Then she hardened her jaw and, turning to the door-slave, drew herself up and nodded her head.

The house filled immediately with well-wishers and gossips. There was loud wailing and angry shouting as Ismini dealt with them. There were gifts and questions. Her manner didn't change from controlled fury until Eirini came and embraced her without words. Then there were tears.

Themis watched and listened to the hubbub in disbelief. He sat on the wooden stairs up to the women's quarters slowly shaking his head. He had just seen Gulkishar take his leave of Ismini. He had looked around the courtyard one last time, picked up his two baskets of belongings, and slipped out of the house via the kitchens.

Frog was standing by the stairs. 'What're you thinking?' he whispered.

'They are all horrified at such an obvious miscarriage of justice,' Themis whispered back. 'So upset and angry, so loud and repetitive. But no one is talking about *doing* anything.' Themis stood up to look over the crowd in the courtyard. 'And where is Uncle Panainos?' he said out loud.

'I'm here, nephew,' said a quiet voice from under the stairs. 'They let me in the back door while you were in the stable.'

'Can we talk somewhere, Uncle?' said Themis quietly, not turning from his scrutiny of the crowd.

'Meet me at the spring under Apollo's shrine on the Peripatos at dusk,' said the voice.

Themis turned to Frog. 'Come on, Frog. We'd better get home.' He waved to his mother and signalled that he wanted to leave. She nodded her consent.

'So, Uncle Panainos, what do you think we should do?' said Themis.

They sat on a bench in the near darkness as the Agora below them emptied of its daytime vendors and torches were lit. The water spouts beside them covered their voices with their splash and gurgle. The only woman at the fountain finished filling her jar and left.

'Firstly we have to make an official appeal to stay the execution, tomorrow at first light,' said Panainos. In the dim light his usually jolly face was pinched and deeply lined. 'Phidias employed an orator to do this before his trial. He'll suggest exile.'

'And if it is not successful?' asked Themis.

'We will have to remain faithful to our laws and see my brother executed. He can choose how this will be effected.' Painainos was so angry that his voice was almost a squeak.

Themis had been debating with himself all day as to whether he could trust his uncle with his idea. That angry squeak made him think he could. 'There's another way,' he said quietly.

Panainos turned to him in alarm. 'What are you planning, young Themis? I know you. You get an idea and never let it go. You're not going to put your own life in danger, as well, are you?'

'Of course not, Uncle,' said Themis lightly. 'But a couple of friends and I have a plan. I just wondered if you would like to know about it.'

After a long pause, Panainos said, 'I think it's best if I don't.' Themis could hear the relaxation in his voice. 'However, if you find yourself embarrassed for cash, I know of someone who might like to help.'

Themis grinned in the growing dark. His heart was beating fast with mounting excitement, but he spoke lightly. 'That's tempting, Uncle! I may have to call on you tomorrow.' He stood up. 'But I must go now and … er … comfort my mother. Thank you for meeting with me, Uncle.'

Panainos stood up too. He held his arms open and Themis stepped into his corpulent embrace. He smelled of sesame cake with a hint of rabbit skin glue. Panainos held Themis tight and whispered in his ear, 'Be very, very careful, dear nephew. Your mother needs you, and so do I.'

Themis hugged him reassuringly, then watched as his uncle walked away, slowly shaking his head. But his gait was less dejected than it had been.

In the darkening labyrinth of streets south of the Agora boundary, there was a tiny triangular yard between high walls. There he found Frog and two companions. They spent the next hour making plans. Then, in the black dark of night before the old sickle moon rose, they collected the pieces of a contraption borrowed from the men building the Great Gates of the Akropolis nearby. They silently broke into a derelict building that leaned precariously against the strong back wall of the prison, and there they hid their loot. In the starlight, they examined the low, flat roof for obstacles, checked their measurements, and then left Frog on guard.

Early next morning, they heard that the appeal had been rejected. So Themis sent food and water to Frog and spent the day purposely visible among the outraged crowds.

At last, in the evening he made his way to the little triangular yard.

'Did you get the clothes?' he whispered to Frog.

Frog passed him a pair of Median trousers from a dark heap beside him. 'All black, but a bit whiffy,' he whispered, as the musty smell of stale sweat enveloped them. 'But that's chorus-leaders' storerooms for you.'

'Our master-thief,' said Themis in mock seriousness. 'Anything important happen?'

'Lots of rats,' whispered Frog. 'And a visitor in the yard – old man with a big beard and a bag of something that stank. I pretended to have the plague and he turned back. A prison guard came through on his way home, but didn't see me. I kept out of sight of the workers on the Great Gates.'

'The other buildings all open into other streets,' murmured Themis. 'I checked, and no one lives in them – they're just workshops or warehouses. So our gods are with us.' He grinned.

'All set then,' said Frog.

'Pantarches and Photios?'

'We're here,' said Photios' voice quietly from the dark of the empty building.

'Thanks,' whispered Themis, taking a hand of each in his and squeezing it hard. 'Quiet now.'

They all four dressed in the black theatre costumes.

Frog hid their pale clothes inside, and a few seconds later Themis felt the ends of two ropes thrust into his hand. Then his other hand was placed on a rung of a ladder that leant against the outside wall beside the door. Pantarches and Photios climbed silently up onto the roof. Themis followed them. Then he attached the ropes to beam-ends above the door. Up here, there was a faint light from the partly clouded stars.

Along the other side of the roof, the wall that was the upper part of the back of the prison was about five feet high, topped by its roof of terracotta tiles. It was one shade blacker than the dark sky behind.

'The diversion should begin any minute,' whispered Photios in Themis' ear. 'I don't know how long they'll be able to keep it up.'

Themis was thinking, *It'll be a miracle if it starts at all,* while his heart pummelled his ribs. He whispered, 'Does Phidias know we're coming?'

Pantarches murmured, 'I think he understood. As I left him, he said he hoped they didn't move him to another cell.'

'And have they?'

'Not that I know of.'

'Is there a guard in with him?'

'There wasn't at sunset. Being alone is part of the punishment.'

Themis leant over the low side of the roof. 'Ready, Frog?' he whispered.

'Ready!'

Themis threw down the ends of the ropes. Frog had a bundle of parts ready. He tied it to one rope in silence, then signalled with a tug. As Themis was pulling this up trying not to make the least sound, he could hear Frog tying another bundle to the other rope. Pantarches took the first bundle from him and ran to the prison's back wall to start setting up its contents. Photios took the next bundle and joined him.

'Where's that diversion?' Themis whispered to the air. Frog tugged on the rope again and Themis pulled up the last bundle. He ran silently with it to what was now a recognizable crane.

Voices began calling, out of sight in the street that ran past the front of the prison. Torchlight flickered there, too far away to light the roof.

'At last. The diversion,' breathed Themis.

They could hear an excited crowd gathering, with voices getting louder. There was obviously some contest going on, because phrases like 'got him by the throat' and 'odds on Bruno wins' were audible.

The three young men worked frantically, assembling the crane against the prison wall. Photios pulled up the ladder from the yard and used it to climb up to the tiles. He removed two of them and slipped an arm under the frame of the roof. He was attaching two large hooks on the ends of ropes to the supporting roof beam. The other ends of these ropes were wound round the axle of the crane now more than ten feet above. Under cover of the noise in the main street, he spoke into the hole he'd made.

'What does Phidias say?' hissed Pantarches from the foot of the ladder.

Photios turned to him. 'He's too old for a rope and needs a ladder,' he said with a gleam of white teeth.

Themis called quietly down to Frog. 'Can we have the other ladder?'

Frog pushed it up towards Themis. Themis grabbed it and leant it against the wall next to Photios. 'Time to lift?' he asked as he tied a string to its bottom rung. He handed the end of the string to Photios, who was still looking down into the prison from his ladder.

Photios nodded. The street noise was now a riot, lights wavered wildly.

Themis and Pantarches heaved on the spokes of the crane and the axle began to turn. The hooks under the roof beam engaged and the roof began to lift away from the top of the prison wall.

The beam creaked, the crane creaked, and the gap between wall and roof grew. Photios grasped the second ladder, leant through the gap and fed it down into the cell, keeping the free end of the string in his hand.

After a few seconds, Phidias' bald head appeared.

But the gap was still too narrow for Phidias to climb out. Photios signed to Themis and Pantarches to lift some more. The beam made a cracking sound. A man's voice in the next door cell called out, 'Have mercy! Mighty Zeus, have mercy on me – I'm no thief. Just a poor saddler!'

Photios slid down the outer ladder. 'Quick,' he urged. 'They'll come to see what that was.'

Phidias wriggled and pushed his way over the top of the wall under the beam. He got himself headfirst onto the outer ladder and Photios helped him slide down onto the roof.

Then Photios was up his ladder again and pulling the inner one up and out of the cell by the string. Phidias took a deep breath and stretched towards the sky. 'Thank you for not cutting me in half,' he whispered to Themis and Pantarches with a grin.

Photios changed places with Pantarches at the crane. Pantarches took the longer ladder and slid it down to Frog on the ground. Phidias turned to Themis and Photios and gave them each an awkward hug as they went on lowering the roof.

'And thank you for my life,' said Phidias in Themis' ear. 'Now dear old Polykleitos can take over as the best sculptor in Athens!'

'But you will be the best in Egypt. May the gods be with you,' panted Themis in reply.

At the edge of the roof, Phidias stood looking back at the crane, still grinning and shaking his head in disbelief. Tears shone in his beard.

Pantarches whispered to him, 'I'll be travelling with you.' Phidias turned and climbed rapidly down into the darkness of the yard.

Pantarches raised a hand to Themis and Photios and slid silently down after him. The street brawl was louder than ever now. Only the unfortunate saddler had heard the cracking beam.

Themis and Photios lowered the roof back onto the top of the wall. Photios climbed up quickly to get the hooks and ropes and replace the tiles. One of the great hooks thudded against the wall as Photios came down the ladder for the last time. The saddler prayed louder than ever.

Once all the equipment was back in the storehouse, Photios ran off one way, and Themis another. Frog stayed an extra few moments to lock the door and sweep the area in front of it. From the corner, Themis looked back and watched for a moment as Frog made other trails of footsteps all over the triangular courtyard. They raised a hand to each other and Frog ran off after Photios.

Themis wove his way through the narrow streets until he was almost under the Akropolis. From there he walked towards the street brawl.

From the crowd, he learned that a travelling entertainer had been attacked by his own bear and there had been a protracted fight in which the bear had eventually come off worst. Now, those who had bet on the bear were protesting angrily.

The prison guards were lined up watching as the crowd dispersed, still with lit torches. 'How long did it last?' Themis asked the man beside him.

'Eh. Only a few minutes,' he said. 'The traveller knew his beast,' he added. 'It was never going to kill him and turn on us like he said it might.'

'Hmm,' said Themis with a regretful nod. 'Seems I missed a good show.' He turned without haste and walked back towards the Peripatos.

But once out of sight, he ran as fast as he dared to Phidias' house.

There, Frog had beaten him to it, and Mrs Ismini and Phidias' two daughters were just getting onto a cart, dressed in their visiting clothes and trying to look sad and depressed.

'Themis, we're going to see Panainos,' said Ismini loudly. 'He went over to Kolonos to see some elderly relatives to tell them about poor Phidias and they have fallen ill with the shock. We'll have to stay there overnight and maybe tomorrow night, too.'

'I'd better drive you,' said Themis in the same tone. 'Frog, go home and tell my mother.'

Frog nodded sadly and walked off dragging his feet. Mrs Irini's slave got down from the driving seat of the cart and Themis took his place. The cart pulled slowly away from the house. No one spoke. Tears poured down the faces of the slaves as they stood by the door in silent farewell.

Once out of sight and sound, Themis turned to the three women behind him and laid a finger on his lips with a broad smile. He motioned to them to make themselves comfortable in the bed of the wagon and cover themselves with the tarpaulin. He turned the cart towards the southern Kynosarges gate of the city.

There they were held up. The gate was shut at sundown and anyone who wanted to pass had to pay. Themis had the fee ready.

'You want to be careful this late on a dark night like this,' said one of the guards officiously, while the other opened the gate. 'You might get robbed. What you got in the back here?' And he laid a hand on the tarpaulin covering part of the bed of the cart.

Themis turned in his seat. 'Just some barrels of rotting fish,' he said, preparing to urge the horse into making a dash for it if necessary. The man moved his hand off and the guard at the gate called, 'Come on. Get a move on! Can't spend all night with the gate open.'

Much later, a long way from the City on the coast road beyond Faliron, the cart rumbled to a stop. Here, the road was separated from the beach by a screen of feathery trees. On the empty beach beyond the trees, two boats were drawn up, a small fishing boat and a much larger Phoenician ship, standing stern-first in the shallows. The sea rippled quietly against its bow and it seemed deserted except for a one-man guard. The sky was clearing and stars were visible.

The guard sat under the stern beside the boarding ladder. Themis stopped the cart and jumped down to speak to him. It was Pantarches.

'Got them?' he asked.

'Yup,' Themis said, his throat tight with excitement and sadness. 'Everything ready?'

Pantarches nodded and looked up at the towering side of the ship. Themis followed his gaze. A shining bald head was looking over the rail.

'Get below!' hissed someone on board, and the head disappeared.

Themis ran back to the cart. He looked both ways. No one in sight. He knocked gently on the side of the cart and Mrs Ismini and the two girls slipped from under the tarpaulin. They ran silently down to the ship, each carrying a travel basket. Mrs Ismini stopped in front of Themis to hug him and whisper, 'Thank you'. Then all three ran up the boarding ladder.

Another ladder appeared at the bow. Two lines of silent men came down the ladders. They formed up along each side of the ship. At a quiet signal they began to push it into deeper water. Themis joined them. Within seconds the ship was afloat and they were climbing back up the ladders, like ants up stalks of barley. Themis stood up to his thighs in the water.

Pantarches was now on the stern beside the ship's commander. He looked down at Themis and lifted a silent hand. He was joined by the taller and heavier figure of Phidias, his head shining in the starlight.

Under the sound of the oars being set, he called quietly, 'No words suffice.' He flung open his arms for a moment, almost knocking Pantarches into the growing expanse of water between the ship and the beach. Then, with an audible laugh and tears gleaming on his face, he hugged his arms to himself as though Themis was within them.

Themis raised both his arms and grinned silently as the rowers began to work their whispered rhythm. The ship gathered speed, heading south past the few lights showing on the island of Egina, on its way to the mouths of the mighty Nile, four or five days away.

The heartbeat of the oars faded slowly in the darkness, taking with it the man who'd been Themis' much-loved mentor for most of his life. When he could neither see nor hear the ship any more, Themis wiped the tears from his cheeks and ran back up to the cart.

He drove the cart to Holargos and ran back to the City down the valley of the Illisos. He found Frog and Photios replacing the original lock on the door of the derelict building by the prison. They'd already returned the dismantled crane to the Great Gates site. He helped them criss-cross the triangular yard with footprints again, this time both donkey and human.

He finally got home just before the sky began to lighten. He sat on his bed to take off his sandals. He was asleep before he'd lain down.

He woke when his mother shook him. She stood over him and said, 'What do you know about this divine disappearance of your uncle?' She was trying to be stern but Themis could hear the joy in her voice.

He groaned. He ached all over. 'What?' he asked groggily. 'Did you say Phidias was saved?' He sat up. 'How?'

His mother ignored the question. 'I said disappeared, not saved. And it seems that a fight between your friend the bear trainer and one of his bears took place outside the prison last night.' She sat down on the bed. 'He was eventually arrested but the guards were afraid of the bear and let him go.'

'Do I have a friend who's a bear trainer?' asked Themis seriously. 'The only one I know of had something to do with Diodotos out at the farm.'

'That's the one. He's itinerant, of course. You and Diodotos made friends with him last year when we were all trying to get news of what the Spartans were planning.'

'Oh yes,' said Themis. 'I remember. But last night I didn't realize it was the bear man from the farm. I heard the crowd from the Peripato, but I got there too late to see the fight. But what – ?'

'Meanwhile,' interrupted his mother, her eyes shining but her face serious. 'There was divine intervention it seems and Zeus lifted your Uncle Phidias out of his cell through the roof and up to Olympus.'

Themis couldn't stop himself from laughing. 'What! I thought Zeus had given up visiting Athens and was enjoying the company of the athletic Spartan ladies these days,' he said.

'Don't you be blasphemous!' said his mother. 'The man in the cell next to Phidias says he saw a great hand, just like the statue you worked on in Olympia, reach down, lift the roof, and lift Phidias up into the sky.'

Themis shook his head. If the saddler thought he had seen the god, it could only help the confusion. 'So Uncle Phidias is free? That's a wonder – a miracle!' he said. 'Where do you think he is now?'

His mother stood up. Her expression was serious and strict. 'That's what worries me. The court authorities are very concerned about their missing prisoner. They've started a search of all Phidias' relatives' houses, so they could be here any minute. It would probably be a good idea if you were out when they come.'

'Well… I'll go to the gym,' said Themis, getting out of bed and stretching. 'I suppose we'd better carry on as normal.'

'Nothing with you is ever quite normal,' said Eirini. 'But yes, get to the gym. There'll be an enquiry of course. Ismini and the girls seem to have disappeared as well. But we know nothing about that, either, do we?'

Themis frowned and slowly shook his head.

'And there's a rumour that a Phoenician war-ship that had brought some Egyptian dignitaries to visit our glorious city has left some of its passengers behind and sailed off to the Hellespont. I don't suppose you heard about that while you were following up on angry bears, did you?'

Themis was doing up his sandals. 'Not a word,' he said.

Eirini went on, 'I'm going to Vravrona in a day or two. I was planning to leave after Phidias' execution anyway. So I shall stick to my plan, but you'd better get out to the farm as soon as is "normal" today, and help Diodotos. Then I shall give you permission to take up the invitation to Massalia from my brother, Leokratis. You and Frog could be gone all winter if you got away before the autumn storms … '

>>>

Chapter 16: assembly

(Breeds of Sheep 10 – I've learned more about Phidias now, and I think that was in 430 BCE when Themis was 14. Phidias was such a one-off – designing, engineering, sculpting, singing, dancing, boyfriends – everything full on, electric energy. But he disappears from the written record without a trace after being found guilty of what seems to have been a trumped up charge of blasphemy. Could this really be why?)

<<<

It had been a long night. Themis had spent it remembering some things and trying not to remember others. The hum had been noticeable once or twice. It made him feel less alone. He'd given up trying to sleep and picked up his brushes again to work on his current 'private painting'. Not long after dawn, he heard Frog's feet on the stairs. Frog came into the workroom and put a platter of cold cooked duck and barley bread on the table by the door. He handed a beaker of water to Themis.

'I saw the torch light in the night. Did you sleep at all?'

'Not a lot,' said Themis. He was holding a woman's mirror in his hand. Frog gestured to it.

'So that's where it is! Mika was asking me if I'd seen Mrs Eirini's mirror,' he said. 'Tidying yourself up for the Assembly?'

Themis put down the mirror and picked up his brush again. 'I'll return it when I'm done,' he murmured.

Frog stood and watched as Themis added eyebrows to the face reflected in the painted water. Above the pool, a slim, smooth-haired nymph in strange, rather skimpy clothes, was gazing into the water. After a few moments Frog stepped back in surprise. 'That reflection's *your* face,' he said. 'It's not the nymph's at all.'

Themis looked at him for a moment and watched the understanding dawn. Then he said pointedly, 'You're not supposed to see this yet.'

'I didn't,' said Frog. 'I haven't seen it. I have no idea that it exists. At all.'

'Mister Chairman, Men of Athens,' declaimed Kallias, striding back and forth on the speaker's dais, his rich purple himation wrapping itself round his legs in the stiff breeze. 'As I'm sure you all know by now, two nights ago there was a partly successful attempt to burn the ships in the Zea Harbour.' Kallias' voice reminded Themis of a crow, but it carried well.

Themis turned to put a hand on Photios' shoulder as a murmur rippled through the thousands of men gathered on the Pnyx. The pre-amble and sacrifices from the officials and the priests were over at last, and now it was down to real business.

Photios, his friends and Leontis, were standing quite near the dais. By half turning their heads, they could see most of the men assembled. The crowd was angry and alert, horrified by what could have happened in Zea, but calm so far.

Kallias hurried on, his allotted time being short. 'The majority of the perpetrators were apprehended. They have admitted their guilt, and will be punished accordingly. They are all either metics or foreigners. But, as you may or may not know, they testified that there is one man who is a citizen of Athens, without whom the plot could not have been carried out. His name is Photios, son of Leontis, of the deme of Diomea. He was the new Yard Master for the shipyards at Zea, including the armoury, appointed by this very Assembly. He replaced Damianos, an experienced and stalwart professional shipyard manager, who tragically drowned some ten days ago. The maintenance of the defences of Zea, and the upkeep of the ship sheds and triremes kept there, is ultimately the Yard Master's responsibility. But we were hoodwinked, Men of Athens. Photios had his eye on a greater prize, a prize promised to him by our enemies if he aided them in destroying our navy. It is our navy they are afraid of – our navy so invincible in battle. But even our navy cannot stand up to the primeval power of flames set by a traitor.'

The Assembly shifted uneasily at this rhetoric. As well as the thousands sitting and standing on the flat semi-circular meeting ground, there were men on the low cliff that bounded it to the south-west, opposite the dais. There was a small temple to Zeus on top of that cliff, exactly opposite where the speaker stood. One man sitting on the steps of the temple stood up and shouted, 'Zeus is watching you waffle, Kallias!' Themis recognized him as a fellow member of his and Photios' gymnasium.

There were guffaws in the crowd at this. Kallias drew himself up. 'Mister Chairman, I wish you to put to the vote that this man, Photios, should be tried in the Court of Areos Pagos or here in the Assembly as a traitor. This Photios gave the criminals access to Zea Harbour. He says they said they were speciality slave merchants. But if you want to take merchants into our shipyards, why not use the main gate? I'll tell you why. Because too many guards and curious onlookers would have witnessed his treachery. So no, he surreptitiously took the two men into the yards through the back gate, which has only three guards. He knew what they were planning. He aided the attackers in their nefarious intent with his knowledge of the security procedures, using his own personal ability to pass into the yards whenever he wished.' The last few drops of water fell from the klepsydra beside the Chairman.

The Chairman stood up and declared 'Time! Who wishes to speak?'

Photios raised his hand and began to push his way between the few men in front of him. Themis could see the tension in the set of his shoulders. But as Photios gained the open space around the dais, another voice rang round the Pnyx, a rich, melodious voice with a slight lisp.

'I wish to make a statement, Mister Chairman!' Alkibiades leapt up onto the dais with a swirl of his blue and ivory cloak.

'Your floor,' said the Chairman. 'But only one xestis till this matter is decided,' and he nodded at the official with the timer. This man chose the right sized vessel and poured water from it into the klepsydra, then placed the vessel under the hole where the water would emerge. As Alkibiades took a breath, he unplugged the hole and the water began to run out in a thin stream.

'Men of Athens,' called Alkibiades. His voice rang clearly across the space and echoed against the low cliff. 'Kallias has told you of the circumstances of the attack on the triremes as he sees them. But he has given no detail, as he is only intent upon accusing the Yard Master, rather than unraveling what actually happened.' Alkibiades' hair suddenly shone gold as the sun lifted over the shoulder of Mount Ymittos to his left. His himation stirred in the dawn breeze, its blue rivalling the sky behind him. Themis' anger at his pre-empting Photios dissipated, and he concentrated on what Alkibiades was saying in his unhurried, modulated voice.

'The truth is both simple and surprising. Photios, son of Leontis, met with two men who had agreed to provide him with skilled carpenters. Carpenters are of particular importance to the upkeep of the triremes, as I'm sure you will agree. In informal circumstances like these, it is normal to use the back, rather than the main, gate of the yards, also well-guarded. Even if he mistrusted his visitors, Photios would have believed that they could be overcome by our trained guards. But three other men were waiting in hiding. They came forward, pushing guards and Yard Master through the gate. Inside, they knocked Photios out and killed the guards. Photios has the bruises to prove it.

'Then this group of at least five criminals began preparing tinder heaps beside certain triremes. The fleet was in dire peril.

The crowd murmured. 'Exactly right!' someone called out.

'But …' went on Alkibiades, holding up his right arm, himation stirring elegantly, 'someone had noted something amiss at the back gate. Our alert onlooker was suspicious and managed to enter the shipyard with the help of a tower guard. He crept forward in the dark. Two men were preparing the tinder heaps against a hull. The first man he killed, the second he rendered unconscious. As he was looking for a third, he came upon two others attacking Master Photios, who had recovered enough to stand. Our chance onlooker accosted these two, preventing the death of our Yard Master. Meanwhile, the guards on the main gate had understood that something was wrong and were grappling with a fifth man, who was setting fire to the triremes at the east end of the harbour. Much as I'm sure our unwitting hero wanted to, he could not be in two places at once.'

The men in the Assembly were now mainly standing. 'Who?' some shouted. Others were saying Themis' name.

Alkibiades smiled. 'I still don't know the man myself, but I cannot hide my gratitude to him. I am told his name is Themistokles, son of Kallistos of Diomea. Perhaps Photios himself can tell us more, or maybe he would like to speak himself?'

The last drop plopped into the one-xestis vessel. Alkibiades bounded down into the mass of men.

Leontis growled to Themis, 'None of his business and yet he manages to interfere. You want to speak or let Photios go first?'

Themis shook his head. 'Photios is prepared, I'm not. I won't speak today unless I must.'

The Chairman had called for the next speaker, so Photios stepped up onto the dais. 'One or two?' asked the Chairman quietly.

'One's enough,' said Photios. The timer poured the water. Photios nodded to him and he unplugged the klepsydra.

'Kallias has tried to make me sound like a traitor today.' Photios voice was lower and less authoritative than Alkibiades', but he had the attention of everyone now. 'I am no traitor. I had no plan to betray my beloved City. I stand here however, with a great weight in my heart. I see that I was too trusting in my dealings with the criminals and so put the navy in danger.' He went on as he had practised to tell the story of what had occurred as he 'remembered' it, though a little less dramatically than Alkibiades.

Then, with his voice cracking, he added, 'And so, men of Athens, I have to tell you that I owe my life to my friend Themistokles. I would never knowingly harm the city of my birth. I believed I was discharging my responsibilities to the City, her gods, and her navy, by keeping the ships well served for repairs. My failure has been in my judgment of men, not in my love of my city. Therefore, if I must be punished, I ask you to consider replacing me as Yard Master, and exiling me for five years.'

The Assembly erupted. Kallias could be heard demanding to speak again, while Alkibiades urged the Chairman to call the vote now.

The Chairman stood up and held up his arms. 'Quiet, Men of Athens,' he called. The clamour subsided. 'Have you heard enough to vote?'

A few voices called 'no' but most called 'yes'.

'We will vote then, on whether Photios should be arraigned for trial as a traitor.' Silence fell. 'Stand here please, Photios.' The Chairman showed Photios the place in the centre of the dais to stand so that everyone could see him. Photios stood still with his hands clasped behind his back. Themis could see he was trembling and trying to breathe slowly. So was Themis.

'Does Athens try Photios as a traitor?' came the call. 'Hands for yes?'

A few arms went up in a group by the foot of the cliff, and another larger group round Kallias near the dais.

'Hands for no?'

A forest of arms went up across the Assembly.

Photios stood as before, but Themis saw his shoulders relax and his breath come deeper.

'Does Athens banish Photios for five years? Hands for yes?'

Quite a lot of hands went up, but still only about a quarter.

'Hands for no?'

A definite majority voted not to exile Photios.

Next, the Assembly was almost unanimous that Photios had lost his job and that he should pay the expenses of this Assembly. But the voting was inconclusive as to whether he should pay to replace the burned ships.

'I shall postpone this decision,' declared the Chairman. 'We have more pressing matters before us, such as how to put the men caught at Zea Harbour to death. They are still being examined as to who employed them but must be dealt with once that is over. Now we must vote on the budget for more stringent security at the Naval harbours.

'However,' the Chairman went on, 'before we deal with that, I must remind the Assembly of a point made by Alkibiades earlier.' There was an audible groan from the more conservative area of the Pnyx. 'By the grace of our patron goddess and her almighty father Zeus, we have to thank Themistokles, son of Kallistos, and our vigilant Scythian Archer guards for saving us from a disaster that beggars the imagination.'

The groan turned into a roar of applause that rose into the crisp sunny air, sending all the birds up from the trees around the Pnyx, and setting all the dogs in the city barking.

Chapter 17: archons

Photios and his father left immediately. Themis stayed alone sitting on the ground to listen to the speakers concerning the possible uses of the security budget. He felt a touch on his shoulder.

He turned to see a Council messenger standing over him. Themis stood up and listened as the man quietly gave his message word for word as he had learned it. 'Archias, the eponymous Archon, and Apollodorus, Archon of the City Watch, request your presence in Office Gamma as soon as you are able after the dissolution today of the Assembly.'

Themis nodded. 'I'll be there,' he said. 'Do you know why I've been summoned?' Office Gamma was particular to the policing of both the City and the surrounding State. It was through that office that the money now being voted for would be administered.

'They didn't say,' said the messenger, as he turned to go.

Later, as the citizens left the Pnyx after all the speeches and votes, Themis was surrounded by well-wishers. Among them, he saw the two men from the symposium, Nereus and Eteokles. Themis was disappointed that there was no sign of Alkibiades, whom he wanted to thank.

'What a hero you have become!' said Eteokles in his rapid-fire way, raising his voice above the general clamour. 'I would be honoured … if you would come more often to our brotherhood dinners.'

Nereus' smile was carefully constructed. 'You'll have a lot of such invitations now, I imagine,' he said. 'Quite a feat – though achieved only with the help of your more-than-faithful slave, I gather.'

Themis ignored the insult in Nereus' voice. He smiled and nodded to them and everyone else and hurried on. He was surprised to be stopped by Agorakritos' firm hand on his arm.

The older man looked tired, his beautiful face deeply lined and the grey in his beard more pronounced. 'Melissus has gone missing,' he said abruptly. 'I thought he might be at your house.'

'Not that I know of today,' said Themis. 'He came by briefly yesterday.'

'Right,' said Agorakritos. 'Nereus has agreed not to bother Melissus again, now that my daughter Melissa has just arrived from Paros. Nereus does not wish to appear gullible.' A glint of Agorakritos' old humour shone in his eyes, then died. He went on, 'If you see my … son, ask him to come home.'

'Of course,' said Themis.

Agorakritos turned away without another word.

Themis took advantage of a gap in the crowd and ran down the hill to the Agora. Two of the most important men in the government of Athens were waiting for him in Council Office Gamma.

Apollodorus was taller than Themis but possibly twice his age. He wore the garland of his office. Archias, slim, short and with one ragged ear, had taken his garland off. He was running his fingers through his short brown hair in frustration.

'Themistokles!' sighed Apollodorus. 'Where would we be without you?'

Themis had heard this question quite a few times that morning. It thrilled him to the core, but he still had no sensible answer, and so he said, 'You asked to see me, gentlemen?'

Archias stood still for a moment. 'The Zea attack was a symptom of the City's disease,' he said. 'We must find the source of the putrefaction!'

Apollodorus moved closer to Themis. 'We have to learn who was behind this conspiracy,' he said quietly. 'We are hoping that you would be prepared to make discreet attempts to find out. We suggest you say you are trying to clear your friend Photios' name if anyone asks.'

Themis didn't answer immediately. This was exactly what he was doing in any case. But would this official request give him extra resources? Would he perhaps even be paid? 'You wish me to spy on the inhabitants of the City?' he said.

'For the sake of her safety, yes,' said Apollodorus.

'This is not spying,' said Archias irritably. 'This is self-defence. You must let us know everything you find out, even if you think it is irrelevant.'

Apollodorus said, 'Do you have any idea where you would start?'

Themis felt he was being taken for granted. He took a deep breath. 'I am determined to clear Photios' name, with or without your … invitation,' he said. 'He is as dear to me as a brother. As to where to start, I have one or two ideas. But if I agree to your request, would that mean that I am authorised to say I'm on official business?'

'We prefer that you keep our agreement secret for the time being,' said Apollodorus.

'Any official status for you would need to be agreed in Council and that could take many days,' said Archias. 'Now is the time to learn things, while the trail is still fresh. We'll begin the procedure to employ professional spies immediately, of course,' he went on. 'And once that is in place, we may be able to employ and pay you. Meanwhile, not a word to anyone.' Archias turned away to touch the shoulder of the small statue of Athena in her shrine by the window. 'So what is it that you mean to do first?'

'To interrogate the prisoners taken in Zea harbour,' said Themis.

'Then you must hurry to the walls beyond the Dipylon Gate. They will be in the Samian shackles by now and could be dead by dawn.'

'Was there an official interrogator?' asked Themis. 'May I speak to him?'

'I will call him.' Apollodorus walked towards the door. 'Please keep us informed of what you learn. Would each day at dawn be possible?'

While Apollodorus spoke to a clerk outside, Themis said, 'If I have anything to report, you will get a tablet sealed with this,' and he pulled the leather thong he wore round his neck out of his chiton. On it hung a carved boar's tooth, a trophy from one of his father's hunts. His mother had given it to him when he was sworn in to the army. The carving was of a swallow in flight, like the ones on his father's dagger. 'I can't promise to report each day. I'll try to do so immediately if urgent, but definitely once every three days around dawn. Who should I address the tablet to?'

The two men exchanged glances. At the door still, Apollodorus nodded sharply. 'It had best be me,' he said.

'Have a good afternoon, sir,' he said to Archias, who turned and nodded gravely to him. Themis followed Apollodorus out.

An officer was walking to meet them. Apollodorus said to him, 'Please answer any questions this man has. You may talk in the small colonnade.'

When they were alone, Themis asked the officer, 'Have the prisoners from Zea named anyone as the instigator?'

'I am authorized to give you information,' growled the officer, an Athenian, 'only because the Archons have ordered me to. Otherwise, you would have to wait until presentations are made to the Assembly.'

'This is true,' said Themis, humouring the man's air of self-importance.

The officer went on, 'My interrogators did all we could think of that wouldn't kill the prisoners. It seems they were employed by a man they'd only met once. They say he left on a ship to Miletus three days ago. They are both Spartan sympathizers in any case.'

'Naturally,' said Themis. 'But there are plenty more of those, so we need to try and stop the same thing happening again.'

'Well it most certainly won't on my watch!' declared the officer. 'The ringleader's gone, the perpetrators are punished or have fled. No one's going to want to risk being caught now. The Assembly – including you, I assume? – has just voted for money to more-than-double the guards, so they would certainly be caught. We know what and who to look for.'

Themis bit back his impatience and asked, 'And what is the man called who left for Miletus?'

'They said his name is Menestratus, but you can't rely on a man who's been sentenced to death. They talk all kinds of rubbish.'

Themis stopped himself asking why they bothered torturing them, then. Instead he said, 'And what do you know about this Menestratus?'

'Nothing at all.'

'Right. Could I talk to them?'

'I doubt it. They're probably dead by now. Last time we put anyone in the Samian shackles, some kind soul stuck a knife in his heart "so he wouldn't groan so".' The officer stepped away. 'I have to go.'

'Thank you,' said Themis to the stiff back as the man marched out into the afternoon sun.

And the officer proved to be right. Both the men were dead when Themis arrived at the Shackles. They were harshly marked from their torture, with shreds of skin torn from their feet and hands, their faces bloody and their teeth missing. Themis' breath came fast, and not only because he had run the short distance. Someone had cut their throats efficiently. Their life's blood had pooled and dried at their feet. Flies had gathered. But at least they hadn't been disembowelled like the male prisoners Themis had seen killed in Skioni.

The sight and smell of that still haunted his dreams.

He ran home and found Photios waiting for him in the courtyard, caressing Yellow's pointed ears.

'We've been invited to join Alkibiades at an informal evening at his house later tonight,' said Photios, showing Themis a small scroll with a rich yellow ribbon-tie. 'Both of us!'

Themis smiled. 'And why wouldn't he invite both of us?'

'Because only one of us is a hero,' said Photios.

'And the other an honourable man placed in an impossible situation,' said Themis.

Photios laughed. 'A chastened man, though free, at least!' he said. Then he went on seriously, 'Did you know Alkibiades was going to speak?'

'No,' said Themis. ' And I've been wondering why he came to the prison to see you, too. Is he a friend of your father's?'

'Far from it,' said Photios. 'Father sees him as a "bumptious cub" who can't live without constant attention from the crowd.'

Diodotos came out of the andron to join them. 'Whatever the truth of that,' he said, 'Alkibiades has brains and charm and can make even the crustiest old campaigner excited about a new venture.'

'I think this was an event that everyone has an opinion about, so the perfect vehicle for drawing the attention of the crowd to himself. However, of course, it might be because, as Frog insists, he's in love with me,' said Themis with a comical expression.

'Why not?' said Photios with a grin. 'But then again, I heard Damianos was a good friend of his, so …,' he shrugged.

Female laughter sounded from above.

'You have a houseful, little brother,' Diodotos said to Themis. 'Chloe and that boy Melissus are here.'

Themis looked up, then asked Photios, 'What will you do now?'

'Off to the farm,' said Photios with false cheer. 'Father has a project for me. Something to do with wells.'

'When?'

'Tomorrow.'

'Time for a visit to Keramikos before going to General Alkibiades', then,' said Diodotos with a laugh, 'to celebrate your non-traitor status!'

Photios looked a question at Themis.

'There's something I need to do,' he said. 'I'll try and meet you before we go to the General's. Where will you go?'

'We'll start at the Double Door in Keramikos,' said Diodotos. 'If we move on, I'll leave a message.'

When they'd gone, Themis started up the stairs to speak to his sister. He wanted to tell her where he was going, and anyway, he felt he must tell Melissus to go home as his father was worried. He could hear suppressed giggling from the women's rooms. Yellow padded at his heels.

Halfway up the stairs he heard Melissa say, 'But surely we don't *have* to get pregnant, do we?' Her voice sounded less aggressive when she wasn't pretending to be a boy.

Themis stopped and sat down quietly on a step. The dog collapsed with its head on his thigh.

'What d'you mean,' asked Chloe. She sounded amused and a little patronizing.

Melissa's voice said, 'Well, I know it's the white stuff that makes the babies. I've watched my brother. He gets big and moves his hands up and down faster and faster until it comes out, and then he falls back laughing. So obviously, it doesn't *have* to end up inside a woman.' Melissa was trying to sound worldly.

Themis took a deep breath. Not only was Melissa in his house after all, but she was seriously embarrassing his sister. He made a move to get up and Yellow growled very quietly. 'So you think I should eavesdrop?' Themis whispered to the dog. Yellow stared into his face with limpid eyes. Themis stayed where he was.

Chloe's amused voice was saying, 'Ah. You've realized that at least.'

'Of course, Mother says it's a gift from the gods if you get pregnant,' said Melissa.

'If you're with the right man, yes,' said Chloe quietly.

'And that girls are born just to get pregnant and give birth themselves,' Melissa went on. 'But that's *not* what *I* want to do.'

'Having children can be a full-time occupation,' said Chloe. 'So that's how things are here in Athens. Women stay at home, look after the house and expect to have babies. That's what marriage is for.'

Melissa was shocked. 'You mean if there are no babies, no marriage?'

'It's been the reason for a lot of divorces – and for marriages that didn't happen.'

'What do you mean?' There was a catch in Melissa's voice.

'Well, if a girl doesn't get pregnant after the engagement, a man is entirely within his rights to cancel the wedding and return the dowry.'

'What?!' Melissa seemed to collapse onto a bed. 'It's *that* important?'

'What's really important is having a bit of control over when you fall pregnant and when you don't,' said Chloe more seriously.

Themis was fascinated – against his better judgement, of course.

'So how do you do that?' asked Melissa. She sounded chastened somehow, as though she was only partly listening.

'Obviously,' Chloe said, 'in a war situation or after a religious fertility festival you can't do much except wash yourself out with vinegar. It's a good idea to have ready one of the right preparations made up by the apothecaries, if you know beforehand you might be …'

'Raped?' asked Melissa, more herself now.

'Or just have to conform,' said Chloe. 'If it's just one man and he's amenable, you can make sure you don't carry his seed.'

'How?'

'One way,' said Chloe, 'is to offer to take him in your mouth.'

'*Woah!*' thought Themis, blushing all over to think of his sister saying – or doing – such a thing. In his experience, this was only done with explicit agreement between men, or paid for with available women.

'Yuck!' said Melissa. 'They stink!'

'True,' said Chloe, 'but better that, than a child you have to spend more than two hundred and seventy days carrying. And who may kill you at birth, or which may die or have to be exposed,' said Chloe. Themis remembered Chloe had given birth to a baby girl with twisted legs. She'd disappeared within hours and been officially declared stillborn.

'But that's disgusting. Isn't there another way?' asked Melissa.

'Well,' said Chloe, 'If there's oil or clean grease around you can slather it on your hands and hold him and slide up and down until the seed comes out, like your brother does himself.'

'That sounds a bit … easier,' said Melissa doubtfully.

'Sometimes it comes out in a rush,' said Chloe, 'and you have to duck!'

They both burst out laughing. Themis stood up. The dog growled.

'And there's the way they like, of course.'

Themis stood still.

'Which is?' asked Melissa.

'They stick themselves in your bum and leave the seed in there.'

'But that's where I stink!' said Melissa. 'What a lot of trouble! Can't they just deal with it themselves?'

'It's a drive they can't resist. And women have it too. Perhaps you haven't felt it yet …' Chloe was further away. Themis strained to hear. He believed the women he'd been with usually enjoyed fornicating, but he wasn't sure about married women. He was learning as much as

Melissa!

'What d'you mean,' asked Melissa, alarmed.

'Oh, they'll go into all that at Vravrona,' said Chloe. 'But if I remember correctly, they don't tell you much about avoiding little visitors!'

Melissa said, 'The best way seems to be the oily hands …'

Chloe laughed. 'That's the name of one of the brothels down by the Dypilon Gate,' she said. 'Philandra's Oily Hands.'

'Oh … so that's what they do there!' exclaimed Melissa. 'I know the place, but the street kids told me it was something to do with cooking.'

'*And how does Chloe know about Philandra?*' Themis thought. His descent of the stairs with Yellow was masked by the sound of their laughter.

He would send Frog to Agorakritos to tell him that his *daughter* was with Chloe for the day. Then they needed to get to Piraeus

>>>

As the gym was closing for the day, Keir, a Lancashire County athletics trainer, took both Suzanne's hands in his and turned them over. 'We need to work on strengthening your right wrist,' he said. 'Being left-handed is good in team games because it confuses the opponents. Work your wrists now.'

Suzanne moved her clenched fists up and down.

'See the difference?' asked Keir. 'The muscles in your left arm are more defined because you use them more. But you need both wrists to be equally strong for pole vaulting. You need to pull up and then push away with both.'

'Oh yeah. I see that now,' said Suzanne. 'Should I work with weights?'

'Yes. I'll show you a couple of exercises that'll help. But it must be every day.'

'That's fine,' said Suzanne.

Keir smiled at her. 'You're doing really well,' he said. 'I've never had a student in the running to be chosen for the Commonwealth Games before.'

Suzanne smiled back. He was a good trainer. He gave her confidence, and was prepared to give her some of his spare time, too.

But she'd have to type even quicker if she was going to do extra training.

Chapter 18: basket of jars

(Breeds of Sheep 11 – I can't always remember the names of new people when I'm writing this up. I look them up if I have time, but they're not usually there (or maybe I get the spelling wrong). But that man who spoke up at the Assembly for Photios *was* the famous Alkibiades/Alcibiades!. Plutarch and a load of others wrote about him, but ages after he died. When Themis sees him, he really is fit – thick wavy blond hair, soft smiley mouth, sexy voice, totally self-confident – and seems rich!

I also looked up Skioni. Small coastal town by the sea in the north. Revolted against Athens' rule. When the town was finally re-taken after nearly three years, all the men were killed and the women and children made slaves. This seems to have been common after a siege. Perhaps that's where Themis' memory of tipping the bodies into the cliff cave is from. These things really shock me when I check them out. But when I'm living them with Themis, they're just the way things are! Upsetting, but fascinating, too.)

<<<

'Frog around?' Themis asked the Skionian in the kitchen. The girl was kneading bread. She pointed through to the back yard with her chin. It was nearly three years since he'd brought her back after the eventual success of the siege of Skioni, and she still wouldn't speak or give her name. But Mika and Frog seemed to understand her well enough.

Frog turned from the potted vine he was tending in the courtyard and looked pointedly up at the window of the room where Chloe and Melissa were still talking. 'Will Melissa be in your mother's care in Vravrona?' he asked with wide, innocent eyes.

Themis laughed. 'None of our business, Frog,' he said. 'But I need you to run an errand and then to come to Piraeus with me.'

Frog stood up. He rolled his tools in a bundle as he spoke. 'Is the errand about Melissa, or Melissus?'

'Just go and let Agorakritos know that his *daughter* is with my sister. Tell him she'll bring her home soon.'

'Then … ?'

'Then meet me at Kimon's tomb and we'll go down to Piraeus on Parilios. I want you to talk to someone there for me.'

'Right,' said Frog. He left the tools where they were and set off.

Themis called out, 'Melissa, are you there?'

Chloe looked down from the window. 'She's here,' she said.

'Her father's looking for her. I don't think it's anything to do with

Nereus. He called her Melissus when I saw him. Can you take her home later? I have to go out, but you're staying the night, aren't you?'

'That's the plan,' said Chloe.

Melissus' head appeared. 'Me too?'

'Not you,' said Themis. 'You know that!'

Melissus made a rude sign to him.

'All well with you and the family?' he asked Chloe.

'Fine. They send kisses,' she said.

'I may not be back until the morning as Alkibiades has invited us. So see you next time you're here, then,' said Themis and went through to the stable to have Tanu saddle Parilios.

Themis and Frog rode at a walk through the streets to Zea harbour.

'You had one of your Skioni dreams last night,' said Frog from behind.

'I don't remember.' Themis turned to glimpse Frog. 'Did I shout?'

'You woke Yellow and he came and got me, but by the time I reached you, you'd quietened down.'

'Having the Skionian living in the house doesn't help,' said Themis. 'Can't we just give her a name?'

'I'll try again to find out what it is,' said Frog. 'I'll tell her I need it to make a song about her.'

'Then she'll never tell you,' said Themis.

'And maybe you'll find flies in your soup next time I bring you some!' Frog chuckled.

'We're nearly there,' said Themis. 'See if you can get Inaros to say who made him change his mind about giving evidence. I have a name, but don't use it unless you have to. It may be wrong, anyway. It's Menestratus.'

'OK,' said Frog. 'Let me off here.' He slid down off the gelding's back and disappeared into an alleyway.

Themis walked the horse across the market square to the huge Cantharus Harbour where the commercial ships came in. At the Wings of Victory tavern, he handed him over to a groom and went in. The clamour and smells of men eating and drinking, trading and betting, hit him like a fist. He climbed the stairs to the quieter room above and found a place by the balcony rail. A boy came for his order and he asked for wine and water separately and a quick word with the boss.

While he waited, he sorted some coins in his pocket and watched the waterfront below. From here he could look west across the busy harbour to the island of Salamis and the mountains of the mainland beyond. Layer upon layer were pleated against the bright sky. The small lump of Akrokorinthos showed clearly in the gap that marked the isthmus between the mainland beyond Megara and the Peloponnesus. Masts, warehouses and ship sheds hid the island of Egina to the south. But south-west, a good half-day's rowing away, the dark bulk of the Methana volcano was leaking a fine veil of white smoke into the still air. The water in the harbour was blue, but nearer to Salamis it was almost black, speckled with hundreds of vessels now that the spring journeys had begun in earnest.

'What can I help you with?' asked the tavern manager. 'You haven't been to see us much lately, but we heard of your exploits in Zea.' He set the wine and water pitchers on the small table by Themis.

'Thank you, Nikodemos,' said Themis. 'It's about that that I'm here.'

Nikodemos was an old man now, with a slight stoop and skin as lined as a walnut. He reached up with a hand on either side of Themis' face and said, 'Ach, my child. It wouldn't be to do with the price of sweet Achaian wine now, would it?' He was referring to a drunken night many years before. He still had four teeth to smile with.

'That was a long time ago,' said Themis with a laugh. 'No, this is important. I need to learn about a man called Menestratus. He left on a ship to Miletus three days ago. Who would know about that?'

'The name of the ship?' asked Nikodemos.

'I don't know that.'

'To Miletus, you say?' mused Nikodemos. 'Give me a few minutes.' And he went back downstairs.

Themis poured himself a little wine and mixed in some water. He remembered the hangover he'd suffered when he and Photios had tried the dark sweet wine of Patra that first time. He watched absently as two men came to blows on the quay below.

A sailor tapped him on the shoulder. 'You wanting to know about Menestratus from Miletus?' he said.

Themis nodded and offered the man a cup.

'No thanks,' he grunted. 'Menestratus left on the Heron three mornings ago, before the fracas at Zea. He asked for boats from Vravrona in the east, but the Heron was leaving immediately from here, so he took that.'

'What was he like?'

'Dark, your height, tough, but high voice,' said the man, eyeing Themis' garments for a heavy pocket. 'Seemed to have a stomach problem.'

'Was he staying here in Piraeus before that? Or in the city?'

'In the city. He didn't like sea voyages. Said something about offering to Poseidon of the green shrine to see him home safely. Guess it was near where he stayed.'

Themis hid his surprise. 'You sure?'

'Never seen a green shrine, myself. Seemed odd.'

Themis took out a half-drachma and said, 'Yeah. It is odd. Nothing else you remember?'

'Drank no wine,' said the sailor. 'Used happy powder.'

'The mushroom powder or the expensive stuff?'

'Mushrooms. But he had plenty of money. Gave us a good time.'

'Well, thanks, anyway,' said Themis and handed him the half-drachma.

The sailor nodded his head and disappeared back into the tavern. Themis waved at Nikodemos and threw the serving boy an obol as he left.

'Inaros wouldn't talk at first,' said Frog, as Parilios took them back to the City. 'But it turned out that it was his boss who threatened him with losing his job if he gave evidence.'

'The heavy man with the scar?' said Themis. 'Frightening type, even if he's not your boss.'

'Yeah, well. Very sure of his own importance. I asked him if he realized he'd been used and did he want to get the user punished,' said Frog.

'Oh, beware the Frog,' said Themis with admiration.

'He said the man was completely shrouded in a long cloak and hood and held a cloth to his mouth. He'd accosted him out the back of the tavern.'

Themis asked, 'Big man? Little man?'

'I didn't think to ask,' said Frog. 'But he did say the man threatened to close him down if any more information from his tavern about the arsonists was mentioned in the City.'

'Nothing to identify him at all?' said Themis.

'The cloak was dark grey and the man had a cough,' said Frog. 'A real cough that made him double up in a spasm.'

Themis sighed. 'That might help but it's not much. Could be temporary. Let's get back,' he said. 'I want to have another look at that house where Photios disappeared.' He urged Parilios into a canter.

The sun was setting when they left the horse at home, borrowed a lamp and a burning ember from the kitchen, and ran up to the crossroads past the green shrine. Someone had lit a torch in the niche below the god. The wavering flame threw shadows of the statue's abundant hair and its trident against the green ceiling.

Themis stopped and looked. 'Quite clever,' he said.

'Very … watery,' said Frog, his head on one side.

Themis rolled his eyes. 'Come on!' he urged. They ran on past a couple of busy shops towards the crossroads where the traffic of people and mules thinned a little. Themis knocked on the front door of the house even though no lights were showing. No answer.

They both went round into the alley. The back door Themis had beaten on the night he'd seen Photios was closed. Frog tried it and it opened with a groan. Themis saw two rats scuttle away at the noise.

'Empty?' he said quietly.

'You going to have a look?' asked Frog.

'Keep watch up in the street. If I find a way to open the front door, I'll let you in.'

'Fine.' Frog went back to the main road.

Themis stepped into complete blackness. There was a definite scuffling. He shut the door, then blew on the little ember in its terra cotta box. He lit the wick of the lamp and in moments had a bright light.

He was in a tunnel. The wall to his right was raw rock. The ceiling and wall to the left were built and whitewashed. He walked twelve steps along it and came to another door. This one had a catch but no lock. He lifted the catch. It made a quiet click.

'This must be the next door house,' he thought. *'No wonder the slave girl had heard no one.'*

He was now in a windowless room with shelves on two walls. Some were full of large plain pots, some of boxes made of wood or terra cotta, some of folded sacking and other fabrics. On one shelf there was a basket full of tiny unlabelled jars. They were the same as the jars Chloe had bought at Zotikos' shop.

'There's enough Lethe's Ladder here to kill a dozen people,' he thought as he lifted the basket down to get a closer look. On the wooden shelf underneath it, he counted thirty-five short lines, a tally. Six of them were crossed through. *'How in heaven and Hades did they get so much?'* he thought. *'Someone's keeping a record of the doses – used or sold, I wonder.'*

He didn't disturb the basket and put it back on the shelf. He looked for a maker's mark on the little, undecorated jars and couldn't see one. On the larger pots he could see one clearly, though, pressed into the clay of the rim round the bottom. It was not a mark he knew – a triangle with four dots, one in the middle and one halfway along each side. These larger pots were of a paler clay, unusual for unpainted ware. Could this room have been where Photios had gone?

A heap of fuel logs filled one corner, and beside it, a stair led upwards. Themis began to climb, listening at each of the fifteen steps.

Above him there was now a high ceiling. The beams were red ochre against a pale plaster. This corridor was narrower and ended in a wall. To the right was a curtained doorway. Themis gingerly held back the curtain, then stepped silently into a large, unoccupied room. There was little furniture, just a long table and two folding chairs. There were no windows, but two tall doorways opened side by side onto the central courtyard where the last light of day was fading. The floor was of old limestone slabs, discoloured with stains. The walls of this room had once been frescoed with a forest in shades of green, but it had peeled off in patches to show the plaster beneath.

The loud sound of the street door opening made Themis jump and blow out his lamp. Three men walked into the dim courtyard. A large hunting dog on a rope followed them.

'Got anyone in the cage?' asked one man.

'Nah,' said another. 'Boss said to have it ready, though. He may need it in a day or two.'

'I'll check it out,' said the third. He walked into the green room, past Themis, who shrank against the mottled wall between the doors and held his breath.

Themis heard the two men outside cross to the other side of the yard. 'Haven't seen the boss myself for three or four days,' one said. The other coughed harshly as their voices faded.

Did they take the dog? Themis couldn't tell. If it scented him he would be in trouble. He followed the 'cage' man to the curtain he'd come through. He waited there until he heard the man's feet on the stairs, then he looked along the corridor. The man had lit a lantern, which shone up from below. Themis ran silently to the top of the stairs. As he reached them, the light disappeared. He flattened himself against the wall and looked down. The man had pulled the section of shelves full of folded sacking open like a door!

Themis could see the light moving around in a room beyond the shelves. He crept down and watched from behind the rolls of sacking. The room was small with one tiny opening high up in the back wall. The man shook out a straw mattress and then swept pieces of straw and what looked like broken pot out into the larger room with a broom. Themis hid between the shelves and the wall as the man took an empty pitcher from another shelf and ran up the stairs leaving his lantern on the floor.

Themis stepped quickly into the 'cage' while he was gone. The walls were painted with a complicated pattern of stripes and squares. There was a stone floor with a hole in the farthest corner which stank of faeces.

Themis turned to leave the way he had come in – and came face to face with the man with the pitcher! Themis was swinging his fist when the pitcher hit him full on the side of the head.

Chapter 19: cage

When he woke, he was lying on the straw mattress, damp, cold, and in the dark. He'd dropped his lamp and his tinderbox was gone. Only the faintest glimmer of paler blackness came through the tiny window high above. The pitcher had been full of water, most of which had sloshed over Themis. He stood up, his legs untrustworthy. He felt along the wall he knew had the door, but could find nothing that indicated where it was.

He wondered whether Frog had also been caught. He whispered, 'Frog, you here?' but got no reply. He felt round the rest of the room. There was no one else with him.

He called softly as near to the window as he could, 'Frog! You there?'

Nothing except a low growl. The dog – or a dog – was on guard.

He sat on the straw mattress. 'Not clever,' he said to himself, 'to end up here. No weapon, no light, no Frog…' He was thinking, '*Who runs this house? What do they use it for? Organized thieves? Smugglers of stuff banned by the Assembly? Is this really where Photios came to get his orders when under the influence?*'

Had he stumbled on the headquarters of the gang trying to destroy the navy. How could he use his capture to learn who the gang leader was? Playing dead might give him a chance to make a dash for it, '*But I wouldn't learn who it is*,' he thought. No, he'd need to seem more badly injured than he was.

It wouldn't be hard. His cheek was on fire and he could feel the side of his face was so swollen that his eye had closed. He really wanted to get news of this house to the Archons. Would Frog work out that he was working for them and tell them where he was last seen? If he got out of this alive, he'd take Frog into his confidence, whatever they thought.

'*Rest and prepare*,' he thought, the soldiers' motto. He lay down to rest his body, but his mind would not be still. They almost certainly didn't know who he was. Their boss would have to decide whether to kill him, keep him indefinitely, or find a way to keep him silent and let him go — blackmail? drugs? A worm of fear was constricting his throat. He ignored it, deliberately imagining the confusion of his captors — but it hurt to smile.

Then he heard a much-loved voice in his head. 'Don't ignore it. Name your fear. Take control of it.' It was the voice of Asterodia the priestess, mother of Xenovia, in the days after his accident, when he had no memory and dreamed horrendous dreams. Asterodia, who had called him out of his coma and given him the courage to recover in this bewildering world.

'*Well, I've named my fears*,' he thought. '*So now rest and prepare*.' The hum in his chest intensified. The nymph was with him at least, even if Asterodia was now dead. The last time he'd seen her, she'd been so very old.

He deliberately relaxed, laid his right hand on his chest and, with his left hand free and ready and his mind partly on listening for danger, he allowed himself to remember …

She was sitting in the late sunshine. Her wicker chair supported her back and legs. Its soft cushions and coverlet were of finest undyed linen.

Her eyes were shut. The deep lines from nose to mouth were softened by the warm light. Themis had never had an opportunity to examine her unique beauty while she was unaware before. She was, of course, from the famously good-looking family of religious leaders who served at most of the City's temples, and that family resemblance was clear. But her face was perfectly symmetrical, the bones now visible under skin like a dried rose petal. The pattern of tiny wrinkles round her eyes changed as she opened them. He felt the familiar shock as their intense green focused on him.

'Themistokles.' Her voice was a musical creak in the peace of the sacred courtyard. 'You came. Please sit where I can see you.' She took a deep breath and tried to raise her body a little in the long chair. An acolyte stepped away from the wall, but Asterodia waved her gently away.

'Yes,' said Themis. 'Mama said you wished to see me.'

'For many years,' said the old priestess slowly, 'I have known something that I feel you should know, but I have no way to prove it.'

Themis frowned. 'And now you do?'

'Sadly I do not have the kind of proof you may wish for. But now is the time for me to tell you, even so. I shall be leaving this world soon and there will not be another chance to speak to you.'

Themis wanted to jump up and shout 'No!' He stared at her in horror but she smiled serenely at him. Her veins showed blue through her skin. She held out her hand and he took it carefully in both his.

'It is only natural,' she said. 'I was already old when you were born. I cannot extend my stay here much longer.'

'It may be natural,' said Themis, 'but I don't have to like it. You gave me back my life when I was twelve and nearly died. You have been the stable centre of what Mama calls my wild youth ever since.'

'There are others younger than I,' she said with a teasing smile. 'It may be that you can turn to … Sokrates or Lysimache.'

'I know of no one who has your understanding of the good in us all,' said Themis seriously. Asterodia closed her eyes and it was as if the sun went in. 'But you wanted to tell me something,' he said quietly.

Taking a deep breath, she withdrew her hand from Themis' and held both hers calmly in her lap. 'Once I had a daughter, Xenovia,' she began in a story-teller's tone.

Themis breathed in sharply.

Asterodia went on, intense eyes open now but looking at her hands. 'She was a powerful priestess, but embittered. She knew your mother well.'

Themis couldn't restrain himself. 'And murdered my father and tried to kill me,' he said distinctly. Was Asterodia's mind wandering?

The green gaze came to rest on his face again. 'She also stole from the temples and lied to men and the gods. But most people wouldn't believe any of this because she was so beautiful. That was my daughter.'

'I know this only too well, sacred lady,' said Themis gently.

'Of course you do,' said Asterodia. 'But this is the last time I shall ever mention her name and it must be done according to the procedure.' She closed her eyes again. 'My husband's family is large and powerful, but it seemed I could give them no children. After he died,

Xenovia was born, a child of the Dionysia. I was the humble means by which she came onto this earth. I did not feel, nor expect to feel, any close attachment to her. She grew to adulthood among the priesthood and both men and women were slaves to her beauty.'

Themis remembered his own infatuation with the perfection of Xenovia's face and figure. How he had longed to sculpt her! And how ashamed he had been later, when he learned the truth about her.

Asterodia went on in her sing-song voice. 'But you were the means the gods used to punish her at last, and this is our bond. She rode at you and missed, leaping off the high cliff. She fell into the Vathonero and was drawn into the depths of the earth in the waters of the river.'

Themis gritted his teeth. The vision of woman and horse, hair, mane and cloak billowing in the moonlight as they fell into the black shadow of the gorge, had the power to wake him from sleep even now.

'They found the horse as had been foreseen,' Asterodia continued, eyes closed. 'And the stolen treasures with it. But no one has seen Xenovia again, alive or dead.'

Themis had thought about this many times. 'Hades must have kept her with him as she was so beautiful,' he said.

Asterodia opened her eyes and smiled at him. 'What I know, and I want you to know, is that she did not die in the caverns and the hidden rivers under the mountains of Elis.'

Themis was shocked into silence for a moment. Then he remembered. 'But sacred lady, you said you have no proof.'

'I have none. Only that the one object I had that was hers, has disappeared. And that I can feel her life, still here with us.' Asterodia leaned forward a little, her eyes impelling as she looked at him earnestly. 'You need to know this,' she said. 'It may be that she will never appear again in your life. But you need to know that she could. She wished you great harm, and it is possible that she could still cause you pain.'

Themis relaxed his shoulders and smiled. 'Sacred lady,' he said. 'You take more care of my soul than my own mother does. I thank you for this warning and I will hold it in my heart. But you must not think about it any more. If Xenovia is alive, and if she wishes me or my family harm, I will now be ready.'

Asterodia lay back again. The down on her cheek shone in the last of the sunlight. 'If Xenovia is alive, she will soon be the only part of me left on this earth, albeit unwished for and unlovable. So if you can find it in your heart, please make offerings to Athena to cleanse her soul,' she said. Her eyes held his one last time. The touch of her fingers on the back of his hand was light as a cobweb. 'Go always to the good, Themistokles. You are very dear to me … Now, may I see your mother for a moment?'

Themis stood and bent over the ancient priestess. He took her hand in his and kissed it. 'Farewell,' he said. 'I will always carry your strength with me.' And he made sure his tears did not show until he was through the door to the colonnade where his mother waited.

'She wants to see you for a moment,' he said.

Later, as they walked slowly home, Eirini was weeping silently. Themis pulled her arm through his. His own tears fell on their joined hands.

'She said she knows Xenovia is still alive,' he said.

'You don't think so?'

'If a horse couldn't survive that underground river, I think it's impossible a woman could,' he said.

'You didn't say that to Asterodia, did you?'

'Of course not. I thanked her for the warning and said it would help me to protect my family if Xenovia re-appeared. She asked me to pray for her, but I'm afraid I'll never be able to do that.'

'But you have a kind soul, my son,' said Eirini. 'Asterodia is perhaps ninety years old and could well be wandering in her mind.'

'But not in your opinion?' Themis said as they turned into a busy street.

'No,' said Eirini. 'And I think you would do well to remember her warning, although it seems unlikely to be needed.' She stopped outside a shop and looked up at him with a tired smile. 'Now, I want to get an offering to Hermes. I don't suppose you've made anything suitable lately, have you?'

'No,' he said with regret. 'I was painting wedding scenes all week. Not really the thing for the passage of our favourite priestess to Hades. But if you don't find anything you like, it wouldn't take me long to …'

'We may not need an offering for a few days,' said Eirini. 'But let's just have a look, anyway …'

Themis must have passed out again, because when he opened his eyes he could see. A lamp was being held through the window. A dark head appeared beside it for a moment. Then both were rapidly withdrawn. Themis stood up and called out, 'Who's that?! What do you want of me?'

A while later, the hidden door opened silently and light bled through the gap. The door into the tunnel was open, and the one into the alley beyond. No one appeared. No one spoke. Themis stepped through the 'cage' door. There were no sounds from the house above. No dog. No captors.

He walked across the storeroom lit by a torch in a wall-bracket. He saw that the basket of Lethe's Ladder was no longer on the shelves, then stumbled along the tunnel and emerged into the alley without hindrance.

When he got to the main road, he saw Frog running towards him up the street with Yellow and a torch.

Diodotos was with him and shouted, 'What the hell happened to you?' as he saw his brother. 'You look like you disagreed with a bear!'

'Full water pitcher,' Themis managed to say out of the healthier side of his mouth. 'You see anyone there in the street?' he asked Frog.

They were beside the green shrine. Frog was examining Themis' face in the light of their torch and the god's lamp. 'No one came out. But I thought I heard something fall. Two men came out of the house next door and turned down the next street, so I guessed the noise had come from that house. I ran down the alley and tried the door but it was locked. Did you lock it?'

Themis shook his head. Pain shot through his jaw. He mumbled, 'That door leads along a tunnel to the next house. The noise you heard was probably me being knocked out. There were three men and a dog. They could lead us to their boss. You only saw two?'

Frog nodded. 'I stayed a long time, but I didn't see any others. I called quietly a couple of times, by the door. You didn't answer, so I went to get your brother.'

'We should look for the third. He might lead us …' Themis turned back, stumbled and would have fallen without their support. Yellow nudged his thigh. 'Got to ask – '

'Let's get you home,' said Diodotos.

Themis freed himself from his brother's grasp and strode back towards the house by the alley. 'One of them had a cough,' he said to Frog. 'And someone looked in at me through a window, high up. At the back. Maybe from the rocks behind. Mustn't lose the chance …,' he murmured. 'Got to tell …' He stopped himself saying the name.

'You're in no state,' said Diodotos, catching them up.

A male slave was sitting on a stool by the house where the wedding had been. He had a short spear and a torch. Themis walked over to him. His eyes opened in shock at Themis' face.

'He's harmless,' said Diodotos. 'You on guard?'

'Yeah,' said the man standing up. 'Been some strangers seen round here lately. No thefts yet, though.'

Themis' lips would hardly work. 'Did you see anyone leave there just now? Perhaps a man and …'

'… and a dog?' he finished for him. 'Yup. They ran off together that way, just before you came out of the alley.'

'Can you describe them?' asked Diodotos.

'Nah. Just caught a quick glimpse. Man was small, dog was big.'

Themis swore under his breath. 'Thanks,' he said. He turned to his brother. 'Alright. Let's go.'

Diodotos took his arm again. 'It's a pity you were … er, busy,' he said. 'Photios went on his own to Alkibiades' party. You'll have to send an apology tomorrow.' He looked sideways at his brother and laughed. 'Your face is a real picture.'

'Chloe at home?' Themis realized he was dribbling as he spoke.

A door opened and a man stood staring at them. 'Keep walking now,' said Diodotos. 'The locals are thinking we're the would-be thieves.'

At home, Frog sent Mika to wake Chloe and they all sat in the kitchen while she washed Themis' face and spread salve on the bruises.

'Nothing broken,' she said with a sleepy smile. 'You really must stop waking me up for such minor ailments.'

'You do a better job than Mama,' said Themis from the side of his mouth.

'Don't tell her that,' said Chloe. 'Sleep now. You can explain to me in the morning what you thought you could achieve by breaking and entering the house of a total stranger.' She took her bag of remedies and went back to bed.

'Didn't break in,' mumbled Themis. 'Door was open.'

>>>

The weight in Suzanne's right hand slipped and fell.

'Oh shit!' she yelled. 'Oh, shit shit shit!' She dropped the second weight with a crash and sat down on the floor trying not to groan or sob. She rocked herself as she rubbed the fast-swelling bruise on the top of her right foot.

Keir dashed across the gym to her. 'What've you done?' he said as he squatted down beside her.

'I dropped a weight on my foot.' Suzanne wailed.

'Let's get your shoe off and see the damage.'

128

Keir's strong fingers pulled gently at the Velcro. Suzanne gritted her teeth. 'Now the sock,' he said.

'I'll do it,' said Suzanne.

They stared in silence at the reddening groove across her now unrecognizable instep. Keir said, 'I'll take you to A&E. You need an X-ray.'

In the car on the way to the hospital, Keir said, 'You've been looking very tired lately. Are you overdoing it?'

Suzanne was clenching her jaw against the pain. 'Don't think so,' she said.

Keir smiled. 'I asked Natasha and she said you were preoccupied and spent a lot of time writing something on your computer.'

Suzanne's eyes filled with tears. The tone of Keir's voice was so kind, so sympathetic. She wasn't used to having a man be so caring. She said, 'There's a long story that I'm trying to get down.'

'You write?' he asked as he slowed for traffic lights, then looked at her with wonder. 'What sort of story?'

'Oh just something … I … see in my head sometimes,' she said.

'I've heard professional novelists say that about their characters.' He drove forward. 'The characters don't let them alone till they've written them down.'

'Yes,' agreed Suzanne. 'It is a bit like that … '

'Would you let me read it some time?' Keir said.

'Oh no!' Suzanne shook her head vehemently. 'No. No one gets to read it!'

<<<

Chapter 20: to be a woman

(Breeds of Sheep 12)

Themis took an empty tablet from the andron and left the house silently in the quiet before dawn. He could see nothing from his left eye but had slept for a while and felt surprisingly well. He'd come to the conclusion that he'd been recognized and released by the third man. Whoever the real traitors were, they must want him alive for some reason. Perhaps they'd try and contact him again.

The Council offices were just opening. He sat on the steps to write a brief account for Apollodorus of what had happened at the house near the green shrine. He included the Heron, the ship Menestratus had left on, and added a request for information about who owned that house and whether there had been any other illegal activities connected with it.

By the time he had sealed this and delivered it to Apollodorus' clerk, the Agora was coming to life. As he passed the statues of the ten heroes, he saw a notice announcing a muster of troops from his part of the city for that evening. A campaign in the Peloponnese was to begin within seven days. Money for this, with Alkibiades as its leading general, had been voted at the Assembly the same day as Photios' treason accusation. The list of names would be put up the next day.

This could mean that Diodotos, a cavalry soldier, would be absent for the harvest. Themis was usually called up as an engineer, a builder or a reservist rower. None of these was mentioned on the notice.

As he walked home, he pondered whether he should volunteer anyway. Part of him longed for the action and excitement. Campaigning meant there were no domestic worries, no money worries, and lots of fun, sex and wine. But the other side of the coin was that the worst might happen and both he and his brother be killed... Assuming Kallistos was in Hades and they met, it would be hard to face his father's eternal disappointment.

No one was stirring when he got into the house, except the slaves. A note had arrived from Photios.

'*You didn't miss much,*' it said, '*except the cheetah! Alkibiades had it with him all the time. Magnificent creature, from Egypt it seems, taller than your Yellow. He'd invited quite a few young men and we all had a chance to touch it. Softer hair than a dog. He told us about his latest ideas for harrying the Spartans – nothing new. There was food and wine and he chatted to each man a bit. He asked me where you were and if you were working on any building projects in the City. I don't think I made much of an impression as I could only say I didn't know! But he did tell me to show up at the muster, so I may see you there. Some were unhappy no girls were offered. We all left quite early. Let me know what happened. Everyone was in a bit of a panic when I asked at your house on the way home. Photios.*'

Themis wrote quick notes to Alkibiades and Photios for Frog to deliver, then went back to his practice wall with his paints.

Sometime later, he heard the rustle of a chiton and smelled the sweet scent of Chloe's fresh lilac garland.

'That's not very erotic,' she said.

He stepped back to be beside her and assess his efforts. 'No?'

'In my opinion, suggestion is more arousing than realistic detail, however beautifully drawn.'

'Give me an example,' said Themis through his misshapen lips.

'Well, how about two hills the shape of breasts – or buttocks for that matter – with a river between and a long slim boat speeding towards them?'

'Perhaps a bit of a cliché?'

'Or Aphrodite leaving her bath but a little obscured by some bulrushes – or maybe just one, strategically placed?'

Themis tried to smile. 'Since when were you an expert on such things, Chloe?'

'Oh, Hipparchos and I have our moments,' she said. 'The time he spends with hetairas and at symposia isn't entirely without value to me. I like him to show me what he's been learning!'

Themis put his arm round his sister's shoulders. 'He's lucky to have such an … enthusiastic wife,' he mumbled affectionately.

'Come on,' said Chloe, touching his swollen cheek gently. 'Let's see what we can do about your face. You're in no fit state to start work on Zotikos' walls today, anyway.'

'Got to get them done soon,' lisped Themis, allowing himself to be led to the water trough. 'Going to be a muster for troops for Alkibiades' next campaign this evening. If I joined them, I'd be gone in three days.'

'And what does he think he's going to do this time?' asked Chloe as she laid out her remedies on the table under the colonnade. 'Build a wall all round the Peloponnese to keep the Spartans in? Sit here.'

Themis sat. He had been wondering the same thing since he'd seen the notice. Of course, the allies of Sparta were never still. They fought among themselves as well as with the allies of Athens. So far the treaty between Athens and Sparta had held for more than three years. But there were those who believed that Alkibiades' aggressive little campaigns against enemy cities could put it in jeopardy. Others backed him as the champion of Athens' superiority.

'Ouch!' Themis exclaimed as Chloe pushed firmly on his cheek.

'Just checking there's really no break in the bone,' she said cheerfully.

A knock on the street door made them both turn their heads. 'That'll be Melissa,' said Chloe. 'I forgot in the excitement last night to tell you. She sets off for Vravrona today. Agorakritos told us when we delivered her home. It seems Nereus is impatient after all.'

Frog had let Melissa and her slave girl in. Melissa was dressed as a girl and her hair had been plaited and arranged like a woman's. She was bowing to the house shrine when she caught sight of Themis' face.

She ran across the courtyard to where he was sitting. 'What have you been doing, Uncle Themis?' she cried. 'Did you fall off a scaffold?' She touched his swollen, multi-coloured cheek.

'Got hit with a jar full of water,' Themis said ruefully.

She stepped back a little and put her hands on her hips. 'What happened to the left hook?'

'No time,' said Themis. 'He hit me almost before I saw him.'

'Why?'

'I was trying to find out who is behind the attack on Zea ...'

'... and sneaked into a house you were suspicious about,' Chloe broke in, 'without permission, or official – or even unofficial – help! Why do you bother?'

'Did you find anything?' asked Melissa.

'Nothing really helpful. A basket of doses of Lethe's Ladder was on a shelf when I got there but not when I left,' said Themis.

'So this is how I shall have to remember you all the weeks I'm going to be in Vravrona?' Melissa complained, her tone that of a scolding mother. But there was real anguish on her face. He tried a reassuring smile in spite of the pain.

Chloe laughed. 'You won't have time to think about Uncle Themis,' she said. 'You'll be too busy learning about how to run your household and when to steer your man to bed so that he gives you a son.'

'You know I don't care about any of that!' said Melissa, stamping a foot. 'It's all so pointless when I know I could manage the sculpture yard and the quarries far better than my brothers ever will – *and* look after a house while doing it!'

'Anyway,' Chloe went on, 'from what your father said, he may have to call you back if your mother has any more trouble with her pregnancy.'

'Anthoussa?' said Themis. 'Is she ill?'

'Not ill exactly,' said Chloe. 'The baby started to come too early, it seems, but it stopped again. The midwife says that can happen when you've had five or six already. But she lost some of the waters, so that makes it all more ... uncomfortable.'

'And Father thinks it's proof of what you know he believes,' said Melissa to Themis with a look.

'If you get the chance,' Themis said to her, 'tell her I'm looking forward to being free to visit again.'

Melissa's eyes suddenly filled with tears. 'You really love her, don't you?'

Themis shook his head kindly. It wasn't like Melissa to cry. It must be all this learning to be a woman. 'I love you all, Melissa,' he said. 'As you know, when I was your age, your mother was who I measured every other woman against. But that's a long time ago, and I've met quite a number of … interesting women since then.'

Melissa looked at him with an exaggerated frown, tears still on her cheeks. 'None you're going to marry before I get back?'

'Of course not!' said Themis. 'But I shall miss having Melissus drop by and give me the family news. I might have to hang around the sculpture yard more often.'

'You'd better practise with your left hook, then,' said Melissa. 'My dad would love to add to your bruises.' Then she turned to Chloe, scrubbing the tears off her face with the corner of her chiton. 'Will they teach me how to make Nereus hate me so I don't have to marry him?'

'Not at Vravrona,' said Chloe. 'But there are those who might be sympathetic once you're back in the summer.' Her voice sank to a whisper. 'And we could always arrange a curse – that he goes crazy and jumps down a well, perhaps.' She and Melissa laughed silently behind their hands.

Themis smiled painfully and stood up. He held out his arms to Melissa. She came up to his shoulder, so his face was not in danger as he hugged her. She smelled of chamomile and hyacinths as well as slightly of menses. He was surprised and angry with himself that his body reacted to her as a woman. He hastily held her away from him and said, 'Go and learn about being a woman, but in your private moments, don't forget how to be Melissus, too. He's been a good friend since he moved back to the City.' Melissa smiled and looked down.

Chloe twisted her mouth and said, 'Whatever Themis says, it might be better if you *did* forget what it's like being a boy. That way, you won't get so frustrated by the daily chores and limitations. And you'll be able to persuade yourself that learning how to manage those chores is more important than anything else in the whole wide world.'

Themis shot a look at Chloe who shrugged back with a wry smile.

Melissa turned away from them both to hide angry tears. She cleared her throat and called her slave. 'Leila! We're going.'

Frog let them out. As he returned he said quietly, 'Never seen a boy turn into such a pretty girl, tears or no tears.'

'It's a shock, growing up,' said Chloe.

Themis sighed. After that embrace, his emotions felt as mangled as his face. Or perhaps it was because his mind was on Zotikos' erotic commission. Whatever the reason, it was a timely reminder that he should get himself a woman soon.

And he'd have to make sure it never happened again with Melissa.

She was out of bounds, Nereus or no Nereus. She wasn't eligible to marry, being a non-citizen. Nor was she a candidate for a more casual arrangement. He couldn't imagine a greater insult to Anthoussa and Agorakritos, assuming things returned to normal once the baby was born.

'I never heard anything so stupid!' shouted Diodotos as they came in from the muster.

There were two lamps burning in the courtyard by the house shrine. He picked one up and marched into the andron. 'What are they thinking? How can I be of more help here in the city than with the army on campaign?'

Themis lay down on a couch. His head ached. In fact he ached all over. He remembered his mother saying, 'Wounds are always worse at night'. The muster had not taken very long, but both he and Diodotos had been refused for active service this time.

His lips were a bit less swollen but somehow stiffer. He said, only half ironically, 'Chief Quartermaster is an important and responsible position. Imagine if the stores aren't got together and delivered to the right place at the right time. As they say, the hungry bear won't dance.'

'Those are jobs an old man can do, or a man who's lost a leg or an arm!' interrupted Diodotos, striding up and down between the couches.

'We'd have mutiny in the army,' Themis went on, pretending to ignore him, 'and soldiers living like pigs, digging up roots to eat.'

'It's an insult to me! Why would they take old Chryses, who can hardly lift his shield any more, but leave me mouldering at home?'

'Well, it could be a mistake,' said Themis more seriously. 'You can appeal in the morning. They won't leave for three days at least.'

'What about you?' said Diodotos, stopping mid-pace. 'Don't you want to get a chance at some action?'

'Just now? Not really,' said Themis.

'Why not, in the name of all the gods!'

'I have two good reasons to stay here,' said Themis. 'One is my work because with you flouncing off to war and the harvest not yet in we need the money. And the other is finding out who was trying to burn the navy.'

'Why are you still bothering with that?' asked Diodotos. 'Photios is out of it now. They even put him in my supplies team. No,' he said, standing in front of Themis with his hands on his hips, 'I'd lay money your reason is something to do with Anthoussa.'

Themis tried pulling a you-are-joking face. It hurt. 'Way out of date, brother,' he said. 'Nothing to do with her. In fact, Agorakritos seems to be more convinced than ever that I'm the father of Anthoussa's child. That would be a good reason to *leave*, not stay.'

'Huh!' Diodotos resumed his pacing. 'I shall appeal,' he said. 'I don't want to miss the excitement of being on campaign with Alkibiades!'

>>>

Chapter 21: Methana wall

(Breeds of Sheep 13 – I don't know whether Themis 'got himself a woman' that evening. I lost him after that. But later he was back with this next bit. Again it felt different – like a dream. Or perhaps talking with Diodotos had reminded him of when they were on campaign together.

But then I had a thought that I can't get out of my head – I wonder if he's deliberately remembering things to show me …)

<<<

Themis was searching the heap of stones for a perfect fit as he added to the growing Methana Wall. Beside him, Kallikrates supervised as other young masons added stone upon uneven stone. Themis was used to dressing the stones he built with. Using odd-shaped stones was confusing, though satisfying when they did fit. And using mortar to hold them in place instead of perfectly aligned joints meant they could build much faster, and that's what they'd been ordered to do. The Wall wouldn't last long in an earthquake of course, but it would serve its present purpose.

He cast a quick glance at the temporary town of tents and shacks between the Wall and the huge Methana volcano that reared towards the northern sky. The noise and dust were tremendous as slaves chipped away at the living rock in a newly opened quarry. Others gathered stones of varying colours and sizes from the ground where the volcano had thrown them, adding them to the mounds that the masons were choosing from. Their rhythmic songs of sweat and sex and satire mingled with the sounds of the mortar mixers and the carpenters sawing and splitting their logs into beams and planks and struts.

The mortar in Themis' hod was almost finished. He cemented his dark red stone in place with the last of it, then straightened his back and signalled to the mortar slave to fetch him some more. The sun had passed its highest point, but still burned through his sweat-drenched tunic.

Standing like this, on top of his section of the partly built Wall, he could look along the spine of the narrow wooded isthmus between the mountain and the mainland. Just a stade or two away on each side, the sea glowed blue in the east and west bays. The Wall would be five feet wide and ten feet high, with a smooth inner surface to which a wooden walkway would be attached for the garrison's future guards. So far it was about three feet high on the outer side facing the enemy. They would attack from the south, the mainland.

He turned and looked up in awe at the multiple cones of the volcano. Without this thread of land, it would have been an island. The summits were streaked with tongues of forest between uneven areas of dark, petrified froth from past eruptions. Today there was no sign of smoke, but he had often seen, from Piraeus across the sea, billows and streamers of smoke from one or more of the vents. Now swarms of vultures and gulls circled and swooped on the growing rubbish heaps by the shores.

The forest at the bottom of the slopes and across the isthmus was thick, though the trees themselves were small. From here, Themis could see the altar set up by the wall-builders half way up the mountain in a clearing. He had joined in the sacrifice and offerings to Hephaistos, god of crafts and volcanos. This had been their first action on arrival the morning before, after their nighttime row from Piraeus.

Ships full of supplies and soldiers were coming and going in the eastern bay to Themis' right. Scores of triremes of the Athenian army were arriving in the wider bay beyond it. They'd beach on the sandy shores near the town out of sight round the mountain.

The Athenians had set guards, some among the builders of the wall and some patrolling a hundred feet or so away in enemy territory, at the edge of cleared forest. They were changed, one at a time, for fresh men from the tent camp. There'd been no sign of an enemy so far, in spite of all the noise and dust clouds.

Kallikrates cleared his throat. His exuberant eyebrows frowned in Themis' direction. So Themis bent to his work again, nodding to an armed guard who was clambering up from the mainland side.

Themis heard another man in armour step up, ready to replace him. The new guard stood behind Themis to look over the wall.

'How's it going, little brother?' he said.

Themis turned and looked at the man's face in surprise. 'Diodotos!'

he exclaimed. 'You weren't wounded?' He threw open his arms and grabbed his brother in a hug. 'We heard about the battle at Solygia.'

Diodotos was laughing. 'Hades seems in no hurry to claim me, though sometimes in the past couple of days, I've felt his breath.' He drew back. 'But, by Hermes, you stink! Have you been bathing in goat's shit?'

'Not for a while,' Themis said with a grin. 'But everything here smells of sulphur. You on duty?'

'Yeah. Protecting you guys from local raiders and snipers.'

'They're keeping quiet,' came Kallikrates' gravelly voice. 'They've been frightened by your actions further up the coast. I heard you lost fifty men at Solygia two days ago.'

Diodotos turned to the grim-faced architect. 'We did, but the Corinthians lost four times as many. General Nikias has sent the wounded home and promised the rest of us that we'll be on our way as soon as this wall is up and garrisoned.'

Kallikrates watched as the mortar slave delivered Themis' full hod. 'At the rate we're building, that should be in two days,' he growled.

Diodotos climbed up Themis' section to the top and jumped down on the enemy's side, knocking off a stone and a gout of wet mortar. The wall came up to his waist. 'Seems unlikely,' he said. 'But my little brother – who is now quite a lot bigger than I am, you notice – has done miracles before.'

He ran towards the trees, and Themis called after him, 'Only when no one demolishes my work!'

Diodotos' laugh was muted by the stunted pines.

The following day Themis had brought his section of the wall to seven feet high by mid-morning. He went to have a word with Kallikrates, suggesting that a scaffold be built all along the inside of the wall to hold the joists needed for the garrison walkway in place. Kallikrates sent him down to see the carpenters.

He had just finished a discussion about the design of the scaffold with the head carpenter when Diodotos appeared at his side, holding a flower.

'Flowers, brother? Are you off to honour Demeter?' he asked.

Diodotos sighed. 'Not exactly,' he said. 'Anyway, Artemis would be more appropriate in this wilderness, don't you think?'

Themis took the flower Diodotos was offering. 'So why the sand lily?'

'Smell it,' said Diodotos.

Themis took a deep breath of the sweet scent. 'Mmm. A bit different from sulphur,' he said, setting off back to his section of the wall. Diodotos walked with him, sniffing a similar lily.

'There's loads of them on a beach near the town and the hot pools.'

Themis was examining the white petals as he walked. 'So you've been to the hot pools this morning?'

'Obviously not. While you've been sweating in the sun, I've been spying out the hinterland.'

'Oh, yes, of course,' said Themis with heavy irony. He laid the flower carefully in the shade and turned to his brother. 'I shall make a painting of it later. I like its shape. Elegant.'

'Ever the artist,' said Diodotos with a snort. He looked at the Wall. 'And the builder, I see. You've done a lot already today.'

'We're up high enough to start on embedding the joists,' said Themis.

'And a staircase?' Diodotos pointed at the first three steps of what would be the access to the walkway.

'Yeah. That's keeping us busy while the carpenters build the scaffold to support the joists.'

Diodotos ran a hand over the uneven inner surface of the Wall. 'You going to plaster this a bit smoother?'

'So they say, once it's all built.' Themis was stirring mortar in his hod.

'Be a great help if it was a lighter colour. Then the garrison could find their way better in the dark. I fell off a staircase like this at Pylos because we couldn't see where we were going.'

'Good idea,' said Themis. 'Even if we don't plaster, we could whitewash. You on duty now?'

'From mid-afternoon, like yesterday,' said Diodotos. 'Why?'

'Thought you might do me a favour and fetch my painting things before this flower wilts any more. I'll take a break when I've finished this hod.'

'Where will you be?'

'In the shade of the three pines by the road. They bring water and bread and olives for us there.'

Themis held the small square tile at arm's length, looking critically at his painting. He'd used white and a greenish yellow to paint the petals – the graceful upward curve of the outer ones, and the jumbled profusion of the inner ones. He'd added another similar flower further back with a longer stem, and in the far background the mountain was a single line that rose then fell. The flower was limp now, drooping as it lay across his thigh. He added a suggestion of yellow among the petals to depict the stamens.

Then he lay back on the earth under the pines and breathed in their sharper scent with closed eyes …

On the third afternoon, the builders were exhausted and the Wall was finished. But Diodotos' suggestion that the inner surface should be plastered had been agreed, so the building process was prolonged, provoking many good-natured complaints. Themis enjoyed smoothing the white plaster over the rough stones. It was one of the skills he'd learned as an apprentice back when the war with Sparta had just started and he was still glowing with his Olympic success in the boys' boxing.

'You nearly done?' asked Kallikrates. 'It'll be dark soon.'

Themis had finished his section where it stopped at the staircase. But he still had half a hod of plaster.

'You need a bit more on your patch?' he asked the mason on the staircase section.

'Yeah. You could fill in this bit between the joists and the steps,' he said. 'I don't have enough to do that.'

As he loaded his trowel again and swept it up from the bottom of the wall, Themis had an idea. Diodotos had mentioned that, at Pylos, just three months before, a soldier had scratched maple leaves, sacred to Ares god of war, onto the rough stones of the fort they were hastily building. The Athenians had surprised even themselves by eventually winning the engagement and taking Spartan prisoners, even though 'Spartans never surrender'.

There was an almost flat stone beside the joist nearest the steps. Themis held his painted tile against it and plastered it in place. As he did, he murmured a prayer to the goddess Artemis, whom his mother served in Vravrona, to protect her and his remaining sister from the horrors of war.

The man whose section this was straightened his back and sighed. The last raw stones were now covered. 'No one'll see that there,' he grunted. 'It'll be under the walkway.'

'True,' said Themis. 'But it's for the goddess. She'll see it wherever it is.'

'Pity,' said the mason. 'It's charming. You're good.'

>>>

'So what does the doctor say?' asked Keir impatiently as Suzanne limped into the gym the next day.

'It's not broken, not even damaged except for the bruising,' she answered. 'I can train as long as I don't overdo it. And she didn't actually say so, but I think she thought I was fussing too much!'

'Not too much when you consider your place in the Commonwealth squad may be at stake,' said Keir with his sympathetic smile.

After the session, as the others were leaving, he came up to her and said quietly, 'I'd just love to read what you're writing. Would you let me if I promise to put in a good word for you at the selection meetings? I know two of the selectors and truly believe you should be in the Australia squad.'

Suzanne's heart leapt with excitement at the thought of Australia, but plummeted at the thought of anyone at all seeing her files on Themis. Why had she even mentioned them to Keir? Just because of his film-star smile?

He went on, helping put the weights back on their stand. 'We could have a meal together this evening and talk about it if you like. Make a night of it ...'

Suzanne's foot was throbbing and all she wanted was to get back to the house and put it up as the doctor had said she should. 'That's really kind,' she said. 'But I'm just so tired today. Can we leave it for a day or two?'

Keir crinkled his sky blue eyes and said, 'You get that foot up and some supper into you and we'll think about it again tomorrow.'

Suzanne nodded and smiled at him. On the way home on the bus she kept on smiling. If Keir could make sure she was in the Team GB that went to the Gold Coast, everything she was working for would be worth it.

And this evening she could catch up a bit with Themis, without feeling guilty she wasn't at her ballet class for gymnasts. That last bit had been intriguing. Was there still a volcano at the place where they'd built the wall? She'd love to explore it. And why had Themis wanted her to remember it with him? If, in fact, he did. It seemed irrelevant to his present problems.

'Not much chance of an answer!' she said to herself as she got off the bus and limped the few steps to her front door. 'Yet another enigma.'

Chapter 22: sacred gifts

(Breeds of Sheep 14)

'You awake?' Frog was looking round the door.

Themis opened his good eye and groaned.

'Messenger from Agorakritos here,' said Frog.

Themis sat up. 'Good or bad news?' he asked. His lips and jaw were stiff and his tongue felt too big in his mouth, but it all seemed to be working.

'Can't tell,' said Frog and disappeared.

The messenger was a slave Themis knew well. He repeated his message immediately. 'Agorakritos requests you to stop by his house before you leave for Vravrona to see your mother.'

'What a nerve!' said Themis to Frog, who had reappeared by the door to the kitchen. 'Throws me out then asks me back.' He rubbed his aching face. 'And, as far as you know, am I going to see Mama?'

'Not that I heard,' said Frog. 'But perhaps the message is not directly from him …'

Themis thought a moment. He turned to the slave. 'Tell your … master I understand the message and will visit his house before the end of today.'

The slave nodded and left.

Frog brought his hand from behind his back. 'This came, too,' he said. 'In a basket of onions and herbs.' He handed Themis a tablet that gave off a hint of garlic.

'Who brought it?'

'The Skionian and I were shopping, just in the square here. We found it in the basket when we unpacked it.'

'Ah. Thanks,' mumbled Themis.

'And are you going to Agorakritos' later?'

'Yup,' said Themis. He held the tablet up. A dirty label on the outside said 'Themistokles only'.

He took it into the andron and slit it open. It said, 'The house with the tunnel behind it was rented as living quarters and a workshop by a man, his mother and some slaves. They make remedies and poisons. They have expanded and moved, but no one in that neighbourhood knows where they've gone. The house beside it with the secret room in the basement belongs to someone living in Evia. There's no sign of any occupants now. We are following up. The Heron puts into Vravrona before heading for Miletus. It'll take some days as it has three islands to visit on the way. We have people in Miletus on the alert.'

There was no signature, and no other identifying sign.

Themis walked over to the kitchen.

'Chloe?' he asked.

'Gone home. Left you these,' and Frog indicated a couple of small packets and a phial.

'And Diodotos?'

'Gone to Army Headquarters to appeal about going on the campaign.'

'Hmmm. And the barley harvest?'

'Starts tomorrow, he said, and Melanas can manage,' said Frog. 'But you're going to the farm today, aren't you?'

'If the gods are willing,' said Themis, nodding sagely. 'Then tomorrow, one of me will be there, scything … while another will be painting at Zotikos' shop here in the City … and a third will be arranging for building supplies at the Quartermaster's stores. A fourth will visit Mama at Vravrona. And the fifth Themis will be at rowing practice in Faliron.'

Frog said, 'Your face must be feeling better. You hardly said a word, yesterday.'

The same slave as had delivered the message let Themis in at Agorakritos' house that evening.

'The Master is out,' he said. 'The Mistress is expecting you.'

'Thank you,' said Themis. Frog had been right. Perhaps Anthoussa wanted to tell him what had triggered Agorakritos' jealousy.

He was led into her salon. She was sitting upright near the window, embroidering. On a small table beside her were a jointed terra cotta doll painted in yellow and white, and a toy cart made of wood with a bag tied with a green ribbon in its bed. The light from the sinking sun fell across Anthoussa's lap. Her feet were swollen in their soft slippers, and the skin on her face, though almost unwrinkled, seemed oddly transparent in the evening light. A slave woman sat sewing in a corner.

Anthoussa made a move to stand, but Themis took two long steps towards her and took her hand.

'Don't get up,' he said. The slave placed a chair for him beside her.

'Melissa said you'd had an argument with a full water jar,' said Anthoussa with a twinkle in her hazel eyes. 'Your face could almost stand in for a rainbow.'

Themis sat down. 'It is so good to see you,' he said. 'How are you?'

'I'm heavy and feeling the heat, but otherwise the same old me.'

'Agorakritos sent for me,' Themis said. 'Why?'

'I asked him to and he agreed. You will notice that we are not alone.' Anthoussa's eyes were laughing as she gestured towards the tall female slave that Themis hardly knew. 'But this is women's business, so he really would be … ill at ease.'

'And I won't?' said Themis.

'I doubt it,' said Anthoussa. 'It's to do with Melissa.'

'Ah, yes.' Themis wondered if Anthoussa had guessed at his disconcerting attraction to Melissa, which if he was honest with himself, made him feel ashamed. He looked down at his hands.

Anthoussa was saying, 'She went off to Vravrona without her offerings.' She picked up the bag with the green ribbon. It sounded like marbles. 'She should have taken these with her for the ceremonies and sacrifices to Artemis. I believe she forgot them on purpose.'

'And you would like me to take them?'

'Yes, as you are going – or is it Diodotos who is going?'

'How do you know either of us is going?' Themis asked.

'The slave grapevine is aware of every decision we make before we make it. You know that,' said Anthoussa with a good-natured shrug and a glance at the slave woman.

'Diodotos was officially told to stay home and harvest,' said Themis, 'but he managed to get that decision reversed this morning.'

'Plenty of time for the grapevine.' Anthoussa stopped smiling. 'The assumption must be that he'll be visiting his mother before he leaves for the campaign. What about you? Will you go to Vravrona too?'

'Possibly,' said Themis. 'Officially I'm staying in the city but must expect to be called upon at any time to go and build siege engines and walls – assuming Alkibiades decides who is our latest inseparable ally.'

'Ah,' said Anthoussa. 'Alkibiades. I heard he's decided to subjugate Epidaurus to open a shorter route to Sparta. An unstoppable force of nature, that man… So you may still be here when the baby comes.' She stroked her rounded belly. 'I would like you to see Agorakritos' face when it is clear who the father is.'

Themis caught the bitterness in her voice. 'So would I,' he said. 'Your note suggested you'd discovered what set off his belief that it's mine. Can you tell me?'

Anthoussa looked at his face for a long moment. He could see a struggle in her eyes. At last she looked down at her work and said, 'I do know, but I have promised someone very dear to me not to tell you – at least not yet.' She looked up again. 'I wish I could, but I promised. But I can say that I don't think you will be upset when you finally find out, and that Agorakritos made a thoroughly understandable mistake.'

'I can't imagine what you're talking about,' Themis said with a shrug. 'But I'll keep the peace and be patient, if that's what you want.'

She smiled and tears gleamed in her eyes. 'It is. Thank you,' she said.

She paused a moment, then added, 'I take it that nothing came of my suggestion that you ask for Thalia in marriage?'

Themis was exasperated and shook his head at her, then rubbed his painful jaw. 'That was months ago. And no, nothing came of it.'

'Don't be cross with me,' Anthoussa said with a smile. 'I like Thalia. She's a quiet, intelligent girl from a decent family. And I like you. You're a noisy, belligerent man from a decent family. It would have been a good match.' She turned to the small table. 'Anyway, if you're going to Vravrona, could you take these with you?'

'But they're new,' said Themis. 'I thought the toys for the offering were supposed to be her old toys. Where's the doll I made her, the one with the short straight hair?'

'Oh, the younger children broke that and everything else years ago,' Anthoussa said with a laugh. 'Of course these are new. Melissa hasn't played with such things for years now. Too busy helping her father.'

'Well, either I or my brother will take them. Which reminds me, as you've gone into the matchmaking business, it's Diodotos you should be helping to find a wife, not me,' said Themis.

'As I'm so unsuccessful at it, I'll leave the matchmaking business to widows and spinsters,' Anthoussa replied. 'So far I've been lucky not to be the former and will never now be the latter!' She patted her belly, then made to rise.

The woman slave stepped forward and helped her. Once standing, she said to her, 'Adrasteia, take these and wrap them carefully. Put them in a bag for Themistokles to take with him.'

The woman made as if to protest, but Anthoussa said with pointed intensity, 'Now.' The woman took the toys wordlessly and left the room.

Anthoussa took Themis' arm. 'I do hope you go to Vravrona with your brother.'

'I'll try to, but there's a lot I need to see to here.'

'If you do, please give your mother this,' she said, taking a small scroll out of her peplos pocket and handing it to Themis. 'Again it's women's business, so don't let anyone else see it or read it!' She was teasing him, guessing he would try to learn what it said.

Themis stood still in the doorway and turned to face her. She hardly reached his shoulder. 'I was worried about you from what Melissa said. But you seem well now. It's been good to see you.'

'It's stupid not to be able to talk to you,' said Anthoussa spreading her hands. 'And I have another, more serious favour to ask you.'

Themis looked down at her, his heart lifting as it always did when he looked into her perfectly proportioned face, even now. 'Go ahead.'

'From now on, I want you to take care of Melissa's interests whenever you get the chance. I doubt Nereus will be able to handle her. Certainly her father can't, and I have difficulty myself at times. You are perhaps the only one with any influence on her at all and, furious though it makes him, Agorakritos knows that.'

Themis smiled wryly. 'A dubious distinction!' he said, and leant forward to kiss Anthoussa's hair in farewell. He breathed in her perfume and the strangely comforting smell of her pregnancy. 'I will of course do what I can, but Nereus is not an easy man.'

'And he may accuse you of the same crime as Agorakritos does – he seems to be a jealous type. You shouldn't be so nice!' She reached up and brushed Themis' swollen cheek with her fingertips. 'Watch out for those flying water-jars.'

Chapter 23: Vravrona

'So you won't take Melanas with you on the campaign?' Themis asked Diodotos, as they rode away from their farm near Athmonon on their way to Vravrona next morning. He was going with Diodotos partly because he wanted to see their mother, and partly because of what Apollodorus had said in the garlicky tablet about the Heron and the man Menestratus. As for seeing Melissa herself, he knew there was no chance. And anyway, he didn't want to.

'Melanas can join me when the harvest is in,' said Diodotos. 'His son, Protos is too young, so our new boy from Kerkyra is coming with me this time.'

'Is that why Melanas had a long face today?'

'He's getting too old,' said Diodotos. 'He was Father's shield slave, and I took him to Delium – what? six years ago? – but I haven't needed him since then. Especially not with the lousy commissions in quarter mastering they keep giving me.'

'D'you think Mama has a hold over some of the generals?' said Themis as they rode through the dust raised by the crowd of slaves and women at a roadside spring. 'Is she making sure we don't get any real fighting?'

'You have the strangest ideas, little brother,' said Diodotos. 'No woman can influence the generals like that. And no proud mother would want to.'

'Hmmm. You may be right … But hey, look!' said Themis, pulling off his wide-brimmed hat. 'There's almost no traffic. Race you to Paiania!'

Diodotos laughed, and urged Astrapi to a gallop. Themis' horse was one from the farm, so Diodotos soon overtook him.

'Mama!' cried Diodotos from the terrace of Eirini's small house, overlooking the river mouth and the small harbour of Vravrona. 'What a wonderful view of the Spartans you will have if they dare to sail up this coast again! You'll have plenty of time to flee to the safety of your smart, new temple precinct.' He gestured towards the sturdy walls and columns of Artemis' newly renovated precinct among the trees to his left.

Eirini's house was near the top of a gentle hill between the precinct and the sea. She and Themis followed Diodotos out onto the shady terrace. She turned to Themis. 'We'll go down later and see how your colleagues have been getting on with the new buildings,' she said. 'They've been following your suggestions, but you were right, my son, the draining of the marsh has caused a lot of trouble.'

'But marshes have to be drained,' said a voice from the shadiest corner. 'Dangerous, festering places, marshes.' It was Uncle Zephyros.

The brothers greeted him and made themselves as comfortable as possible on their mother's small chairs while Eirini picked up her spindle.

Before Zephyros could start talking, Diodotos said, 'Do you know what Themis believes you've been up to, Mama?'

'Me?' said Eirini. 'What could I possibly be "up to"?'

'He believes you've been influencing the mighty generals of the Athenian army and navy to give your sons safe positions in the campaigns, so that they will come home to you in one piece.'

Themis laughed. 'That's not what I *believe*,' he said. 'I just wondered about the fact that almost all the men of our age and deme were called to active frontline service, and we weren't – again.'

Zephyros bellowed, 'Is that true, Eirini?'

Eirini shook her head. 'Yes, it seems to be. But, much as I wish I had that kind of influence, I have to admit I have no part in these decisions,' she said, halting the rhythm of her spinning for a moment. 'And anyway, I'm proud that you got it reversed, Diodotos, and that you are off to fight for your homeland. You will be a credit to your father.'

A little breeze fluttered the gleaming new vine leaves in the trellis above their heads. Out in the bright sunlight, the sea was a deep, translucent blue.

Zephyros stood up, gazing at it. 'The campaign is to be run by Alkibiades, I hear,' he said. Then he turned and looked directly at Diodotos. 'You keep a wary eye on that Alkibiades. He's a skilful orator and a charming man, but from my point of view, his actions seem ruthless and self-serving.'

'He defended Photios, though,' said Themis.

'He'll have had some other reason than compassion,' said Zephyros. 'Perhaps he wanted to recruit the hero of the hour to his latest enterprise.' He winked at Eirini. 'After all, I'm trying to recruit him myself!'

'Themistokles of Diomea being the hero of the hour!' said Diodotos with wry emphasis. 'He did invite you to his place that same night.'

'True,' said Themis doubtfully. 'But it ended up a not very heroic, and totally confusing, evening for me!' He rubbed his bruised face gingerly.

'Well, I'm glad Chloe was there to patch you up,' said Eirini.

'Ah! I've just remembered,' said Themis. 'I have something for you, Mama.' He went inside to where he'd left his saddlebags.

'You brought me enough from the farm to feed me for a month!' Eirini called from the terrace. 'What more could I want?'

Themis came back with the bag of toys and the little scroll. 'This is from Anthoussa and is probably a secret, so open it later,' he said.

'Oh, it'll be about Melissa,' said Eirini with a tired smile. 'Anthoussa warned me how difficult Melissa would be, and she's right.'

'What d'you mean?' asked Diodotos. 'How can she be difficult? She's betrothed already, isn't she? Not even a question of finding someone crazy enough to take her on any more.'

'Well,' said Eirini, 'She's finding it hard to accept the differences between life for a man and life for a woman. She does try. But it doesn't always work.'

'In what sense, doesn't work?' asked Zephyros, intrigued.

'She brings things up that the other girls don't,' said Eirini. 'Yesterday, for instance, she said to me, "Could a woman cause the death of the man she loves without meaning to?"'

'Hera in Heaven! What on earth could she mean by that?' exclaimed Zephyros.

'Perhaps that you can damage someone you care about without realizing it,' said Themis. 'He – er, she said something to me the other day about having to live with yourself after … er … doing something silly.'

Eirini said, 'I asked her what she meant and she clammed up in front of the other girls. I can't imagine any of *them* having such anxious thoughts.'

Diodotos pulled his chair closer to his mother's. 'I've been meaning to ask you, Mama, about this year's girls. You haven't got a likely one for me in your classes just now, have you?'

'Surely you haven't finally decided to take a wife, my son?' Eirini asked ironically. 'Are you sure you are not too young still?'

Diodotos sighed elaborately. 'Well, actually, I heard that a girl called Niovi was here now. I saw her in the procession at the Panathenaia and thought you might arrange for me to see her here for a few minutes.'

Eirini leant towards her elder son and looked into his eyes. 'You know I cannot do that, even for you,' she said seriously. 'The girls cannot leave their quarters in the precinct, and no man can visit while they are there. But if you wish, I will speak to Niovi's father when I am next in Athens.'

Diodotos smiled. 'You don't think that, as head of the household, I can do that myself?' he said.

'Of course you can,' said his mother, sitting back. 'You have every right to. You are a successful farmer and cavalry officer, and the legal head of our family. But sometimes the older generation can oil the axles of a tricky social situation.'

'Indeed,' growled Zephyros.

Diodotos twisted his mouth. 'I doubt it,' he said. 'Niovi's father is a famous misogynist.'

Eirini caught his hand and slapped it, her eyes flashing. 'Time, then, to remind him that you men wouldn't even be born if it wasn't for us!' she said. 'And another thing, I know her family is not wealthy. Niovi won't bring you much of a dowry unless you bargain hard.'

'Bad deal,' murmured Zephyros.

'I can get a matchmaker to do that for me tomorrow,' said Diodotos. 'I don't need to wait for months for you to come to the city.'

Themis could see Eirini getting upset. He broke in with a sad expression on his wounded face, 'So there's no chance that I could get to say hello to Melissa while I'm here, then, even though I brought her her toy offerings?'

Eirini shot an angry glance at Diodotos and stood up. 'Certainly not,' she said. Then she realized that Themis was joking. 'Ach, my children!

You will drive me mad. I have to go now, but I expect to see you tonight – and you, Zephyros – for the evening meal. You'll be staying the night.'

Diodotos began, 'We weren't planning to ...'

Themis put a hand on his arm. 'As you say, Mama. We'll stay the night.'

Eirini nodded. 'Good. Now I suggest you both spend some time at the shrines of Poseidon and Afrodite down in the town. Perhaps they'll be kind enough to bless your various future plans.' She went into the house.

Zephyros laughed wryly. 'She wants you to live longer than her husbands and her brother. Must be lonely, being an old woman.'

Themis looked sharply at his uncle. Perhaps there was more to Zephyros than he'd thought.

Diodotos went into the town immediately, but Themis stayed to talk to the builders. The purpose-built hostel where the girls now lived had made life at the sanctuary much easier. The colonnades of the new public rooms were still uncoloured, but their foundations were at last solid and strong. The river had been tamed and now ran in a single channel through the precinct instead of spreading out as a marsh.

Along its banks white egrets fished and sweet-smelling mint flowered pink and white. The hillside above Eirini's house was flushed with spring cyclamen. Themis imagined Melissa drawing the scene and peopling it with her fellow acolytes of Artemis. But not a single inmate appeared while they were touring the site.

And, as he'd expected, the quays were quiet when he got down to the harbour. The loading of ships bound for Miletus and other Ionian ports had stopped in the heat of the day, although this was not yet as searing as it would be in high summer. The slaves had disappeared and the overseers had dispersed to the taverns. There was no one to ask about Menestratus, and Themis couldn't see Diodotos in any of the taverns.

So he roused a stallholder and bought two small pottery horses to offer to Poseidon. They were made by a potter he knew in Athens and were not cheap, but they were so beautifully painted that he did not begrudge the god the money. He climbed up to the sea god's small temple on the hillside and went inside to see the statue. It was old, standing stiffly with a grim face and a trident in its right hand.

'Athens needs you on our side against Sparta,' Themis whispered, 'however confidant Alkibiades is of her strengths.' He recited a gratitude prayer and added a request for help in tracing the saboteurs. A flute player was filling the temple with a gentle melody. Zephyros' last remark about loneliness still echoed in his head, and the sea gulls' cries reminded him of the grieving women at the funeral of his relative and mentor, Panainos, Phidias' brother. '*Ach, Panainos,*' he thought, '*I always miss you when I visit Poseidon. You denied his existence until you got seasick, and then promised him the world if you could just get safely to land. If you really are down there in Hades, please protect us when you can, dear Uncle.*'

Back by the harbour, Themis felt drawn to an empty couch under a woven willow awning outside his favourite corner tavern. From there, he could see the whole curve of the quays. Surely someone he could ask about the harbour traffic, or even his brother, must pass that way. He ordered honey-water and almonds. The sun was warm on his legs. Calculating the possible profits of the farm seemed to be easier with his eyes shut …

'That's not Menestratus' way,' someone was saying. 'He doesn't just pay his assistants. He makes sure they can't say no to his "suggestions".'

Themis looked around and could see no one near him. Where was the speaker? And was he really talking about Menestratus? No. It must have been a dream.

'When do you expect him back?' asked another voice.

Themis sat very still. The voices were above the willow canopy. The men must be sitting on a balcony or perhaps the roof of the tavern.

'The message said eight days.'

'Is that time enough to get the right men together?'

'I'll have to make some changes because a couple are off to the Peloponnese with Alkibiades. But I'll manage ten or twelve easily.'

Themis heard the thuds of cups put down on wood. He smiled and sent a thank you to Poseidon – or Panainos. He sprang up and out from under the awning, pretending he had been stung by a bee. Looking up, he just caught a glimpse of one of the men before he disappeared into the dark of the upper room. Themis couldn't see his face or head, but the man trailed the corner of a sulphur-coloured himation with grey embroidery. His sandals were old with visible wear on the sole.

'Ah, there you are!' called Diodotos as he approached along the quay. 'What's the wine like there today?'

Themis turned but didn't move. He was hoping the two men would come down and out of the tavern onto the quayside. The light off the water splintered and dazzled as the sun slanted across the harbour.

'Not bad,' said Themis. No one appeared. They must have gone out the back. 'Look I just have to follow something up,' he said as his brother took his seat. 'I'll see you back at Mama's house as soon as I can. All right?' And he ran round the back of the tavern before Diodotos could answer.

He heard a horse leaving at a canter. He ran to the stables and asked the stable boy, 'Who was that man who just left?'

'Don't know his name,' said the boy. 'But look what he gave me!'

'I've never seen a coin like that,' said Themis, 'but it looks like silver. Did he say where he was going?'

The boy shrugged, but looked happy. 'What's it to you?' he asked.

Themis searched his pocket for an Athenian obol. He held one out, saying, 'I think you'll find this is even more valuable.'

The boy reached for it. Themis held it away from him. 'Where?' he said. Of course the boy could tell him any place he could think of.

'Something like … Athmonon or Athlonon,' said the boy.

Themis gave him the coin. 'Nothing else?' he asked.

The boy was examining his treasure. 'Called his horse "Sunny",' he said. 'But it was black.'

'Thanks,' said Themis.

Back at Eirini's house on the hill, Diodotos was washing at the well.

'Can I take Astrapi back to the farm?' Themis said. 'I have to go now!'

Eirini came into the courtyard. 'Themistokles, are you trying to avoid dinner with your Uncle Zephyros?'

'Mama, I have to follow someone and he's on his way back to Athmonon. Maybe someone at our farm there knows who he is. It's to do with the arson at Zea.'

'And we need to discuss the farm, in case – ' Eirini interrupted herself. 'Oh, just come back as soon as you can!'

Diodotos was drying his hair and beard with a towel and spoke over her. 'What's the point? Isn't it enough that you are already the hero of Zea?'

Themis clapped his brother on the shoulder with a cheeky smile. 'I knew you wouldn't mind.' To his mother he said, 'If I don't get back tonight or tomorrow, ask Uncle Zephyros to be sure and call in at the house when he comes back through Athens.' He took his mother by the shoulders and kissed her forehead. 'Don't forget to read Anthoussa's message so you can tell me what it says!'

Before Eirini could answer, he ran out towards the stables. Diodotos called after him, 'How much is Leontis paying you to get Photios back into favour?'

As Themis jumped onto Astrapi's back he wondered if his brother had guessed who he was really working for. He hadn't told him. Diodotos drank too much to keep a secret.

Themis galloped into the fading sunset towards Athmonon, his eyes searching the traffic on the broad, dusty road for a black horse in a hurry.

>>>

'Keir asked me out, so I can't make it to the jazz club next week,' said Suzanne as she came out of the bathroom, towelling her hair.

'Asked you out?' squeaked Natasha. 'But he's your trainer!'

'I know, but he wants to help me get selected and offered to give me supper to discuss it.'

'Bullshit!' Natasha exploded. 'Don't be an idiot. Keep away from him socially. He's a ski jump into a cesspit.'

Suzanne stopped her towelling. Melissus' voice echoed in her mind. '... once you've jumped into the sewer you have to live with the smell.' '*I still don't know what that really meant*,' thought Suzanne. She looked at Natasha. 'Well, it seems a very glamorous and possibly helpful cesspit,' she said.

Natasha's face was screwed up in disgust.

Suzanne sighed and added, 'But I'll see if I can avoid actually going out with him, if that'll make you happy.'

Chapter 24: go to the good

(Breeds of Sheep 15 – The only Menestratus I can find on-line fed a booby-trapped breastplate to a dragon that died eating his lover… Obviously not Themis' man! And there may have been another one who fought the Romans, but that was centuries later. So I can't help him, even if I could, so to speak.

His countryside is full of the signs of wild pigs and rabbits – and birds. Sometimes there are five or six species in the sky at once and their calls are loud and mixed together. Themis doesn't take much notice of them, but I saw Eirini looking up a few times.)

<<<

Themis knew the road well. From Vravrona it ran across the Mesogeion Plain between vineyards and olive groves. Villages and country estates had been built along it in the rich times before he was born. But many had suffered during the Spartan raids during his absence in Massalia and later. Since the peace began three years before, crops had grown to harvest. But burnt-out buildings still gaped at the sky in patches of rampant weeds.

Ahead, in the wide valley between the mountains of Ymittos and Pendelikon, that sky turned the deep red of ripe pomegranates as he rode. Beyond the gap between the mountains, the road would divide, right to the north-west and Athmonon, left to the south-west and Athens.

Themis kept Astrapi at a canter while he thought about where in Athmonon the man on a black horse called Sunny would be likely to go. Athmonon was a loose community of rich farmlands and vineyards on the skirts of Mount Pendelikon. Tributaries of the Kifisos River ran down from Pendelikon, cutting deep little valleys into the land but watering the farms. On the lower slopes were almond and apricot orchards. Higher up were olive groves. There were three farms Themis knew of near the main road that might put a man up for the night.

Of course, the man in the yellow cloak may not have been going there at all. It did seem a strange place to be heading for, if he was planning another sabotage of the navy.

By the time Themis came to the roadside spring he had passed with Diodotos in the morning, the sky was dark and a slim moon had lifted above the bulk of Ymittos to his left. He had not seen his quarry again. Now the spangled sky above Pendelikon to his right was slowly being blotted out by cloud. It was cooler, and a skittish breeze teased the pale olive leaves so that they shimmered and rustled, anxious ghosts in the starlight.

There were two or three riders resting at the spring, their horses tethered to the rail in the dark shadow of the one wide plane tree. All the horses seemed black.

Themis rode past and round a bend. The low cliff at the side of the road had a faint path up to the right. Themis dismounted and took Astrapi up it and into the olive grove above. He tied the mare to a tree, and made his way back to the main road as if he were walking towards Vravrona. His stomach reminded him he hadn't eaten since noon.

The riders were discussing a shortcut towards the city of Athens. Themis approached and bent down to make an unnecessary adjustment to his sandal. He recognized the voice of one of the riders. It was the one who would 'manage ten or twelve' men.

Themis stood up and went over to the spring. He washed his face and hands under a spout and took a drink. In daylight his lack of luggage might have been remarked on, but he wasn't the only walker, and the riders were busy with their discussion.

Themis loitered in the shadows near the horses. A man approached. He murmured a few words to one animal, which whinnied quietly in reply. The man mounted and set off at a fast walk. He was not wearing a himation, just a riding tunic, a short warm cloak, and long boots.

Themis watched him go round the bend. Then he fetched Astrapi from the olive grove and walked onto the road about a stade behind the black horse. They would come to the junction soon. There were still a few other travellers on the road, but they were probably going to Athmonon. If his man was also going there, following unseen would be easy as the road ran beside a small stream and wound back and forth with many bends through steep woods and farms. But if the man turned for Athens, the road was straight and open for a long way. Themis would be visible and that might well provoke a challenge.

The man turned for Athmonon. Themis followed, still at least one stade behind.

The bends were tight as the road climbed out of one valley and over into the next. Themis lost sight of the black horse more than once. But it was clearly ahead, black against the paler road, as they crossed a high point and began down into the next valley. But when the road straightened out again alongside the river, Themis could neither see nor hear the horse. The clouds had covered more than half the sky now, and the only other travellers were a group of three men with laden donkeys.

The black horse had disappeared.

Themis noted exactly where he was, but it was not near any of the places he thought might put a man up for the night. There were many other pinpricks of light among the trees all around, too many to knock on all their doors looking for his man.

Themis sighed. He was hungry and so was Astrapi.

'Come on, old girl,' he said quietly. 'Who knows where our man has gone? We'd better get to the City and report to Apollodorus. There'll be something to eat there, or on the way.'

So it was after midnight when Apollodorus, wrapped in a warm grey himation, showed Themis into a room lit by one tall lamp. When

Themis had reported his news, they sat down and the Archon leant back in his chair. 'What kind of thing, in your opinion, can they be planning?'

Themis shook his head. 'I can't imagine. But that obviously has to be our next objective – to learn what they are going to do.'

'You lost him on the road between the junction for Athens and Athmonon village? Personally I don't know the area well. Is there a tavern he could have gone to to sleep?'

'There might be one I don't know,' said Themis. 'Or a farm where he knew he would get a welcome. There were no lights close to the road, but many further back among the trees. I can take a better look for tracks on foot in daylight.'

'I'll send someone else,' said Apollodorus. 'Don't want you showing your face. The locals probably know you as your farm is near there. It's a help knowing who to look for.' He stretched and then sat forward. 'Did you get my tablet about the house in the city?'

'Yes,' said Themis. 'Did you hide it in garlic as a hint of how I should treat this?' He grinned and touched the bruises on his face.

'Garlic, eh?' Apollodorus smiled. 'No, but well done my messenger! Well, we now know that the owner of the next door house lives in Evia. His agent has a table here in the Agora and rented the house to the apothecary and family as I said. It is now completely empty. The house where you were held is also empty. The Scythians went in and found nothing at all – no furniture, no shelves, no bags and boxes, nothing. Except a pile of logs in a corner.' He stood up. 'Is there anything else you can tell us about your rider?'

'He may be a bit vain. He has a dark yellow himation with heavy silver embroidery which he was wearing in Vravrona. That's not the kind of thing to wear if you are trying not to be noticed. But his sandals were noticeably worn.'

'True,' said Apollodorus, making a note on a tablet and replacing it on a shelf. 'Now we both need some sleep.'

'If there's a new plot,' said Themis as he stood up, 'it would exonerate Photios, wouldn't it?'

Apollodorus looked up at him steadily. 'You'll need more than overheard conversations by disappearing foreigners to prove that to the Assembly if he ever has to face an accusation again,' he said.

Themis went home feeling exhausted and annoyed.

He leant on the herm as he waited for Frog or Tanu to open the door. No one came for quite a while, though he could hear Yellow whining. Then the window in the door opened and Frog called out, 'Who's there?'

'Let me in, Frog,' said Themis. 'And call Tanu to look after Astrapi.'

Frog disappeared. The window closed. The door opened, Yellow ran out, followed by Tanu, who led Astrapi off to the stable.

'So that's what was wrong with the dog all evening. Thought you were gone for two days,' said Frog. His short hair was standing on end and he had a garment wrapped round his waist. He held a small lamp.

'So did I,' said Themis. 'Go in, Yellow! I'm coming.' He looked at the garment. It was the Skionian's working chiton. He chuckled. 'I'll look after myself. You go back to bed. Did she tell you her name yet?'

Frog looked at Themis under his lashes, as he clutched at the chiton with his free hand.

Themis said. 'Just give me the lamp. Tell her I'll need some well-cooked eggs, olives, cheese and a barley loaf first thing in the morning. Oh, and get the stuff you'll need ready to go over to Zotikos' shop to prepare whichever wall he wants done first. '

Frog said, 'Fine. Sleep well,' and disappeared into the gloom of the kitchen and slaves rooms.

'Go carefully, my son,' said Eirini the next afternoon. 'It has been very good to see you – twice in two days!' She opened her arms as she looked up at Themis.

He had left Athens at first light. After a breakfast in Vravrona with his Uncle Zephyros, during which he began to feel there might be one or two small advantages to working in Greater Greece, he'd spent some time with his mother, only to realise he could never leave Athens. Now he and Diodotos were setting off for the City from the steps of the newly built precinct. The pale, unpainted columns threw fitful shadows in the erratic sunlight. Lilac bloomed nearby, scenting the restless breeze.

Eirini and Themis embraced and she whispered in his ear, 'And persuade your brother to marry someone other than Niovi if you can!'

Themis stepped back but held his mother's shoulders as he kissed her forehead with a laugh. 'Give me an achievable task, Mama, like walling off the Peloponnese in a day!'

Eirini put her hand on his chest and pushed him away gently with a wry smile. 'Go to the good,' she said, 'and come back soon.'

Then she turned to her elder son and took him in her arms. Themis saw the sparkle of unshed tears as she held Diodotos. He thought, 'She is finally getting old. There have never been tears when we leave before.'

Diodotos held her close and said, 'I'll be back before the figs ripen. I'll bring you a Spartan slave – and perhaps myself a wife!'

Eirini pulled back and looked full into Diodotos' bearded face. 'Each time you leave I know you may be going to join your father rather than returning to me. But whichever way you go, you will be warmly welcomed. Make me proud to be your mother. Travel a good road, my son.'

The brothers rode in silence. The weather was blustery and cool for the time of year. When they got to the spring, they stopped to drink.

As he cupped water in his hands, Themis said, 'Shall we change horses at the farm?'

Diodotos frowned. 'I'd rather go straight on.'

'There's something I need to ask Melanas. Let's just drop by. Or, if Astrapi is fine, you go ahead and I'll catch up later.'

'That's a plan,' said Diodotos and drank.

As they remounted he said, 'We ought to listen to old Uncle Zephyros, you know. He just wants to keep his family business going and we know what that's like.'

'Some of his ideas are fine,' said Themis, 'but I doubt I could bear him constantly. And, with you away cheering on Alkibiades against the Spartan allies, Chloe married, and Myrto and Menelaus in Hades with Father, I have a minor responsibility to a family business myself now and again.'

'True,' said Diodotos. 'Especially if I don't come back, as Mama so considerately pointed out. There are times when I think she tempts the Fates, you know,' he added with a laugh.

Themis shook his head. 'She trusts the gods to look after you but she's just trying to be realistic.' After a while he said, 'We can split up at the turning for Athmonon. I'm guessing you've got a date with Iole tonight.'

'Perhaps,' said Diodotos with a falsely indifferent shrug.

'She's worth the uncertainty?' asked Themis.

'To me, yes,' said Diodotos shortly. Then he relaxed and sighed. 'I know she's a professional, I know she could choose any man – or woman, of course – that she wanted. But I still laugh more with her than anyone else.'

'Fornication and laughter,' said Themis looking straight ahead at the midday traffic. 'Can't ask for more than that.'

Diodotos cleared his throat. 'I've been meaning to say, I know about your … er … moment with her.'

Themis turned to him. 'Moment?'

'When you met at the Dionysia a couple of years ago.'

'Ah,' said Themis. 'That.'

'She told me she'd followed you and snared you at her door but you decided not to join her inside.'

'How delicately she describes it,' said Themis, moved by the memory of expert hands caressing him in almost pitch darkness. 'I only recognized her from her perfume.'

'And you refused her. Why? She still seems surprised by that.'

Themis sighed. 'It wasn't exactly easy,' he said with a twisted smile. 'But at the time you'd been telling me that she'd agreed she would give up the profession and consider becoming your wife.'

Diodotos snorted with laughter. 'I must have been drunk,' he said.

'Oh you were,' agreed Themis. 'Often.'

'So I suppose I should thank you.'

Themis shook his head. 'No point,' he said. 'I can choose whether to live with *you* or not, but I can't choose whether to live with myself.'

Diodotos nodded. He reined in Astrapi. They were at the fork in the road. 'And that's an immutable truth,' he said, with a wry smile. 'So, this is where I choose to live without *you* and go left to Athens.'

'See you later then,' said Themis. He raised a hand as he kicked his farm horse into a trot on the road to Athmonon.

The farm was quiet as he rode up. It had been his mother's first husband's, and the cause of his death. While Eirini had been away at a shrine, the farm had caught fire and burned to the ground killing her husband, small daughter and all the slaves but two.

The only sign of this catastrophe now was a blackened and tumbled wall that Eirini had turned into a shrine to her daughter Phrynis. This was on one side of the entrance. On the other was a splendid herm carved by Themis from a piece of marble he had been given by Kallikrates after the Methana campaign. He had carved the herm to have a look of his dead father, Kallistos. They had sold off Kallistos' own farm earlier that year.

At the sound of the horse, Melanas came out to welcome Themis. His black skin seemed dull and Themis noticed for the first time that he stooped a little. But he was grinning.

'Welcome again, Master Themis,' he said in his deep voice.

Themis dismounted and gave Melanas the reins. 'Greetings, Melanas,' he said. 'Is there another horse I could take on to the city? I'm only stopping by for a few minutes.'

Melanas was leading the horse to the stable. 'I'll get young Protos to prepare you one. There are three gone with the mules to start the barley harvest.'

In the kitchens, Themis greeted the farm cook, Kalliope, and his old trainer, Arianos, now a carpenter and wheelwright. When Melanas came in, Themis said, 'Have any of you heard of a stranger in this area? Someone who stopped over near here for the night last night?'

The two men shook their heads, but Kalliope looked thoughtful. 'I heard about a man who asked this morning at the bakers for those Ionian honey pastries your father used to like. No one else round here has asked for those since he died.'

Themis' heart beat a little faster. 'Maybe I should check at the baker's on my way to the City,' he said. 'You're sure about this?'

Kalliope nodded. 'It's gossip, of course, but he seems to have made an impression, and he was definitely a stranger.'

'In that case, I'll try to get it investigated. Thanks, Kalliope, and don't mention it to anyone else, please.' Themis looked around the kitchen. 'So now I'd like some bread and our ambrosial cheese for the road. And Melanas, could you help me with something?' He went out into the yard.

The horse was waiting. Themis thanked Protos, Melanas' son, who was standing back out of earshot. Themis turned to Melanas. 'I understand my brother is taking the Korkyran boy with him on campaign this time.'

Melanas sighed. 'Mikro? Yes. I have to admit, I'm getting old now,' he said. 'I can't keep up with Master Diodotos, and Protos is still only a boy.'

'Could you be free to come with me, though?' asked Themis. 'I may well be called upon as an engineer or builder within the next month or so.'

Melanas smiled. 'I'll see the harvest in and be ready,' he said.

Themis mounted the horse, a young bay gelding with a blaze like his first pony. 'I'll send for you if I can't come myself,' he said. Kalliope brought out a linen-wrapped bundle and pushed it into Themis' saddlebag.

'I'll be here,' said Melanas. He stood and watched as Themis trotted out of the yard.

Chapter 25: Asklepion

After leaving a message for Apollodorus about the man with a taste for Ionian honey cakes, Themis went on to the Corner of Paradise and began work on the wall prepared for him by Frog.

After a while, he discovered a problem. *'How is it possible,'* he thought, *'that I have no exact image in my mind of this part of a woman when she's excited? Been a bit preoccupied when the chance to notice arose, I suppose … '* He put down the brush he was sketching with.

'Need to check something,' he called to Zotikos as he left on his quest.

At the Asklepion clinic on the south side of the Akropolis, he found Androklos, a healer he knew from his army training days. Androklos was coming out of one of the newly-built examining rooms, spattered with blood and pus. He led Themis to the waterspouts, where he washed while they spoke.

'From my limited experience,' he said with exaggerated seriousness, 'Each woman is different. All I can suggest is that you experiment again.'

Themis laughed. 'That's the kind of prescription I like to be given,' he said. 'You've never been involved with a birth, then?'

Androklos rolled his tired eyes. 'What woman would want a man to be there at that time? I have dealt with one or two of the rarer problems during pregnancy, but the actual birth is always seen to by women. It's the one time, I hear, that none of them faint at the sight of blood!'

Themis thanked his friend and left. The shadows of the columns striped the bright floor as he walked rapidly along the colonnade. When he'd been a boy of twelve, brought here after his head injury, there had only been a spring, an old shrine and a wooden 'dreaming house'.

As he stepped out into full sunlight, a woman was being helped out of a litter. Heavily pregnant and veiled, she leaned on a slave woman whom Themis recognized.

'Is that you, Anthoussa?' he said quietly to the woman.

She pushed back her veil impatiently. 'Oh Themis. It's too hot for all these layers! What are you doing here? You're not ill, are you?'

'No, I'm very well.'

Anthoussa indicated a seat under the shade trees with her chin as she held onto her slave with both hands. 'Let's sit a moment together.'

Once sitting, she asked before he could speak again, 'So did you see

Melissa in Vravrona?'

'Sadly no, but Mama says she's fine, learning to make reed baskets and behaving well, except for a tendency to prefer her masculine life!'

'That's what my note to your mother was about. I suggested a way or two I learned to help Melissa adapt.' Anthoussa looked at him seriously. 'So, if you're not ill, why are you here today?'

'Ah, well,' he hesitated, but the woman had withdrawn and the litter bearers were washing by the entrance to the precinct. 'You see, I am painting a wall with erotic scenes and needed to check a detail of … um … female anatomy,' he said wryly.

'Something we never explored together,' said Anthoussa with a grin. 'But surely you have plenty of experience?'

'Ah, there are so many variations …' he said wistfully.

She restrained a laugh as if it hurt. 'You always make me smile,' she said.

'And how you used to make me cry!' he replied grinning. 'Eight whole years until I realized there were other women in the world.'

She touched his cheek. 'Your face looks better.'

'Not quite like when I arrived at your father's house in Elis after being beaten in the adult Olympics by Kleomachos?' he said. He caught her hand and held it for a moment. 'How kind you were to a lovesick loser.'

She rested her head on his shoulder. 'And what good fortune I had to be loved by such a youth,' she replied. 'You know that I have also always loved you, but as a sister loves?'

'Yes, you told me on that day, too,' said Themis, leaning his head against her elaborately dressed hair. 'And that has given me such strength, knowing you care in spite of my – and your dear husband's – idiocies.'

She sighed. 'And my father's, I lately learned. You men are so impetuous when you're young… but I'm glad you've grown up enough to accept the weaknesses of people you idolize…' She shifted slightly on the seat.

'Whatever your weaknesses,' said Themis with a smile, 'for me you are a rock and a refuge – and someone I wish I could do more for, to make things easier.'

She looked into his face. 'To me it is a help just that you are there somewhere, like a younger brother. Even now, when you may leave for the Peloponnese at any time,' she said with a wry smile. Her hands stroked her bulge. 'But I want you to do me a favour.'

Themis smiled down into her lovely face. There were lines of pain round her mouth now, but the sculpting of the bones still seemed to him too fine to be real, and her eyes still shone like a woodland stream in spring sunshine.

'Tell me,' he said.

'If you find yourself near Elis, please spend a little time with my father. He is old now and both my sisters have married and left. He doesn't travel any more and will probably not see his new grandchild. But I know he particularly hopes to see you again before he goes. He mentioned it in a letter I got only last month.'

Themis took a breath to speak but she suddenly pulled his face to her and kissed the battered cheek near his eye. 'Be well and happy, dear friend.'

Themis' eyes filled with tears. He sighed deeply and blinked them away. 'See what you can still do to me?' he joked. 'I'll go and see your father, I promise, though I shall avoid Olympia and the scene of my shame.'

'It's no shame to be beaten at Olympia,' said Anthoussa. 'You have to be the best to get there in the first place. It only means you're not as rich as the winner when you leave.'

Themis laughed out loud. 'How right you are!' he said. 'And that reminds me, I have a day's work to do in the hope of paying some bills.' He stood and offered his hands to help her up.

She took them and rose carefully. Her woman ran over and they helped Anthoussa up the steps towards the entrance between them. He had not managed to ask what was wrong and he knew she wouldn't tell him now. At the top of the steps, she turned a joyful smile on him and waved, her eyes sparkling with fun. Then she and the woman went in to see the doctors.

Themis ran twice all the way round the Akropolis on the Peripatos path for no reason whatever. Then he went back to his waiting wall.

>>>

Keir came up behind Suzanne and moved her arm into a more dynamic position. 'Practise like this,' he said.

'Thanks,' she said and stepped away from him to begin the exercise.

He came round in front of her. 'So shall I call my friends on the selection board? Can you get away for the evening today?' He smiled charmingly, and winked.

Suzanne let the weights drop to her sides. She looked into his handsome face and smiled back. 'Keir, that's really nice of you.' She said the words she'd practised. 'But I just feel it's not appropriate, your being my trainer and all.'

Keir's lips twitched and the smile faded. 'What do you think I was talking about? I didn't mean anything "inappropriate"! You've got the wrong end of the stick, my girl.'

'If I have, I'm sorry,' said Suzanne, hefting the weights a little. 'You're a really good trainer and I don't mean to make it difficult for either of us to carry on as before. But I feel that meeting socially – just the two of us – wouldn't be right.'

'Who said anything about just the two of us?' asked Keir, frowning now. 'You're jumping to conclusions. I was going to invite some of the others.' He gestured round the gym.

Suzanne was suddenly angry. So what had the wink been about? What was all that 'make a night of it'? But she said, 'Excuse me, Keir, but my foot is killing me. I'll have to pass on this training session.' She marched over to the weight rack, put the weights in their places, and left the gym, limping a little.

When Natasha came in later, she said, 'You ok, here in the dark all by yourself? Need company?'

'Thanks,' said Suzanne. 'Yes. That would be good.' She stood up from the sofa. 'Today ... well, today you'll be pleased to know, I sidestepped the cesspit – though it's possible I'm in another one now. Anything funny on Netflix?'

Chapter 26: drinking games

(Breeds of Sheep 16 – Feeling pretty grumpy cos it seems men then and now can't be trusted. Didn't they have anything better to do in this next bit than sit around gossiping about nothing in particular, eating, drinking, and smelling like hyacinths so you can't breathe? And that Eteokles gives me the creeps. In mythology, Eteokles was one of two sons of Oedipus and he killed his brother who killed him back in a duel!!! Not even sure I can be bothered to get it all down, but it might be important later. You never know ...)

<<<

'Master Themistokles?' said Zotikos' slave. 'A man here has a message for you from Master Ilarion.' He pushed forward an elderly man in a good but plain blue tunic.

Themis stood back from his painting and took a breath. 'Go on,' he said.

The old man chanted, 'The supper club will meet at my house this evening to wish Master Diodotos well in the Peloponnese.'

Themis turned in surprise. 'That's kind of Ilarion,' he said. 'Does Diodotos know?'

'I was sent first to your house with the message for your brother.'

'Thank you. In that case, please thank your master and tell him that we will both be there at the usual time.'

The slave turned to leave. Themis said, 'Will there be any special events? Should I bring an offering?'

'Nothing was said to me,' answered the slave. He smiled. 'But you might like to bring your most accurate wine cup.'

Themis laughed and turned back to adding toe nails to the female foot he was painting as the slave left. The foot and its partner were pointed enthusiastically towards the ceiling.

The man had gone but Zotikos' newest employee had not. Her name was Lidha and she would be busy once the 'treatment room' opened. While Themis worked, she came in every now and again to see how the decorations were going.

Now she said over Themis' shoulder, 'You could give her my face. It would enhance my customers' experiences – and I could enhance yours in exchange …'

Themis turned to her. She was professionally alluring, of course, but there was also a freshness about her that he found particularly attractive. 'It's a deal,' he said. 'Stand here in the light …'

Themis and Diodotos were sitting on one of Ilarion's luxuriously cushioned couches at the host's end of his large andron. They had just been given garlands of scented broom flowers, white hyacinths and iridescent bee-eater feathers, which fascinated Themis. The lamps had already been lit as it was a stormy evening. The walls of the room glowed with painted sunset skies teaming with roosting birds over the Marathon marshes.

Ilarion's couch was next to theirs, but placed so as to have a view of all his guests. After the ritual prayers, he asked, 'Were you involved in the sinking of that training trireme this morning, either of you?'

'Haven't heard anything about that,' said Diodotos, adjusting his garland. He'd had his hair cut short and the garland was too big.

Themis shook his head. 'Nor have I,' he said. 'I was working all day on a new commission.' As he settled his own garland on his head, he watched Eteokles removing cushions from his place on the opposite couch. He thought, '*I never noticed before. Eteokles prefers to be uncomfortable* ...'

Ilarion gestured to the slaves to bring in the wine and water. 'It seems the rowers were on top form and the helmsman was not,' he said wryly. 'They hit that rock off Fleves Isle at speed, tore a hole in the hull and she sank – rapidly.'

'And the crew?' asked Themis.

'Seems most of them got to safety on the island. They lit a signal fire and were picked up later. Fifteen or so needed rescuing, so their swimmers worked hard.' Ilarion laughed. 'But no one drowned like poor Damianos.' He turned to Themis with a long cool look. 'And, as you said at the time, Damianos was a brilliant swimmer.'

Themis felt a prickle of excitement. Was this symposium not just as a send-off for Diodotos? Glykon caught his eye from across the room.

'You were in a sinking last year, weren't you, Themis?' said Diodotos.

'Hmm. More of a capsize as we tried to beach,' said Themis.

'What exactly happened? You had to rescue some of your fellow rowers, didn't you?' Diodotos knew quite well what had happened.

'Yes,' said Themis shortly. 'The wind was wild and the waves were as high as the ship, tipping us one way then the other. Some of the men were washed into the water on the open sea side.' He elbowed Diodotos to stop asking questions and let their host direct the conversation.

But Eteokles was interested. 'So you rescued them from an angry sea?'

'He's not just a rower and an artist, you know,' laughed Diodotos. 'We're actually descended from Glafkos the merman. However, only Themis inherited the webbed toes. He can swim as fast as I can walk.' Diodotos pointed at Themis' feet.

Themis held up his demonstrably un-webbed toes and said, 'Diodotos has been drinking already!' He threw an amused glance at Ilarion.

Eteokles looked into his winecup, saying rapidly, 'Ah well, swimming on the surface is easy. It's swimming under water that's the real test.'

Themis knew better than to rise to the bait of Eteokles' belittling tone. But Diodotos said pointedly, 'Under or over, Themis is more fish than man in the water.'

Ilarion clapped his hands. 'Let's have the first course!'

As the slaves brought in the food, Glykon said, 'What happened to the trireme?'

Ilarion said, 'They left the poor trireme on the bottom. With Damianos gone and Leontis and Photios not responsible for the fleet any more, no one has been appointed to deal with salvaging as yet.'

Glykon was stroking his silky brown beard. He said, 'Every spare man is part of the security detail now. Never seen so many guards in the towers and at the gates as I did this morning. That new Yard Master, Talaos, has already spent all the extra money assigned by the Assembly.'

This was a subject for after the first course, so, as host, Ilarion said, 'Has anyone seen the new painting by Timanthes? It's displayed by the Council Offices, destined to grace the walls of the new gallery beside the Great Gate to the Akropolis when that's finished. Fine view of the temples at Sounion from the sea. I do wonder how Timanthes painted it from that angle. He did these walls, you know.'

'Perhaps he took a small boat out on a calm day,' suggested Themis.

Eteokles' thin voice was hardly ironic at all as he said, 'Has the City approached you, Themistokles, to do one of your extraordinary scenes of the building of temples?'

'That,' said Themis cheerfully, '*is* the kind of commission I'd like. It's all very well painting Herakles on hydrias, and erotic heaven on the walls at Zotikos' place to pay the bills, but I'd like to do something a bit more permanent – partly to honour Panainos. No offers so far, though.'

'Probably only a matter of time,' babbled Eteokles. 'Will you continue your commissions with your brother away? Who will see to the harvest?'

Diodotos' hand hovered over a duck tart. 'That's all taken care of. We have very experienced slaves at the farm.' He looked up at his brother. 'Themis can carry on with his favourite plan for a whole wall of ships.'

Glykon raised his wine cup to Themis. 'Are you going to re-paint Eteokles' andron, then?' he asked with the slightest of smiles.

'My plan is for the long wall of the stoa in Vravrona,' said Themis. 'My mother wants the girls there to expand their horizons.'

'Would you like to discuss your designs by the light of day, Themistokles?' said Eteokles. 'I might have another customer for you.'

Themis wasn't sure he'd understood correctly. Was this the reason he was here? He chewed his mouthful of hare in wine sauce slowly, then said politely, 'I'd be obliged, Eteokles.'

Eteokles washed his hands together even faster than usual. 'I'll send you a message,' he said. Then he stood and turned to Ilarion. 'May I bring in a little music?'

Ilarion inclined his head. A boy of about 15 came in with a harp. He settled himself on a stool beside Eteokles and played a quiet air. As the men discussed other news, the boy's eyes often searched out Themis' face. They were outlined with kohl and reminded Themis of a baby seal.

Later, when Ilarion had brought girls in to join them and they were playing kottovos, Eteokles came over to stand behind Themis. It was Themis' turn to flick the last drops from his cup into the bowl on the low table in the middle of the room. His drops fell beyond the table, almost on the lap of the boy, who gathered his feet in under his stool. Eteokles laid a hand on Themis' shoulder. 'An indication of your interest?' he asked quietly.

Themis looked up at him. 'Interest?' he said. 'No. Just inadequate practice.'

'Ah,' said Eteokles. 'You should take what's offered,' he said with irritation. 'Soon you'll be too old,' and he bustled back to his place.

'Hmm. The boy will be Eteokles' gossip spy, I imagine,' thought Themis.

Now it was Diodotos' turn. He flicked his drops of wine towards the bowl with a practised hand. They fell perfectly in its centre, on the torso of the naked flute girl painted on the bottom of the bowl. All the other guests had failed to reach it, leaving a spattering of wine lees on the floor and the tabletop. They groaned in defeat.

'You are humouring me, gentlemen,' said Diodotos with a grin.

'I think not,' said Ilarion. 'You have won fair and square. Your prize is this satchel and its contents.' Ilarion nodded at his house slave who lifted a tooled leather satchel from behind his couch. It was dark green, with a raised design of acanthus leaves and a four-horse chariot on its flap. The slave took it to Diodotos, who tipped his companion off his lap and stood up.

'This is an unexpected gift,' he said, taking it from the slave and looking at Ilarion with wonder. 'I thank you with all my heart.'

'Always look inside before accepting,' said Ilarion with a serious nod.

Diodotos opened the bag and gasped. Then he laughed and lifted out a long smooth snake, made of a thousand carved pieces of wood. 'Ah,' he said. 'The symbol of Asklepius and Athena to keep me safe. A fine gift. Thank you, Ilarion. I may need their help in the Peloponnese.' He wrapped the wooden snake round his neck and lifted its head to wave at the company.

'Master!' It was Frog's voice. 'Where are you?'

With his brush poised to paint a tree tossing in the wind, Themis growled in quiet frustration. He looked down into the courtyard from the window of his workroom. Frog only called him Master if they had visitors.

'What is it, Frog?' he said.

'Master Eteokles has dropped in, hoping to speak with you.'

Themis sighed. With no word from Apollodorus, and Zotikos suspending the painting work as the City prepared to see its army off on campaign, he had determined to spend the morning working on his 'private painting'. The nymph had been appearing in his dreams again and he wanted to give her a suitable background. She'd had an air of power and anger that he wanted to capture before it faded from his mind.

He leaned from the window and said, 'You'd better give Eteokles something to drink. I may be a few minutes.'

When he came down, he found Eteokles on a bench in the shade under the colonnade, nibbling obsessively at a handful of pumpkin seeds and tapping his foot.

'Are you well, Eteokles?' he asked as he approached.

Eteokles stood up. 'Of course I'm well,' he said. 'Why would I not be?'

'We all drank deep last night of Ilarion's stimulating wine,' said Themis. 'I was concerned it might have left you feeling a little jaded.'

'Not at all, not at all. I have been out and about making petitions on your behalf.'

'On my behalf?' said Themis. 'What do you mean? Have a seat.'

Eteokles walked up and down under the colonnade, his sandals slapping a rapid rhythm on the paving. 'You said you had never been approached by the City to paint a wall yourself?'

'True,' said Themis. The hair on his arms rose. 'Although there was that time when Nereus mentioned it. Is this something to do with him?'

'Nereus? No. Not at all. Far from it. This offer will come directly from the City's Architecture and Planning offices.' Eteokles marched on, backwards and forwards. 'A man there called Eryx is expecting you after today's muster of the troops for the campaign to support Argos. Do you have some ideas you could show him?' Eteokles stopped in front of Themis. A merciful silence fell.

Themis stood up and said, 'Of course. I'll get them ready now.' He looked steadily into Eteokles' eyes and said, 'What have I done to deserve such a favour from you?'

Eteokles looked away. 'Well, er, you are of course the hero … of our supper club,' he blustered. 'I don't like to see a man's talents wasted, you know.' He turned and walked out into the sunlight in the courtyard.

Themis followed him to the street door and said, 'Thank you, then. I hope your … er … involvement will bear sweet fruit – for us both, of course,' he added as Eteokles stood by the door fidgeting. 'Eryx, you said?'

Eteokles nodded impatiently. Themis opened the door and Eteokles hurried out.

'Seems like a busy man,' said Frog as he swept up the pumpkin seed husks. 'And he mixes with some odd people.'

His tone made Themis say, "Tell me,' with his foot on the bottom step up to his workroom.

'One of his slaves and I are – were – good friends,' said Frog. 'This slave died a few nights ago. When I heard he wasn't well, I went to see him. He mentioned that Nereus had been at Eteokles' one evening and he and another man had come out of the andron to pee. While they were watering Eteokles' vine, they talked in whispers.' Themis moved impatiently.

Frog went on calmly. 'One man said he'd just got a new contract, a profitable one, and he needed Nereus to get him enough "stuff" to deal with two adults. Nereus said he couldn't supply that much at once. The other man asked how much he would need. He'd heard Damianos had only needed two doses, so he reckoned he'd need four to be sure.' Themis stared at Frog, who went on, 'Nereus said he'd have to go straight to the supplier for that much and whispered something else very low.'

Themis was standing quite still. He said, 'Are you sure it was Nereus? Or is it just slave gossip?'

'My friend was dying and knew it. I doubt he was passing on slave gossip on his death bed.' Frog picked up his sweepings and made for the kitchen.

Themis shook his head thoughtfully. No one could officially believe what a slave said. But this confirmed his own feeling that Damianos had been 'eradicated' for a reason. It also justified the fears he had had for Photios until he was freed. And it indicated that Nereus might be behind this latest offer to him. But most of all, it heightened his concerns for Melissa if she became Nereus' wife.

When he'd finished painting it, the nymph's tree was spectacularly twisted, and Themis was no nearer guessing what Nereus might be mixed up in, or whether it could have anything to do with the Benefactor.

Chapter 27: an offer

(Breeds of Sheep 17)

Astrapi was stamping and shifting, infected by her rider's excitement.

'So, little brother,' Diodotos was saying, 'While you're pleading with the intransigent City beautifiers for a decent fee tonight, I'll be eating roast goat on the beaches of Salamis.'

'I'm envious enough. You don't have to rub it in.' Themis looked up through the dust haze at Diodotos on Astrapi's back. 'You saw I'd repainted the eyes of the boar on your shield?'

'Yeah. I saw. Much fiercer now,' said Diodotos.

'And have you got the spare shield-grip Mama gave you?'

'Oh, stop fussing like a woman!' Diodotos said, looking along the line of mounted cavalry in front of him. Flutes and drums sounded from the front and a cheer rippled down the line towards them, 'Alkibiades is here!'

'Hah!' laughed Themis. 'I'll be expecting my call from him to come and close off the Isthmus with a twenty-foot wall.'

Diodotos' glance was serious. 'Better if you got yourself a lucrative commission with the City. Seems to me you spend too much time snooping and there's no recompense for that.'

'You know I'm only doing it to prove Photios innocent.' Themis let go of Astrapi's bridle as she shook her head, eager to be off.

'A pointless, and possibly thankless task, little brother. Friends come and go in life. You'd do better to go to Apulia with our irritating uncle. He'd make you rich, which I doubt you'll ever manage on your own. And Photios' family are famously tight with their sizeable fortune.'

'No need,' said Themis with a theatrical shrug. 'You'll make us rich with all the loot you'll bring back from Korinthos and Epidaurus.'

Diodotos threw back his head and laughed. 'But you won't always be able to rely on me to keep the family solvent, you know.' A trumpet sounded. 'Ah! We're off to show them what a real army is like!'

The drums intensified and the column began moving from the front. Diodotos put on his helmet and squeezed with his knees. Astrapi began to walk forward. Themis grabbed Diodotos' hand and held it tight for a moment. 'Aris, Apollo and Athena be with you, Diodotos my brother,' he shouted over the increasing din.

'And you, Themistokles, brother of mine and son of Kallistos,' called Diodotos. 'Paint me a picture of this for when I get back!' He raised his hand as he turned to look forward and Astrapi danced up closer to the rider in front.

Themis ran up a path at right angles to the road, then up the steps of Meton's Observatory above and behind the Pnyx. From there he could see all the way to Piraeus and across the sea, south-east to the island state of Egina, and westwards to the Methana volcano.

He watched the column as the hoplites changed to the brisk march. The cavalry rose to a trot once they were through Kili Village. Not far beyond, where the Long Walls came closer together, the column began to move even faster, lost in its own cloud of dust.

But Themis could still hear the trumpets and the drums and voices calling out names as the army passed by. He sat on a step and allowed tears to fall at last. They were tears more of frustration than sadness. '*If he saw me cry*,' he thought, '*he'd think I was going to miss him.*' He smiled wryly and wiped his face on his chiton as the sounds of the army slowly faded. He could now hear birds calling and people going about their daily tasks in the suburb below.

At last, even the dust cloud disappeared among the streets of Piraeus. He sent into the ether his prayer to Athena and Apollo for his brother's triumphant return or honourable death, as his mother had requested.

When he turned to go to his meeting with Eryx, he found Frog standing behind him. They walked down to the Agora in silence.

Eryx's left ear was missing and there was a great dark scar down the left side of his face and neck. The other side of his face was hardly marked at all but was pale as Egyptian alabaster.

'There's a table over here where you can show me your sketches,' he said. His mouth was unscarred.

Themis laid his satchel on the table and unrolled a series of sketches on papyrus and linen.

'I understand,' said Eryx, watching him, 'that you have managed to avoid going with Alkibiades to teach the Spartan Allies a lesson this summer?'

Themis looked up at his ironic tone. 'You do?' he asked, intrigued.

'They are saying that the hero of Zea is disillusioned with the lack of reward he received and has turned his back on those he tried to save …' Eryx was now looking carefully at a drawing of a trireme passing a cliff.

'That's strange,' said Themis, genuinely puzzled. 'Not something I know much about, market gossip.'

Eryx looked up. 'What we have in mind for this commission is something truly patriotic, so the City wouldn't want it to be by someone who is more sympathetic to the Spartan than the Athenian.' His irony was calculated to insult, in spite of the musical lilt of his voice.

This confused Themis, but he was used to being provoked by those wanting to test his legendary left hook. He said mildly, 'Eteokles didn't say where you are expecting to use my work, assuming you like it.'

'Ah, the enigmatic Eteokles,' said Eryx. 'He never tells you the whole story. Well, as you know, we are expecting the new picture gallery up beside the Great Gate to be finished soon. We have Timanthes' work prepared for the westerly wall on display in the Agora at present – just to see what people think of it. Timanthes is very young, but has a formidable talent.'

'So would you be looking for something for the easterly wall?' asked Themis.

'I was considering the long northern wall, myself. I have seen one or two of your paintings and others you designed for Panainos' School. You ran it for a couple of years, didn't you?'

'Hardest work I ever did,' said Themis cheerfully. How Panainos would have crowed at the thought of Themis' work on the North Wall, the position of honour! 'Uncle Panainos was a slave driver. Fair, but tough.'

'A talent sadly lost,' said Eryx. 'So let's see …' He smoothed out Themis' drawings.

'And what was decided?' asked Frog, taking Themis' satchel from him as he stepped out of the Planning Department into the late sunshine.

Themis said thoughtfully, 'He wants me to do a panorama of the campaign at Pylos seven years ago and the capture of the Spartans on Sfaktiria Island. He asked me if I could paint Demosthenes and

Brasidas the Spartan as portraits.'

'Well, you know Demosthenes from our Assembly, and Brasidas from the campaigns near Skioni,' said Frog.

'And he wants it for the long North Wall.'

'Excellent!' said Frog. 'Sounds like you may at last be recognized for your pictures instead of as a boy boxer gone soft.'

Themis laughed. 'Who says that? Diodotos?'

'No, actually. I overheard it ages ago from a friend of Melissus. Made Melissus so angry he punched him. Odd to think he's a girl … She packs a good punch!'

'Anyway,' said Themis. 'Eryx is making me an offer that I'd be a fool to refuse, but perhaps I'd be more of a fool to accept.'

'Meaning?'

They were walking along the Street of the Tripods towards home. Themis stepped aside to allow a cart to pass. 'Two things. The first is that there's usually a competition for such an honour,' he said. 'There should be notices up in the Agora to announce it, with a date for submissions and so on. They're not in a hurry, after all. The Gallery isn't even finished yet.'

Frog indicated a bakery down a side street. 'You hungry?'

'And the second,' said Themis, turning towards the bakery, 'is that he tried to provoke me with stupid gossip about my changing my allegiance to Sparta because Athens didn't pay me enough for saving Zea.'

'Ah,' said Frog, breathing in the smell of baking with relish. 'I heard that too. Someone's jealous and wants people to think you're a traitor.'

'Really?' Themis was shocked. 'They're really saying that? Any idea who started it?'

'Let's get a cheese and sesame pie. We can think about that better on a full stomach, and anyway, no one I've heard believes it. It's just gossip.'

>>>

Next day in the gym, Keir seemed to have forgiven Suzanne. He paid particular attention to her technique and was complimentary about her coordination, holding her up as an example to the others and citing ballet as a contributing factor.

At the end of the session, he called her over and asked her to sit down on one of the blue plastic chairs near the door.

'You're not limping today,' he said, leaning against the wall bars.

'Not as much,' replied Suzanne. She felt wary and uncomfortable.

'I contacted the trainer of your home team, Cassie Wilson. She says you are a gem and should be encouraged to keep working out.'

Suzanne smiled. 'She knows I hardly need encouragement,' she said.

'She also mentioned that you'd had some mental troubles after an accident,' said Keir, his voice warm and sympathetic. 'I didn't know about that.'

Suzanne frowned. 'But it's in my membership file, I'm sure,' she said. 'I've never pretended it didn't happen.'

'Yes, I had a look. A possible residual tendency to fantasy, it says.'

'That's a strange way to put it,' said Suzanne.

'But it's not wrong?'

'Not exactly. But it has no bearing on my training. In fact, I believe it helps me try harder.'

'But it might cast doubts in the minds of the selectors, mightn't it?' Keir's smile was kindness itself. 'Even if it's what helps you with your writing.'

Suzanne looked a question at him.

He said, 'If you'd let me see your writings and were prepared to spend some time discussing them with me, I would know better whether to ignore any doubts or to make a point of mentioning them to the selectors.'

Suzanne sighed and looked straight ahead. She wished for a split second that she really was Themis with his invincible left hook. 'What exactly do you want, Keir?' she asked.

Keir laughed, and his hips twitched involuntarily. 'On a personal level, only what I'm sure you want too. And I'm prepared to help a lot professionally. I could get you on that plane to the Gold Coast in Australia, no trouble at all.'

Suzanne stood up and turned to look at him. He was a head taller.

'Let me think about this,' she said. She turned on her toes and left the gym.

'What is there to think about?!' said Natasha. 'If your rule is that no one sees your stuff, then why change it for him?' Theo had come over and was playing some kind of war game on Natasha's computer. The noise was giving Suzanne a headache.

'What will he do if I say no?' she said. 'Can he really influence my chances?'

'Probably not,' said Natasha.

'And even if he can,' Theo said, stopping the slaughter for a minute, 'you'll never know whether you were chosen because you really are good enough or because he interfered. Not a healthy foundation to build a career on.'

<<<

Just before dawn, Themis left a small package by the house shrine for Frog to send to Eirini, and slipped out into the street. Inside the package was a quick sketch of the departure of the army and a note that Diodotos had got away on a calm sea, wearing his father's armour, and raring to get to the action.

He asked at the Council offices for Apollodorus to see him as soon as he could and, to Themis' surprise, he was ushered in immediately.

The Archon didn't give him time to speak before he said, 'I have news of the apothecary.' He indicated that Themis should sit down. 'The owner was a man who died lately after a long illness it seems. The business has been taken over by an employee and moved to nearer the Eastern wall and the Eridanos river.'

'Not far from Agorakritos' house, then,' said Themis.

'My agent asked the woman in the shop if they still had dealings with the owner of the house near the Green Shrine, but she said an emphatic no.' Apollodorus sighed. 'So there seems to have been a falling-out there and the whole story seems to be a dead end. And I have no news yet of Menestratus.' He looked hopefully at Themis. 'Do you?' he asked.

'Not directly, no,' said Themis. 'But I wanted to tell you two things. Firstly, some slaves' gossip but from a trusted source.'

'Go ahead.'

'It seems Nereus was overheard talking quietly while urinating in company with a man who asked Nereus to supply him with four doses of "stuff". The man said that, "Damianos had only needed two doses", but he needed enough for two adults. Nereus refused to get it for him but seems to have told him where to go.'

'But the point is,' said Apollodorus, visibly shocked, 'that Damianos was poisoned, and that Nereus probably knew.'

'Exactly,' said Themis.

'We can't act on slave's gossip, however trusted, but we can make a point of investigating Nereus and his connections.'

'I hope you do. Nereus and I are not on good terms, so I can be of no help there.'

'And the other piece of news?'

'An odd offer is being made to me and I wonder if it's relevant to the Menestratus business.'

Apollodorus put his head out of the door and called for breakfast and a scribe. Then he shut the door and sat down. 'Go on.'

'The Architecture and Planning office want me to paint a panorama for the unfinished Gallery on the Akropolis. There has been no competition and the fee is enormous. It must be a trap of some kind.'

'Hmm,' grunted Apollodorus. 'Almost certainly. Someone wants you to do something in return for this "golden opportunity".'

'But what could I do?'

'Well that's what's intriguing, isn't it?' said the older man as the door opened and two slaves came in. 'It could be anything. But you'll probably find out soon enough.'

'You think I should agree to this commission, then?'

'I think you should accept it with open arms and a grateful heart,' said Apollodorus with a wry smile. 'You won't get an offer like that every day.'

Themis nodded. 'And there's one more thing …'

'What's that?'

'Someone's spreading rumours in the Agora that I'm dissatisfied with my rewards for the Zea business and –'

'That would be me,' said Apollodorus, leaning back in his chair.

'You!'

'Yes. I asked a couple of … friends … ' He waved at the slave with the food to put the tray down on a table by the window. The slave went out, closing the door. Apollodorus went on ' … friends to put this idea into certain heads to increase the chance of your being recruited by certain other people. I was going to tell you today, but they've worked fast. I hope you didn't give any indication that this is not the case?'

Themis thought back. His calm refusal to rise to the accusation could be seen as accepting its truth. Eryx might well now believe that he was a Spartan sympathizer with a tendency to greed. 'I ignored the suggestion,' he said to Apollodorus. 'It could have been taken either way, but the official did seem to relax as though a question had been answered.' He glanced at the scribe who was now sitting with his tablet open.

'Good,' said Apollodorus. 'We may finally be getting somewhere.'

'It would be good,' said Themis, 'if it led to useful evidence in support of Photios.'

Apollodorus stood up. 'Even better if it provided a bargaining tool with the Spartans.'

'But if it doesn't,' Themis went on pointedly, 'the destruction of my reputation will be pointless – and disastrous.'

'We can remedy your reputation later if necessary,' Apollodorus replied. Themis wanted to ask how, but Apollodorus was saying,

'Meanwhile, I need you to always be in communication with me,' he said. 'So don't leave the City again without my knowing where you are going and when.'

Themis sighed. 'I'll get a message to you if at all possible,' he said as he stood up too, and moved towards the door.

'Who did you speak to at the Planning offices?' asked Apollodorus.

'His name's Eryx. He has a bad wound to his head and face.'

'I know him. Who introduced you to him?'

'Eteokles, son of Adrastos of Diomea. He's a member of a supper club I started going to lately.' Themis did not pass on Frog's opinion that Eteokles had Spartan relatives.

'Not a man I've met, though I heard well of his father,' said Apollodorus. 'Could he be dangerous?'

'Seems too smug and a bit ridiculous. Eager, intense. Someone may be manipulating him, though. Some time ago, at a symposium in Eteokles own house, Nereus tried to bribe me to join an army unit of swimmers. His offer was similar – a commission for a large, public wall-painting.'

'And you said no.' Apollodorus wasn't surprised.

'I said I preferred to learn of such opportunities officially.'

Apollodorus nodded, then looked at the scribe. 'Got those names?' he asked. The scribe nodded. 'Good. Well, you have my blessing and best wishes for your new appointment as a painter for the City,' he said.

Themis had a thought. 'Could you let me have a couple of tablets that you are sure are yours?'

Apollodorus looked at the scribe, who pulled two lightweight tablets from his large bag. Apollodorus took them and stamped a tiny horse's head into the wax inside with his seal ring. He handed them to Themis. 'My messengers,' he said.

'Thanks,' said Themis. He nodded to the scribe, noting the man's greying hair and button nose. As he was closing the door behind him he thought, *'I hope Apollodorus can trust his servants.'*

>>>

Suzanne looked in the bathroom mirror and whispered, 'So – both you and I are being manipulated, Themis. But at least my worries are only about myself. You have a whole city to worry about. And you're brave and going along with the manipulation, to see where it leads. Would you really like to paint a wall with the horrible fire on the island of Sfaktiria off Pylos? I know what happened, you know. Athens captured a load of Spartans and held them prisoners for years, as bargaining chips…' She finished shaping her eyebrows.

'But I'm *not* going to be manipulated, I've decided. I'm going to tell him today to stuff it. I bet he can't stop me getting to Australia, anyway. He is clever. He's been careful not to do or say anything I can prove as harassment. So he might be very nasty in other ways in future. Somehow, I'll just have to manage… I bet you'd like to tell your man to "stuff it".'

She smiled into the mirror. 'Then again, I guess some people enjoy that kind of challenge. You don't want to prevent the manipulators, do you? You want to provoke them.' Her smile broadened to a grin. 'You're a self-made hero … Well, I just hope you can deal with the consequences.' She put toothpaste on her toothbrush. 'Is it just a man thing? Or is there maybe a lesson there for me?' She began brushing her teeth.

<<<

Chapter 28: first installment

(Breeds of Sheep 18)

Lidha picked up her tunic from the floor of the empty therapy room and began to put it on. Themis held her arm.

'Wait a minute,' he said. He led her away from the mess of clothes they'd thrown off earlier. 'Stand here by the lamp,' he said. 'I want to include the shine on your skin in the painting.'

Lidha put a hand on her hip and her head on one side. 'You said the girl in the picture would be me, but she's not tall enough.'

'You wouldn't fit on the wall,' said Themis with a shrug. 'But she has your delicious face. Imagine! You'll be looked at and longed for, for years and years. And now the light on the curves of your delectable body will make you even more beautiful.' He made curves in the air with his hands.

Lidha looked pleased and struck a different pose. 'Come on then. Don't take all day.'

Themis laughed and picked up his abandoned paints. 'If you stand like that my hands will shake too much to paint.'

'Good,' she said with a giggle. 'There's more to life than painting.'

A new voice said, 'Not for everyone,' and Eryx appeared through the curtained doorway. 'They said you'd be here working, Themistokles.'

'Eryx! Good to see you,' said Themis, waving a brush. 'Lidha, we can carry on later. Get the stool over there for Eryx to sit. Then send in some wine and a couple of pies. I'm sure Eryx would like a bite to eat and I'm starving. I came straight here from trireme training.'

Lidha moved the stool for Eryx, then picked up her tunic and put it on. She offered Themis his, but he shook his head, attention on the painting. She dropped it on the floor near him and disappeared through the curtain.

'Painting the shine evenly across a surface is difficult,' said Eryx.

'Mmm,' said Themis, concentrating. When he'd finished, he stood back with a deep breath. 'That'll do.'

He hadn't noticed anyone come in, but there was now a tray on the only table in the room, and the smell of the pies was assaulting his stomach.

He threw on his tunic, grabbed a pie and sat cross-legged on the floor near Eryx. 'What brings you here?' he asked through a mouthful.

'Our conversation yesterday,' said Eryx. 'I've been authorized to make official arrangements with you to paint your version of the Pylos campaign. I was told to authorize the first instalment of the fee we agreed and see that you have all the materials you need. I thought you would like to know this immediately.'

'Well, thanks be to the gods – and the Council, of course,' said Themis. He stood up and gestured to the wall. 'I was wondering how to cover expenses once this was finished. And I will be eternally grateful to you, Eryx. Your commission is an ambition I've had for years, as I'm sure Eteokles told you.'

Eryx ignored that and said, 'And a tribute to Panainos, your teacher, whom we all have to acknowledge in spite of his brother's transgressions.'

Themis bowed.

'Please come to the office this evening,' Eryx went on, 'to make the official arrangements with my colleague.'

Themis thought, *'This evening? So soon, and when the offices are officially closed?'* but he didn't say another word and saw Eryx out. Then he came back to the painting. His heart was beating too fast to paint well and his mind was full of speculations about what he might be blackmailed into doing. Lidha came in for the remains of the food.

Later, as his brush stroked the last crease of the garment that dropped in soft golden folds at the feet of the woman on the wall, Themis heard a movement behind him.

'Not just now, Lidha,' he said.

'I'm not Lidha.'

Themis spun round. 'Melissus! What in the name of Athena ..?'

'Don't send me back, Uncle Themis!' warned the 'boy' vehemently. 'You're the only one I trust!' Melissus was filthy. The hair escaping from his cap was tangled and his face was streaked with sweat and dust. But his eyes shot green fire and his mouth was a stiff arch of stubborn fury.

Themis put down his brushes. He took Melissus by the shoulders and steered him to the stool. 'Sit,' he commanded.

Melissus sat, but did not relax, although he was obviously exhausted.

Themis put his head round the curtain and called, 'Lidha? Send someone for sweet wine and water and some more pies or something.'

'More?' called Lidha.

'Not for me, for my … apprentice.'

He squatted down in front of Melissus. 'Right. Now tell.'

'I went to your house, but Frog was outside, talking to a harness maker. I think he saw me and I was afraid he'd shout my name, so I came here.'

'That's fine. But why run away? Why aren't you still at Vravrona?'

'Because – well, it's complicated.' Melissus took a breath and his words tumbled over each other as he spoke. 'They said at Vravrona – when we first began – your *mother* said – that most of the time we women have to lie – because we're not as strong as most men, because men don't understand our bodies, we have to lie and get good at it. She said the gods have made rules for us and that she would teach us how they work. But she said it was safe to tell the truth *there*, because there, the goddess would protect us.'

'But that's true of everyone, Melissus,' said Themis, thinking of his present situation. 'Men *and* women. Sometimes we have to lie to get what we need.'

'OK,' said the 'boy', his eyes wide and furious. 'But do I have to lie about the gods when they speak to me?'

'What?'

'I was walking past the new altar there, and heard one of my voices say, "Athena needs to keep watch on the sea for the smoking lightning".'

'You heard what?' asked Themis. The hairs on his forearms had risen.

'It's not the first time something like that has happened, but never such a … fierce voice.'

'I didn't know *you* heard voices!' murmured Themis.

'I took no notice as usual. I mean, what's smoking lightning, anyway? But I heard the same voice again as I was going to sleep. And then again in the dawn, as I was getting ready to get up. So I told your mother. And she said many people hear things like that at Vravrona. It's a place where it's easy for the gods to reach us. She also said it might be best not to tell anyone in case the other girls were jealous.'

Themis stood up. 'Quite right!' he said. 'Ah … But of course, you did.'

'Yes. I thought that was just a polite way of saying she didn't believe me herself. After all, the day before, she had said we didn't need to lie if we were there. Anyway, the girls laughed at me and called me names at first. One of them said I was just showing off and that lightning never happens at sea – which is irrelevant and anyway, it does.'

Themis nodded. 'True. I've seen a few dead fish after a storm. So then what happened?'

'Then they started pulling my hair and pinned me in a corner. The guardian women didn't stop them, either. There was a bit of a riot and Mrs Eirini had to take me to her house. I'd punched a few by then.'

'So you ran away. Does my mother know?'

'Of course not. I stole these clothes from her slave and the guards actually chased me away.' Melissus' fists balled and beat on his knees. 'Uncle Themis, if we go there specifically because it's a good place to contact the gods, why do people behave like that when we do?'

Lidha came in with the food. She winked at Themis as she set it down, and looked over her shoulder with a sway of her hips as she left.

Themis raised an eyebrow at her, then turned to Melissus, who was looking ferociously at Lidha's retreating form. 'It seems to me,' he said slowly, 'that most people believe it must be … more exciting – or fun, or interesting – to be someone else.' He watered a cup of wine and handed it to Melissus. 'They aren't happy with what they've got and always want something they can't have. I do it myself sometimes.' He also handed a pie to the 'boy'. 'We should send a message to Vravrona that you are safe.'

'No!' Melissus leapt up, spilling the wine. 'No. You're always trying to interfere in my life. Don't tell anyone! No one!'

'Well, … all right. But they'll be looking for you. When did you leave?'

'Last night.'

'You ran all that way since last night?'

Melissus put his cup and pie on the table.

'Look. I'll write a note to my own mother to say I'm fine, but I won't go back there, ever!' He flung out his hands. 'You can't make me. You're not even related to me!'

Themis grabbed the hands and held them down. He looked into the wild eyes and said, 'Tell me about the voices. How often do you hear them, anyway?' His mind was racing. Should he admit to his own, less palpable experiences?

Melissus looked up at him with a shrug. 'Almost every day,' he said.

'What!' said Themis. 'You've never told me! Does your mother know? What sort of things do they say?'

'No. I never told her. And just personal things, usually. It's not like they are oracles or foreseeing stuff. I'm not a Cassandra. It's almost always when I'm going to sleep or just waking up. Just ... explanations. My dad being jealous of you, for instance. Or ... your being cleverer and kinder than your brother. Lots of stuff like that.'

'Which gods?'

'I don't know. Sometimes it's a man's voice, sometimes it's a woman's.'

'And this time?'

'It was a woman. A very ... anxious woman – anxious, but used to being obeyed, so I assumed she was Artemis herself.'

'And what did she say exactly?'

'I told you. "Athena needs to keep watch on the sea for the smoking lightning".'

'All three times the same?'

Melissus looked up at him with dawning comprehension. 'Yes. D'you think it's important?'

Themis thought for a moment. 'I'm not sure what it means, but I *am* sure it could be important,' he said. 'It could be very important. We'd better get you home. Eat up.'

Themis led Melissus in through the empty kitchen. He put his head out of the door into the courtyard, looked around and listened for a moment. Then he turned back and said quietly, 'No one around.' Melissus followed him through to the foot of the stairs up to the women's rooms.

'You'd better sleep upstairs in the same room as Chloe,' said Themis as they went up.

'I thought you did your painting up here,' whispered Melissus.

'I'm only using Mama's old weaving room. The other rooms are still furnished as before for when she comes home.'

Melissus looked round at the three beds strewn with blue and yellow striped cushions and the cedarwood chests against the pale frescoed walls. The window looked out onto the courtyard. Frog was calling to Mika in the kitchen about the fish for the evening meal.

'I bet you could hear everything the women say when you're down in the yard,' said Melissus in a whisper. 'All the private women's things?'

Themis shook his head to hide his embarrassment.

'Which bed was Myrto's?' Melissus asked quietly.

'They burned it after she died,' said Themis. 'This is a new one.'

'Did you do the frescoes?' asked the 'boy', gesturing round the room at the scenes of tumbling, woodland streams and, on another wall, the distant Akropolis and city between saplings in new leaf.

'Yeah. When I was about the same age as you are now.'

'Not bad,' said Melissus as he sat down and pulled off his filthy cap. Hair fell down his back in a shining copper cascade. 'He' was suddenly 'she'.

Themis was shaken by a bolt of desire. He turned his back to her and controlled his breathing as he ran a hand over the lid of a chest.

'She died in the plague, didn't she? What was it like, the plague?'

'I wasn't here – I was away in Massalia with Mama's brother, Leokratis – so I don't remember it myself. And you were a toddler. I think your mother took you to Elis.' He opened the chest. 'They told me that everyone from the farms was crammed into the city to be safe from the Spartans. People died in their hundreds, usually just a few days after they started feeling ill – but some got better. The dying fought for water round the reservoirs and springs. And their bodies were piled in heaps and began to stink before they could be taken away and dealt with. Surely you've heard about it from other people?'

'And the Spartans were burning the fields all over Attica?'

'That's what I remember,' said Themis. 'Coming back and finding the farms all burnt.' He pulled a couple of garments out of the chest, one green and one wine-red. He was in control now. He turned to her. 'After you've washed, you could dress in one of these … The burnt farms, and then learning that Myrto and her husband and the little boys were all dead.' He laid the long chitons on the bed opposite Melissa. 'Yes, that was a very bad time. Mama told me that Myrto died a couple of days after her husband and children. She didn't want to live without them.'

'No wonder no one wants it to happen again.' Melissa looked at the clothes on the bed. 'I think it's better if I dress as a boy still,' she said.

'I'll get Frog to find something clean, then,' said Themis. 'And Chloe will be here by tonight. Her bed is the one nearest the door.'

Melissa whispered fiercely, 'No! You can't tell her as well!'

Themis spoke equally quietly and fiercely. 'And you can't stay here without a woman companion! I won't have Nereus challenging me just because I gave you sanctuary tonight. As you say, you are not a blood relative. Tomorrow you'll have to go and stay in Sacred Artemis' Vravronium on the Akropolis. It's too late now and they won't let you in.'

'Well, it won't matter what Nereus thinks,' Melissa snapped, 'because I won't be marrying him anyway. But I'm sorry if I'm being … inconvenient.'

'Of course you'll marry him,' said Themis, appalled at the pain in his chest as he said this. 'What makes you think you won't? You've been promised.'

'I just know. I was told,' said Melissa emphatically.

'Ah,' said Themis ironically. 'Well, I can't really argue with your gods, but even if it's not Nereus, it'll be someone, someday and so the situation doesn't change.'

Melissa shot him a glance and said, 'I'll sleep here, then.' She lifted her satchel off over her wild hair and threw it on the bed nearest the window in a puff of dust.

'I'll send the Skionian up,' said Themis at the door. 'She never speaks so she won't tell on you.' '*And I'll let your mother and mine know where you are,*' he thought as he took the stairs down to the courtyard at a run.

Chapter 29: dangerous bet

And later, as it was getting dark, he took the steps up to the City's Planning Offices three at a time. When he got to the top, a man appeared from behind a column. 'Themistokles?' he said.

The man was dressed in a dark himation. He had a square head and a jutting nose, with short white hair and beard. Themis didn't know him personally. He did know that he owned marble quarries on Mount Pendelikon and had been chosen by lot to serve this year in the Planning Offices. His name was Hyllos.

'Please, come this way,' Hyllos said to Themis. 'My name is Hyllos. I work with Eryx.' And he led Themis into the building and down a corridor with a statue of Athena against the wall at the end.

They entered a small room looking out onto the gardens. Stars and the distant torches on the Akropolis reflected in a pool surrounded by ferns. Frogs competed in a deafening chorus. Hyllos had some papyrus sheets ready on a small table beside an armchair under a lampstand.

'This is the agreement for your North Wall painting,' he said.

Themis sat down on the offered chair. He read the standard official contract to provide a work of sculpture or painting. The fee was twice his usual earnings for a year. It would of course take many months to complete, assuming the offer was genuine, but still it was too much. The signature of the relevant Archon was clear, however. '*A forgery?*' thought Themis.

'It all seems in order,' he said loudly over the frogs. 'When will the building be finished and ready for me to start?'

Hyllos turned from looking out at the garden. He held a heavy purse. 'The start of this project is expected within the month. Your official remuneration will begin at the same time.' He laid the purse on the table and stepped back, his hands pressed together as he looked down at Themis. 'It is funded by a private benefactor who has asked me to discuss something quite unconnected with you, in the hope that you could help him with another project in the meantime.'

'*Here it comes,*' thought Themis. He said, 'I'm not much good at anything but painting.'

'You are too modest, Themistokles,' said Hyllos smoothly as he turned to walk around the room. 'I have been making enquiries and find that you are also an engineer of defence systems. You have been involved in designing and building walls in Methana, Patra, and to a lesser extent at the sieges of Amphipolis and Skioni. You were once a student of the great Phidias, your mother's cousin, before he fell into disfavour.' He began counting things off on his fingers. 'You also managed his brother Panainos' painting studio and school, sold or gave pictures to many discerning citizens, painted much-praised frescoes on the walls of many private houses, and worked as a mason on some fine stone sculptures for the public buildings on the Akropolis up there.' He gestured to the great rock that filled the horizon. 'You deserve much greater fame.'

Themis laughed. 'You make me sound very important,' he said.

Hyllos tilted his head and began counting on the fingers of his other hand. 'And that is not all. You won the boys' boxing wreath at the 87th Olympic Games fourteen years ago. You row Athena's triremes and serve as a hoplite. Your self-discipline is such that you train every second day at the palaestra, every third or fourth day as an oarsman, and regularly as a swimmer...' He smiled. 'You are particularly lauded as a strong underwater swimmer.'

'How could any of these things be of interest to your Benefactor?' asked Themis with a slight shrug.

'He has made a private bet about something and wonders if you would be prepared to prove him correct. There is somewhere that his friends insist no one can access, even by swimming under water.'

A great peace spread through Themis. He kept his expression curious. 'And that is?' he asked.

Hyllos' eyes were dancing with humour. 'The harbour of Zea.'

'Really?' said Themis. 'Surely many have succeeded in that. Some trireme maintenance is done in the water.'

'Of course, by entering the water from inside the harbour,' said Hyllos. 'And not by night, naturally enough. But the terms of the bet stipulate "without discovery, in total darkness".'

Themis arranged his face to show apprehension rather than the triumph he was feeling. 'I see ...' he murmured.

'The discussion seems to have arisen in connection with a possible attack on Zea again,' said Hyllos. 'The Benefactor insists that a determined enemy could penetrate our defences that way, while his drinking companions insisted that the harbours are safe from such an assault.'

Themis said, 'I'd be inclined to agree with them. The water is extremely deep in the approach to Zea harbour. Even on the brightest day, you can't see the bottom from my seat on a trireme.'

'Oh come now!' said Hyllos. 'A man like you in the prime of his strength could surely demonstrate that it is at least a possibility. And imagine succeeding and winning the bet for the Benefactor. You would also have the pleasure of being able to report to the City authorities that you have breached even their expensive new security measures. You would be a hero all over again!' Hyllos was quite charming when he smiled like that.

Themis nodded as if he was surprised and enthusiastic.

Hyllos went on, 'The size of the bet involved is considerable. Of course, if you succeed and our Benefactor wins, the man who did the swimming would be paid a good portion of the winnings.'

Themis knew there was a net across the harbour mouth of Zea that was drawn up by winches each night. During the day it lay in the depths of the approach. Once it was hanging in place in the water, a good diver might be able to pass under it. He asked greedily, 'And if I agree? When are we talking about?'

'The moon is completely dark in a couple of days,' said Hyllos with a slight shrug. 'I imagine that is when the notion is set to be tested, but it may be even sooner. The moon doesn't rise until after midnight as it wanes. We'll meet again tomorrow, when the decision has been made.'

'May I involve a companion?'

'The notion is of course, an exciting challenge but it is illegal, and you might get arrested before you can do anything. So better to keep this entirely to yourself at the moment.' Hyllos leaned slightly forward, pushing the purse towards Themis. 'I'm sure you understand,' he added with his charming smile, but looking pointedly into Themis' eyes.

Themis needed a drink! He had expected Hyllos to offer him wine to clinch the deal concerning the painting, but nothing had appeared. He crossed the road from the Planning Offices and sat on a stool in the first tavern he found. The wine was very sweet. He watered it and poured half a cupful into the dust as a libation to Hermes, the god of deceptions. Then he ordered some soup and barley bread.

He was angry with himself. In spite of his excitement at finally having a chance of learning who was behind the harbour attacks, his mind was full of the picture of Melissa shaking her hair down and looking up at him with her sparkling green eyes. It was playing havoc with his concentration. 'Focus on the task in hand,' he said out loud to himself.

The soup came – bean and walnut – the colour of Melissa's hair.

He turned his attention to the traffic on the street. There were torches alight at the entrances to the public buildings. Two or three men came down the steps from the Planning Office, obviously leaving work late. It was the time of evening when men went out to their supper parties or to meet business partners. They walked in groups of two and three, some talking loudly and others in discreet, hushed tones.

'*But I doubt anyone's affairs need keeping as quiet as mine,*' he thought. His heart was beating fast with a kind of glee. '*I'm going to have to keep it a complete secret, even from Frog.*' He drank some wine. '*Then again,*' he thought, '*that might be foolish, whatever Hyllos said.*' He would need Frog to know where he was going to be, even if he couldn't go with him.

An older man led by a boy slave with a torch had stopped in the road. It was Leontis, Photios' father. He had almost passed when he recognized Themis and now he came over to greet him.

'Will you join me for a cup of sweet wine?' Themis invited, wishing he could tell Leontis what he was celebrating.

'I can't stay,' said Leontis, 'but I just wanted to say that Photios begs me every day to stop by your house.'

'Why don't you?' asked Themis standing up.

'To tell you the truth, I'm not sure what to say to you,' said Leontis. 'He is so deeply in your debt and yet seems to expect even more from you.'

'Tell him, that's what friends do,' said Themis with a laugh, 'and please tell him I'll drop by to see him myself in a few days.'

'Very well. We would be very pleased to welcome you.' Leontis backed away and then walked off briskly, the boy running to keep up.

Themis' soup had begun to look less appetizing as it congealed. He sighed and thought, '*Ah, Diodotos. Where are you now when I need a drinking partner?*'

As he prepared to leave the tavern, he saw a man detach himself from the walkers in the street and climb the stairs to the Planning Offices. This seemed odd so late in the day. Then he saw that it was Glykon.

He sat down again, and ordered more wine. Glykon was another man well known for being a strong underwater swimmer.

Glykon reappeared some time later. He walked with a bounce in his step and met a friend and a torch slave at the bottom of the steps. They turned and walked west towards the Pnyx. Themis grabbed his satchel and followed.

They took the road towards Piraeus. He watched from a distance as they turned into a tavern in the village of Kili. They went in to the well-lit inner room and sat in a corner under a window. Themis took the alleyway at the side, up some steps, and sat with his back to the outside of the wall they were sitting by. If he stood he would be able to see in through the window. As it was, he could hear their voices clearly.

Glykon was laughing and his friend, whose voice was deeper, was congratulating him.

'You'll be eating larks' tongues in a day or two, then,' he was saying.

'Not me,' laughed Glykon. 'Waste of money. But I'll be able to pay for that gelding your father's selling, and a new saddle!'

'When will you know how much?' asked the friend.

'Oh, in the next day or two I guess. They'll have it ready for me when I come ashore,' said Glykon.

'Ashore?'

'Oops!' said Glykon. 'Giving too much away.' And he laughed again.

'Here, let's drink to Hermes and our health!'

'To Hermes the God of trickery!' said the friend. 'And may he keep your secret for ever!'

Themis walked home, wondering how to get a message safely to Apollodorus.

Early next morning, the boy Melissus came down the stairs into the courtyard. In his clean boy's clothes with his hair tidied away into a hood, he was not too disturbing. Themis was angry with himself for spending much of the night dreaming of tumbling hair and green eyes that seemed lit from inside.

'Where's Chloe?' He was surprised at how grumpy he sounded.

Melissus laughed. 'We talked for ages. She's still sleeping.'

'And what are you planning to do today?'

'It's ok, I'll move on,' Melissus said mischievously. 'I'll give my brother Skopas a note for Mother on his way home from school, but don't worry, I'll stay out of your way.'

'Actually,' Themis made himself sound more friendly. 'I was wondering if you could help me with something that's come up.'

Melissus looked suspicious. 'I don't need you to take responsibility for me,' he said. 'I'll be fine as long as Frog and Mika don't tell on me.'

'It's nothing like that,' said Themis. 'It's just that I need to know the movements of a man I'm thinking of working for, but I don't have time to follow him myself.'

'And you want me to, even though you want to send me back?'

'I just thought you might enjoy a bit of an adventure,' said Themis.

Melissus paused. 'Who is he, then?' he asked wryly.

Themis stopped himself from smiling. 'His name is Hyllos and he works in the City Planning Offices. He should be there now, but he said he'd be going out to visit a colleague or two later in the day.'

Melissus looked excited in spite of himself. 'What are you going to make? An Athena in marble? Or a bronze?'

'No. It's not a sculpture. We're in negotiation for a painting. But it's a secret for now. Can you keep an eye on him? He's about 50 years old with very white hair and beard, and a nose like a jug handle. Make sure he doesn't know you're there, but I need to know who he sees and particularly if he gossips about me to anyone.'

'And would I get another night's sanctuary if I do this?'

'You know I can't promise that. If Chloe can help, that's fine. But …'

'It's all right. I have somewhere to go if not.'

'And where would that be?'

'You don't need to know,' said Melissus coolly. 'At least, not yet.'

'Come back here, anyway,' said Themis, gathering up his painting satchel. 'I'll finish at Zotikos' today. You can tell me what Hyllos has been doing over some food this afternoon. I have an appointment with him tonight. Then we can decide where you spend the night. Oh, and don't say a word about this to anyone!'

Themis stood in front of his last wall painting in Zotikos' therapy room. He was staring at, but not seeing, the dishevelled hair of the naked girl he had painted the day before. Frog had done a good job of the wall preparation while he was at trireme practice – in another life, it seemed.

'What's happening to me?' he asked himself. 'I haven't been fixated on someone I can't have since Anthoussa – eight, ten years ago? And of all people, it's her daughter! This is driving me crazy...' He took a deep breath and shook himself. 'You'd better sort yourself out,' he whispered to himself. 'The gods, or whatever facets of our own characters we give their names to, are taking revenge because I don't always take them into account. Maybe I should pray, as well as try practical ways to discover whether Nereus is a criminal.'

He turned to the paints on the table and began preparing his colours. An almost silent footstep sounded behind him and he was not surprised when Lidha's hands slid round his waist and came to rest in exactly the right place.

Chapter 30: instructions

(Breeds of Sheep 20)

'This is where Hyllos bumped into the Persian,' said Melissus later, waving an arm.

'Here?' Themis asked. 'So near Dionyssos' Temple? It's a bit public for a secret meeting.'

'Yup,' said Melissus, hands on hips. 'I was playing ball-in-the-hole with some other boys across the road.'

'Did you say Hyllos and this man acted surprised to see each other?'

'Yup. They tried hard to make it look like an accident – too hard,' said Melissus. 'I'm sure they already knew each other. Hyllos' voice was too loud. The other man was dressed like an Athenian but he spoke quietly, and when I got nearer, I heard his voice properly. He certainly wasn't from here. He had a really thick accent, like the man from Sardis who used to come to Father's yard in Rhamnous.'

'A Persian,' said Themis thoughtfully. 'And they walked off together?'

'Yes.'

'Which way?'

'Along here, back the way Hyllos had come.'

They set off together in the direction Melissus was pointing, along the Street of Tripods.

'Did you hear what they were saying?'

'A few words. I pretended to be deaf and Hyllos had to grab me out of the way of a donkey cart.'

'Did he guess you were a girl?'

'Why would he? I have as much bicep as most boys my size. Anyway, the Persian was saying he'd need more money to be sure of his special "operators".'

'Did he say what the operators were going to do?'

'He said something that sounded like "meeting a merman or two". But otherwise I couldn't hear. Something to do with keeping the dolphins happy, I think. All a bit fishy, it seemed to me...' Melissus eyes sparkled.

'Did either of them mention when the operation is due?' Themis asked.

'Just that they only had a day or two because it has to be done during the "pause".'

'Pause? Pause in what?'

'They didn't say.' Melissus shrugged and pouted. Themis looked away, along the street.

'And where did they split up?' he asked.

'Hyllos went into the City Planning Offices and the other man ran through the city gate at Kili Village – to that stables just under the walls. He jumped on his horse and set off for Piraeus. I watched him go … Do you think this is something to do with "smoking lightning"?'

Themis stopped in the shadow of a tall portico on the corner of a narrow alley. 'At the moment, I can't say,' he said seriously. 'But some of what you just told me is going to be really useful – I'm just not sure which bits. And I'd rather Hyllos had never seen your face, filthy though it is. Anyway, thanks, Melissus. You go back to Frog now. If Chloe is coming back, you can stay at the house. If she can't make it, I'll have to take you up to the Vravronion on the Akropolis and they'll get you back to Vravrona tomorrow.'

Melissus looked up at Themis, his mouth a pugnacious line. 'There's something wrong, Uncle Themis, isn't there?' he asked, hips forward, arms folded.

'What d'you mean?' Themis felt the sudden sick thudding of his heart must be visible in his neck. She mustn't guess.

'I mean … you're angry with me, aren't you?'

Themis breathed out in relief and nodded slowly. He looked along the street, not at Melissus. 'You're right. But I am trying to be sympathetic,' he said carefully. 'It's no good your trying to go on being a boy when your body is so obviously a girl's. So I'm angry *for* you, that you have to accept this. But I'm also angry *at* you, because you don't see that you will have to go back to Vravrona sooner or later...'

Melissus' eyes were green slits. 'You have no idea how useless and boring the life of a woman is, do you? It's just glorified slavery, you know. And if you think I'm going to be meek and sweet and do as I'm told, you'll soon learn that I'm not like the others. Don't imagine you or anyone else can make me change.' He turned on his heel and ran into the alleyway.

Themis ran after him. The alley was completely made up of steps and was in deep shadow. Above, it gave onto a brighter street at right angles. There were seven or eight people carrying loads on their heads coming gingerly down the steps. Themis threaded his way desperately between them as he ran up calling, 'Melissus! Stop! We can talk about it with Mama!'

But when he got to the junction and scanned the crowd of busy pedestrians, there was no sign of either Melissus or Melissa.

Themis marched back into the Agora. He didn't notice where he was going until he heard a burst of laughter from a group of young men. Sokrates was sitting at the top of the steps of the Painted Arcade, discussing life with a group of young men sitting beside and below him. Themis stopped and listened.

'So now we have a better idea of the nature of efficiency,' said Sokrates. His smile embraced them all as he stood up. 'Shall we see if there are any duck pies left at The Hungry Bear?'

On a whim, Themis stepped forward and intercepted the philosopher.

'May I have a quiet word?' Themis asked him as the younger men dispersed towards the tavern.

'Themistokles?' said Sokrates, standing still and looking up into Themis' face. 'Shall we sit down again here?'

Themis inclined his head and they sat on the steps again, in the shade of the colonnade. *How do I begin?* he thought.

'Is it something to do with this latest discussion?' asked the older man.

'No, not at all,' said Themis. 'I hope you won't think me disrespectful, but I truly would value your thoughts on … on … a voice – a kind of presence – that I hear and feel sometimes. It seems to be someone quite specific and distinct.'

'Ah,' sighed Sokrates. 'You have a visitor, a daemon.'

Themis laughed a little. 'That's exactly what I have. I call her my visitor.'

'It seems you're not the only one. And it's a she?'

'Yes.' Themis nodded. 'It's a young woman. She's very wise about some things, and ignorant about others. And often, she's just … there. Present, but not doing or saying anything.'

'Not a goddess, then,' said Sokrates. 'They can't resist interfering.' A wry smile creased his face so that his twinkling eyes almost disappeared into his bulging cheeks.

Themis shook his head. 'I thought she might have been a nymph in the beginning, but now I am almost sure she's a real person. I keep thinking I might meet her …'

'And how long has she been visiting you?'

'Since I was twelve and had a serious bang on the head. Not constantly, though.'

'So you think the injury caused her presence?'

'Yes.'

'And do you feel her in your head or your heart?' Sokrates' was looking directly at Themis with speculation in his eyes.

Themis thought a moment, then replied, 'Both. Sometimes I just feel her presence like a hum in my chest. Sometimes I hear her voice as though it's in my ears, inside my head.'

Sokrates said, 'You know, of course, that I have the reputation for hearing the voices of the gods?'

'That's why I wanted to talk to you,' said Themis.

Sokrates was looking at his gnarled hands in his lap. 'There are times when I am brought to a standstill by what I hear, what I see. I, too, am not sure whether it is in my heart or my head. There are times of blinding white light, of total surrender to silent bliss. And there are other times when a jumble of voices vies for my attention, particularly when I may be in the wrong.' He looked up at Themis and smiled. 'And that's when they remind me how extraordinary it is that we are alive at all, and that we are just specks of dust in the endless cosmos.'

Themis smiled back. 'One way the gods try to save us from hubris?' he said quietly.

Sokrates laid a hand on his arm. 'Do you wish me to advise you?'

Themis shook his head. 'Not unless you think there is some danger I am unaware of,' he said. 'I merely wanted to ask whether our experiences are similar.'

'Yours sounds more similar to what young Melissus has let slip. It seems he "hears" the voice of a god at times, warning him, usually.'

'Melissus? Is he one of your followers? Did he tell you he hears voices?'

'Not in so many words. But I guessed he probably does one day when he said something like "But that's not what she told me".'

'She?' asked Themis. 'Did he explain?'

Sokrates went on, 'We were talking of Athena of the City. We'd just been told she was demanding a larger sacrifice than usual at the Panathenaia. When I asked him about what she had said to him, Melissus coloured and muttered something about a warning.' Sokrates raised an eyebrow. 'As it turned out the demand was not from the goddess, but from a corrupt mortal who stood to gain from the larger sacrifice. So Melissus was right … Would you say that your nymph warns you?'

Themis frowned a little. 'I can't remember a specific warning ever. In fact, sometimes it seems she's actually laughing at me.'

'As you say,' said the older man, standing up with a chuckle, 'a way for the gods to stop you being too sure of yourself. Nothing is ever exactly what it seems.'

Later, Themis again sat waiting on the steps of the City Planning Office. His anger with Melissa had cooled a little after his conversation with Sokrates. Now he was watching the area around for anyone who might be stalking him. But no one seemed in the least bit interested. He jumped when someone tapped him on the shoulder from behind. It was Hyllos.

'Thank you for coming,' Hyllos said with his charming smile. It was a tinge more patronizing than it had been the day before. 'Follow me, please.'

They went through the portico and across an atrium. The frogs were just beginning their evening chorus. Under the columns on the other side, Hyllos led the way into a small, dark room. He indicated that Themis should look at the plan of Zea Harbour and its surroundings on the large table. Then he shut the door. There was no window, and a plain lamp stand supported a smoking flame. There was no other furniture.

'The Benefactor,' said Hyllos, 'has asked me to arrange for our enterprise to go ahead tomorrow night.'

'Tomorrow!?' Themis exclaimed.

Hyllos smiled his most charming smile and said, 'It is the first night that will be dark enough.'

'I see,' said Themis, turning to the map. 'Where should I enter the water? There are walls with guards all round the peninsular of Piraeus.'

'I have arranged that you will approach by boat.'

'But boats in that area are always challenged.'

'I don't think that will be a problem,' said Hyllos lightly. 'You will be accompanied by an interested party, who will watch you enter the water.'

'Of course,' said Themis. 'And another will watch as I emerge?'

'Naturally.'

'It's a long way into the harbour from the bay. They may have to wait a while, depending on how quickly I can swim that far.'

'And depending also, perhaps, on how much you wish to continue with the project of the Pylos painting?' Hyllos was still smiling broadly.

Themis sighed. 'Of course,' he agreed.

Hyllos turned to the map. 'So I suggest that you meet your companion at this gate out of Piraeus. He will go with you through this one in the Long Wall.' Hyllos tapped his finger on the relevant gates in the defensive walls. 'From here, there's a wide track down to the shore where fishing boats are pulled up in their scores. Do you know it?'

'You want me to swim all the way from there?' asked Themis.

'No, no. As I said, you will be on a boat. You will be the third man with Lukos and Linas. Ask for them on the beach, and go out with them into the bay, along with all the other fishing boats that leave around that time. Your companion will return to the walls where he will engage the guards in conversation until he sees you enter the water. Lukos and Linas will manoeuvre themselves to get as near as possible to Zea's harbour mouth without rousing suspicion. You will slip over the side with a light rope tied to your waist. Do not make a splash. The only man to notice you must be the watcher.'

Themis said, 'There will be starlight.'

'Indeed. So you will need to be underwater as much as possible, and from here.' He pointed on the map to where the long narrow passage into the harbour mouth began between high defensive walls. 'Constantly. You will be visible to the harbour guards and winch workers on both sides of the passage if you surface. The whole point of the wager is that you are invisible as you swim into the harbour entrance.'

'At night there is the net stretched to hang vertically across the inner entrance under the water,' said Themis.

'True.' Hyllos nodded. 'You need to swim under its ropes, as near the bottom as you can. I suggest you surface really close to the entrance inside, here on the left, where there is shadow from the walls.'

'And the Benefactor will be there to check that his wager is won?' Themis asked innocently.

'Perhaps. But whoever is there, you will be asked, "Does the starlight reach the bottom?" Don't show or give up the rope until you are asked that, and then give it only to the man who asks that question.'

Themis nodded sagely.

'Once you have delivered the end of the rope,' Hyllos went on, 'and it has been checked to be lying on the seabed, you should swim back the way you came. If no alarm is raised, I'm sure your reward will be waiting for you when Lukos and Linas get you back to shore.'

'And have you any idea what I can expect as my reward,' asked Themis.

'The bet is large, and my Benefactor suggested I offer you a tenth of the winnings, so it should be around a thousand drachmas. You could buy a fine house with that!' said Hyllos.

'And is there no one else involved? No help I could summon if, for instance, I tangle with a giant octopus?' Themis looked at Hyllos quite seriously.

'Your sense of humour becomes you, Themistokles,' said the civil servant with his charming smile. 'I am sure you are more than a match for any monster of the deep.'

'You are very kind,' said Themis. 'But it will be a lonely business swimming all that way in the dark.' He allowed his apprehension to show on his face. 'Knowing there was someone I could rely on for help would make it less … daunting.'

'I'm surprised a hero of your calibre would be daunted at all,' said

Hyllos. 'We covered that last time,' he went on decisively as he put a friendly arm round Themis' shoulders. 'Absolute secrecy is the only way.'

When Themis got home some time after sunset, he found Frog preparing to go and join Melanas at the farm in Athmonon for the last couple of days of the harvest.

'So you are going to leave me to the smothering ministrations of Mika, are you?' said Themis.

'And the Skionian,' said Frog wistfully.

'She's not the smothering type,' said Themis.

'How would you know?' asked Frog archly.

Themis shook his head with a half-smile. 'And what have you done with Melissus?'

'He's taken some food and I gave him the money you told him to take.'

'What!' Themis exclaimed. 'I didn't tell him any such thing!'

'Ah,' said Frog.

'And he's gone?'

'Yes,' said Frog.

'And you don't know where?'

'He said you knew,' said Frog.

'Athena, Hermes and Mighty Zeus!' exploded Themis. 'What am I supposed to do now?'

'Tell his – er, her – mother?' said Frog. 'Melissus is not really your responsibility.'

'And you'll be up at Athmonon for how long?'

'Two or three days,' said Frog.

'Come with me,' said Themis and swept into the andron. Frog followed calmly.

'Sit!' ordered Themis quietly as he shut the door.

Frog shrugged. 'Where?'

'On that couch. I have to talk to you seriously.'

Frog rested his bottom carefully on the edge of the couch opposite Themis. 'What has happened?' he asked.

'Two things,' said Themis, jumping up again and marching up and down. 'One, we've now lost Melissus, who is furious with me for not managing to save him – her – from Vravrona in spite of the fact that she brought me an important warning which is proving very useful. She could be anywhere in the city, or kidnapped and lost for ever.'

'She is still not strictly your responsibility,' Frog insisted.

Themis forced himself to stop marching and sat down. 'True, but I do feel … grateful. And two, I have purposely put myself in the position of being conned into making the next attack from within on the triremes in Zea Harbour.'

Frog sat back a bit and whistled. He folded his arms and said, 'The market is buzzing with tales of your dissatisfactions. You'll need good evidence that you haven't turned traitor if this gets out.'

'If I can learn who is setting it up, it should clear Photios of all involvement with the last one.'

'And can you? Otherwise you'll both be dead meat.'

'I know the names of some of the small fish, and there's a chance I will even meet one of the more important ones, but I can't get anyone to tell me who the shark is.'

'So you want to tell me who they are in case anything happens to you.'

'Good idea,' said Themis, 'and I will. But what I really wanted to say is that I need your presence tomorrow night, all night, so I want you to postpone going to the farm.'

'The harvest can't really wait for postponements,' said Frog. 'But this time I think you need protection more than the barley needs cutting.'

Themis relaxed a bit. 'Thank the gods my father fished you out of that swamp,' he said. 'You can pay a man – or two even – to go and help Melanas.'

'Fine. So what's the plan?' asked Frog, sitting forward, his eyes glowing with excitement.

Chapter 31: Adrasteia?

(Breeds of Sheep 21)

Over breakfast next morning, and after his regular trip to the gymnasium, Themis asked Frog to sit down with him at the table in the courtyard.

'Did you send the message to Anthoussa,' he asked.

'Before dawn,' said Frog. 'The Skionian took it. She brought back a rather short reply written by Mrs Anthoussa herself.' He handed a piece of folded papyrus, obviously much erased and re-used, to Themis.

It said, 'If you find her, bring her straight here! No detours!' Themis sighed and turned to his food again.

'Was she followed?'

'We don't think so. But you were.'

'Yes, to the palaestra at the gymnasium. So I couldn't deliver a tablet to … someone.' He grinned his apology for the secrecy.

'Was your sticky stalker the seller of melon seeds?' asked Frog. 'He's standing at the corner of the street with his tray resting on his belly.'

Themis frowned with his mouth full. 'No. It was a groom, with horse shit on his tunic. He trailed me all the way there and back.'

'They've probably just changed over,' said Frog.

'Look. I really need to get out without being seen. How can I do that?'

'Under a large sack of straw from the stables?'

'They'd probably recognize my legs. I'm a different shape from you …'

Frog nodded, looking down at his small feet and wiry legs. 'True. Your legs are more like tree trunks.'

'Huh! Not ancient oaks? You're not being very kind today, Frog.'

There was a tumultuous knocking on the front door.

Frog raised an eyebrow at Themis who shook his head and shrugged. Frog went to the door calling, 'All right, all right. No need for the battering ram! Who is it?'

A female voice came from outside. 'What have you done with the girl?!'

Frog opened the door and Anthoussa's slave woman charged into the courtyard. Themis stood up to face her. 'What girl?' he said loudly so that anyone listening in the street would hear. But he made a sign with his hand to speak more quietly.

'Melissa!' hissed the woman. 'Her mother is beside herself with worry, and she should be calm and carefree just now. This may kill her!'

The woman was sweating and wild-eyed. She was tall and strong and her voice was crackling with distress. Themis raised his own and said, 'Melissa hasn't been here for seven or eight days.' Then he spoke quietly near the woman's ear, 'The last time I saw her she was dressed as a boy. It was late yesterday afternoon, on Tripod Street.'

The woman clutched at her garments in anguish. 'Oh, that child!' she exclaimed. 'She'll be the death of her mother. Why can't she just relax and get on with growing up?'

Themis offered her a stool. Frog shut the street door with a bang.

'Melissus has been taking care of himself – I should say, herself – for years in Rhamnous and in Athens.' Themis soothed quietly. 'She'll be fine. She has some money and food and a gang of friends. She'll reappear when she's ready.' He squatted down in front of her. 'Did Mrs Anthoussa send you?' he asked.

'She'd have me whipped if she knew,' she said in alarm. 'It was the old nurse who comes by now and again.'

'Well, I won't say a word,' said Themis. 'Tell me, though, what's the matter with Mrs Anthoussa?'

The woman looked at him, wiping tears from her cheeks with the back of her hand. 'This pregnancy is not going well. She has fainting fits and can't breathe sometimes. The doctors say she must be calm and stay quiet.' She jumped up, almost knocking Themis over. 'So this is just the kind of thing she doesn't need! Her other children are behaving so well … '

Themis stood up. They were almost the same height. Frog made a gesture to Themis from behind the woman's back. It took Themis a moment to understand. Then he nodded slightly.

'I'm sorry, I've forgotten your name,' he said to the woman.

'Adrasteia.'

'Adrasteia,' said Themis seriously. 'Please sit down a moment and let's think what to do.'

She sat down again and Themis pulled up another stool. 'I have two problems today, Adrasteia. I am concerned about Melissus and I want to find out where he is,' he said. 'But my other problem is that every time I try to leave the house I am followed by some doubtful characters who have decided I am very rich and need to be robbed or kidnapped. I want to ask a couple of influential people to keep an eye open for Melissus, but that means going out. Could you – er, would you? – lend me your clothes for a short time? I wouldn't be long.'

Adrasteia looked shocked for a moment. Then she sighed. 'At least we would be doing something that might help,' she said. 'Mrs Anthoussa has the old nurse with her today.' She stood up and turned to Frog. 'Who will lend me something to wear meanwhile?'

Themis left by the slaves' door, raising a hand to Mika, who stood and called, 'Goodbye, Adrasteia'. He had shaved his face and wore Adrasteia's hooded cloak pulled over his head, as if to ward off the midday sun. He carried a bundle and tried to walk like she did as he made for the main road towards the Akropolis. The melon-seed merchant watched him go.

By the time he arrived at the Archons' offices, he was more suitably dressed in his own short chiton and sandals.

Apollodorus came out to meet him. He seemed a little surprised by the lack of beard and the last vestiges of bruises but said nothing as they walked together to a small building beside the law courts. They talked amicably about the state of the harvest. A table and two chairs stood by a wall in the square room they entered. Once inside, with the door shut, Apollodorus turned to Themis.

'Did I understand you to say it's tonight?' He spoke quietly and his dark eyes glowed with enthusiasm.

'Yes,' said Themis. He took the heavy purse Hyllos had given him from his bundle and handed it to Apollodorus. 'This is the payment,' he said. 'It should go back into the city's coffers, as I'm pretty sure that's where it came from.'

Apollodorus weighed the bag of coins in his hand. 'A serious sum,' he said. 'I'll get you a receipt when we're done here. But tell me what you have to do to earn it.'

'I am to invade Zea Harbour from the depths of the sea!'

'Ah…' Apollodorus smiled and nodded. 'And how will that work?'

'I go on to the shore with the fishing boats, join two men in their boat. One has the same name as the man who found Damianos, by the way. They will take me out to near Zea Harbour mouth. There I slip over the side and pull a line in under the protecting net. I deliver the end of the line to someone just inside to the left, swim back to the boat without getting tangled in the net, and am carried to the shore to get the rest of my reward.'

Apollodorus had walked slowly to the other side of the room. He turned and said, 'Why?'

'I am assuming they will pull something into the harbour under the net with which to booby trap the triremes.'

Apollodorus nodded again. 'So. They'll be depending on our not believing that lightning can strike twice in the same place.'

Themis shivered as he remembered the words of Melissa's goddess.

'So simple!' Apollodorus went on, sighing happily. 'Sit down, Themis. We have plans to make.' And he went towards one of the chairs.

'But I don't think I'll be the only one,' said Themis.

'How not?'

'A man I know from swimming training and my supper club also seems to have received the same proposition. His name is Glykon. I couldn't get Hyllos to admit that he would be there too, but I'm pretty sure he will.'

'Did he tell you himself?'

'No, I haven't spoken to him. But I saw him leaving Hyllos' offices and then heard him boasting to a friend how rich he was going to be soon.'

'Could he be making a similar sortie into Mounichia Harbour where the other triremes are kept?'

Themis said, 'Of course! That would make sense.' He sat down.

Apollodorus spread out a plan and went on. 'But we'll be ready, and catch whomever receives the line, and anyone waiting for you at the shore. We'll send a detachment to Mounichia, too, and see what we find.'

Themis nodded. 'But no one must make any kind of move until the moment when I hand over the line,' he said. 'My own man will watch as I set off from the shore, but he won't do anything and will be invisible.'

'Don't worry. We'll be ready. At both harbours.' Apollodorus stood up and walked up and down rubbing his hands together. 'Information from other sources has made me expect something like this, but we were thinking it would be more complex. This could be an important day, Themistokles. I have a notion whom we will capture, and it would be the culmination of a long and tricky investigation.' He stopped in front of Themis. 'Thank you for taking this on. It's not going to be easy. The water is deep going into Zea.'

Themis took a deep breath and stood up. 'And now I have a small request you may be able to help with,' he said.

A cloud sped over Apollodorus' face and disappeared. 'Which is?'

'A young friend is missing,' said Themis. 'When I last saw him, he was dressed as the son of a citizen, though not a wealthy one. But in fact …' Themis only hesitated a moment. 'In fact "he" is a girl. Her name is Melissa, daughter of Agorakritos the sculptor, a metic with special priviledges. This is of course a deadly secret. She has long reddish-brown hair and green eyes. She has run away from Vravrona, where she is partway through the initiation course my mother is responsible for there.'

'Hah! An enterprising young woman,' said Apollodorus with a laugh. 'Is she by any chance betrothed to someone she doesn't like?'

Themis nodded. 'You are not surprised, then?'

'My own daughter tried it, as have many others. Surely your mother has encountered the problem before?'

'Perhaps, but not with quite such a … an intractable character.'

'I'll mention it to the Archers,' said Apollodorus. 'It's not you she's betrothed to, is it?'

Themis shook his head. 'No, thank the gods,' he said emphatically. 'Her father and I are old colleagues, that's all. And she's my mother's student, of course …'

'And who is the future husband?'

'Nereus, the prospective general.'

Apollodorus stepped back a little. 'Really?' he asked. 'Nereus, eh? He's an old … acquaintance of mine. He hasn't mentioned her to me. Hm … She'll be very rich,' he said with a laugh.

'If she can be found,' said Themis. A spasm gripped his stomach.

'I suppose she calls herself Melissus?' asked Apollodorus.

'Yes.'

'We'll get onto it.' He went to the door. 'And am I right in assuming you're being followed since you agreed to this outlandish wager?'

'Not this time. I came in disguise,' said Themis, holding up his bundle. 'But there was a melon-seed seller watching the house this morning, and a man dressed as a groom at dawn.'

'Well, next time you leave home, you may find that your follower has a follower of their own, but we'll be discreet and not declare ourselves till it's all over – and probably not then, either.'

Themis nodded his thanks as they walked out into the heat of the day.

Chapter 32: fishing

Themis reined the horse in at a narrow street corner on the east side of Mounichia Hill in Piraeus. Away to the northeast starlight gleamed here and there on pale walls and cliffs. Hardly a light was showing between the Long Walls that ran inland across the plain, except where they joined the great walls of Athena's city.

The three distant mountains, Parnitha, Pendelikon and Ymittos, formed a semi-circular barrier against the spangled sky on all sides except the sea.

The shapes of the buildings close by were indistinct and, now that the horse was still, all was silent. One light showed in an upstairs window.

'Did Adrasteia get home all right?' Themis said quietly as he slid down from in front of Frog.

'Yes. I saw her home. The old nurse was just leaving.'

'Thanks,' said Themis, looking all around. They seemed to have lost their follower, but Themis was not convinced. 'Did you see Anthoussa?'

'No. The house was very quiet, ' said Frog. 'I'd say she must be quite ill.'

Themis sighed. 'With any luck, I'll be able to go and see them tomorrow.' He beckoned Frog to dismount and spoke in his ear.

'I have to meet someone at the gate between the Long Walls. I want you to keep an eye on him. See where he goes when I've left on the boat.'

Frog nodded.

'But keep away from him. Don't want it assumed you're his associate!'

'Unlike you, who really are!' breathed Frog.

Themis laughed silently. He was very excited. 'Look, I'm not sure how this will end,' he whispered, 'so I won't expect to see you again tonight.'

'You want me to take the horse home?'

'Yes. I'll get back somehow to hear what you've learned.'

Frog remounted and walked the horse noisily away from Themis as if he was going to ride to the top of Mounichia Hill. Themis ran silently down through the steep, dark little streets to the gate.

He stood just outside it in the light of the torches. He was wearing his oldest cloak, with the hood off at the moment. A hooded man in a longer, smarter himation approached him.

'You're supposed to have a beard,' he said with irritation. 'Lukos and Linas are expecting you.' It was the voice of the man from the Vravrona tavern who'd been riding Sunny. Themis resisted an urge to pull back the hood and see the man's face.

'Swim faster with a smooth face,' Themis said. 'They ready to set off?'

'Follow me,' said the man, taking the road to the gate in the southern Long Wall that led to the shore where the fishermen beached their boats.

Themis was bouncing on his feet and felt as powerful as before a boxing tournament. 'Are they taking anyone else out with them?' he asked.

'Just you,' snapped the man.

They were approaching the gate. This was closed for the night, but a guard seemed to be expecting them and opened it for them immediately. The hooded man handed the guard something. The guard grunted. Themis had pulled up his own hood and kept his face in its shadow.

Once through, they were on the small flat plain that was bordered by the sea ahead and the wall behind. Themis deliberately slowed down.

'Come on!' said his companion. 'No pulling out now!'

Themis heard the gate open behind them. He bent down to adjust his sandal and managed a glimpse back. Two men were following them on the main road, and he saw two other men emerge separately from buildings under the wall. Otherwise there was no one around in this gloomy area of small houses and sheds.

As they neared the straggling jumble of warehouses and waterside shops by the shore, however, they could hear raised voices and the sounds of rope slapping and wood on shingle. The smells of fish and smoke enveloped them in the suddenly busy night.

There were thirty or more small boats, black against the lighter pebbles or floating on the uneasy sheen of the sea. Most of them had two or three men clambering on and around them, preparing for the night's fishing. His companion gestured for him to go forward. He went over to the nearest man and asked quietly for Lukos and Linas.

'They're on the Seahorse,' said the man. 'You their third tonight?'

'Yeah,' said Themis. 'Are there fish?'

'Poseidon knows! Conditions are good, though. Slight breeze to stir the surface but not enough to send them to the depths.'

'May the gods give you a good catch!' whispered Themis as he made for a boat leaving the shore while raising a pale sail with a dark seahorse on.

The hooded man in the good cloak crunched across the pebbles to Themis. 'Better hurry,' he said. 'They're leaving without you.'

Themis whistled quietly and the two men on the boat turned and beckoned. He waded in and climbed aboard, setting the Seahorse rearing and dipping.

'Ah, our merman,' said the larger of the two men. Themis smelt wood smoke as well as fish on his clothes. 'Late,' said the other man, who stank of fish, and only fish.

'Thanks for waiting,' said Themis as he took off his tattered cloak. Other boats were pulling up sails now and they were in a group of fifteen or so heading south with the wind filling their sails from the northwest. Themis looked back at the shore and lifted a hand. The hooded man turned away. There was no sign of Frog, of course. But

Themis could still see the two men who had come through the gate. One headed for a boat at the other end of the shore. The other dissolved into the shadow of the wall.

'If you want to be over by the harbours,' said the smoky man. 'We'll have to tack.'

'Earn our money tonight,' muttered the other. 'You'd better get to work on that net, merman. Make it look like you know what you're doing.'

Themis stripped off his chiton and adjusted his belt and loincloth. Then he sat on a gunwale to unravel the top edge of the net that was heaped in the bottom of the boat.

'You scared something might nip your dog?' said the larger man as he brought the boat round on its next tack, gesturing at Themis' unusually well protected genitals.

Themis looked up at him with a wry smile. 'Once bitten, twice shy,' he said. He had noticed the men were naked under their stinking tunics.

The breeze was hardly moving them, so the larger man handed the sail ropes to the other, set an oar in the stern rowlock and began to skull. They moved slowly across the bay towards the high walls and cliffs of the peninsula of Piraeus. Other boats fanned out, most heading for open water. Themis noticed one with an egret on the sail, keeping close in, almost parallel with the great walls between the mouths of Zea and Mounichia harbours.

'Strange business, that with Damianos,' Themis said to the oarsman.

The man gestured to the east. 'Yeah. Found him floating over that way. Just his back showing, like a seal.'

'No wounds?'

'Nothing I could see. Delivered him to the Scythians. Friend of yours?'

Themis shook his head. 'Nah. I don't mix with the likes of him.'

He had the net almost ready now. The smaller man said, 'Eh, Lukos. The buoy's here. Keep her steady.'

Themis stood up. 'What buoy?' he asked.

Lukos shipped the oar and reached into the water. He lifted a thin rope from the buoy, flicked its knot undone and presented it to Themis. 'All yours, merman,' he said.

The fishy man (presumably Linas) snorted and pulled the ropes to bring the boom across on another tack.

The sail came snapping over and Themis only just avoided being cracked on the head as he tied the rope around his waist.

A few moments later, Lukos leaned down in a whiff of burned pine and said quietly in Themis' ear, 'This is just about the nearest we'll get to Zea's mouth. I've got us out ahead of all the others. You can go over the bow out of their sight here.'

Themis looked around. The Egret was not far behind them, just slipping behind Stalis Island as though heading for the smaller harbour, under Mounichia Hill. All the other boats were some distance away. He nodded. 'Ready,' he said.

As Lukos held the boat steady, he slid into the water without a sound. It was cool, but not cold. He took a deep breath, turned his face towards the great walls, and dived.

The water was clear. The starlight reached down a foot or two. It gleamed and flickered on the backs of hundreds of silver and black striped fish. None of them touched him, in spite of their huge numbers.

Themis estimated he'd have to surface four times before he got to the dangerous area. Each time he did, he stayed still in the water so as not to disturb the surface, and breathed three times before he went on. The walls looked twice as high as they did from his rowing bench on a trireme.

He stayed in the middle of the channel. As he came up to breathe between the two great buttresses at the outer harbour mouth, he looked at the guards up on the wall. None of them seemed to have noticed his slowly rising head although they were looking in his direction. Perhaps they were focused on the further horizon or thought his wet head was just a seal. He kept his newly pale face bent towards the water while he took a longer series of breaths. There was no sign of the hooded man, but then he would be waiting at the inner mouth by now. Themis sank quietly into the world of flickering fish, and swam on.

He came to where the ropes were stretched across from tower to tower under the water. He surfaced cautiously, knowing his burning lungs would not allow him to do the deep dive under the net without more air. The rope round his waist was thin and light. It had caused no problems so far, but now seemed to be quite taut.

He checked all round and saw no sign that anyone had seen him. He took three deep breaths, relaxed his muscles, took one more and dived.

He had to feel for the bottom rope as it was completely dark down there. With his hands out in front of him, he found it and slid under it, but the rope he was trailing was now very tight. It was not long enough to allow him to surface again without untying it. He pulled hard on it in case it was caught somewhere on the seabed. Bubbles rose from his mouth with the effort. It didn't move.

He yanked at it again, then tried to untie it. But wet rope in the dark is not easy to loosen. He could feel the beginning of the burning in his lungs. He would have to go back under the bottom rope. As he turned something gave. He was suddenly free and surfaced faster than he liked inside the harbour. He prayed the guards were still more interested in the horizon.

The last foot of water flashed by and he took a breath. He was back under the water in a count of five, swimming to his left. He found himself in three feet of translucent water with the foundations of the great walls rising in front of him. He kept further left in the shadows right under the wall. The water lapped on a deep step. He pulled himself quietly onto the underwater shelf along the bottom of the wall. He could see no one. He sat with his back to the wall and untied the thin rope under the surface. The square, dark mouths of the ship sheds stretched away from him round the curve of the harbour. He'd never seen them from this angle before. Their painted eyes glared and their bronze rams gleamed dully. '*Dragons in kennels,*' he thought.

He could hear a group of men talking in the ship shed nearest his part of the wall. Between hammerings and curses, they were discussing the advantages of goatskin over pigskin for containing wine. They must be a detail of trireme repairers and there were at least five of them. He had no weapon.

But nothing happened. His teeth began to chatter. He bit on a finger to silence them. '*Is this right? Should I leave?*' he thought. Was he visible in the starlight? If he was found here by anyone other than his contact, he would be arrested and tried for treason as Frog had predicted. He slid silently back into the dark water.

Then he heard a voice say, 'I wonder, does the starlight reach the bottom? What do you think?'

Another voice, very near now but still invisible, said, 'Why don't you go for a swim and see?'

And suddenly there were four men on the slip between the ship shed and the water's edge. None of them was the hooded man.

'Where shall I go from?' said the first man. 'Over there by the entry tower?' And he came striding towards Themis.

Themis raised himself a little out of the water, holding the rope hidden but ready.

'Do you have something for me?' asked the man as he approached the base of the wall.

'Ask me again,' said Themis quietly.

'Does the starlight reach the bottom?' said the man. Themis lifted the end of the thin rope and gave it to him. Drops fell from it, briefly gleaming.

The man with the hood appeared from nowhere. Was he the Benefactor after all? 'Congratulations, merman,' he said quietly. 'Our friend's wager is won. You can go and I'll visit you tomorrow.'

Themis raised a hand, took a breath and dived deep. He would recognize the hooded man's voice and a couple of the others if he heard them again, but the whole point had been the hope of coming face to face with the Benefactor. He was disappointed, though not surprised.

Meanwhile, if he found out what the rope was tied to, he could still learn more. So he took loose hold of the thin rope as he swam down and down, under the net.

He surfaced again carefully beyond the net, and then set off along the rope, keeping it running through his hand and staying as close to the bottom as he could.

While he was still under the watchtowers, the rope went taut as someone began to pull it. He let it move towards the harbour through his hands. He could feel the puller's impatience to get whatever was tied to the other end. He almost lost it when his hand delayed a large knot from slipping by. This second length of rope was much thicker.

He kept swimming along it, deep under the surface, out into the bay, his hand now sliding easily as its tension increased.

Suddenly it went slack. He gave a gentle pull towards the harbour. The rope came towards him. He gave another, and more came towards him. Whoever had been pulling on it had let go for some reason. He thought he heard a whistle in the air above.

'*They've either cut it or dropped it. Maybe they've been caught,*' he thought.

He surfaced and pulled the thin end of the rope in, coiling it as he trod water. The breeze had strengthened and the sea had little waves now. He would be less visible. And he could hear a commotion in the harbour, so no one would be looking for him out here.

There was no sign of the Seahorse. '*They must have heard the noises and left me to the fishes,*' he thought. '*Or maybe they never meant to stay.*'

With the thin rope coiled round his elbow, he swam for the buoy where he tied it on, and added his loincloth to identify it. The fishing boats were a long way out now. He rested at the buoy, considering whether to explore the other end of the rope now or in daylight.

'What might be there?' he asked himself. 'Some kind of rotting agent, maybe. Or a barrel of wood-eating worms?' He smiled grimly, took a deep breath and dived through a shoal of fish.

Back down in the flickering blackness, the rope ran between two rocks. This was where it had snagged.

From there, it slanted steeply to the blackness of the bottom. He felt his way down it and found something that was not a rock. It felt like a coarse- meshed net round a large wooden chest. The chest was under an overhanging roof in a shallow cave. It was difficult to be sure in the dark how big the cave was, but the rock it was in was deeper down than the height of three men. So it wouldn't have been a hazard to ships. He got a hold on the net to see if it would move. It seemed to give a little, but was too heavy for him to lift. He went for a stronger hold, but his hand fell on the soft body of an octopus in the dark, giving them both a fright. The octopus must have sped off because Themis felt no eight-armed embrace.

'You would have been dinner if it wasn't so dark,' he told the octopus silently as he surfaced, heart hammering. He decided there was nothing he could do about the heavy chest. *The Archon's men will have to salvage it themselves in daylight,*' he thought, and swam back to the buoy on the surface, careful not to splash.

At the buoy, he stopped long enough to hear that things were still noisy in the harbour. The sounds travelled clearly across the water. Then he struck out at a leisurely pace for the shore, wondering what he had left in the depths of the bay.

As he neared the beach, he saw three mules on the shingle in the starlight. They were harnessed to carts, ready to pull catches of fish into the city when the boats came back. Behind them was a man with a horse.

Wearily, Themis waded out of the sea. The man led the horse down to the water's edge.

'Dogfish got your pouch?' asked Frog, as he threw a blanket over Themis' naked torso. 'I hired this one. Parilios might be recognised.'

'Thank the gods you did,' Themis said through chattering teeth.

'Lost your man almost immediately in the dark. Later heard the Archers catching their men,' Frog said as he helped Themis dry himself. 'Seems you did what you set out to do, even if you did lose a garment or two.'

Themis chuckled as he put on the chiton Frog held out. 'Certainly did!'

'Come on,' said Frog, offering his cupped hands as a stirrup. 'Probably a good idea if we get out of here fast.'

Themis mounted, then hauled Frog up behind. 'Got any of that sweet wine you're addicted to?'

A small leather flask appeared over Themis' shoulder, as they set off for the city at a trot. Themis was looking forward to reporting back this time.

Half way through the village of Kili, where the sound of hooves was louder on the paved road, a cart blocked their way. Frog dismounted and walked ahead to speak to the driver. Two men in black cloaks appeared silently from alleyways on either side of the road. They converged on Themis, and before he even understood the threat, he was pulled off the horse, his mouth was stuffed with a cloth and a net was thrown over his head. He struggled to free himself, making muffled shouts.

There was a thud and he lost consciousness.

Chapter 33: betrayals

(Breeds of Sheep 21)

When he came round, Themis found himself in a room with a painted ceiling. He was no longer gagged, and there was no sign of the net. He sat up gingerly. His head was bruised but not badly. He looked around.

This was a very fine house, and he was sitting in a large room on a soft couch. The double door was guarded by two uniformed archers. On the low table in front of him were water and a bowl of fruit. He shook his head in disbelief. It didn't hurt. One of the guards opened the door a little, nodded to someone beyond it, then closed it again.

Themis fingered the bruise in his hair. No blood. He wondered whether this was the home of the 'Benefactor'. He said to the guards, 'Water but no wine? Our host is being uncharacteristically parsimonious.'

The guards made no move or sound. '*Not helpful*,' Themis thought as he swung his legs off the couch and poured himself a cup of water. He sniffed it, and then drank. He was very thirsty.

'Seen my slave, either of you?' he asked. The guards remained silent.

The door opened and a man came in. It was Apollodorus! Themis stood up, his jaw slack with surprise.

'My apologies for abducting you,' said Apollodorus with a shrug and a grin. 'You were being followed and my agents felt we couldn't risk your being caught.'

'What about Frog, my slave,' said Themis in alarm.

'Oh, we got him too,' said Apollodorus with a laugh. 'He's eaten a whole chicken while you've been … er … asleep. If you hadn't made so much noise my men wouldn't have knocked you out.'

Themis sighed. 'We were on our way to see you,' he said.

'Of course,' said the Archon. 'So we had to make sure they didn't discover that.' He sat on a couch at right angles to Themis' and gestured that he should sit, too. 'Frustratingly, we do not seem to have got the main man, or evidence of who he is – so far. But now you are going to tell me all you learned, then have a meal, be re-wrapped in your net and dumped in a questionable part of town to recover your senses and stumble home.' His dark, deep-set eyes were unusually wide open and direct.

Themis smiled and sat down.

In the chill of dawn, they rolled him off the back of the cart into the drain of a back street near the Sacred Way outside the city wall. This was where the poor sold scraps from the trash heaps of the ceramics factories, and even the dogs were thin. Frog had gone home in the back of an elegant weaver's cart, under a layer of scented linen.

Themis hardly dared breathe in for the stench. He was pretending to come round from a drunken stupor. He peeled off the now damp and filthy net. His chiton was hardly less disgusting. He shrugged and made his way to the nearest spring.

'You want to poison us all with your filth?' an old woman screamed at him as he crouched to let the flow from the stone ram's mouth pour over him. He took no notice and rubbed energetically at the dirt on his garment and the salt in his hair. Then, dripping and shivering, he made for the Dipylon Gate at a run, and so into the City with the dawn crowds.

The tombs of the great (but not always good) lined the way to the Agora. Rows of decorated steles stood like teeth nibbling at the brightening skyline. He smiled as he passed the tomb of a friend of Phidias. The stele was carved with a relief of a man waving goodbye to his family. This had been Themis' own first assignment in Phidias' sculpture yard. He'd been thirteen. The movement in the carving of the robe and the tilt of the noble head still pleased him.

As did the memory of his interview with Apollodorus. The arrests in the night included the hooded man, two of the men from the ship sheds, and later the two fishermen. The hooded man had left the harbour before all the others and an archer had followed him to a private house. There they had arrested a further three men, and one of them seemed to be Persian.

Glykon, meanwhile, had been caught swimming out of Mounichia Harbour, but he had been released as there was no evidence that it had been he who brought a second rope to the waiting conspirators there. He had been one of three young men out swimming near Stalis Island, and they had all sworn they were competing with each other after an evening of drinking. Two men had also been arrested in Mounichia Harbour. Glykon must have delivered his rope to them, and they would probably give evidence of his presence there. But the rope itself, though seen during the arrest, had disappeared.

Themis had offered to show the investigators where the chest he'd found was himself. But Apollodorus felt that would advertise his working with the authorities. This might result in his 'disappearance' at the hands of the gang. So Themis had drawn a map of the position of the buoy he'd marked and where the chest was in relation to it. The Archon had sent for divers before Themis had left.

Now traffic into the Agora was heavy. Themis slipped between two carts as he turned off to the left, towards the Hungry Bear. This tavern had been a favourite eating place of Themis' Uncle Panainos. It backed onto the somewhat unhygienic Eridanos river and had survived somehow through the plagues and sieges of the last fourteen years. Apollodorus had given him a few obols to buy food on his way home and his chiton was beginning to dry. He felt it was a very fine day.

As he loped towards the tavern, past the Painted Arcade, he noticed a group of young men sitting on the steps. They were earnestly debating around Sokrates. Themis slowed to hear the conversation.

'In that case,' Sokrates was saying, 'is loyalty to your family the same as loyalty to your city?'

A boy with his back to Themis answered. 'Not at all!'

The hair on Themis' forearms rose. He knew that voice. It went on, 'If your city is threatened, the whole fabric of your life is in jeopardy – the place itself, the society you belong to, your friends and your very life – you have to try to protect it. But if only your family is threatened – or threatening – you can turn elsewhere for your survival.'

'So for you, Melissus,' said Sokrates, 'Loyalty is based on the practicalities of survival?'

'Of course,' said Melissus. 'Most abstract ideas are to do with staying alive.'

The other young men murmured, some shaking their heads, some nodding.

Themis stood irresolute. He couldn't very well grab Melissa without causing uproar. But he couldn't let her slip away again either. Anthoussa, and also Apollodorus the Archon, would never forgive him. Apollodorus wanted Melissus to be found so he/she could identify the Persian as the man Hyllos was talking to. Themis quietly sat down behind her, close enough to touch her. She smelled of the stale urine used by the leather tanners, with undertones of cedar and … was that pigshit?

What with trying to work out how to speak to her without her running off, and his body's acute awareness of her nearness in spite of the stench, he missed most of the debate on loyalty. He focused again when he heard Sokrates say to the whole group, 'So betrayal is the opposite of loyalty?'

Melissus raised his voice again above the thoughtful murmurs. 'Not exactly. You can only be betrayed by someone who knows you are loyal to them. If you have never told them or sworn to them that you are loyal, then it's your own fault if they behave in a way that harms or hurts you.'

Another voice added, 'In that case, they wouldn't know they are betraying you so you couldn't really call it betrayal. But sometimes loyalty is implicit in your relationship with someone – as within a family, or as a soldier in an army, for instance – then betrayal *is* possible even without your having specifically declared loyalty to them.'

'You make a clear point, my friends' said Sokrates. 'Loyalty can be declared and undeclared, and each must be considered separately. Which in your experience is the more binding?'

Themis had decided what to do. He sat cross-legged behind Melissus and wrote with his finger in the dust on the marble paving to her left side, 'Persian caught. You identify?' Melissus was so intent upon the discussion that he didn't notice until Themis pulled gently on his sleeve. Melissus half turned with a frown. His eyes widened in anger when he saw Themis, but he relaxed a little when he saw the message in the dust.

After a moment's thought, he turned to look at Sokrates. There was a lull in the discussion and Melissus stood up. 'Excuse me, Sokrates,' he said bowing his head respectfully. Then he looked round at the seated young men and said with an impish smile, 'I have just been asked to prove my loyalty, so I'll have to leave the discussion for a while.'

Sokrates looked at Themis with a small silent nod of recognition, while the others all laughed. 'Go to the good,' he said, turning to Melissus. 'Come and find me – whenever you can.'

Themis heard Sokrates' emphasis on those last words and guessed that he knew Melissus was Melissa, and so unlikely to return.

They walked through the busy Agora in silence until they were out of earshot. Then, looking straight ahead at the Akropolis, Melissa said fiercely, 'Don't try to make me go back!'

'I can't make you,' said Themis. 'But I hope you will think about it when we've dealt with this.' He looked sideways and down at her.

Melissa's jaw was set. 'No chance,' she said, in the slang of the street. She stopped suddenly and said, 'Where are we going?'

Themis smiled. 'Relax,' he said. 'I'm won't kidnap you. We'll start with Apollodorus' office and see from there. Probably to the prison …'

'But we both stink,' said Melissus. 'I doubt the Archon will let us in.'

In his airy office, Apollodorus, who pointedly ignored their filth, said to Melissus, 'I understand that you are clever at drawing. Could you draw the Persian man you saw speaking to Hyllos?'

Melissus was suspicious, although Apollodorus had spoken to him exactly as if he was a boy. 'Most of my drawing stuff is in Vravrona.'

'We have papyrus or tablets here, whichever you prefer.'

Apollodorus gestured towards the open door into an inner courtyard. 'You can work there.' He turned to Themis. 'And perhaps you can give us some visual idea of the men you encountered. I'd like to have evidence that the organizer you met is among the men we arrested at the scene.'

Melissus looked sharply at Themis. 'What happened?' he asked fiercely. 'You didn't tell me anyone had been arrested.'

Apollodorus ushered them both into the courtyard. 'We are trying to keep it quiet for now,' he said. 'But last night another attempt was made to infiltrate the naval harbours. Themistokles had volunteered to be part of the infiltrating team as a spy.'

For a moment, Melissus' face glowed with affection as he looked up at Themis. 'Still trying to clear Photios' name?' he whispered. 'That's loyalty!'

Themis nodded. 'Ye-es. But mainly trying to learn who the real traitor is – and perhaps find any "smoking lightning",' he added.

Melissus' face hardened again. 'In case I was talking rubbish?' he asked.

Apollodorus frowned, but Themis replied immediately. 'You know I believe you, Melissus. It was one of the reasons I agreed to do this.'

'So what exactly did you do?' asked Melissus.

'He can tell you about it another time,' said Apollodorus. 'Just now I need to have your drawings as soon as possible, so as to proceed with the courts today. Please don't write anything on them. If any of them are in the jail, you can tell me later exactly where you first saw them.'

Themis and Melissus sat side by side and drew on the papyrus that Apollodorus' scribe gave them. Themis drew the face of the hooded man as best he could, and the man who took the rope from him. He also drew Linas and Lukos. Melissus' drawing of the Persian and Hyllos talking was more detailed.

When they'd finished, Apollodorus said, 'I'll have these taken to the jail at once. Go and get some food and come back soon so we can check who each man is.'

'Fancy some breakfast?' asked Themis.

Melissus looked at him stonily. 'Food, yes,' he said. 'Lectures, no.'

'Just food,' said Themis. 'I haven't eaten properly since yesterday midday, and I have been quite busy.'

They left Apollodorus' office and went out into the Agora.

As they walked, Melissus asked, 'What were you doing last night? Was it to do with the merman, or dolphins?'

They were among the stalls along the east side of the Agora now. 'We can talk about that later,' Themis said quietly. 'We are probably being followed now, so let's talk about something else.'

'No,' said Melissus. They had stopped under the awning of a bakery. 'I know what you want to talk about and I'm not going to. Let's just eat. Oh, and clean up a bit.'

When they got back, still awkwardly silent, the Archon called them into a different office and closed the door. The windows were shuttered, so two lamps were burning and individual chairs were set out round a low table covered in maps.

'Sit down, sit down,' he said, quietly opening the papyrus rolls he had brought in.

Melissus sat like a man, legs apart. He was wearing canvas trousers and a close fitting but battered cap covering his hair.

Themis sat down beside him. All the faces he and Melissus had drawn were marked 'Yes'.

'So the Persian *was* my Persian,' said Melissus.

Apollodorus nodded. 'And these, Themistokles? Who are they?'

'This one,' said Themis, 'is the man whom I followed that night from Vravrona. He wore a hood last night and was my "handler".'

'His name is Tydeus,' said Apollodorus. 'And the others?'

'I hadn't seen this one before. He was the man who took the rope from me. The other two are the fishermen on the Seahorse. I doubt they knew what was going on at all, even though Lukos was the man who found Damianos' body. I asked him about it.'

'Fishermen?' exclaimed Melissus.

Themis shook his head slightly at the boy and asked Apollodorus, 'So, are we any nearer knowing who was behind this business? We still don't know who the Benefactor is?'

Apollodorus shook his head. 'Not yet. But the men in prison may well be persuaded to tell us… and we've let the fishermen go but we're following them in case they lead us to others in the gang.'

'Who is us?' asked Melissus pointedly ignoring Themis.

Apollodorus was rolling up the scrolls, nodding slowly. 'Hmm. Please excuse me a moment,' he said, and left the room.

'So what happened?' Melissus was impatient. 'What were they all doing?' When Themis didn't answer immediately, he jumped up from his chair with an exasperated glance at Themis and bent to examine the maps.

Themis stood up and bent over the table next to Melissus. He spoke close to his ear. 'Last night I was employed by a group of men to sabotage Zea Harbour. As he said, the Archon knew about it and his men kept watch. Your report on the meeting between Hyllos and the Persian helped us to learn more. It'll be common knowledge soon that the attempt was made and foiled, but no one is supposed to know that I was involved, so never mention that to anyone.' He laid a hand on Melissus' shoulder. 'All right? Never. It could cost me my life.'

'All right.' Melissus nodded seriously but excitedly. 'And were they going to try burning the ships again? Were you a merman? Was it "the smoking lightning" from the sea?'

Apollodorus came back in before Themis could speak. He answered Melissus' questions. 'Themistokles marked a buoy that was near a chest hidden in the depths of the bay. It seems they were going to pull the chest into the harbour under the security net.' He turned to Themis.

'We have been diving for it all morning. If we could find it, we'd know what they were planning. But we haven't yet.' He started opening the shutters. Sunlight bounced off the white marble floor and flooded the room.

Melissus shook his head and shrugged. 'I have no idea what you're talking about, and of course I won't say anything. But I'm glad I could help a bit, and it sounds like the warning I got was right.'

Apollodorus was looking at Melissus speculatively. 'I can't confirm anything, of course,' he said, 'but now, I hope you'll sit down and consider helping us in another way.'

Chapter 34: going back

Melissus looked up at Apollodorus, then at Themis. Themis nodded slightly, so the 'boy' sat down.

'Now, from what I understand,' Apollodorus began, 'you're pretty good at keeping secrets, Melissus.'

Melissus looked at him steadily with a slight frown.

'So firstly,' the Archon went on, 'I want you both to behave as if last night's incident did not happen. Show no interest in any trial. Do not, Themistokles, appear in the Assembly that will probably be called. Be surprised when anyone, anyone at all, mentions it. But note who does.'

Themis and Melissus looked at each other. Then Themis said to Apollodorus, 'As you wish, Archon.' Melissus nodded curtly.

Apollodorus then said, 'Secondly, I'm afraid that your own secret, Melissus, is in danger of being betrayed by the shape of your body and the smoothness of your face.'

Melissus' smooth face went pale. He stood up and looked desperately around the room.

'I sympathise,' said Apollodorus. 'I really do. However, even if you could get out of this room, there's no escape in the long run, you know.'

Melissus turned and glared at him.

He went on, 'You have been a help with this incident and even as a woman, you could easily be a help in the future. Married to Nereus, you would have power over many issues, both by influencing him and due to your own elevated position in society.'

Melissus was rolling his eyes, not looking at either of them. Apollodorus' voice had a new, harder edge when he said, with slow emphasis, 'I want you to go back to Vravrona.'

Melissus looked at the floor, his jaw clenched and his breathing heavy. Apollodorus looked at Themis with a rueful shrug. Themis nodded slightly to him. Apollodorus touched Melissus' shoulder and said in a kinder voice, 'While you are there, discuss the worst and the best things about being female with your tutors. If you divide the problem up into smaller pieces, it will seem more manageable.'

Melissus turned to the two men with a proud tilt to his head. 'The problem cannot be divided up. It is purely that I will not spend my life spinning and gossiping and married to Nereus. He is an arrogant, shrivel-hearted man, whatever my father thinks of him, whatever you tell me about him, however rich he is. One of his closest friends is Kallias, and we know what that means! I've learned this from his slaves, and people who know the criminals he secretly associates with. Being an unmarried woman is bad, but not as bad at that would be. I will find a way to avoid this marriage, even if it kills me. I know that it's not meant to be.'

Apollodorus turned to Themis, 'Do *you* have any influence with either Agorakritos or Nereus?'

'None,' Themis said. 'Agorakritos has taken against me lately and accuses me of adultery with his wife. Nereus tried to manipulate me into some scheme of his and failed, so I doubt he would even speak to me. Has your investigation of him and his activities had no results?'

'Nothing as yet. He mixes with all kinds of people, some of them a little dubious, but no one as yet that we can say is a criminal. He's a very effective, energetic man in many ways.' Apollodorus seemed loath to think badly of Nereus. He turned to Melissa. 'Melissa, please listen to me.'

Melissus looked up at him coldly.

'I want you to return to Vravrona. If, as you say, Nereus is corrupt, you could disclose his crimes once you were sure of them from your position as his wife.'

Melissus looked at the Archon pityingly. 'You know that evidence given by a wife isn't considered trustworthy. There is no way that any Athenian court would convict such a "pillar of the community" on that alone.'

Apollodorus sighed. 'Perhaps you have a point. In that case, if our investigations show that Nereus is a criminal, I will personally find a way out of the agreement your father has made with him. Meanwhile, as I have known Nereus a long time, I shall suggest to him that he will be very unhappy with someone who is determined to hate him.'

Melissus shook his head in disbelief. 'That won't do any good at all,' he said. 'It'll just be a challenge! He'll marry me and then beat me.'

Apollodorus ignored this and went on, 'But whatever the outcome, I want you to know that you are not the only girl of your age who has been in this predicament, nor the only one who has run away to avoid a marriage she thought was going to be unhappy. In my experience, these girls, once they accept their position and turn their energies to being a proper wife and raising a family, are thoroughly content.'

Melissus held his eyes with a cold green stare. 'You are a free man,' he said. 'You have not heard the stories I have heard. You cannot possibly understand what it means to be a "proper" wife.'

'Will you go back to Mrs Eirini if we promise to try and get you out of this engagement to Nereus?' Apollodorus was almost weedling.

Melissus was looking at the floor again and seemed not to hear him. When he looked up, his eyes had filled with angry tears. 'If Uncle Themis will take me home and then to Vravrona, I will go.' He dashed the tears away, leaving dirty streaks on his face. 'But one day, if my engagement to Nereus is not called off, you'll remember this conversation.'

At the door to Melissa's home, they knocked and waited. Themis asked, 'Was it a god's voice? What did it say?'

Melissus looked up at him. 'Goddess. She said, "Give way now. Give way, and the road forward will appear."'

'Would you like me to come in with you?'

'I'm not afraid of my father,' she said. 'I just think he's obsessed with some sick ideas. Anyway, he's probably out. But if you did come in, it would be worse than if you didn't. So thanks, but no, don't bother.'

Themis sighed. Still no one opened the door. 'Is it locked?' he asked.

'Not usually,' said Melissus and tried it. It was locked. 'I have other ways in, of course,' he said.

Just then, someone drew back a bolt and the door opened. It was Skopas, frowning with worry. The frown was replaced by exasperation on his young face.

'Where on earth have you been?' he said. 'Mother isn't well and the slaves are taking over.'

'Where's Father?' asked Melissus, striding in.

'At the yard,' said Skopas. 'And I'm supposed to be at lessons, but Mother asked me to stay till he gets back.' He looked a question at

Themis.

'Uncle Themis is just leaving,' said Melissus over his shoulder.

'I'll come back tomorrow morning and collect you,' said Themis. 'I promised I'd take you to Vravrona and I will, assuming your father allows me to.' He turned to Skopas as Melissus disappeared into the house. 'Can I do anything to help your mother?'

'I doubt it,' said Skopas. 'But I'll ask her and let you know.'

'Thanks,' Themis said. He added, 'Tell Melissa I'll come for her a little after dawn.'

Skopas nodded and shut the door.

'Skopas wasn't surprised, so he must know about her dual life,' Themis thought as he walked away. He turned back hoping to see Anthoussa or her slave at the only window looking into the street. It was empty, but he glimpsed a figure looking over the low wall that edged the roof, black against the sunset sky. It disappeared before he could see who it was.

Next morning, Agorakritos was at the door when Themis turned into the street riding Parilios. Frog was following him, driving a small mule cart, in which sat Yellow as though on a throne. Agorakritos stood beside his house herm, his hand on the crown of its perfect stone curls.

'I'm sending Adrasteia with you. Leila is no longer ours,' he said, his voice harsh, his face sour under the beard. 'Please be kind enough to escort her back here on your return.'

Themis dismounted slowly. 'Stupid of me not to think of that myself,' he said pleasantly. He'd spent the night cursing himself for agreeing to this trip at all. It was clear to him that he needed to stay away from Melissa. By dawn he'd decided to ask a matchmaker to find him a quiet, 'suitable' wife as soon as possible. Now he said apologetically, 'My cart is too small for two passengers and luggage. Could you lend us a horse or a mule?'

Agorakritos snorted. 'Ha! Adrasteia will walk,' he said, and called out, 'Are you ready, Melissa?'

Adrasteia came out, carrying a large and a small bag. Melissa followed her. Her hair was braided and bound. She'd been crying but was holding her head proudly now. She was wearing a fine, plain linen peplos, belted with a wide woven sash. Themis was amazed to see that her small breasts stood high and firm under it. He'd never even noticed she had breasts before. He looked away quickly.

Melissa turned to her father. 'Please take care of Mother,' she said calmly. 'Listen to her, believe her. She needs kindness now. She has been more than kind to us all and is the best mother anyone could have.'

Themis saw conflict in Agorakritos' face. With his jaw jutting, he said, 'As you made such a fuss, I am forced to trust Themistokles to take you back to Vravrona. But I'll be there to fetch you back in two months' time.'

Melissa grabbed one of his hands and said earnestly, looking directly into his face, 'You used to be such a dear man, and you taught me so much and allowed me to learn so much more in my freedom.' Tears ran down her cheeks. Her father looked at the sky. 'You may yet lose faith in me, but you must never lose faith in Mama, or Uncle Themis. Even if you won't wish me "good journey", I say to you "be well until I return".'

She let go of her father's hand, brushed the tears from her face, and said to Adrasteia, 'You get in the cart with the bags. I'll walk for a bit.'

Themis shook his head. 'Not while we're in the city, Melissa. We can all walk once we're among the farms.'

Melissa smiled a false smile at Themis. 'Of course,' she said. 'What *would* people say?'

'Out, Yellow!' Themis ordered and Melissa climbed into the cart. Adrasteia put the bags in beside her and stood behind. Themis remounted Parilios and nodded to Agorakritos. 'My greetings to Anthoussa and the children,' he said. 'And for what it's worth, my wishes for your own recovery from this … unhappy state.'

Frog said, 'Walk on,' to the mule and the little procession set off down the busy street. Agorakritos went straight back into the house.

As they turned the corner, Themis looked back. Among the people in the street there were two mounted men. He thought either or both could be following him. And on the roof of the house, three children were waving. Melissa waved back with a falsely cheerful smile.

>>>

'Cassie?' Suzanne said into her phone.

'Hey, Suzanne! Great to hear from you.'

'I've just heard I've been refused for that training camp the university are arranging in July. They say there aren't enough places for us all. Are you running any special training days, or could you help me keep fit if I come home and work on my own?'

'You're way beyond our levels now, girl,' said Cassie proudly. 'I'll look around for something more helpful. Our next pole vaulting star deserves the best. I'll get back to you.'

'Got to get a job, too, over the summer. I'm totally broke.'

'Ok. I'll be in touch. Keep lifting that pole.'

Suzanne's day seemed brighter as she closed the call. Keir had probably made sure she lost the free training place, but it looked like he wasn't going to ruin her programme, after all.

Chapter 35: Eros

(Breeds of Sheep 22 – Just loving the way everyone is self-confident and not worrying what other people say about them. No Twitter in those days, of course. Jealousy and trolling by Internet *feels* dangerous, though you can always switch off. But jealousy in person – how do you switch that off?)

<<<

They stopped for a meal around noon. There had been little scope for talk or song due to a lot of heavy goods traffic on the road. They were still some way from the town of Paiania on the River Erasinos, which was half way, but a pleasantly shady shrine by a single waterspout gave them a chance to get out of the dust and heat of the road for a while.

When they'd settled themselves in some shade, they noticed clouds building from the north, streaming from the summit of Mount Pentelikon.

'Are they going to catch us?' asked Melissa as she sat by the shrine and bit into her second cheese and honey bun.

Frog chanted, 'Need to be there before the night, / In time for evening offerings. / Or all the doors will be locked up tight / And long and wet our sufferings.'

Adrasteia looked apprehensive.

Themis said, 'Don't worry, Adrasteia. I suggest that you ride in the cart while Melissa drives. Frog can travel up behind me, and Yellow can run alongside. That way we should manage a trot or even a canter now and then.' He was looking at a man on a black horse who was just dismounting under some trees on the other side of the road. '*Not Tydeus, who's under arrest in the City,*' he thought. '*Perhaps the man he was talking to in Vravrona?*'

Melissa swallowed her mouthful and shook her head. 'No way can I drive that beast,' she said. 'I've watched it trying to pull the cart off the road every time a horse gets too near.'

Frog looked at Themis over his bread and olives and said, 'I suggest you take Miss Melissa up behind you. She's lighter. And that mule really can be a problem sometimes.'

Themis said, 'But she is not dressed for riding. Imagine what my mother will say if she arrives on a horse.'

Frog made a comic face and Melissa said, 'Since when have you really listened to your mother's opinion? And if you're worried, we can change over just before we get there.'

So when they set off again, Themis rode with Melissa's arms round his waist and Frog drove the mule. Themis told himself that his thudding heart was due to the faster pace they were making. They were well beyond Paiania when the rain caught them.

Thunder boomed and echoed, quietly at first, chasing them along their road towards the sea. When the rain came in huge splashing drops, Frog shouted over the noise, 'You go ahead. You'll find somewhere out of the rain in the next village. We'll catch you up.'

So Themis and Melissa flew before the wind, cantering down the road lined with cypress trees, tall and straight as columns in a city arcade.

Soon the road bent to the left and then to the right over a low bridge. The stream under the bridge was raging and had almost topped the banks. As they took the second bend, Themis could see back down the road they had come. Yellow was just behind them, but there were very few people still on the road. The man on the large black horse appeared through the rain some way back. Themis turned and spurred their horse to a gallop. Yellow barked and kept pace.

'I know where there's shelter,' Themis shouted over his shoulder.

Melissa's grip on his clothes tightened. 'Good!' she called back.

A sudden, deafening crash of thunder overhead made the horse shy. This shook Melissa off. As she fell, she rolled to the side of the road. Themis only just managed to stay on, controlling the horse as it danced and bucked. It was a few moments before he could dismount and get to her. But by then she was on her feet, one hand on Yellow's soaking neck.

Just ahead, up a narrow track, there was a farm whose buildings had never been repaired after the Spartans marauded five years before. Themis glanced back. The haze of rain was opaque. He grabbed Melissa's hand and the horse's cheek-strap and ran towards the buildings. They turned off the track behind an almost roofless barn.

'In here, quick!' he said to Melissa.

'The others will miss us if we stay here,' she said. 'We can't be seen from the road now.'

'Exactly,' said Themis. 'But they'll probably stop here anyway. Frog knows I know about this place. And Yellow will keep watch.'

He pulled the horse into the end of the barn where the roof was still intact. There were two doors in the high walls but no windows. One door faced away from the road into the derelict farmyard. The other door faced the track, not the main road.

'We'll wait here till the rain stops,' he said from the doorway. He could hear galloping hooves. As he watched, a dark shadow flew past the end of the track, cloak flapping.

Melissa spread the saddle blanket where the ground was dry. Her travelling cloak was dripping and muddy. She took it off and laid it over the small fig tree that grew in the corner. 'Are they coming?' she asked, sitting down on the damp blanket.

Themis turned back from the doorway and joined her under the roof. 'Can't see them,' he said.

'That's not who you were looking for though, is it?'

Themis looked down at her. 'It's not who I'm worried about, no.'

Melissa patted the blanket beside her. 'Sit down and stop worrying,' she said. 'If he's seen who you're with, he'll know where you're going anyway. Of course, you might have trouble on the way back to the city,' she added mischievously.

'Perhaps it's you he's after, not me,' said Themis in the same tone.

He really did not want to sit down beside Melissa in her sodden clothes. The curves of her body were as visible as they would have been if she were naked. He turned to the horse and stroked its cheeks and neck gently.

Melissa shook with an involuntary shiver.

'Are you cold?' he asked her. 'I can look for a warmer place.'

She shook her head. 'Not cold, no. That was just because I remember a time when I was little. Skopas was even smaller than me and he fell into a whirlpool in the river. I jumped in and grabbed his feet and we both ended up on the bank, muddy and dripping like we are now. Our mother scolded us so much, we've never forgotten it.'

'She must have been very frightened.'

'She said it was the worst moment of her life.'

They were quiet, listening to the rain and the grumbling thunder. The horse whinnied and Yellow was shivering. With a hand on each, Themis murmured to them, 'Don't be afraid. It's passing.'

'What was the worst moment in your life?' Melissa asked. 'Was it when you went to Olympia the second time and lost?'

Themis thought for a moment. For many years he would have answered yes to that. But something else had actually been worse. 'No. I don't think so,' he said. 'Perhaps it was learning that my father was dead, but I still don't remember that, so I can't be sure.'

'What then?' Melissa patted the blanket again.

Themis sighed. He just wouldn't look. He sat down as far from Melissa as the blanket allowed. Water seeped into it from his clothes. 'Have you heard the story of what happened the first time I boxed at Olympia?'

'When you beat everyone without even getting hit? Yes, of course. But that was a marvel, not a bad thing.'

Another clap of thunder sounded, less aggressive this time. Parilios whinnied and stamped twice. Yellow looked at Themis, then stayed sitting to attention. Themis started to go to them, but Melissa put a hand on his arm. 'It's all right,' she said. 'They're not so frightened this time.'

Themis sat down again. 'True,' he said, 'but that wasn't the only thing that happened in Olympia that year.' He risked a quick look at her face.

She said, 'I heard you helped Phidias with the great statue of Zeus.'

'Yes … but no, that wasn't a bad thing, either. The worst thing was when I went for a run after winning the boy's boxing garland and was chased by a priestess on a horse. She was so intent on catching me that she rode off a cliff into a river gorge.' He was looking sightlessly at his muddy feet.

Melissa's sudden intake of breath was audible over the rain. 'Off a cliff! Did she die?'

'She must have,' said Themis. 'Her horse was found later, further down the river. It had been battered to death by the water.'

'Why was she trying to catch you?'

'She'd stolen gold and jewels from the statue of Athena in the temple on the Akropolis in Athens. My father was Chief of the Akropolis Guard at that time and he guessed who the thief was, but he had no other evidence.' Themis swallowed. He hadn't talked about it for years. But at least it kept his mind off Melissa's effect on him. He hugged his knees and looked at the carpet of chamomile growing over the old flagstones.

'Go on,' she said.

'I learned later that … she'd killed him before he could prove anything.'

'What!' Melissa's voice was almost a shriek.

'Then she came after *me* because she thought I remembered seeing her with the jewels in her pocket. But I didn't.'

'And so she was trying to kill you too?'

'I assume so …'

'But *she* died instead.'

Themis sighed. 'I shouldn't have answered your question about the worst thing,' he said. 'It's not … But it's haunted me for years, watching her and her horse fly off that cliff … hearing their screams cut off …'

Melissa put a warm hand on his forearm.

'I'm sorry,' she said. 'No wonder you don't like being followed.'

Her hand didn't move. After a pause, he turned to her.

He knew he wasn't hiding the surge of feelings her touch was causing in him. He knew she could see he was breathless and his heart was drumming in his throat. Surely she couldn't miss it. He swallowed, steadied himself, then dared to look into her eyes.

She looked back at him quizzically. Then her hand shook on his arm and her breathing became ragged. Her eyes widened in surprise and her lips parted.

Themis leapt up, strode to the doorway and looked out. The rain immediately soaked his hair and shoulders again. His hand on Yellow's head steadied him as he leant against the charred doorjamb, legs trembling. She'd felt it too! A grin spread over his face before he could stop it.

But stop it he must. Her father or Nereus would murder him if he didn't take control. Or they'd kill Melissa herself, because she'd never sit still to be locked up … And of course he couldn't marry her. She wasn't a citizen. Her family was from Paros, not even Attica. He took a deep breath.

When he turned to look back at her, Melissa had her hand clamped over her mouth. She was sitting huddled against the wall. She noticed his look and relaxed, letting her hand drop. 'So. That's what he feels like,' she said with a grin.

'What who feels like?' Themis kept his tone flippant.

'Eros,' she said with a laugh.

He could hear hooves again, but slow, plodding hooves this time, and the jangle of harness. Yellow stood up and went to the doorway, looking at Themis for permission to run out and meet the others.

Themis nodded at the dog, which sprinted away. 'Ah well,' he said lightly, 'what's a little Eros between friends?' But inside he was swearing and begging, '*Eros! Get off my back!*'

Melissa stopped smiling and stood up, looking at him anxiously. 'And we still are loyal friends, aren't we, Uncle Themis? Eros can't destroy that, can he?' She stepped towards him.

He said jokingly, 'If you come any nearer, my legs will probably give way.' She stood still. 'Thank you,' he said, then swallowed hard. 'And so that we can remain friends, because, as we both know, that's all we can ever be, I think we need an agreement.'

'We do?'

'Yes,' Themis felt more in control now. The cart with Frog and Adrasteia was in sight coming up the track. He smiled down at her. 'It seems to me that Eros is out to cause mischief. Neither your father nor Nereus would hesitate to lock you up if they got the least hint that there's ever that kind of feeling between you and me. I suggest ... that we each promise to tell the other if Eros begins his tricks. That way we'll know to forgive each other any unsuitable – or disloyal – behaviour.'

Melissa's eyes suddenly filled with angry tears. 'What?' she exclaimed. Then a sour expression twisted her mouth and she nodded. 'Fine!' she said, her tone sharp as a chisel. 'Fine, Uncle Themis. You are, after all, just a man like any other. I'll make sure I don't feel like that again around you. And I'm sure you'll do the same around me.'

Themis froze, appalled. '*This is far worse than with her mother – not even in the same game!*' he thought. '*Can she really believe that will be possible?*'

Melissa had also heard the cart arriving. She turned and gathered up the saddle blanket and her cloak.

Adrasteia dashed past the doorway looking desperately around, her toilet sponge in her hand.

Chapter 36: blighted

'Would you like me to drive the mule?' Melissa asked Frog, going out into the easing rain.

Frog considered this very carefully, rubbing his dripping chin and pressing his lips together. 'I'm not sure it would be safe,' he said, his eyes on Themis.

Themis looked up at the sky, which was clearing from behind them. Sunbeams were already slicing between the clouds.

He looked sideways and nodded at Frog, who grinned and said, 'Well, as the rain seems to be passing, perhaps you can manage her after all. It's worth a try,' and he handed the reins to Melissa.

When Adrasteia came back from behind the buildings, she stood quite still, watching Themis pull Frog up behind him on the horse and Melissa turning the cart in the yard. Themis saw her take a deep breath and send up a silent prayer as she climbed back into it. Yellow took up his station beside the mule. No one spoke and they set off again.

The road followed the valley of the Erasinos eastwards towards the sea. The sunshine caught up with them and they followed their own shadows. These grew longer ahead of them as the afternoon wore on. Frog tentatively began to sing a current song about the fate of a sandal-maker and his ugly sister. Themis felt his shoulders relax and joined in the choruses. Yellow and the mule seemed to walk in time to the music and it behaved itself perfectly.

There was traffic through each village, but there were times when they were alone on the road. Themis kept turning to check that the road behind was empty. The dark horse and rider did not reappear.

He caught Melissa's eye once. She gave him her false smile and gestured to the mule. 'You see? She's fine,' she called.

He nodded and turned to the front.

The buildings of Vravrona finally appeared, throwing shadows across the road. The new, impressive entrance to the precinct shone white against the willow and plane trees around it. *'They still haven't painted it,'* thought Themis, as the gatekeeper bowed them in.

Melissa called, 'Whoa!' to the mule immediately inside the compound. She jumped down, swept her bag from the cart and touched Adrasteia's hand in farewell. Then she walked briskly towards the bridge over the water channel. The bridge led to a porticoed doorway in the middle of the wall of the new hospitality block. Along its outside wall, the offerings shelf was bright with food bundles and flowers, coloured garlands and ribbons. The precinct was bustling with visitors and parents of girls Melissa's age.

As Themis dismounted, Melissa ran from the end of the bridge to the portico, and a familiar voice called from in front of the small temple on the rise to his right.

'The goddess be praised!' It was Eirini with laughter in her voice as she hurried down the steps. 'How I prayed that you are well, Melissa, my child.'

'Yes, I am well, Mrs Eirini,' Melissa said, as Themis' mother and she met by the great doorway through to the sacred court. 'I'm sorry if I have caused you to worry.'

Eirini took Melissa by the shoulders. 'You are not the first,' she said, loudly enough for Themis to hear. Then she said something quietly by Melissa's ear. Themis thought he heard the word 'cleverest', and both Eirini and Melissa laughed. Eirini called across the stream to Themis. 'Will you meet me at the house before dark?'

A crowd of parents and girls were entering and leaving the temple. Themis nodded briefly to his mother and raised a hand as he turned to go round by the road outside the precinct to her little house on the hill. He didn't trust himself to say anything to Melissa, or to watch her disappear under that shadowy portico into the world of the goddess.

'Has there been any news of Diodotos?' Eirini asked Themis later, as they ate on her balcony. The lights of the town twinkled across the inlet and the hill above loomed dark against the stars. Themis could see the bright lamp in the tavern where he'd heard Tydeus talking to his colleague.

'Nothing specific, Mama,' he replied. 'We know the army was on its way to Argos a few days ago, but he's sent no news himself.'

'And has Uncle Zephyros left the city yet?'

'I haven't seen him again,' said Themis. He was finding the fish dumplings difficult to swallow.

'You must have seen Photios, though,' his mother went on. 'I understand his punishment has been reduced and he's back in the army. It's been confirmed that he has the job Diodotos was to do in the stores.'

'Really?' said Themis absentmindedly.

'His young cousin is one of our inmates at present. It seems he sent her a message about it. She now worships you from afar, of course. She says Photios said his liberty is all due to your heroism.'

Themis just shrugged. Eirini laid a hand on his shoulder. 'What's wrong, Themistokles?' she said quietly.

'I'm just tired, Mama,' said Themis.

'Too much work, or too much play?' asked his mother.

'It's ... complicated. There's been a lot of ... covert stuff. And I'm not sure what the outcome will be. I'm glad it made a difference for

Photios.'

After a pause, Eirini asked, 'How did you find Melissa?'

'*She* came to *me*,' said Themis. 'But I was … quite hard on her and she ran off again.' His mother was looking at him disapprovingly, so he went on. 'Then later I was in the Agora and I heard her voice by chance. She was in her boy's clothes but I needed her help and, surprisingly, she gave it.' He managed a smile. 'And she had foreseen something very important. I owe her thanks, not … all this.' He gestured to the precinct below by the river, its torches gleaming on the new, pale columns and walls, its doors securely locking in its student virgins for the night. 'She hates me now.'

Eirini ignored that. 'Foreseen?' she said. 'You didn't believe her about hearing the gods talking to her, did you?'

'What she said she heard was in fact what was being planned,' said Themis.

'But the lightning had already come from the sea and you stopped it.'

Themis took a breath to speak but his mother went on, 'She was just using something from the past as if it was going to happen again.'

'No, Mama,' Themis broke in. 'It did happen again — at least, someone far more organized tried to make something even more sinister happen. But we stopped it. And that's why I'm tired.'

'I can't believe it,' said Eirini, rising from her chair and walking to the balcony railing. 'Melissa is not the type to get messages from the gods!'

'Well, this time she was right,' said Themis. He suddenly felt completely exhausted and had to stop his head falling forward.

'Oh, my child, I'm sorry,' said his mother coming over to him. 'The gods know what you've been dealing with. You obviously need some sleep. Get to bed now, and I'll wake you at dawn.'

Over breakfast, Eirini said, 'What were you up to down by the harbour so early today?'

'There's a man I wanted to meet,' said Themis wearily. 'But it seems he's left already, although no one I spoke to knew where he'd gone. A wasted effort. I need to get back.'

Eirini sighed. 'Frustrating,' she said. Then she put a hand on his. 'Before you go, I wonder if you'd do me and your brother a favour?'

Themis frowned, then shrugged. 'What sort of favour?' he said.

'There is a lovely girl, much richer and better behaved than Niovi, that I would like you to make a drawing of. Her name is Tyro. Diodotos needs to see that there are other lovely girls eligible for marriage this year.'

'Where do I find her?' he asked. '*And will Melissa be nearby?*' he thought. Then he sighed angrily.

'I'll get her to come here where the light's good,' said his mother, misunderstanding his anger. 'You needn't move. I'll find a tablet and stylus.'

Themis hardly noticed the journey back to the City. He only focused briefly when Frog called to him to say the turn off to Athmonon was soon. Frog was finally going to help Melanas with the harvest.

When Themis stopped but didn't dismount, Frog prompted him. 'Shall I take Parilios and you drive on to the city with Adrasteia in the cart? I can send someone with Parilios to the City tomorrow.'

Themis nodded and slid to the ground. He took the mule's reins from Frog, checked that Adrasteia was sitting safely in the cart, and set off towards Athens. Far away, the toy-like buildings and walls of the City were shining through a golden haze of dust as the sun sank. The sea was pale silver and the mountains of the Peloponnese soft grey silhouettes against an apricot sky. Themis looked back along the way they'd come.

'Any followers you can see?' he asked, as Frog rode alongside.

'No one suspicious,' said Frog. 'Do you want your saddle bag?'

'Oh! Yes,' said Themis vacantly. 'Of course. Thanks.' Frog handed it down and Adrasteia put it on the floor of the cart.

Frog rode on to the turning, shaking his head. As he took the road to Athmonon, they heard his voice raised in song fading into the distance. 'It came from the earth, it came from the sky, / It came from his bones, it blinded his eye. / His mind filled with cloud, his gut filled with fire … '

Themis shook the reins and the mule moved off noisily with Yellow following.

Some time later, Adrasteia asked, 'How long will we be on the road?'

Themis roused himself and saw that the mule was hardly even ambling. 'Sorry, Adrasteia,' he said. 'Are you in a hurry?'

'The nurse I left with Mrs Anthoussa is old and has a bad leg. She's not strong, so I worry…'

'Quite right,' said Themis. 'Come on, old girl,' he called to the mule. 'Let's get there before midnight!'

Later, when Themis turned into his own street, a man who had been lounging by the herm at the corner stood up and followed the cart. Tanu the groom was waiting at the door and took the mule's cheek strap as Yellow leapt off the cart and Themis climbed stiffly down. He nodded at the lounger, who was now standing waiting by their house herm.

'What is it?' asked Themis.

'I have an important message for Themistokles, son of Kallistos,' he said quietly.

Themis forced himself to concentrate. He took his saddlebag from the cart. His dagger was in the bottom. 'Can you tell me here?' he asked.

'Although I am not wearing the uniform, I come officially from the Office of the Archons,' said the man quietly, and he lifted the flap of his satchel to show the running horse emblem of Apollodorus.

'Come in, then,' said Themis, and led him through the street door while Tanu led the mule to the stable.

The man sat calmly on the water trough bench, so Themis took the time to lay his offering of wild rosemary on the shrine of Zeus of the house. Then he washed his face and hands in the water trough. His mind was blank, refusing to consider the possible contents of the message.

'Come into the andron,' he said. 'Mika!' he called, and Mika appeared at the door of the kitchen. 'Please bring wine and water.'

The man stood in the middle of the room while Themis lit a lamp.

'Go ahead,' he said, when Mika had gone.

'Apollodorus sends greetings,' the man said in the lilting tones of the professional messenger. 'He hopes your mission was successful. He informs you that in your absence, the Assembly elected new Archons as always at this season, so he will be in office for only thirty more days. Also, the Assembly was told of the second attempt to destroy part of the navy and the perpetrators' names. It voted to reduce the penalty for Photios, son of Leontis, for the first attempt, from five years to nothing, but at present could offer no other employment except as a soldier. However, the examination of the men arrested has been unsatisfactory. All insist that the second attempt was made to show that it was possible, not to cause actual damage. The aim was to prove that security is not tight enough. The evidence you say was hidden in the bay has not been found. The men in custody will have to be freed without charge. You should be on your guard.' The man stopped.

Themis asked him to repeat the message. The man did so. Themis gave him a short message of thanks to take back to the Archon, and saw him out. He went and lay down on one of the couches.

Later, Mika woke him and told him to go and sleep in his bed so that she could tidy up.

The nymph looked very tired and hot. Themis could see her face and naked body right down to her waist. She had muscles like a man and small breasts, probably smaller than Melissa's. Everything was misty and he could hear water running. On the wall behind her hung a series of large blue and red cloths on hooks, thicker and softer looking than any fabric he recognised. '*Someone spent a lot of money dying those,*' he thought. '*Red is expensive, but blue is astronomical. They must be towels. So much money just to dry yourself?*' A strange bird called and the nymph put a small, flat black box to her ear. She was anxious and said something, though Themis couldn't hear the words. Her eyes lost focus for a while, then she laughed and said clearly, 'Wonderful! Thank you Cassie, thank you!' She talked some more, it seemed about money, and then moved the box away from her ear, took a deep happy breath – and vanished!

The mist swirled towards Themis and the expensive towels faded into it as he stirred in his bed. He sat up sweating and pushed off the blanket. The buzz was loud. 'You were talking to someone, weren't you?' he said to the nymph with a smile. 'Someone who wasn't there with you and yet you could hear each other. Were you alone? Was it a bathhouse? You had no clothes on! I wasn't supposed to see that, was I?' Yellow put his feet up on the side of the bed.

'Sorry, Yellow,' murmured Themis, rubbing the dog's head between its ears. 'Nothing to do with you – or me, probably. It didn't feel quite like a dream, but not a warning, either.' Cooler now, he lay down again.

At the palaestra next morning, Themis worked his body so hard that the trainer suggested he should stop. He took no notice.

Photios arrived for his first session since being arrested.

They were doing a series of squats and lunges side by side and Photios' face was shining with joy and sweat when he whispered breathlessly, 'He's right ... You're going too fast ... Listen! ... You've lost the rhythm.'

Themis slowed down to synchronise with the flute and drum. 'Breakfast at my place?' Photios panted.

Themis nodded. His mind was coming out of its fog. That 'dream', and the thought of chatting with Photios made him feel more alive.

'No! Breakfast at Foot-of-the-Wall tavern,' he gasped. 'On me.'

Photios was too breathless to speak, but he nodded with a grin.

'So, you're back in the army, now,' said Themis, his mouth full of barley and walnut bread. 'And how are the wells going?'

'We gave up on one, but the other is finally showing water,' said Photios. 'At least, it was yesterday when I left the farm. And yes, I'm back in the army as a quartermaster. I may be off to the Peloponnese soon. There's another campaign being planned, Father tells me.'

'Is there?' asked Themis. 'I'd better get down to the Agora and check out the news. There might be something about Diodotos' unit.'

They ate in silence for a moment.

Then Photios looked up. 'So why are you punishing yourself?'

Themis choked. 'Get straight to the point, why don't you?' he said when he recovered.

'Well, you often do this,' said Photios with a shrug.

'Do what?'

'Exercise as if a fury possesses you, but don't say why. I'm just giving you the chance to discuss whatever it is, before you kill yourself outdoing Herakles.' Photios grabbed an apricot from the dish between them.

'Hmm.' Themis thought for a moment. 'Basically I have two problems. One I can't discuss, even with you, and one I don't want to discuss.'

'Oh, stop being enigmatic,' said Photios. 'It doesn't suit you. I know the first problem is to do with the security of the city. You got mixed up in that because of me originally – a fact I will always be grateful for. I promise not to ask questions in case your own safety is now threatened. That was a knife I saw you strap between your buttocks, wasn't it?'

Themis nodded.

Photios said, 'I am constantly shocked by the perfidy of men.'

Themis said, 'I remember Phidias saying that nothing men – or women! – did, ever surprised him any more. Only what the gods did.'

Photios nodded. 'Hmmm … women. I've been thinking about the ideal woman lately. It'd be good to have someone to tell you how perfect you are, even when you're not.'

Themis shook his head. 'No woman I've ever met would do that.'

'But that's what a perfect wife would do.' Photios began counting on his fingers. 'She'd make you feel invincible, look after you, give you children, be frugal, keep you laughing, and make you want to stay home with her instead of going out looking for sex on the street.' Photios was teasing.

'Of course. She'd give up everything that makes her an individual to gratify your wishes,' Themis agreed, dipping his bread in his goat's milk.

'Well that's what we're taught to expect,' said Photios with an elaborate shrug. 'And how else can we guarantee our way of life?'

Themis looked Photios in the eyes. 'I don't know,' he said seriously. 'It seems to me that one in each couple has to sacrifice their true selves for our "way of life" – and it's almost always the woman.'

Photios nodded. 'So … from that, I guess that your second problem is to do with love, as you never seem to have money worries for long.' He looked steadily at Themis.

Themis looked back, then down. 'Love? Hm! Lust, more like.'

'Why be worried about that?' asked Photios.

'Because I don't want to feel it for this particular person,' said Themis. 'Because that would cause me and a lot of other people endless conflict.'

'So you try to ignore it, but it "clouds your mind, distorts your vision and burns your entrails". Is that it?'

Themis nodded and sighed. Then he suddenly laughed out loud, making Photios jump. 'I've just realized,' he said, 'that *that* was the song Frog was parodying when we split up yesterday. What a monster he is!'

'I'd say *he's* more like a knowing shadow than any woman could be,' said Photios. 'Look, you obviously need shaking out of this – if you really are sure there's no hope of consummation?'

Themis shook his head. 'None at all,' he said. He took an apricot. 'I have enough trouble with friends who seem to think my latest pastime is seducing their middle-aged wives. I can't imagine the chaos if …'

Photios smiled as if he knew whom Themis meant.

Themis said, 'I can't say who, but it's not who you think it is!' He sighed gustily and bit into the apricot. A juicy maggot waved at him in protest at being disturbed. Themis and Photios both burst out laughing.

>>>

Chapter 37: one too many

(Breeds of Sheep 23 – He saw me in the mirror! With no clothes on! But he didn't think anything gross, or get embarrassed. That is really weird – like 'worm-holes in time' weird. And confusing, but not actually scary. And this next bit was confusing at first, too. There's a time gap. It seems to be a month or more later, though it ran straight on during my connection. Now the City feels different – hot and dry, and people seem more stressed, on edge.)

<<<

Themis was running into the City through the gate in the southern Long Wall. Just inside the gate, a grove of pines and holmoaks grew around the small temple to Zeus the Saver. There was a group of men standing under the trees beside the road. Themis looked at them as he ran past and thought he recognized a face from the diving incident that had led nowhere. They were all free again, of course.

He ran a little faster. But some signal must have been given, because a man on a horse galloped towards him and flung a large piece of sacking over his head.

Themis ran on, avoiding the horse and trying to disentangle himself. He was deliberately tripped but managed to fall sideways rather than face first, and the cloth fell away. Then three men jumped on him. In spite of his shouts and struggles, he found himself trussed up like a goose and lifted onto a cart. No one on the road took any notice. One of the men stuffed something disgusting into his mouth. The cart turned and a tarpaulin was thrown over him as they approached the gate.

He decided not to struggle and to conserve his strength. He didn't know who these men were. They might have been 'friends' like the last time he was abducted, though that seemed unlikely. The gag stank of rotten fruit. He listened carefully but he couldn't hear much under the canvas. But there was a knot he could reach with his left hand so he began to work on it. The men hardly spoke. Themis thought there were four of them.

After some time, the cart stopped. The tarpaulin was removed. Someone grabbed Themis' feet and pulled him to the backboard.

'Get off!' ordered a deep voice. When Themis struggled to obey, the man dragged him off the cart and stood him up like a statue. The man was wearing a bag as a mask and his eyes glittered through its holes. 'Walk!' he said, and pushed Themis towards a wooden door.

They were in a mudbrick courtyard with high walls. The ground was baked earth with dying weeds round the edges. Themis walked slowly and deliberately to the door. From the shapes of the distant mountains, he knew they were between the sea and the road to Sounion.

The door opened and he was pushed inside. In the darkness, strong hands manoeuvred him until he came up against a post. Here he began to struggle as he realized they would tie him to it. He got a punch on the chin for that, and another in his stomach when he tried to butt his attacker on the bridge of the nose with his forehead. He felt blood or spit drip onto his forearm from his mouth as they turned his back to the post. They tied him firmly to it with a rope round his neck and another round his ankles. And he still had the rope round his hips that immobilised his hands.

Feeble light from a small window behind him revealed that they were in an empty storeroom. It smelled oddly of dust and walnuts as well as the usual stale sewage. There were three men, all masked. One of them seemed to be the right shape for the man he'd recognized under the holmoaks. The thin, shrivelled-looking one had a cough.

The tallest one said, 'If you talk, you'll be out of here in a flash. If not, I'll drop you in the bay – way out in the bay – in a sack – with stones.' It was an educated, confident voice that Themis thought he'd heard before. But where?

'Who are you?' Themis asked, not expecting an answer.

'I'm your Nemesis,' said the man and laughed inside his bag mask. 'So. Let's get down to business. What were you doing in a fishing boat out near Zea Harbour forty days ago?'

'What are you talking about?' asked Themis.

'We know your story so don't lie. I'm just checking it out.'

Themis knew suddenly that this was the man who had locked him in the 'cage' under the house where the Ladder to Heaven had been stored – and who had hit him with a jug full of water. He must be part of the gang that attacked the harbours. Perhaps he hadn't been present that night. Something must have happened to make them believe their official stance of testing the security of the harbours was in doubt. Had the chest been found at last? Had someone sold a secret to the new Archons?

'Winning a bet for someone,' he said.

'And who knew you were there?'

'At the time, no one.' The rope pressed on his larynx and made it difficult for Themis to talk normally.

'So who brought you the horse?'

Themis chose his first lie carefully. 'I don't know who he was,' he said. 'It's a long time ago. I saw him there and promised to pay him. I was tired. The men with the boat had left me to swim all the way back to shore.'

'Of course.' The man walked up to Themis and hit him so that his head struck the post behind him with a crack. He saw stars. Did they in fact know it had been Frog waiting for him?

It seemed not. 'Who set the whole thing up?' was the next question.

Themis mouth was full of blood and saliva. Swallowing was painful. He said, 'A man called Hyllos said I'd get a load of money if I took a string under the net into the harbour under the noses of the guards. It was for a bet by someone he knew.'

'Go on.'

Themis shut his eyes and breathed as if he was fainting. He was working with his left hand on that knot. It was weakening, but the other two men might notice his hand any time. He said, 'What do you want to know?'

'Who did you tell?'

'Hyllos said to tell no one. I agreed with him.'

'What happened to the string?'

'I gave it to the man I was told to and swam back. I don't know what happened after that. I was under water.'

'So you told no one and know nothing,' said the tall man, 'but you didn't get arrested like everyone else.'

'Hyllos had said it was just an exercise, a bet.' Themis took a breath. 'I just wanted my money. I didn't even know they were arrested. On the way home, I got beaten up by some robbers in Kili and heard about the arrests the next day.' Themis' voice was a rasp now and he was really beginning to feel faint. The rope seemed to tighten even as he tried to push his aching head back against the post. He spat some of the bloody liquid in his mouth onto the floor and went on, 'Hyllos said I'd be paid enough to buy a house. Did he tell the robbers? Did they think I'd have that money on me? I never got it, by the way. And Hyllos has left the City.'

'Oh, he'll be back,' said the man with a laugh. 'Perhaps when he is, he'll find it for you.'

Themis felt the knot give way. He coughed and spat again to take attention away from the movement of the rope around his hips.

But the man had gestured to his companions and they made a tight group, muttering together. No one was watching, so Themis freed his hands. He pulled his knife out of the sheath between his buttocks and almost strangled himself cutting the rope round his neck. He made an involuntary choking noise, but no one turned round.

He leant down and slashed the rope round his feet, then stood back in position against the post.

They finished their consultation. The first to turn to him was the tall, educated man. He met Themis' left fist full in his face, and fell like a log. The men behind him came dashing forward. The one on the right tripped over the first man and fell forwards. Themis kicked his head while attending with his left fist to the hooded face of the third man.

There was a suddenly silence. Then the first man groaned. Themis was still holding his knife in his right hand. He stepped rapidly to the door, expecting the man outside to appear at any moment. He could hear the mule moving in its harness.

He opened the door a crack and looked out. The mule was munching on the dry weeds by the wall, but he couldn't see a fourth man. He pulled the door open, expecting to be jumped on, but nothing happened. Either there had never been a fourth man, or he'd gone.

A loud groan and an oath sounded inside. Themis sprinted the ten paces to the mule, cut its traces from the cart and leapt onto its back. He leaned down to push the rotting gate open and urged the animal into a lumbering trot. He heard the crash as the door of the storeroom slammed open.

The track from there to the main road was empty. Themis could hear the men shouting at each other to run after him. The mule seemed pleased to be rid of the cart, and did some little kicks as it accelerated into a canter.

By the time they were on the main road among the traffic, he could see the men had given up. He kept the mule to a trot, weaving between the carts and pedestrians. Near the city walls, he allowed it to slow to a walk, and headed for the palaestra.

There he left the mule with the resident groom and managed to wash and borrow a clean chiton. As he left on foot on his way to the Agora, a veiled woman collided with him. They apologized to each other and he continued on his way, holding in his hand the scrap of papyrus she had given him. From the smell of her sweat mixed with leather he guessed she had not been a woman at all.

As he moved through the crowds on his route to the Agora, he took a look at what the papyrus said. There was the name of a street corner and one other word. 'Now!' with a sketchy running horse.

As he arrived at the relevant corner, a door opened at the bottom of some steps to below street level. He touched his dagger, now back in its sheath, and went down. As the door shut behind him, he turned. A guard stood on either side. The cellar was full of wine barrels, quietly growling in the gloom. And ahead of him were Apollodorus and his scribe, and Archias, the chief magistrate, sitting on stools. A lamp burned on a barrel. Archias stood up.

'We've been waiting for you,' he said to Themis. 'We learned you'd been abducted. Congratulations that you got away.'

Themis tried to smile. It hurt. 'Thanks,' he managed to say.

'Our runners had set out to get you when you were seen riding a mule up to the walls,' said Apollodorus. 'But this is one too many abductions. As you know, we cannot produce clear evidence that the underwater attempt forty days ago was in fact an attack.'

'But haven't you found the chest?' said Themis.

'The chest is still elusive,' said Apollodorus. 'So we still have no proof. I am handing over to my successor soon, so I had our men check out where those we had under arrest for this case are now. As you know, they all went free due to lack of proof. Hyllos was made to leave the City, but we're watching him. He has friends who've already begun proceedings about his coming back, though, including Kallias and Nereus, who suggested to me the other day that the planning offices were understaffed without him! He still seems to be the only man who ever saw the Benefactor. He swears he didn't of course, and that it really was all a joke to persuade the Assembly that the navy is still vulnerable.'

'Hah! Then he's talking out of his – ' Themis began.

'Possibly,' interrupted Apollodorus, 'but it really looks as though our "smoking lightning" from the sea must have been to do with the previous attempt. We have nothing on Hyllos or Eryx, or any of the others, including Glykon, except your word. And none of the leads we've followed up so far points to anyone specific.

'This all puts you in a vulnerable position – however much we know it was a real sabotage attempt, at present we have no proof. Your abduction today shows that someone is frightened of you, but we didn't act fast enough to learn who. They could just murder you, but more likely, if it's a "respectable citizen", they'll employ an orator to accuse you of deliberate libel, so you'd end up in court yourself, ridiculed and ruined financially.'

'What about the document I signed for Hyllos – the contract for the painting?' Themis face and head were throbbing.

'There was no trace of it in the City's archives,' said Apollodorus with a shrug. 'I believe you, and so does Archias, especially after today. We can't imagine your returning the money that Hyllos paid you to the City as you did, unless you were telling the truth. But to others it might look as though you are just trying to ridicule an authentic attempt to highlight the need for tighter security. Or even that that money was a bribe to the Council for some obscure reason. That is something I'm sure you wish to avoid.'

Themis had to agree with that. And perhaps Melissa had been deluding herself about the goddess' message after all. A pain stabbed through his chest. 'In that case, it's better you drop the investigation,' he mumbled. *'But I won't – ever,'* he thought.

'Exactly,' said Archias, standing up. 'Now, as you know, Apollodorus and I are being replaced in the next few days. And Nereus is now a general, though he will stay here in the city, responsible for designing new ships.' Themis stomach twisted, taking his breath away. 'Laches and Nikostratos were also elected generals. Alkibiades is in the Peloponnese already, as you know, and has asked for more troops. He may not be a general this year, but he's still the beloved of the men, with or without his cheetah, and an official ambassador of the City. Laches is recruiting a further four hundred men to join him at Argos. I want you to be among them.'

Themis sighed and nodded painfully. 'When?' he asked.

'They'll be leaving in the next ten days,' Archias went on. 'You'll need a shield slave and your full hoplite armour, but the city will provide any necessary horses and baggage animals. There'll be training every day even if there's no action.'

'Archias will be replaced by Antiphon and I by Lysikles of Kefisia,' said Apollodorus. 'We will brief them both concerning your help to the City.' He smiled. 'You'd better get those bruises seen to before you leave.' He seemed glad that Themis had not objected, only grunted and nodded.

Themis was in fact surprised by how relieved he felt. The pain in his chest lessened. There would be action, the uncomplicated company of men on a mission, good humour and lousy food. Frog could take over the farm and Melanas would be able to serve as his shield slave, perhaps for the last time. Melissa was safe in Vravrona for a while.

There was nothing now to keep him in the City.

>>>

Suzanne closed her laptop hurriedly. Theo, who'd moved in with Natasha lately, always wanted to know what she was doing if he saw her computer open. He'd finally got out of bed and was on his way to the kitchen next door. As he passed her open doorway she stood up and said teasingly, 'Good afternoon, Theo! Look, I'm working on an Anatomy essay so I'm shutting the door.'

Theo grunted and Natasha put her head out of the kitchen. 'See you later, then. Shout if you want anything.'

Suzanne nodded and closed her door. She'd been typing like crazy to catch up with Themis' doings since he'd seen her in the mirror in his dreams. It'd made her wonder how often he did actually 'see' her. Was it only when he was asleep? Did he see her at times she wasn't seeing *him*? She'd come to the conclusion that neither he nor she was controlling the connection. Years ago, she'd sometimes been able to call him up with a series of musical notes. But now the connection was either on or off.

Which was disconcerting but fascinating. She always tried to stay 'invisible', however embarrassed or angry his attitudes to war, or women, or slavery, or sex made her feel, because she was learning so much about his sometimes familiar, sometimes alien world.

And now he was setting off on something even more alien. Could their connection survive? And could she still manage her studies and her training *and* write up his story? And yet her choice was either to carry on, or to ignore him and forget all she'd learned. So no choice, really.

She'd been reading up on the 400s BCE in Greece. There was a great battle later in the summer of 418 at Mantinea in the Peloponnese. '*But Themis is in the engineering corps,*' she thought. '*He won't fight, even if he's still there.*'

It was the expedition to Sicily three years later that worried her more. In 415 BCE, Alkibiades led an enormous occupying force to Sicily. In 413 the army was annihilated there, and hardly any of the men ever came back.

<<<

PART TWO

Chapter 38: Argos

(Breeds of Sheep 24)

Frog had come to the City from the farm for two days, to see Themis off to Argos. He stood at the open door of the andron with a platter.

'Is that food?' asked Themis, who was checking the straps of his armour. Frog put the platter on the table by the door. 'Yes. Mika made duck pie. We've explained to your Uncle Zephyros that you send him greetings but are under orders to leave and have no time to meet up. As you can see, your packs are ready. Melanas will take them down with the mule at dawn – and your shield. You won't want that in the parade.'

'It's not a parade,' said Themis. 'It's just a short march to Piraeus.'

'But it IS a parade.' Frog chanted, '"Here's our hero" they'll call. "Such a man, such a charmer!" / As you pass with a flash in your much-polished armour. / When the gods see their faces in the shine of your helmet / They'll thank your man Frog for his finest work yet.'

Themis laughed and play-punched Frog's shoulder. He was getting excited about going now. 'Pity you're not coming, too,' he said.

'Other duties keep me here,' said Frog, his face mock-mournful.

'Ah, yes,' said Themis. 'The Skionian …'

'Don't forget to eat,' Frog said as he went out grinning.

It took two long, hot days to row to Kios, the port of Argos. With the summer solstice only just passed, there was almost no wind. Themis was rowing in his usual position and Photios was among the zygites on the middle benches. He was accompanied by Numa's son, Orcus, as his shield slave. The convoy was made up of two triremes and four supply boats. They met no obstacles and, half way there, slept a few hours with the triremes hauled up in a tiny bay on the deserted side of Ydra Island. They knew its dusty, goat-grazed slopes and deep blue water from previous campaigns. There was a sweet spring that oozed out under a rock, half a stade up the steep hill behind the beach. The supply boats stayed in the bay while the triremes beached and the men disembarked. They set guards and went about their chores without fuss or noise.

With food eaten and relief guards set, it was time for stories round the fire. One man told how his brother was beaten in the Isthmean Games Pentathlon. He made it a comedy of divine intervention.

As the quiet laughter faded, he added, 'But you have an even better story to tell us, Themistokles. Tell us about your second visit to Olympia.'

'Ah. Yes. Well,' said Themis, rubbing the back of his neck. He nodded at the wine skin with an ironic smile. 'I'll need some more of that. It's embarrassing. But remember, I was younger then.'

'No younger than some of us,' chortled one, handing Themis a full leather wine bottle.

Themis took the bottle, drank a couple of mouthfuls of neat wine and shook his head at its strength. 'Well, you see,' he began, 'in those days I was a famous boxer.' Photios and many of the others nodded emphatically in agreement. Themis added the heightened tones and emphasis of spoken story-telling to his usual voice. 'I'd won the olive crown as a boy eight summers before. I'd beaten everyone in the selection bouts in Athens – the boxers from Kili and Piraeus, Sounion and Elefsis. And I'd beaten everyone in training at Olympia – the men from Massalia and Knidos, Korkyra and Epirus.'

Photios began to play quietly on his lute, a lilting, repeating melody, a parody of the serious, competition-winning pieces they all knew. Over his music he said, '*And* you'd been hunted by the wicked priestess and defeated her by leading her headlong into the ravine.'

Melanas began to tap on Themis' shield as if it were a drum while Themis nodded his head and said, 'Not exactly "leading" her. But I'd been lucky in other ways, too. So, as you can understand, I knew I could trust the gods and that I would be the victor. No one could stand up to my left fist. It was famous throughout the whole Greek world!' There were nods and smiles and jaws fingered in good-natured memory. 'The final bout was going well. My first opponent had submitted, and I'd knocked the second one out. The other finalist, Kleomachos, seemed sluggish and had the sun in his eyes, but I was strong as a lion.' Melanas made the 'drum' purr. Themis went on, 'The crowd was roaring encouragement, Zeus was on my side ...' He paused and looked around at the firelit faces, then up at the glittering mass of stars in the black sky. No one spoke, the drum pulsed and the lyre whispered its rhythm in time to the wavelets on the beach.

Themis took up that rhythm as he said, 'And then ... I woke up ... in the tent ... on the bed ... one eye closed, ... face swollen ... like a water-skin.' There was a restrained burst of laughter. The music stopped. 'My ribs felt cracked, and my neck felt broken.'

An old opponent of Themis at the gym laughed loudly. 'A bit like now,' he brayed. The man next to him put a quieting hand on his arm.

Themis went on. 'Oh, much worse than this,' he gestured to his recovering face and half-grown beard. 'My trainer said to stay still and I knew then I'd lost. They'd unbound my hands after they carried me out of the pit, and scraped me down. I was beaten, a shameful lump of meat, carried away, bleeding, unconscious. I could almost hear the crowd jeering and see Kleomachos dancing his victory dance.' Photios began playing again and Themis moved his head and torso in a sneering imitation of the dance. The men guffawed. 'I thought of how those men who'd bet on me would hound me. I thought of all that wasted training, of how my friends, my family, my city had had faith in me to win – and would now be ashamed of me. I pushed my trainer away, stood up and forced myself to run… I had resolved to die!' he said slowly, with exaggerated dignity.

Photios and Melanas played a steady rhythm which began to accelerate. Themis took a little more wine. The men around him were suddenly silent, their eyes wide, reflecting the flames of the fire.

'I took the way to the ravine where the priestess had tried to kill me.' Themis lowered his voice. 'I could hear Hades calling me. My tears of shame fell in the dust as I ran. It was midday, hot and still. I heard voices calling me to stop. But no one could catch me. I sprinted up the mountain and onto its wide shoulder. The pains in my side and my head made me dizzy, but I knew I would soon escape the pain, *and* the shame, the shame. I flew, taking short cuts, leaping bushes.'

Themis had told the story many times. The first bit always gave him that sinking, shameful feeling, however dramatic and self-mocking he made it. But from here on, he would feel better. Photios' melody became sweeter.

'Now I could see the two trees that mark the invisible edge of the ravine, my gate to Hades. They'd grown since the priestess had ridden between them to her death. And someone had built an altar to the god across the gap. But the ravine beckoned, so I veered to the left, put on a final spurt, my chest bursting, my head pounding… And tripped over a root.' Photios made discordant sounds and Melanas produced a noise like falling rocks from the shield.

As the laughter died down, Themis went on. 'And there was someone there, tending the altar – an old man, badly injured, twisted somehow. He knelt down and gave me water. He had a high, cracked voice, and he said, "It will pass. You will live again, however shamed you feel now. I know. I have lived through shame."'

'But all I could do just then was lie in the dust. I heard the men who had called to me talking to the old man. He sent them away and then left me there … with the water bottle, the altar, and the way to Hades so close, so easy. I knew what to do. When I could stand, I walked to the edge, and got ready to meet the god.'

Themis drank another mouthful of wine. 'But the god of the altar was not Hades. It was Apollo, with his skin and hair of gold. I stood at the lip of that gorge – the sword-cut of a Titan into the mountain. The silent river flexed its muscles far below. And I heard his voice say, 'Remember your family, your work, your city. Live now, it's not the time to die.' I touched his arm as he sat by the altar. It was warm from the sun, and felt alive. I looked harder at him. He was small but perfect, made of a wood I didn't know, sculpted by a master – perhaps even the mighty Polykleitos. I stood looking down into that black cleft and realized that I wanted to live, I wanted to learn to do work like that. I would be humble, accept my fate and ask the great man to teach me. I stepped back from the edge.'

Themis sighed and looked round at the intent, sympathetic faces. He noticed Melanas had been replaced by Orcus, who was making the shield over his knees growl gently. 'And now, although I never met Polykleitos, I'm not only famous for my unbeatable left fist, but also for my brilliant sculptures and paintings!' The ring of faces dissolved in gleeful laughter and knee slapping.

'Where did you go?' Themis asked Melanas as they prepared to sleep.

'I saw someone slinking around by the luggage,' replied Melanas. 'He ran, and I found your satchel open on the ground. Nothing missing.'

'Did you see who it was?'

Melanas shook his head. 'But I'll keep better watch in future.'

Themis lay down next to Photios, with his head on the now closed satchel. 'Then we'll have to be content with Orcus as our drummer.'

Melanas grunted and lay down nearby.

As they looked up at the glistening sky, Photios said quietly, 'It wasn't quite like that, was it? At Olympia.'

'Not quite,' ageed Themis. 'But a story isn't the same as a memory.'

Once they arrived at Argos, Themis and Melanas fell straight back into the day-to-day life of an army on campaign. Up before the sun, combat training, sweat, thirst, stink, guard duty every second night, flea and tick removal, orders, armour repairs, competition dancing, sexy stories, songs.

Melanas dealt with food, water, shelter and latrines. Themis dealt with being fit. He ate and ran and exercised, always aware that Spartan soldiers did nothing but be soldiers – the hardest men and best fighters the world had ever known, with no time for painting or sculpting, logic or mathematics. They believed they were the only people the gods honoured, and that all others should be their servants.

At least, that was their reputation in Athens, where every male citizen had the right to civic power, and an education that encouraged thought and ideas.

Photios with Orcus joined the naval cohort by the shore, maintaining the triremes and supply ships. Themis was sent inland to a camp on the plain under the walls of Argos. General Laches made him responsible for the design of wooden siege engines and stone and earth defensive walls, and for the supply of the materials needed to build them.

The days passed quickly. Melissa was part of a forgotten world that only appeared in uneasy dreams, and Themis rarely noticed or thought of the nymph. He actually felt calmer here than in the City full of latent threats.

There were skirmishes at the edges of the Argive Plain and in the valleys between the mountains that limited it. He was constantly looking for an opportunity to journey overland to Olympia to see Judge Iasos, as he'd promised Anthoussa. But he was kept busy with his engineering duties in and around Argos. Rumours flew as to why the Spartans seemed to be happier to make treaties than to engage this year.

Eventually, the order came down that General Laches' men were to join the other Athenian units under General Nikostratos and to make a joint camp on the plain near the great ruined walls of Mycenae. It was said that Alkibiades would join them there, although he had been offered more luxurious quarters in Argos city, on the other side of the plain.

In the afternoon of the day of this move, Themis and his engineers rode across to sleep in the new camp. Themis thought he might find Diodotos there, as he was supposed to be with General Nikostratos' troops.

But first he needed to find Melanas among the rows of tents and lines of cooking fires. When he did, he opened his satchel and poured a stream of small hyacinth bulbs into a platter by their fire. 'Found these where I was working today,' he said. 'Not quite a hare, but tasty enough.'

Melanas nodded. 'I'll find some mint up there,' he said, gesturing with his chin to the gulleys in the hills behind the ancient citadel. 'But there won't be many snails to go with them at this time of year.'

'You won't need snails,' said a young slave, coming towards them along the 'street' of tents. 'I've brought you some pigeons,' and he laid down four fat grey birds by their fire. It was Mikro, Diodotos' shield slave.

Themis laughed. 'So he *is* here. He must be improving his shot,' he said.

Mikro raised an eyebrow but didn't speak.

'Ah, Mikro,' sighed Themis. 'What would we eat without your catapult?'

Diodotos appeared from between the tents. 'A few bitter bulbs and some stale bread,' he said. 'Aren't you pleased to see me, little brother?'

Suzanne couldn't wait to get away. She was envious of Themis leaving his daily worries behind. Every day she was expecting Keir to drop another bomb. Every day she had to give in some piece of coursework and deal with arrangements for the autumn when she would be back in Lancaster.

Meanwhile, she'd managed to talk to Dr Lawson, the professor of the Sports and Exercise department to which she belonged, to complain about not getting a place at the Lancaster training camp. She told the professor that Keir seemed to have 'taken against her'. Dr Lawson seemed to understand immediately, though neither of them said anything explicit. Dr Lawson said that, as a university employee, she had no power over the people who worked for the Mid Lancashire Athletics Club, although they often used the University's facilities. So Keir, employed by the Club, was beyond her control. She promised she'd try to stop any influence Keir might try to have on Suzanne's degree studies.

But then she began to sing Keir's praises! She told Suzanne how many athletes, some of them her own students, he'd got into county- and country-wide competition and how much sponsorship that attracted.

Suzanne left, knowing she'd get no meaningful support from her department. The simple days back at school in Carlisle seemed a long time ago …

<<<

Chapter 39: siege

Next day, in the cool of the dawn, Diodotos and Themis led eight men up to the ancient citadel of Mykines. General Laches needed a map of the area and this was the nearest high point to view the whole plain. The citadel was now an outpost of the Argive army, which had captured and razed much of it fifty years or so before. But they'd kept a skeleton garrison there, who were now repairing some parts.

'Those old builders were pretty crude,' said Diodotos, looking at some huge, irregular blocks of stone that made up the walls.

'They knew a thing or two about making walls that the gods can't shake down, though,' said Themis. 'The columns of our present-day temples wouldn't have survived the earthquakes these walls have weathered.'

As they marched up the approach road to the great entrance gate, the mighty doors opened and an officer and six men came to meet them. They explained their business and were led in under the triangular sculpture of two lionesses above the massive uncarved lintel. Men were working on the courses of stones above it, using a crane to repair a gap. The damaged faces of the lionesses were turned to look accusingly at those approaching the gate. To Themis they seemed older than ancient. Tradition said that this had been the palace of Agamemnon at the time of the Trojan War. If so, it was hardly palatial now. It was just an army outpost, barracks and practice grounds among ruins that in no way resembled a palace.

Inside the mighty walls, Diodotos turned to his men. 'Each man, choose a local and work in pairs to make a plan of these fortifications for General Laches,' he said. 'In particular, make clear where water supplies are, and how many men and animals can be accommodated. We need to know how long it could last in a siege – and where the other exits are.'

Themis and Diodotos followed the officer, who seemed to resent their presence. There were fine walls in some parts and fallen masonry in others, where stunted trees and sprawling vines had taken over.

'Did you meet any lions during your travels with Alkibiades?' Themis asked his brother quietly, gesturing back to the gate.

'Saw some pug-marks on a path on the mountain above Patrai. We were camped there.' Diodotos had got thinner and darker-skinned since Themis had last seen him. His smile was a white flash in his black-bearded face. 'Tracked it, but lost it in a ravine.'

'And how are the walls we built?' asked Themis. They were walking up a series of steps towards the upper level of the citadel.

'Still standing,' said Diodotos. Then he whispered, 'And you'll be pleased to know that I did not need the little treasure that we hid behind the white stone last summer.'

'It's probably been stolen by now,' said Themis. 'Or claimed by Athena – or Father's ghost.'

'You don't believe that,' said Diodotos. 'And I don't think it's been disturbed. I checked, and the mortar around our stone hadn't been tampered with.'

They came out on the final slope up to a wide flat area where some walls still stood to shoulder height, making corners where there had been rooms. Great dressed stones lay strewn where they had fallen. The sun was up now and their shadows were long as they turned to look south.

'You should get a good enough view from here,' said the officer. 'I'll be over there if you need me.' He strode off to stand to attention in the shadow of a wall.

Themis took a length of white linen from his bag. He laid it out on a large flat rock, weighting its corners with stones, then took out his brushes and paints.

The wide, flat valley of the Inachos River, usually called the Argive Plain, lay before them, stretching south to the curve of the blue and silver sea. The massive walls of Tiryns were a dark brooding bulk of stone near the eastern edge of the plain to the left. They, too, were now partly in ruins, partly occupied by Argive soldiers. Beyond them, under its protecting cliff, lay the city of Nafplion with the best harbour in the Argive Gulf.

Across the plain, the walled city of Argos crouched at the foot of the steep Larisa Hill, and spread out over the lower hill called Aspis. Temples stood on its terraces, a haze of cooking smoke softening their angles and columns. High up, the top of Larisa was crowned with the acropolis, protected by walls and the steepness of the slopes. On the back-and-forth bends of the road, bright colours shone in the slanting sunshine from two temple precincts.

But Larisa was dwarfed by the mountains behind. These rose and rose in an uneven spine running southwards, shielding Argos from the Spartan lands further west, and looming over the far side of the Argive Gulf. Among them shone the summit of the highest, Mount Ktenas, crowned with pale grey rock scored by deep ravines.

Northwards, behind them, the plain narrowed towards lower mountains. White dust roads were a spider's web between the empty brown barley fields, the orderly green orchards, the army camps and the villages. The road from Korinthos entered the plain in those narrows. From time to time a sword or a helmet would flash in the sun where soldiers were on the move.

After a while, Themis put his hand back into his bag and said, 'By the way, Mama asked me to give you this.' He handed his brother the tablet with the drawing of Tyro. 'She says you might like to think about this girl, who is rich, modest, and an example to all the others.'

'Especially Melissa?'

'Probably,' said Themis. He looked up at the view, paintbrush in hand. 'But she's …'

'Spoken for by the trusty General Nereus,' Diodotos finished for him, his eyes on Themis' face. But Themis was focusing on the map, so Diodotos held up the tablet in the growing light. 'Hmm. Tyro is pretty,' he said. 'What did Mama promise you to make her so lovely?'

Themis laughed. 'In fact, I was a bit put out that day and probably didn't do her justice. She's delicious-looking – perfect lines of eyebrow and nose.'

Diodotos closed the tablet with a snap. 'And a few curves in the right places, too, I hope …' He leant over Themis' shoulder. 'See there, under the moutains, the black stain? That was the village of Saminthus. The Spartans destroyed it before this truce with the so-called Argive traitors.'

'Men in my company were arguing about whether they were traitors,' said Themis, 'and we hadn't even got here yet!'

'Well,' said Diodotos, 'with the Spartans plundering the villages in the plain, and their King Agis and his huge army spoiling for a fight, Argos had no chance. If those men hadn't made that truce, Argos would certainly have fallen. And the Spartans would be at the gates of Athens again before the winter.' He looked across at the mountains between Argos and Sparta.

Themis took a drink from his waterskin and handed it to Diodotos. 'So what made them leave? Did they forget how to fight?' he said.

'Huh! Spartans never forget, Spartans never forgive,' Diodotos quoted from a marching song, and drank from the skin. 'They'll be back. And Alkibiades is determined to help Argos hold out against them.'

The officer came over to them. 'I need to get my men to their next training ground.'

Diodotos nodded. 'You done, Themis?'

Themis began folding up the linen. 'Yes. That's all I need.'

'Right. We're done then,' said Diodotos. He put two fingers between his lips and whistled. As they walked back towards the gate, his men joined them, one by one. The officer saw them to the gate, saluted and turned on his heel as the huge wooden doors were shutting.

'So what's the verdict of the generals?' Themis asked Photios a few days later. 'Are we disbanding and going home?'

'No way,' said Photios, watching Melanas blowing on their cooking fire. 'Alkibiades put it to the generals that we have collected the largest and best equipped army we've had for a long time.' Melanas handed Photios and Themis each a hammer and a cleft stick and knelt down again to blow. 'So the generals have agreed to besiege Orchomenos. It's two days' march from here, and as you know, a legend of wealth and luxury. I hear that's funded by the levy of outrageous taxes to travel through their gorge between plains.' He hammered the stick into the ground beside the fire.

Themis was doing the same on the other side. 'So we'll be off on a siege campaign tomorrow,' he said. 'That might be quite restful. Searching out quarries and trees large enough for siege-engine-beams is hard work!'

Melanas got up and laid a horizontal stick in the clefts of the two vertical ones. From it, he hung a large pot and then marched off along the line of cooking fires.

'Did he say rabbit tonight?' asked Diodotos, coming up. 'Mikro only found a couple of quail in the market, but he's cooking up a heap of wild spinach and cracked barley into a stew with them.'

Melanas returned with a skinned rabbit. When he saw Diodotos, he shook his head. 'You should have said you'd eat with us, Master,' he said. 'I'd have brought two rabbits. This little thing won't be enough for five hungry men.' As he'd got older his voice had become even deeper and smoother. Now he saw the exaggerated disappointment on Diodotos' face and his rich, rolling laugh rang out across the camp.

'Ah well,' said Diodotos. 'If we take Orchomenos, we'll have plenty to eat – and other delights.' He sat down a little distance from the now crackling fire. 'In my unit, they're saying the walls are gilded and the roofs are of Parian marble.'

Melanas said, 'I'll ask Mikro to bring your pot over.'

Orchomenos' walls were not gilded, nor its roofs marble (except two of the temples). The acropolis of the city was behind an encircling wall on its own hill to the west of the deep gorge. Themis was intrigued by how the foundations were stabilized on the steep slopes.

The gorge lay between the high, swampy plain to the north and the fertile plain to the south, its almost vertical cliffs not even one stade apart. A barrier blocked the road and a fast stream ran beside it. A solid little fortress squatted on the western clifftop. Facing it, across the gorge, a stout tower rose against the eastern sky.

The way into the city snaked up the hillside, protected by a wall, which became part of the enormous gate installation.

As they approached, Themis noticed that parts of the walls of both the fortress and the much larger acropolis seemed weak, perhaps neglected over years of relative quiet. He had prepared catapults to travel in pieces in carts. They began assembling these immediately and General Laches took Themis' advice as to where to target their bombardment.

The first attack was on the tower on the east side of the gorge. The guards in it had bows and arrows as expected. But they also dropped great boulders that they must have hauled up to the top in preparation. Themis was directing the bombardment from below, shouting the orders to his catapult unit, when a man fell against him and knocked him down.

'Are you wounded?' Themis shouted above the uproar as he picked himself up.

'Not me,' the man shouted back. 'But look behind you.'

Themis turned and saw an arrow quivering where it had struck the wooden side of the cart that carried the catapult stones. If he hadn't been on the ground that arrow would have hit him in the throat. He'd forgotten to guard against the dangerous gap that opened in a man's armour when he looked up. He turned to thank the soldier, but he'd disappeared.

That day, they took the tower and the barrier across the road. This cut off both supplies and money from the city. The fortress protecting the road to the city took two days to fall, partly thanks to a battering ram, hastily made from a mighty plane tree that had been growing by the stream. One evening the fortress guards were there, but when the Athenian troops broke in the next morning, they were gone.

'There'll be a tunnel down through the hill and then up into the city,' declared Alkibiades to the men encamped on the southern plain.

Diodotos' unit was sent off to search for this tunnel, while Themis and his men lined up their siege-engines to batter the wall up to the gates of the city.

The city of Orchomenos fell on the tenth day, with the main walls still standing but the tunnel blocked. A deal concerning hostages was struck and the city elders agreed to join the Athenians and their allies against the Spartans. There was to be no pillaging, at least not officially.

'But there'll be roast pig and honey cakes,' said Diodotos. 'They gave in so fast, they'll still have good stores of food and wine.' He rubbed his hands with glee. 'And no one said anything about keeping our hands off the women.'

Photios winked at Themis and poured Diodotos a cup of water. 'Meanwhile, until we humble hoplites are let into the city, we eat beans and drink water, like the Spartans,' he said.

Themis was glad when General Laches ordered him back to Argos immediately, to plan the building of long walls from there to the sea. He had seen enough of the division of spoils and slaves at Skioni three years before. His plan to ask for leave to go to Olympia to see Judge Iasos would have to wait yet again, but his heart lifted when his unit and part of the Argive army marched away from the surrendered city the next morning.

As their small column came down into the Argive Plain, they were surprised to see spirals of smoke rising from hastily deserted villages. Piles of debris had appeared across streambeds and roads.

'Did the Spartans break the truce?' Themis asked an old man leaning on his stick by the road.

'Nah,' he replied, and spat in the dust as he joined their march. 'It was the Epidaureans. You went off, they took their chance. Cowards. But they've gone now.' He was out of breath, trying to keep up with them. 'They killed the guards, raped the women, went home. Same old story.'

Later that night, in the upper streets of the city of Argos, Melanas found lodging for Themis above a ceramics shop, one of Master Zephus' customers. It was hot and stuffy in spite of being high up with a wide view from the open terrace.

'Did you paint this?' asked Melanas as he poured water into a decorated mixing jug.

'Oh, come on, Melanas,' said Themis, shaking his head. 'Even I can draw Odysseus better than that!'

Melanas grinned. 'Now I look at it closely, you are right of course, Young Master. Your Odysseuses always have more muscular legs.' He put a platter of fruit on the low table by Themis. 'In the market they are saying that Alkibiades wants to take Tegea next. That way he'll control the road north out of Sparta and put an end to this tit-for-tat half-war.'

Themis held out his wine cup. 'Fill it up, Melanas. I'm not sure how much General Laches and General Nikostratos listen to Alkibiades, but I want to offer a large libation to Zeus that good sense prevails,' he said. 'The Spartans haven't won anything important from Athens in fourteen years. Why can't we just leave it at that?'

Chapter 40: Heraion

(Breeds of Sheep 25)

Later, as Melanas was clearing up the meal, a loud knock sounded on the door.

It was a man Themis knew. His name was Chilon and he was in charge of the stone defences of the city of Argos. He was a large man with a blond beard and receding hairline. 'In the name of Apollo, Themistokles, what are you doing cooped up in here, like a mullet in an oven! Come down and join the boys by the fountain.'

'Surely not a mullet,' Melanas murmured.

Themis had to smile as Chilon went on, 'Bring your cup and let's drink to dead comrades. Better than weeping and tearing our hair like the women,' he boomed.

Themis was beginning to protest when Chilon added, 'And there's someone here who wants to meet you. He's working on a statue of Hera for the new temple at the Heraion.'

'You mean Polykleitos?' Themis was stunned. He hadn't even been sure that Polykleitos was still alive.

'That's the man,' said Chilon, turning to go.

Themis had revered Polykleitos from afar for most of his adult life. He made an excited face at Melanas, who smiled indulgently. Themis followed Chilon in a daze.

At the corner of the main square the tavern had spilled its customers out into the open. One man sat on a chair under a spreading mulberry tree. Many others sat on the ground in a circle at his feet. 'But Hera is our mother,' he was saying. 'She must wear the most impressive jewels.'

Chilon had a voice like a herald's trumpet. 'Here is Themistokles who worked with Phidias on the Zeus at Olympia,' he called as they walked across the square.

Polykleitos looked up. He had never been a big man and was now shrunk with age. He had wide brown eyes that rarely blinked. He was clean-shaven and had, Themis noted, a forehead that was as deep as his face was long, his eyes halfway between his thinning hairline and his chin.

'Stand still a moment, please, Themistokles,' said Polykleitos. 'I want to look at you.' His voice was husky but musical, as though years of stone dust and smelter smoke had affected his throat.

Themis stopped at the edge of the circle. The old man examined him coolly, and then said, 'You've changed a bit since Phidias sculpted you.'

'That was just one of his standard boy-victor bronzes,' said Themis. 'It wasn't a portrait.'

'Perhaps not, but there was always something individual about the lines of the brow and cheeks, and even the feet. I can see now why,' said the old man. 'Do you sculpt as well as paint?'

'I have done,' said Themis, 'but not for some time.'

Polykleitos stood up. In spite of his age, he moved with vigour. The men around him got up too. Some murmured in protest but loitered to see what the great man would do next, others drifted away.

Polykleitos said, 'Could you spare some time tomorrow, Themistokles? I shall be at the Heraion and would like to discuss a couple of points with you on the spot.'

'I have army work in the morning. Would afternoon – ?' Themis asked.

'Not too late,' interrupted the old man. 'It'll be hot but we'll need good light.'

The Argive Heraion was larger than Themis expected. From Argos across the plain, it looked like a small town around a temple complex on three levels, great steps supposedly carved by the gods into a rising hillside. As he got closer, the town seemed to grow, with its two-storey houses multiplying. They were all painted in shades of yellow, ochre and cream, the wealthier ones near the precinct, the poorer ones on the outskirts. None had suffered the destruction evident in so many of the settlements around Argos. Hera protected her own, it seemed.

The precinct itself rose on its three great terraces with the administration buildings on the lower one, the grand new temple on the second, and the now tidy ruins of the burnt out old temple on the top one, almost hidden from below.

From half way across the plain, Themis could make out a great altar and a long low wall on that upper terrace. He could see a series of priests and priestesses carrying out some kind of ceremony. Smoke of varying colours was rising into the pale blue of the afternoon sky. As he ran nearer, the music of flutes and drums got louder.

He was met at the ceremonial entrance to the holy precinct by Polykleitos himself.

'Come on up,' said the old man as Themis finished washing at the sacred spring by the gate. They walked along the paved way and up the steps to the second level as they talked.

'I haven't been here before,' said Themis, 'though I've seen the town and precinct from the plain. It's impressive.'

'The marauding armies have avoided it so as not to anger the gods. You'll notice,' said Polykleitos, 'that the whole town and precinct are linked by their golden and earthy colours. This is one of the things I wanted to talk to you about – as a painter you may have an opinion as to which colours to use inside the temple to link it with the town but also to set off the statue.'

They arrived at the corner of the new temple. The tall columns of the long side stretched away from them, parallel to the edge of the terrace. They walked up the steps and in through the great oak doors.

Themis took a deep breath. The smells of cedar wood, stone dust, vinegar, lamps burning and men sweating took him back to working on the Zeus in Olympia with his mother's two cousins, Phidias and Panainos. He grinned.

There was less light inside this temple than at Olympia, but the windows high up under the eaves sent dusty beams down into the corners. Masons tapped with their hammers on suspended platforms near the ceiling. A square mast surrounded by a cedar-wood scaffold stood in the gloom.

'You are working in gold and ivory, I heard,' he said to Polykleitos.

'Yes. As you can see, we've only got the statue's internal structure set up here so far. I'm carving the main parts of the figure in a temporary workshop in the town. It is not quite as comfortable as poor old Phidias had at Olympia, of course.' He was smiling slightly.

'Perhaps that will save you from the jealousy of rivals,' said Themis.

'Hah! It took the gods to save him from that in the end,' said Polykleitos with a wry laugh. 'At least, I heard it was the gods.' He looked at Themis with a raised eyebrow.

'Undoubtedly,' said Themis. 'Zeus leant down from heaven and lifted Phidias out of his jail cell with his own hand.'

Polykleitos nodded sagely. 'And that reminds me,' he said. 'I want you to see the end of the ceremony they are performing on the upper level. It is to appease Zeus as his dear wife Hera is now going to have a statue as grand as his own.'

They walked back out into the dazzling sunlight and turned up the steps to the top level. Polykleitos said, 'I cannot hide from you that I have been a little concerned as to the exact facial features of my Hera. I began by drawing her just as my Kanon dictates, with all the features in their mathematical proportions for Perfect Balance. But she does not satisfy me thus, and I have been in despair as to what to do to make her truly live.'

'I know the feeling,' said Themis.

'Until today, that is,' said Polykleitos with the most genuine smile Themis had seen on his face so far.

They had arrived on the upper level and Polykleitos indicated that they should walk along the wall at the edge of the terrace with their backs to the westering sun, the temple, and the town below. 'We will stand at the side in the crowd and observe,' he said. 'I want you to guess which face I now wish to use for my Hera …'

The slight breeze was from the west and the smoke from the altar fires to their left hovered and swirled along the terrace until it blew away towards the eastern hills. Two perfectly white bullocks, with garlands of yellow flowers and coloured ribbons on their painted horns stood peacefully close to the altars. At their feet were two wide stone bowls.

Opposite where Themis and Polykleitos stood, a long line of religious officials and acolytes waited, one behind the other, their left sides to the back wall of the terrace, the right side of their faces fully lit by the afternoon sun. Just then, they began to pass a large closed basket backwards along the line towards the High Priest at the altar. They held the basket above their heads and passed it on without turning round.

Themis examined the profile of each person in the line as the basket moved along. Both men and women were dressed in simple chitons for the ceremony. The colours alternated: cream, then brown, then cream again. It was hard to see some of the faces as the smoke drifted quite thickly at times, curling white and blue and grey.

The acolyte four places away from the priest had difficulty lifting the basket above her head. Her face was in profile and was quite perfectly beautiful, fit for a goddess.

Themis' jaw fell open. His whole body flushed hot, then cold. He knew that face only too well.

It was the face of Xenovia!

There, through the smoke was the priestess who had murdered his father, the priestess who had tried to kill him too, the priestess who had robbed the gods of gold and jewels, the priestess who was dead in the bowels of the mountains above Olympia.

The smoke billowed and suddenly he was unsure. It couldn't be her. She was dead, after all.

Polykleitos had been observing him. 'I can see you have guessed,' he said quietly. 'Is she not magnificent? Her name is Lythaia. But when you meet her, your heart will break. The other side of her body is in ruins. What a waste! What a ghastly trick the gods have played on her.'

The basket had arrived with the High Priest now and he was opening it. Themis looked again at that face through the smoke. Was it really Xenovia, so lovely and so … poisonous? Could she possibly be alive?

The whole line of acolytes turned on a signal in the music to face the altar. And Xenovia became unrecognizable. The left side of her face was broken and scarred, her arm was twisted and her left leg under her brown chiton was clearly shorter than her right.

'It is *her*,' Themis thought. '*She must have been injured, but survived. Dear Zeus and Apollo! What will this mean for my family?*'

She seemed to feel Themis' eyes upon her, and glanced towards him. Her head snapped back into position immediately. Her stance became one of extreme tension, but she stayed in formation, following the woman in front of her towards the edge of the terrace. '*She knows me,*' thought Themis. '*But how? I was thirteen, a beardless boy.*'

The whole terrace of people was silent as the bulls were brought forward. The High Priest's voice rose in incantation as he laid a hand on each bull's curly forelock. Two priests took the knives from the basket and rapidly slit the throats of the magnificent creatures, so that their blood cascaded into the stone bowls. A sigh went up from the watchers and an echoing chant from the priests. The row of acolytes began to move forward.

'Come!' said Polykleitos, grabbing Themis' arm and moving rapidly along the terrace within the crowd. 'We will wait for the attendants to leave the terrace at the top of the steps. I hope she will be able to pause and speak to us.' Polykleitos seemed as excited as a young lover.

Themis felt sick as he was pulled along. He was thinking, '*Asterodia said she was still alive, and I didn't believe her. But she was right. Oh, dear gods, what should I do?*' His mind was racing, wondering whether he could still find the girl who was witness to Xenovia murdering his father. Could he bring her to trial in front of the Assembly or the Court of Areos Pagos? Or perhaps, with Diodotos, he could take matters into his own hands and exact some kind of retribution. But what? He realized angrily that he would never be able to kill her himself. It would be like killing Asterodia.

The ceremony had finished. The music changed to a lilting melody. The High Priest led the line of acolytes towards the steps and began a rhythmic descent. A woman in cream, then one in brown, then one in cream followed him. Then another in cream.

'Lythaia' had disappeared.

Themis laid a hand on Polykleitos' arm. 'Your inspiration has vanished,' he said. 'I'll see if I can find her.'

Polykleitos looked bemused but nodded, as Themis ran up the steps towards the altar against the flow. He'd noticed a doorway in the sidewall of the terrace. He found that it led down another shorter stairway to a narrow cross street giving access to buildings against the retaining wall of the terrace. At the end of the street more steps went down to a similar street below.

On that street Themis caught a glimpse of a brown chiton as it disappeared down yet more steps towards the main part of the town.

He ran across the roof of the house in front of him and jumped down to the second level. He took the fall as a somersault and was back on his feet and down the next steps without a pause. Shading his eyes from the sun, he could see along this wide street until it joined another at right angles, perhaps two hundred feet ahead. But now there was no sign of a brown chiton, or of anyone limping among the many people in the street.

He ran down the steps and walked fast, looking into the shops, the alleyways, the open courtyards. Nothing.

He returned to the bottom of the steps and looked carefully at the houses on either side. He knocked on both doors, but neither opened.

'Everyone here went up to the ceremony,' said a slave with a basket of bread on her head. 'Who did you want?'

'One of the priestesses left before the others,' he said. 'She looked ill.'

The slave woman shook her head. 'No one came by here,' she said with a shrug and walked on.

>>>

<<<

'And so you lost her,' said Melanas next morning.

'Part of me is saying it can't have been her anyway,' said Themis.

'But the rest of you knows it is.' Melanas said quietly.

Themis and Melanas were in Argos City Hall courtyard. Themis had begun on a model of the joins of the existing walls of the city's lower level to the planned long walls. Joins were always the weakest points.

Melanas handed Themis a rule. 'What did Polykleitos say?' he asked.

'Oh, he just laughed and said we'd find her later. He knows nothing about Xenovia.' Themis measured an angle. 'I want you to see if you can find out what Lythaia is doing at the Heraion. Where's she been all this time? She knew me, and yet I've changed a lot. How is that possible? Polykleitos may have already found her, so try him first. He quizzed me for ages on Phidias' methods. I had to be rude to get away.'

Melanas came closer so that the many hurrying scribes and messengers wouldn't hear him. 'I might need to employ someone,' he said. 'Xenovia would know me, too.'

Themis nodded. 'Someone female would be best,' he said.

Melanas smiled and said. 'I have someone in mind.'

Themis looked at him knowingly. 'Of course you do,' he said.

>>>

'OK,' said Bernie, Suzanne's old school Best Friend Forever, as they strolled along by the River Eden, back home in Carlisle, 'what would happen if you didn't medal in Australia? Would they keep you on in the English team?'

Suzanne stopped. 'I think I'd have to take a lesson from Themis.' She felt Bernie stiffen with discomfort at that. 'I'd have to learn to laugh at it, at myself, however much it upset me. That's what he did. I'd have to show that it didn't stop me wanting to train, to improve, to win! I think they'd probably keep me in the team then. And it'd help me get over it – sorry – pun!' They giggled. 'After all, I've probably got another ten to fifteen years of useful athletic life ahead ...'

'So how long will you be home?' asked Bernie. They turned back towards the river-flow measuring station. They were meeting up with Laila and Gina there, then going on for a girly evening at a pub.

Suzanne skipped a couple of steps. 'That's the wonder! Cassie has arranged for me to go to France, to a specialist training camp. Can't wait.'

'So your dear friend Keir's interference may turn out to be a blessing.'

Suzanne smiled to herself. Bernie was studying Theology and Religion at Durham and used words like blessing now. 'Yup, though it'll cost a bomb. I'll have to borrow a load of money – p'raps Florida Granddad can help. And I was thinking of going back to working in the sports store in town for a few weeks – '

'If they'll have you.' Bernie was smiling herself. 'After your very public Twitter argument with the boss about Nike being the goddess of victory, not sport.'

'Yeah. That was embarrassing,' said Suzanne. 'I couldn't believe it went viral.'

'It was the photo of the statue where you can see her nipples through her clothes,' said Bernie, more seriously. 'It wasn't really the argument.'

'Probably.' Suzanne looked at Bernie, then away across the river. 'I never really thanked you for not telling the reporters about *why* I was – am – so ... into that ancient stuff,' she said. 'My family was surprisingly good about it, too.'

'Ah well,' said Bernie. 'We were trying to ignore it. It's ages ago now, anyway.'

Suzanne looked her friend in the face. 'But he's back, you know. He's been in my mind every few days for weeks, now – months, in fact.'

Bernie suppressed a shiver. 'Well ... you don't seem as ... obsessed,' she said kindly. 'I'd never have known if you hadn't said.'

Suzanne laughed. 'I've got a lot of obsessions at the moment. Themis is just one of them. I'm writing his story down when I have time and otherwise trying to ignore it myself, though it can be pretty exciting. But my own life is complicated enough.'

'When did it begin again?'

'On the day Ron dumped me and I cleared four metres thirty-five.'

'Ah, that momentous day ... '

They could hear Gina and Leila coming along the riverside path.

'Yes,' said Suzanne. 'Life changed up a couple of gears that day.'

Chapter 41: plug the jug

(Breeds of Sheep 26 – According to the internet, Alkibiades wasn't even a general on this expedition. He was supposedly an ambassador. His manner and what he says remind me of some of our British politicians and how they're dealing with Brexit!)

<<<

'Any news of Lythaia Xenovia?' Themis asked Melanas as they began packing up. General Laches' order had just arrived. There was to be a special ceremony at a place called Mantinea to celebrate the final returning of hostages and payments of ransoms to do with Orchomenos' surrender. Alkibiades wanted all units there.

'Nothing,' said Melanas glumly. 'But if this move turns out to be a false alarm like the other alerts lately, there'll be time for your latest offer of a reward to bear fruit. She can't have gone far without being noticed.'

'She stayed hidden for years, so I doubt even the reward … ' Themis sighed. 'And I believe this summons really is genuine. The rumour is that Alkibiades wants to taunt the Spartans by taking Tegea.'

'Dangerous, that,' murmured Melanas, packing his cooking utensils into a basket. 'Tegea's just up the road from Sparta, I heard.'

The journey took almost two days. Once the camp on the western slopes of Mount Alesion had been set up, late on the second day, Themis and his unit set off towards Mantinea. They marched down and across flat land to the hill behind the walled city. As they approached the wide training area half way up the hill where the ceremony was being prepared, Themis turned to look back.

The Spartans were said to be camped forty stades away to the south, near where two mountain spurs confronted each other across a narrow gap at the end of the Mantinean plain. But the land there was forested and he could see no sign of Spartans. He walked on up towards the growing clamour of thousands of men anticipating a feast. They were taking their places facing a temporary dais under five oak trees that stood along the back edge of the flat training area.

The priests had sacrificed goats at the altar of the shrine at the top of the hill. The meat was now cooking nearby and the smell was working on the men's stomachs. They sat on the ground or at tables, laughing and teasing, batting away the flies, ignoring the view of the city below in its plain, and the far away mountains. Somewhere among them lay the valley of the Evrotas and the city of Sparta.

As Themis found a place to sit, he noticed that, on some of the heights around the plain, fortlets and lookout towers had been built. On the furthest slopes of Mount Alesion, smoke was rising. Could that be the Spartan camp? The smoke drifted over the forest as if it were alive – a ghostly dragon, languid in the last rays of the sun.

'Hey, little brother,' said Diodotos, slapping Themis on the back and sitting down beside him at the long table. 'How was the road from Argos?'

'Here to Mantinea? Dusty,' said Themis.

'When did you leave?'

'Yesterday morning. About when you arrived here, I should think.'

Diodotos was looking round for a slave to bring him something to drink. 'No we've been here longer than that,' he said. 'It's three days since the Elians walked out on the commanders' conference.'

'Because Alkibiades wouldn't agree to join an attack on Lepreum?'

'Something like that,' said Diodotos. Slaves were now bringing round loaves of bread. 'Anyway, our commanders agreed to muster with the Argives here at Mantinea and attack Tegea through those narrows to the south. They say the Tegeans are ready to submit, but young King Agis of Sparta needs to prove himself and is determined to stop us and keep Tegea loyal to Sparta.'

'We met messengers on the road from the north saying his allies from Korinthos and Viotia would be delayed.'

'He's sent for them of course.' Diodotos was making energetic signs to Mikro to bring him some water. 'But obviously they'll have trouble getting here as we hold most of the roads. Meanwhile, the Eleans will be back and we're expecting other reinforcements, so the Argive generals – and ours – have some decisions to make. Which means we'll be here or hereabouts for a few days. That'll be why you and the rest of the support stores were sent for.' Diodotos waved a piece of bread at their surroundings.

He bent his head conspiratorially towards Themis. 'Had any more trouble with our personal spies?' he asked quietly, then popped the piece of bread into his mouth.

'Not that I've noticed,' said Themis, reaching for the loaf.

'But pleased to be here?' asked Diodotos with his mouth full.

'Depends what you brought me from Orchomenos,' said Themis.

'Cheese, a few silver coins, and … a girl slave. Will that do?'

'For now,' said Themis with a laugh. 'You must have heard that they're sending us a thousand more men from Athens? Alkibiades is going to tell us all about it before we get to the meat tonight.'

'And I dare say he'll go into raptures about the spoils from Orchomenos, too. Luckily we weren't allowed to take many, so he won't go on too long.'

The slaves were bringing round the watered wine now. Diodotos again lowered his voice. 'I hear from Mikro you may have seen Xenovia.'

Themis shrugged and spread his hands. 'It was a while ago now, and I wish I could be sure,' he said. 'The woman I saw was serving as an acolyte at a ceremony at the Argive Heraion. One side of her face was perfect, just like before – made me feel sick, I can tell you. But then I saw that her whole left side was broken and twisted, so it could well be her. *And* she seemed to recognize me, which is odd as I've changed a bit since she went over the cliff.'

'What d'you mean, recognized you?'

'I was staring at her in horror – disgust, more like – and our eyes met. She looked away immediately and disappeared from the ceremony. I tried to follow her, but she'd vanished – obviously avoiding me. And, as far as I can find out, no one has seen her in the thirty days since then. She called herself Lythaia, and Polykleitos is furious with me for frightening her away. He wants her to model for his Hera. But Melanas has had various spies out and there's been no result.'

'You do look more like Father now,' said Diodotos. 'Imagine murdering someone and then seeing them alive and well years later.' Diodotos poured a generous libation. 'This for our Father in Hades to remind him to keep us safe.' He smiled. 'I still miss him. Whatever the gods did to Xenovia in the river under the mountain, she deserved it. Living as half a person is probably worse than being dead.' He drank some wine. 'Perhaps it's she who was sending people to spy on us.'

Themis turned sharply to his brother. 'You think so? You know, you could be right. It would explain a lot of little things. But out here with the army we haven't been attacked. Would she go after Mama, or Chloe?'

'She may just want to stay well out of our way,' said Diodotos. 'I would! And she never had a go at our women.'

'What about that time Myrto's wagon was sabotaged and she broke her leg and lost a baby?'

'Hmm. That could have been someone else entirely,' said Diodotos. 'I doubt she'll come anywhere near us. And anyway, what were you thinking of doing if you did find her?'

'I'm not sure, but I really want to know what she's planning!' exclaimed Themis. The men around them turned in surprise at his tone. He continued more quietly, 'She murdered our father. She tried to kill me, and possibly you. Is she still plotting against us? It gives me nightmares.'

'She must have been purified if she was serving at a ceremony, so the gods have forgiven her,' said Diodotos. 'If she's a cripple, she'll just be a lower order priestess and lucky not to be begging in the streets. We'll probably never know. The gods never tell us what they're up to, do they?'

The priests were calling for quiet to make the official libations.

Diodotos whispered, 'But *I* want some more wine!'

When the libations and their accompanying hymns were over, Alkibiades appeared on the dais under the plane tree. He wore a long purple himation over his yellow tunic in spite of the heat. The two generals, Laches and Nikostratos stood either side of him. There was no sign of the cheetah. The soldiers thumped their cups on tables and benches. Alkibiades raised a hand and they were quiet. He spoke slowly and clearly, his lisp and his perfect, handsome face charming his audience. He pitched his voice to echo from the city walls at the bottom of the hill.

'Today,' he called, 'We remember with gratitude to our gods that Athens is officially at peace with the Spartans.' The men groaned a comic groan.

Alkibiades grinned. 'But we are not here to fight for Athens, we are here to aid our allies, the Argives, in their age-old conflict with the arrogant men of Lakonia.' He raised an arm and pointed over their heads. 'There they wait, between the dissembling Tegeans and this brave city of Mantinea. Do you see the smoke of their meagre cooking fires rising by the dark forest? *They* are eating sour black soup and hard bread. *You* are eating meat, and cheese, and the best barley loaves so kindly provided by Orchomenos, once their friend, but now at our mercy.' There was a huge cheer at this.

'So celebrate that victory you won!' Alkibiades' voice rose a notch. 'And celebrate the thousand more men who will arrive from Athens within three days. They come to support the Argive plan to isolate the Spartans.' Again a roar from the men made him pause. 'And let us also celebrate the presence of the other Argive allies and our common goal of containing the Lakonians. Especially now that their young King Agis has shown so clearly what an *experienced* general he is.' They all banged their cups on the tables and laughed.

'Oh, that young King Agis,' murmured an older man. 'Which god made him agree to that truce with Argos a month back? The Spartans could have annihilated the Argives, but they buggered off south without so much as a herald's toot.'

Laughing, Diodotos declared, 'And I just heard the Spartans fined Agis for losing Orchomenos when he wasn't even there! They're floundering, aren't they? Don't know which way to turn.'

Themis was enjoying the elation of the army. He said, 'Melanas heard they'd agreed to let Agis off if he won the next battle against Alkibiades. Not much hope of that. They've been essentially impotent for years.' He and Diodotos banged their wine cups together.

When the merriment died down, Alkibiades went on, 'With the help of neighbours from Orneae and Kleonae, our allies Argos and Mantinea, the Messenians in the far west around Pylos, and the Eleans in Olympia, the Lakonians are being surrounded in their rustic valleys. The generals have chosen the perfect place to defend on Mount Alesion for our camp.' Now he raised his arm to indicate the heights to his left, above the plain between Mantinea and the Spartan camps. 'When we are ready, we will advance upon the cowering Spartans and drive them to Tegea's borders and their brutish homeland.

'And thus we will plug the spout of the Spartan jug. We will cut them off from their allies further north, the Corinthians and the Sykionians. We will close the passes in the mountains and seal the Argive Plain to the east against them. They will not break the treaties again. They will not reach beyond the Isthmus. They will not come again to plunder the towns of Attica.' The men were standing up now, chanting 'Plug the jug! Plug the jug!' and the echoes rebounded from the city wall.

Alkibiades waited patiently until the men calmed down. Then he called out, 'Eat now! Enjoy the spoils from Orchomenos. This is just the beginning!'

In the dawn gloom next morning, Diodotos mounted Astrapi. Looking down, he said to Themis, 'So you didn't like my present?'

Themis stroked the white blaze on Astrapi's nose. 'She was sweet and pretty, but I can't afford to send her to Mama, and this is no place for a girl who does nothing but weep. We had enough of that with the Skionian.'

'You could have sold her,' said Diodotos with a shrug.

'True, but men are reluctant to pay for tears. She'll be fine. Melanas gave her some food and put her on a wagon back to Orchomenos.'

'It's not her I'm worried about, it's you!' said Diodotos with real concern. 'I bet you didn't even try her out for fornication.'

'That needs to be fun,' said Themis with a shrug, 'and she wasn't going to provide any fun, poor kid.' He slapped Diodotos' thigh. 'But thank you for the kind thought. The cheese is ambrosia and the money very useful!'

Diodotos' cohort began to move towards the new defensive position being set up high on the side of Mount Alesion. 'See you later in camp,' he called as Astrapi fell into line and the dust boiled up. 'Don't forget the siege engines. We'll need them to take Tegea!'

Themis made a rude gesture to his brother. Then he turned and ran to the mustering place for carts and wagons under the walls of Mantinea.

Melanas was waiting for him there.

'Ready?' asked Themis, leaping up onto his army mule.

Melanas nodded. 'All ready,' he said. 'But did you hear the news?'

'News?' said Themis. He bent down. 'From your face, it's not good.'

'The Eleans haven't come back. We'll need their three thousand men if the Spartans decide to fight.' Melanas' eyes were round with anxiety.

Themis straightened up. 'They'll be back,' he said. 'It's in their own interests. Alkibiades will have been too pushy, so they're saving face. He tends to do that, even with friends. You going to lead the singing?'

Melanas nodded and climbed onto the wagon he was driving.

Themis turned in his saddle and called to the line of drivers. 'Don't move till the hoplite snails finally get started. I'll give the call. And all the gods be with us all!'

A guffaw rose from the nearest hoplite infantrymen as they fell into line.

Melanas' deep voice began a rhythmic chant, which the men behind him took up. 'Heard the rumble of your wagon, saw the glitter of your sword, / Watched a cloud of your arrows hide the sun as they soared.'

The hoplites in front joined in the refrain as they picked up the rhythm and marched along the dusty road.

Themis called, 'Forward!' and rode on beside Melanas.

'But your sword was too blunt and your arrows were too slow, / Your wagon broke a wheel and you ran before your foe. / Run faster, little soldier. I'm right behind, you know. / Run faster, little soldier. I'm right behind, you know.'

Chapter 42: frustration

It was the next morning and the sun was still low in the sky.

The generals were confused. They'd gathered in a huddle under the one remaining oak tree on the west-facing slope of Mount Alesion. Their voices were raised in accusations of betrayal and treason. There was no sign of Alkibiades.

The Spartans had begun an attack up the hill towards them at first light and the Argive and allied armies had been ready and waiting. But the Spartans had suddenly given up their advance. They'd retreated in a hurry and disappeared beyond the forest.

So now the men still stood in their hill-battle formation, fully armed, feeling like boar-hunters deprived of a quarry. They argued about the Spartans' motives. Was it a trick? Some even drew their swords on each other, until General Laches yelled at them from under the tree to calm down and stay vigilant.

'They were almost upon us,' said Diodotos, stabbing the spike end of his spear into the ground in frustration. 'I'd chosen my first victim. He was just there! What in Hades made them retreat? And why aren't we chasing them?'

Themis picked up Diodotos' shield and propped it against his own.

'I want that here!' said Diodotos, keeping formation but squatting down.

Photios joined them and sat on the ground. 'Have the gods deserted the Spartans?' he said, his voice strange inside his helmet.

Themis sat down beside him, pulling Diodotos to sit on the ground. His heartbeat was slowing and he could feel his muscles relaxing. 'Who knows what happened?' he said. 'We were making so much noise ourselves we couldn't hear them at all.' He took off his helmet and took a deep breath. All around the men were sitting down, still in loose formation. 'I don't know what's worse, fighting and losing, or being ready to fight and then having it stopped.'

'The second,' said Diodotos. 'Because there's no resolution, no decision, no outcome. What'll happen now? We should have gone after them.'

They sat in silence for a while, among other silent men. They all took off their helmets. A couple of scouts were talking to the Argive generals under the tree. A herald began to call the news as he ran round the camp. 'The Spartans have retreated, back beyond the forest, to Tegea!'

Helmets and cuirasses were unbuckled. Water skins were passed round. But no one left his position. Other scouts were out in the woods below. It was obvious that no one knew what to do. Had the Spartans really retreated to Tegea? Or were they hiding in the forest? Photios pointed out that there was no sign of activity in the fortlets on the tops of the two spurs that narrowed the plain.

The heat grew as the sun climbed. Sitting in armour without shade was torture. Flies gathered in the sweating creases of their skin. At last the order came to find shade and rest.

Melanas appeared and carried their shields as they walked up into the shade of some twisted old pines above the camp.

Diodotos turned to Themis. 'We were ordered to battle positions so fast this morning, I couldn't ask you, but aren't you supposed to stay with the supply division?'

'Not since I left Argos this time. I go where I'm told, and Laches told me to join this company.' Themis said.

'Ah, so you're just a common soldier now, not an exalted engineer,' mocked Diodotos.

Photios rolled his eyes. 'It *is* extraordinary, Themis, that it took explicit orders from the General for you, a strong and well-trained hoplite, to join the front line,' he said.

'But Mama won't be pleased,' said Diodotos.

'With any luck, she won't know,' said Themis with a pointed glance at his brother. 'You know it's not favouritism. I'm just more useful designing and building things.' The others scoffed loudly. Themis went on. 'But Laches keeps us all fit and on our toes. He relies on his "support staff" to fill gaps that open in the battle lines.'

'On your toes, eh? I did hear there's been extra dance training in your ranks,' said Diodotos.

'More often on my arse than my toes,' said Themis. 'Though I'm getting quite good at the supported jumps.'

'But you used to dance a lot when you were training for boxing,' said Photios. 'Like this!' He jumped up and did a couple of bouncing feints, then screwed up his face. 'Ow! Not so easy in full armour, mind you.'

The tension broke and they and the men around them began to laugh. They laughed and laughed, slapped each other on the back, and took off the rest of their armour. Some began a leaping dance in a line. The flute and drum gave them music. The leader offered Themis his position 'on condition you dance on your arse'.

But when a herald came, running up towards them from the

conference tree, everyone fell quiet. 'The army will move off before nightfall,' he was calling.

The men all sat down to cool off. Mikro and Melanas appeared and checked the brothers' panoplies. Orcus did the same for Photios.

Themis and Diodotos lay down near each other in the shade, resting while there was a chance. The flies took a few minutes to find them again.

Themis watched the pattern of long green pine needles against the bright sky. They moved in the breeze as if painting it an even more luminous blue. 'Are you still thinking of getting married this winter?' he asked lazily.

'Yeah, I suppose so,' said Diodotos, half asleep. 'It's my filial duty, after all, and I can afford it at last.'

'It's been five years since you could afford it,' said Themis quietly. 'It's not money that holds you back.'

'True,' agreed Diodotos seriously but without stirring. 'It's my fear of giving a woman any kind of hold over me.'

Themis chuckled. 'Women have a hold over us from the day we're born,' he said. 'It's only by staging wars and fighting other men that we feel more powerful than they are.'

'You've been listening to the sophists,' said his brother. 'The truth is that we can always take a woman by sheer strength. That's what gives us power over them.'

'Until they present you with your child,' said Photios, joining them in the shade.

'If they can find you and are sure it's yours,' drawled Diodotos. 'No, the best time to show them we're more powerful is during the Dionysia. No one cares if they get pregnant during the Dionysia because they're enjoying it so much. And they never come and complain afterwards or expect help with raising a child.'

Photios sighed. 'Ah, the voice of experience, perhaps?'

Themis rolled onto his side and looked at his brother. 'Will there be a little Diodotos from the last Dionysia?'

Diodotos shook his head. 'Unlikely, little brother,' he said dozily. 'And if there is, his mother won't know who his father is. That night is a complete blank in my memory after the procession, the sacrifices and the feast … What about a little Themistokles?'

'I doubt it,' said Themis. He pulled a sad face. 'I didn't get there till the feast was almost over. And later, the girl I had my eye on disappeared with a man in a lionskin. Anyone in a lionskin deserves what they get.'

Diodotos laughed. 'You didn't tell me that,' he said.

'Nor me,' said Photios.

'I don't tell you a lot of things,' said Themis.

A general stir ran through the camp. The heat was growing and the men were looking for more shade.

But just then, the Heralds' voices called, 'Prepare to march!'

The setting sun lit the tops of the two mountain spurs facing each other across the 'waist' of the plain. The spear-tips of sentries in the fortlets on their tops twinkled. The ground at their feet was already in darkness.

Melanas drove the lead wagon carefully down Mount Alesion with the sun in his eyes. The generals had finally chosen a place between the river and the road, to the north of the narrows for their next camp. As they descended, to their left, almost in among the forest trees, was the precinct of Herakles, the Herakleum, where the Spartans had had their camp until they'd suddenly pulled back beyond the 'waist', towards Tegea. To their right, in a tributary valley, was the Temple of Poseidon Hippios, a Mantinean precinct, surrounded by a village and ancient plane trees.

Further away to the right, was the city of Mantinea in the middle of the plain, with its isolated acropolis hill where they'd eaten two days before.

Themis rode along the line of wagons and back. The orders were to set up a camp near the road on the east side of the plain, a stone's throw from Poseidon's precinct. Once there, Melanas went off immediately to arrange a water supply as the river and streams were almost dry at this time of year. There were wells in the precinct.

The heralds were busy passing on the orders of the generals to the officers. The allies were to rest until the moon had set. Then they were to line up on the flat plain, north of the narrows and the forest, in full battle order, ready to attack the Spartans if they appeared.

The scouts said the Spartans were still digging channels to divert the river and flood the Mantinean plain. They reckoned they'd come back to their camp at the Herakleum some time that day.

In the battle plan the generals gave them, the Athenians would be closest to the eastern hills, not far from Poseidon's temple. The hoplites would be in the main battle line on the flat, while the cavalry would start higher up the slope and attack from there when ordered.

Themis was to be in the third rank of General Laches' hoplite unit, Diodotos with the cavalry. Photios would be in the sixth row of General Nikostratos' phalanx. An order for quiet came round early in the evening.

Themis lay beside his fellow soldiers in full armour in the dark. They set up a whispered chorus of a series of scurrilous songs. Themis knew some of them from Frog's renditions, but the one about the wounded soldier imprisoned in a cave by three nymphs was too explicit even for Frog.

After a while, even the more sentimental songs died away, and most of the men lay silent, gazing at the canopy of glistening stars.

Themis kept control of his thoughts by reciting parts of the Odyssey to himself – the parts about feasting and travelling. He avoided his usual memory of Odysseus' lazy days with Circe as that made him think of Melissa, which made him clench his teeth. He also prayed, and he could hear others doing the same, each to his own favourite deity.

At last, sleep came, but he dreamed of his father in the stable at the birth of Astrapi. In reality this had gone smoothly, but in his dream there was panic as the birth progressed and Astrapi's mother got weaker and weaker. Melissa was there, sobbing and trying to help the mare, stroking her belly saying, 'It's nearly out. Keep working, girl. It's nearly here.'

And suddenly, Melanas was shaking Themis awake. 'The day is nearly here, Master Themis,' he rumbled, putting a water skin into Themis' reluctant hand. 'General Laches wants everyone fully ready "before you can see your fleabites".'

And now they were ready. They'd all drunk water, urinated, re-armed, returned to their positions and were polishing spear heads and spikes as the sun lifted above the hills to their left. The priests were sacrificing goats and a ram at an altar by the road. The word came round that the omens read in the entrails were auspicious.

Themis prayed again, to Zeus and to Athena and to Apollo, who had helped him get over his head injury. He'd left an offering for Artemis at her temple in Mantinea the afternoon before, asking her to care for Eirini and Melissa if he did not return.

He hadn't fought in a phalanx for years. He had trained with the other hoplites this last month to create the shield wall that defended both him and the man to his left, but his other battles had been sieges where such a phalanx had to be ready to break.

Today he would be in the third line, and the phalanx must hold, no matter what. There were reported to be no archers on the Spartan side, so the two phalanxes would advance on each other. Themis' first job would be to thread his long spear between the heads of the front two lines and try to pierce the armour of the first line of the enemy. As soon as the initial crash of shield walls happened, he and the men behind him would begin to push, expecting to plough into the enemy phalanx as the Athenian front line took down their front line.

Diodotos on Astrapi was among the cavalry by the road. They'd saluted each other as the officers were marshalling the troops. Now Themis hoped the Spartans would appear soon. Waiting was the worst thing about war.

And then they did appear, marching out of the wood along the road seven or eight stades away. Shields and spears gleamed, red cloaks and helmet crests billowed, unwavering files of men moved with perfect discipline. Their front unit pulled up sharply, then turned along the edge of the forest, making room for the following cohorts. Within minutes thousands of men were filling the fields by the forest.

The men around Themis commented on this. 'That gave them a shock,' said one. 'They weren't expecting to see us all lined up and ready.'

'Their scouts couldn't see us moving in the dark,' said another. 'That King Agis will have to rethink.'

'Again,' said a third. The laughter was more nervous than humorous.

As the Spartans fell in and organized themselves for battle, Themis could hear the Argive general to his right and other commanders beyond, addressing his men. General Laches rode along his section of the line of Athenians on a magnificent bay horse. His armour shone, his helmet crest was as yellow as the sun.

'Men of Athens,' he cried. 'We are privileged to be here, part of the greatest army gathered in a generation, to face the coarse and boorish Spartans, and to show them that the Peloponnese is not theirs alone. With these honourable allies in your battle line, your victory will not just win glory for Athens, but extend the power of your city and your goddess to these fertile plains. In turn this will save her from the invasions and incursions that we have suffered in the past. Did you see the Spartans check in surprise when they saw us? You are forcing them to face you when they least want to. Show them how mighty you are in your revenge for the wrongs they did to your families at home! Who serves the greatest city the world has ever known?!'

The army shouted, 'We do!'

'Who serves in the greatest army the world has ever known?'

'We do!' The shout echoed all across the plain, and returned from the slopes of the mountains around.

The men laughed and cheered and beat their spears against their shields.

The General turned his horse and took up his position at the front of the Athenians.

As each sector of the allies finished cheering, a hush ran along the line.

Now they could hear the paean from the Spartan ranks, a drumbeat pulsing under the voices. The enemy had begun a slow march across the flat, dusty fields.

Chapter 43: battle

Laches and Nikostratus and the other generals further along the line had turned their horses to face the Spartans' advance. The wall of shields and spears came on agonizingly slowly. The men that formed it sang of their gods and their strength, of victory and the glory that is Sparta, their feet marching in time to the drums.

Themis heard a great commotion to the far right. He turned his head to see through the eyeholes of his helmet. The far end of the Spartan line was in disarray where it had encountered the Mantinean and Arcadian allies. His own end of the line had still not collided with that solid wall of Spartan shields. But if it had broken at the other end, it could not be invincible. The men around him cheered and moved forward, some faster than others causing the front line to bend, but not break.

And yet the Spartan wall came inexorably on, the slow beat of drums and fists on shields relentless. Their King and his chosen guard were to Themis' right, facing the Argives and General Nikostratos' men. The men facing Laches' sector were less daunting. Themis felt a shiver run through his comrades. He repeated over and over to himself, 'Today is the day, today is the day,' although he didn't know which day he meant.

He heard the Spartan order, 'Spears forward!' and saw through his helmet the Spartan spears transferred from left to right hands and point towards him. The thud of the drums got a little faster. He couldn't see much but he could hear his own heart beating louder than any Spartan drum. He transferred his own spear to his weaker right hand. How he would have preferred to wield sword and spear with his left!

At the last minute, the line in front of him stepped backwards, towards him! He had to push the men in front apart to stay on his feet. There had been no clash of shields, no final great cry of attack. The Athenian front line had broken and fallen back, not just here but to his right as well.

The second and third lines stumbled as the Athenians in front turned and fought their way away from the Spartan spears. The Spartan drums did not stop.

Men were turning and pushing past Themis in panic. He looked along his line. He and others were holding fast, but many were trampling over their own men as they ran for safety, tripping and even swearing at those who didn't move.

Now the Spartan wall did break. Some chased the Athenians who had run. Some attacked the Athenians who had remained in position. A sword came stabbing down towards Themis' neck, black against the pale blue sky. He lifted his shield and took his spear into his left hand with one movement, pulling his sword and stabbing forward with his right. He felt the sword go home and the other man's weapon dropped, clanging against his helmet.

Someone collided with him as that man fell away. He forced his way forward to find room to fight. He fell over a body, as the Athenian on his right was cut down by a taller Spartan. This man turned to Themis next, his hacking sword lifted. His shield was coming up to clout Themis' chin. Themis dropped his spear altogether, lifted his shield, and, with all the strength of his dominant left arm, parried his opponent's shorter sword and shield. His own sword, still dripping with blood, glanced off his opponent's cuirass and sliced into the man's thigh. The tall Spartan grunted and raised his hand again to chop down on Themis' neck. Themis crashed his shield under the raised arm into the man's armpit while swinging his own sword high across his body. The Spartan's hand fell to the ground, still holding the hacking sword. He staggered and fell back.

The smell of faeces was added to that of blood and urine and dust already thick in the air. Themis yelled in triumph and turned to his left. Another Spartan was making for him, leaping over the bodies on the ground. Through the groans and screams, Themis heard the thud of horses' hooves and Diodotos' voice bellowing, 'Stand and fight! We're holding them! You're not alone! Stand and fight!'

Themis swung his shield at the man leaping towards him and the

Spartan fell back a step. But he recovered immediately and, with his spear in his right hand, aimed at piercing Themis' neck. Themis ducked and the blow went into the crest. He chopped the spear in half with his sword. The Spartan threw down his remaining half and reached for his sword. Themis led again with his shield while stabbing at the man's neck from the side with his own weapon. He must have cut him at least, as blood began to flow down his cuirass, but at that moment a Spartan voice called an order, directing their forces to their left. Themis' opponent turned and ran off to Themis' right.

Other Spartans followed his lead, leaping on and over fallen Athenians. Themis saw the man he'd just wounded run past three battling couples. Photios must be over there somewhere, he thought, then turned and saw another coming for him from his left.

This man had a sword at the ready but no spear. Themis picked up the broken spear and raised his shield in one movement. The man attacking managed to avoid the iron point of the spear as it glanced off his cuirass. But he ran into the rim of Themis' shield, held horizontally at shoulder height, and almost cut his own throat before his sword could reach Themis. Themis stepped back, aiming the spear at the groin, but the man ran erratically off to the right to obey the order.

The Athenian cavalry was harassing other Spartans also moving to obey the order. Themis could see horses circling beyond the melee of men fighting hand to hand and hear their shouts and cries. He stepped out in front of another Spartan who was running to the right, showing no interest in chasing the fleeing Athenians.

But this one was ready with his short sword out and his shield a constantly moving protection. As Themis raised his own shield, he heard a horse scream close by. Was that Astrapi? He ducked, stabbing with his sword and crashing his shield against the man in front of him. He felt his sword bury half its length in the man's armpit and heard his grunt as he lost his grip on his shield. The eyes behind the holes in the helmet were white with surprise. Themis saw the shield dangle uselessly, streaming with blood.

He turned and ran towards the scream of the horse as the Spartan stumbled away.

There were three horses on the ground that Themis could see through his eyeholes. The furthest one was Astrapi. And under her blood-spattered hindquarters, trapped by his left arm and leg, was Diodotos. He was trying with his other leg to push her off him.

But it was not only the horse's weight that pinned him to the ground in a pool of blood and urine and faeces. The spike of a broken spear had been thrust into his neck on the right side, at the edge of his cuirass. His right arm was useless and his helmet was crooked so he couldn't see.

Themis knelt down in the gore and took off the helmet. Diodotos moved his head, wincing as his cheek hit against the spear. His breath came in gurgling, choking gasps.

'Themis?' he asked, blinking his eyes to try and focus.

'Yes,' said Themis. 'Lie still a minute.' Themis stood up. He checked to see they were not going to be attacked, threw down his shield and sword and leaned hard against Astrapi's flank. 'Move old girl,' he said under his breath.

He was shocked at Astrapi's agonised whinny. 'Move your arse, old thing,' he said again. In spite of her pain, she seemed to understand and shuddered as she tried to shift herself on the ground. Both her back legs lay at impossible angles.

'One put a spear between her legs … and another went for her head,' said Diodotos. 'Bastards!'

Themis retched, directing the vomit away from his brother. He pulled Diodotos' left leg and arm free as Astrapi tried again to roll her body away from her master.

'Thanks, old girl,' said Themis when he could talk. 'That's enough.' To Diodotos, he said with a bitter smile, 'They must have seen you were their greatest threat.'

'You'll have to kill her,' said Diodotos, his legs free and twitching. Blood ran from his mouth as he coughed.

Themis could hardly hear him through the chaos of battle around them, but he didn't need to be told twice. He took off his helmet and dropped it in the filth, picked up his sword and went round to Astrapi's head. The one eye he could see was wide with terror and pain. Flies had settled on its long lashes. He knelt down beside her and fondled her ear. 'Thank you, Astrapi, daughter of Chrysohaiti and Glykovelas. You have served us well all your life and been a fine mother to many foals. Go peacefully to Hades.' He slid his sword under her neck, then lifted it sharply, severing her arteries and windpipe. Her whole body shuddered and lay still. Themis closed her eye.

With his left hand, Diodotos was feeling the spear in his neck. He looked up with clear eyes and a calm face as Themis returned to him.

'So,' he said, 'it's over. We have the Spartans on the run, don't we?'

Themis looked around. The battle had moved away. 'Yes,' he said.

'They're taking a beating from the Argives now.'

Diodotos spat blood. 'I want you to promise me something.'

'Don't talk now,' said Themis. 'I'll get Melanas and we'll get you to the healers.'

'I'm dying, little brother,' said Diodotos. His voice was a mere wheeze. 'I know that, even if you don't. So listen! Come closer so I can see you.'

Themis' whole body went rigid, rejecting what he knew was true. He knelt closer. 'I'm listening,' he said hoarsely. His throat had closed and he could hardly breathe. He was pulling the linen lining and its wadding out of Diodotos' helmet with shaking hands.

His brother took a gurgling breath but seemed calmer. He rasped, 'You have to make sure you get married and have lots of children. I put it off too long.'

Themis' mouth fell open. He'd expected a message for Alkibiades or his mother, not this.

Diodotos went on, 'You are the only son now. You must carry on Father's name, the farm, and the honour of our family.' The ghost of a smile moved the dark, matted beard. The flies that had settled on it flew off. 'Buy yourself a decent wife. We have enough money ...' His breath came as a loud rasp. 'Promise!' he demanded.

Themis took Diodotos' left hand in his to stop it touching the spear spike. His stomach churning and his heart pounding, he said, 'I promise that by this time next year you'll have a nephew and I'll have a son.'

The smile grew for a moment. 'Even if you don't like her much, you know what to do ...' Diodotos body arched in a spasm, and then relaxed. 'Thank Mama for me, and the slaves,' he said, his breathing rapid and shallow, 'and kiss Chloe.'

Themis nodded.

'And do me one last favour,' whispered Diodotos.

Themis bent closer to hear his voice, the wadding in his other hand.

'Pull this stake out of my neck. It's bothering me.' Tears made clean lines from Diodotos smiling eyes to his ears as he lay. His breath came now as shuddering sobs. They both knew that pulling out the spear meant Diodotos would bleed to death within moments.

'You've been a steadfast brother and son,' said Themis. 'Greet Father and Myrto for me.'

The noise of battle was growing in the centre of the fighting lines. Themis stood up. He called out to the sky, 'I charge you, great god Hades, to honour this man I'm sending you, above the others you will

receive today. He comes to meet you with courage and a pure heart.'
He looked down at Diodotos.

Diodotos nodded slightly and took a deep, rasping breath.

Themis put his foot on Diodotos' right shoulder, grasped the spear,
and pulled. The sound as the spike came out made his stomach heave
again. Diodotos cried out. Themis threw the spear behind him and
knelt by his brother. He placed the wadding from the helmet over the
fountain of blood that was pulsing from the wound and pressed hard.
He watched the smile on Diodotos' face grow as the pain seeped away.
He smiled back as his brother's eyes fixed and his body went limp.

'Good journey below,' whispered Themis. 'You will have peace now.'

>>>

Chapter 44: pyre

(Breeds of Sheep 28 – Trying to keep it together to get this written up.
NEVER EVER EVER IMAGINED ANYTHING AS BAD AS THIS! Keep
crying.)

<<<

Themis lifted his arms to the skies amid the sickening clamour and
howled long and loud. At last he picked up both helmets and hooked
them over his arm, then lifted his brother's body over his shoulder. He
heard a clear cry in the chaos. 'Laches is dead. The General is dead!' He
stood up, staggered a moment under the weight, threw a final glance at
Astrapi, and set off at a run, aware that, at any moment, he might be
rounded up by the victors as a hostage.

The army hospital was at the Temple of Poseidon, a little above the
plain. Themis arrived there in a daze. Melanas had appeared beside him
at some point on the last short climb up the paved way to the precinct.

As he laid his brother on the dry grass, for a moment he thought that
Diodotos still lived. Fresh blood poured from the wound in his
shoulder as the wadding fell away and air exited his body. But there was
no breath, and the body settled with its head lolling and its mouth
open. Themis collapsed beside it, sitting with his head on his knees, his
mind a blank. Flies settled on his bloody skin. Their hum was loud …

When he finally looked up, Diodotos' jaw was tied up and Mikro was
taking the armour off his body. The satchel was beside them and the
wooden snake, emblem of the healing god, lay in the dusty grass.

'The Spartans have the victory,' said Melanas, running up with Astrapi's saddle and bridle. 'Laches and Nikostratos are both dead. The Spartan trophy is made with their armour. If you hadn't brought the Master back, they'd have his armour, too.'

'And maybe his body,' said Mikro quietly, now sponging away the blood and filth from Diodotos' face. 'And you. But there was protection.' He meant the snake.

Themis shook his head slightly and stood up. 'No. They'd've left the body.' He took a breath. 'He went well,' he said, gesturing at his brother's body. 'Mother will be proud. He told me himself to pull out the spear.'

Melanas grunted, setting down his burden. Tears streamed silently down his lined cheeks as he stepped close to Themis and began to unbuckle his cuirass. 'You're wounded!' he said suddenly.

Themis looked down. His left thigh had a deep cut into the outer muscle. Blood was oozing from it and more had run down his leg.

'I thought it was Diodotos' blood,' he said stupidly to Melanas.

'There's another wound at the back. The sword went right through your leg. You'd better get a poultice on it now.' Melanas looked at Diodotos with a quiet groan. 'We'll see to your brother.'

Themis arrived in Argos on an army horse that evening. He couldn't remember setting out from Mantinea. Someone must have dressed his wound with a thick wad of clean cloth. Only when it began to throb, aching like a hundred wasp stings, did he begin to grasp the full horror of what had happened.

And then it was only his anger that kept him on the horse – anger at the men in the front line who had turned back in fear, anger at the futility of the battle, anger at the gods who played like this with human lives, anger at the generals who'd allowed themselves to be pushed into it. But most of all, Themis was angry at Alkibiades who did the pushing and then DISAPPEARED and hid among the hills while his followers fought and bled and died for his STUPID pursuit of glory! He ground his teeth all the rest of the way, against the pain in his leg and the rage in his mind. The horse noted the fury and behaved perfectly.

At Argos, he rode it straight to the cemetery precinct. The dressing on his wound was soaked through and blood was running down his leg.

An official approached him grimly as he dismounted.

'You know the news?' he asked the official, a small man with dark, appalled eyes.

'The Spartan emissary said they would not be upon us until after the Carnea,' said the official. 'Time enough to bury our valuables and ship out the women. How many dead?'

'They were still counting when I left,' said Themis. 'With Argos and all the allies together, more than five hundred, perhaps twice that. Someone said they'd cremate some at Mantinea, but others will come here by tomorrow night.'

'We'll need more wood,' said the man. 'The Epidaureans took the opportunity again while the army was away and so we have a few dead here, too. The pyres will have to be communal.'

Themis put a hand on his arm. 'Can I buy wood for a personal pyre now? It's for my brother.'

The man's eyes rested on Themis' thigh wound. 'I'll put it aside,' he said. 'Name?'

'I'm Themistokles and my brother is – was – Diodotos, sons of Kallistos of Diomea in Athens.'

'Diodotos?' The man's eyes lit for a moment. 'I remember him. He lent me money to pay a bet one evening when the wine was particularly good … I'm sorry he's gone. Did you know that your tardy Athenian reinforcements arrived this afternoon in the bay? They'll be camping in the sand by the sea tonight. Your Alkibiades met them there and is not letting them into the town. They'll cause trouble, all excited and ready to fight that they are.'

Themis' leg felt as if it was on a pyre of its own. He breathed heavily through flared nostrils but he set his jaw so as not to groan his pain or scream his anger. 'Where d'you do the burning?' he forced himself to say.

'In the valley between Larisa Hill and Mount Lykoni,' said the official. 'It floods there in winter. You can't see it from here. If the body's here by tomorrow, you can do it tomorrow night, before the rush. Or you can choose somewhere else on public land if you wish. Will you be taking the urn home?'

Themis grabbed his horse's bridle to steady himself. 'Depends on what the remaining commanders order. But that's my plan.'

'Themistokles of Diomea, brother of Diodotos. Got that,' said the man. 'Get to the Asklepion now and get that seen to,' he added, gesturing at Themis' leg.

The healers gave him something that knocked him out. Next morning, he was on his feet, limping and bleeding, making arrangements, ignoring orders. He'd found he couldn't eat.

He watched Melanas drive up to the crematorium at the bottom of Mount Lykoni's east-facing slope. The late afternoon sun was striping the road with shadows from the poplar and willow trees. The back of the wagon was covered in a stained tarpaulin. The stench was choking.

'There's wood here for Diodotos,' Themis said as Melanas drew up, 'but the others have to go to the director of funerals over there'.

Melanas nodded. He and Mikro and Themis' leg wound were black with flies the minute the wagon came to a standstill, in spite of the growing breeze. 'We'll deliver the others first, then come back with him for the wood,' he said. 'Will we have the pyre here? Looks like a storm coming.'

'I've found a good place by the sea,' said Themis. 'Everything's ready there.'

'Master Photios is behind us,' said Melanas. 'He lost a finger but is otherwise whole.'

Themis waited on his horse in the shade of the trees. After a while, Melanas drove the wagon back to him. Then Themis led the way along the road south towards holy Lerna and the sacred lake. But not far from Argos, he took a fork to the left, which led between fertile fields and orchards to the seashore.

The rumble of the wagon wheels suddenly went quiet when they came to the beach. A great stand of canes where the field met the sand whispered as they stopped twenty feet from the water.

The bay was a long unbroken curve to the east. At its far end, about forty stades away, the high crags above Nafplion rose dark in the heat haze. About half way round, a trireme from Athens was beached. Beyond it were another ten and the low harbour mole of Kios jutting into the bay. The ships were empty except for the guards.

Wavelets splashed, curlews and terns cried and, in the trees edging the fields beyond the sand, cicadas sawed.

Themis dismounted and tried to help with building the pyre, but Melanas made him sit on a rock in the shade of the canes. 'Your wound will go rotten if you go on straining it,' he said, handing Themis a water skin. A north wind was rising and the canes swished and fidgeted.

Hoofbeats sounded and Photios appeared. He leapt from his horse and ran over to Themis. 'I didn't hear till noon,' he said.

'He died well,' said Themis, looking up at Photios' tear-streaked face. 'I heard he saved the lives of many of us – those who stood to fight *and* those who didn't – before the Spartans could stop him.' Photios put his good hand on Themis' shoulder and Themis laid his own hand over it and went on, 'They had to bring Astrapi down to get him. She fell on top of him, both her legs broken. So she held him down while they spitted him like an animal.' Themis sobbed suddenly. 'He asked me to release him …'

Photios pulled Themis' head into his chest and held him tight with both arms. Themis sobbed once more, then pulled away, gulping for breath. 'We have to build him the perfect pyre,' he said when he could speak. He tried to stand up.

Photios held on to Themis' shoulder. 'Stay there, we have helpers,' he said, gesturing with his bandaged hand.

Themis looked where he pointed and now saw five men and a woman helping Melanas and Mikro build the pyre. While they'd been speaking, a small cart and other horses and mules had arrived.

'We brought apple wood, and seasoned fir and scented oil,' said Photios. 'And this.' He showed Themis the green satchel Diodotos had been given at the farewell symposium. 'And we have a priest and Evanthi, Diodotos' last lover.' Photios twisted his mouth. 'Her wailing could summon more than a mere Hades.'

Themis sat and rocked side to side as he watched. He knew nothing about Evanthi, but was grateful for the basket of funeral foods she had set down near the wagon. Then she helped Mikro wrap Diodotos in his cloak. Themis stood up and limped over to the bier. Without his armour, Diodotos seemed so slight. Themis' vision blurred and he had to fight to stay upright.

The priest had set up his temporary altar and now lit his incense on it. Melanas and Photios and two other battle-scarred men, whom Themis vaguely remembered from Diodotos' unit, lifted the body up onto the pyre. Themis took a breath to calm himself, got out a small flask he had bought at the funeral shop and sprinkled rosemary oil over the bier.

The priest raised his voice in prayer and the other men beat their chests slowly in unison.

'Great Lord Apollo,' intoned the priest. 'You have declined to send Diodotos back to rejoin his body. Hermes is leading him on his way to the Halls of Hades. And so we wish him farewell, and with the flames that consume his earthly home, hope to ease his journey.'

Themis rolled his eyes at Photios, who shrugged helplessly. Themis stepped forward, quieting the priest with a raised hand. He called out to the sky, 'Farewell, Diodotos, my brother. May you be at peace in the Underworld, with Father and our sister Myrto and her family. You will be remembered at our home and in our hearts for ever.'

Evanthi's keening rose to a crescendo and she threw herself on the pyre. She beat Diodotos' chest with her fists. 'You loved me and left me! How could you do that? How could you let yourself die, when I'm waiting here for you to return?'

Photios took her shoulders and pulled her back. Themis took the torch from the priest and lit it at the altar. He laid the traditional coin on Diodotos' thin lips and ran his hand over the side of Diodotos' clean, bearded face. 'That from our sister,' he whispered. He bent and kissed his brother on the forehead. 'And that from our mother.' He sobbed and felt his tears catch in his beard.

Then he stepped back and looked up at the wide sky, the great curve of the beach, the distant mountains. Diodotos' voice in his head said, *'Do me one last favour.'* Themis looked back down at his brother's thin face, took a deep breath, and thrust the torch into the oil-soaked logs in the bottom layer of the pyre.

'And don't forget your promise,' said Diodotos' voice.

Flames sprang along the whole length of the pyre and began to rise through it. The wind added to their roar. Evanthi wailed loudly. The priest prayed. Themis stepped back. Photios extended his arm and Themis leaned on it, looking through the flames along the beach to the ships. He would be going back alone to tell his mother. Photios put the strap of Diodotos green satchel over Themis' shoulder.

Themis shuddered, shook his head vehemently. He took the whole bag in his hands.

'No!' he yelled. 'No! This brought him nothing but bad luck!' He tried to rip it to pieces but it was too strong. He staggered towards the fire dragging out the wooden serpent. He threw the bag on the flames and tore the serpent apart. It exploded into hundreds of small pieces, scattering into the flames.

Heat rose, distorting the view. Through it and his furious tears, Themis thought he saw a wavering, shrouded figure in grey on the beach, standing far away, nearer the ships than the pyre. It stood completely still, facing him. But its face was covered. After a few moments it turned, leaving the sand to go inland. As it did so, it tripped and stumbled. Then the smoke billowed up and hid it.

Diodotos' woollen cloak had begun to shrivel. Evanthi was tearing her hair and her himation. The priest stood silent and one of Diodotos' friends began a doleful tune on his flute. The others beat time, fists thudding on their chests to the solemn rhythm. Evanthi fell keening to her knees, shaking her wild hair blindly. The heat of the fire and the sound of the roaring flames filled Themis' mind. He watched as the flames caught Diodotos' hair and beard.

Then all went black.

>>>

Someone was knocking on the door of Suzanne's tiny room. She woke with a jerk, dislodging her open laptop. She grabbed it as she sat up in bed and it slid towards the edge. She was dizzy. Diodotos was burning. Her face was wet. She couldn't remember where she was. She called, 'Who's that?'

A woman with a French accent said, 'Are you OK? I didn't see you since yesterday.'

Suzanne said, 'I'm in the loo. I'll open in a minute. I'm fine.'

She 'saved' the file, closed and plugged the laptop in to charge, and went to the loo.

It was 19.03, according to her Fitbit. Had she only been 'away' for 12 hours? It felt like weeks.

But she'd made it to France, she remembered. And France was hot and sunny. She'd been here ten days. The Stadium had a brilliant pole vault pit and the trainer had such a strong French accent she couldn't understand him. A fellow trainee, David, had to translate for her. The trainer had been impressed by her ballet-enhanced skills and had actually said, 'Ooh la la! A veritable bird!' as she flew over the bar at four metres twenty on her first day.

She began washing her hands and Themis' world came back with a rush. Diodotos was dead and Themis wounded but alive. Her mind clamped shut on the memories of the battle. '*I mustn't go there*,' she thought. '*It didn't happen to me. It's just … a story – from long ago.*'

She looked at her face in the mirror and rearranged her expression from stricken to sleepy. She nodded to herself. She was fine.

The woman waiting outside the door was the one who took care of her room and probably all the others in this large, students' block. She was holding a letter. 'This is for you,' she said. 'You are ill?'

'No. I'm fine, thank you,' said Suzanne. 'I think I was just exhausted. Is the canteen open? I'm really hungry.'

The woman laughed. 'Always the athletes, they are 'ungry. Oui, the canteen is serving now.'

Suzanne took the envelope. 'I'll just read this and then come down,' she said. Letters only came when things were too official for email.

The woman left. The building was quiet. Everyone must have gone to supper. Suzanne opened her letter.

Chapter 45: home

(Breeds of Sheep 29)

Themis came round sitting on the sand with his back against the rock. It was night. The pyre was almost out now, glowing red. The wind had dropped. The sky sparkled with uncountable stars and the sea hissed quietly as it stroked the beach. Melanas, Mikro and Photios were still there. Evanthi had laid out the funeral cakes and wine on a board on the sand but she and the others must have left.

Melanas brought Themis a cake and a cup of wine. 'We drank it neat,' he said.

Themis was shocked at how hungry he felt. 'Thanks,' he said. He trickled a libation onto the sand. 'Share this with me, brother,' he whispered.

His anger sat like a stone in his gut, whispering plans for revenge.

'The bones will be too hot to collect till morning,' said Melanas. 'I'll stay on guard and you come back at dawn.'

Themis ignored this. 'Did you see that person watching us just as I lit the pyre?' he asked, lifting his hand to point along the beach.

'On the beach? No, I saw no one.'

Themis frowned. 'Maybe I dreamt it,' he said, 'But it could have been Xenovia. She needn't bother trying to get rid of us now, need she? Our stupid generals are doing that!'

'Eat,' said Melanas, handing him the cake. 'Take the bitterness out of your mouth.'

'Nothing can do that,' said Themis. But he sighed, then took a bite. 'Did you purify the wagon?' he asked with his mouth full.

'It's been in the sea twice.'

'Is it dry? I'd rather stay here while the fire cools.'

'There's even a blanket,' said Melanas, 'though I doubt you'll need it in this heat and no wind. No storm tonight after all.'

By the time Themis got to Vravrona four days later, his leg was healing cleanly. His anger at the carnage at Mantinea was turning to despair at the probable repercussions for Athens of losing the battle. He couldn't face arguing about them with everyone he knew in the City, so he'd gone straight to the farm and left Melanas there, with his own and Diodotos' armour.

Kalliope had prepared a basket of produce from the farm for Eirini. She'd included a bag of apples especially for Melissa, mentioning that Adrasteia, who had brought them a message to be delivered to Eirini, said the red ones were Melissa's favourites.

'Has Agorakritos' got his citizenship?' Themis had asked.

Arianos had shaken his head. 'I heard he thinks it's being deliberately withheld.'

So, even if Melissa were freed from the contract to marry Nereus, Themis himself could not marry her because she was not a full citizen of Athens. When Diodotos made Themis promise to marry and have lots of children to carry on their father's line, he had not meant Themis to have 'foreign' children. And unless there was a change in the law, Melissa could only have 'foreign' children, whoever their father was. He'd have to look for a wife elsewhere, but now was not the time.

Themis repeated this to himself from time to time as Frog drove the wagon to Vravrona. He tried to keep his thoughts on designing a permanent urn and tomb for Diodotos' bones. The temporary urn was wrapped in an old cloak and jammed in a corner of the wagon beside him.

Eirini was waiting at the outer end of the bridge when they arrived at the precinct. She stood very straight but her eyes were red from weeping. Themis got down from the wagon and put his arms around her without a word. She held him for a moment, her body stiff in his embrace. Then she pushed him back and held his face between her hands. 'I envy the Spartan mothers their courageous acceptance,' she said. 'And I thank the gods I still have one son, at least.'

'Your other son died a hero,' said Themis. He gestured to the wrapped urn. 'Will you make his memorial here, or on the farm?'

'Will the City not put him in the cemetery?' Eirini asked.

'There are so many, Mama,' said Themis.

'Then you will make a shrine at the farm. You can incorporate the herm of your father and maybe we can reclaim his bones, too. And perhaps make a stele for Myrto and her family?' Themis had never seen his mother's eyes so anxious.

'It won't bring them back, Mama,' he said.

Eirini looked down and sighed. 'Of course not,' she said. 'But it would give me peace – and be a good use of your talents.'

For once there was no irony in her tone. Themis nodded. 'True. But for now I'll be going to Epidaurus where they are building a siege-wall, so it will have to wait for winter.'

They began walking the wagon towards her house along the road around the precinct. Themis limped.

Eirini stopped and pulled back his chiton. 'You're wounded? You were both in the battle together?'

'It's a clean wound and it's healing fine,' said Themis.

'But why were you both fighting?!' Eirini wailed in anger, her open hands held taught to the skies. 'That's not – '

'The reinforcements from Athens didn't come in time,' he said, his jaw rigid as he gathered her tense body in an awkward hug. 'So Laches put all possible men into the field. You know that's normal, Mama.'

Eirini took a breath to speak, then pushed herself away from him and walked on shaking her head.

Later at her house, Themis stood on the terrace where Diodotos had stood looking out at the bay and the town across the little estuary. Eirini came out with a slave girl. They began to set out a meal.

Themis turned and watched until the slave girl left. Then he said, 'I have a favour to ask you, Mama. I have to go to Epidaurus – '

Eirini threw up her head like a startled horse.

' – but I'll only be building walls,' he added. 'In any case, the Spartans won't fight during the Carneia festival this month, and Autumn's coming so I'll be back here soon. When I am, I need to marry, so I want you to choose me a decent, kind girl from among your charges.'

Eirini stopped with a jug in her hand and looked at him for a moment. 'You mean it,' she said, surprised. 'Well now, what about Photios' cousin, or Tyro that you drew for your brother?' Her voice cracked.

'I'd rather it wasn't Tyro, lovely though she is. Every time I looked at her for the rest of my life I would think of him, and so would you.' Themis looked back out at the view. 'Can you arrange for me to meet Photios' cousin, and one or two others unconnected to us before I go?' He turned back to her. 'I want to marry as soon as I get back in a month or so.'

Not mentioning Melissa was one of the hardest things he'd ever done. Perhaps it would get easier with time.

The next day, Themis and Frog drove back to the city. Frog was very quiet, only humming under his breath at times.

They made a detour to visit Chloe.

'Mama sent me the news,' she said as she came out to meet the cart.

Her face smiled but her eyes were dark with sorrow. Then, as Themis limped towards her, she added briskly, 'But she didn't say you'd been wounded'.

'It's nothing much. I'll be back to normal in a few days,' he said as he embraced her. Then he exclaimed in pain as Chloe's eldest son Canthus hugged his leg.

'Careful, Canthus,' she said. 'Uncle Themis is wounded there.'

'Oh! Can I see?' asked the boy. 'Are you bleeding?'

Frog laughed and Themis had to smile. 'Not now,' he said. 'The healers put herbs and spiders' webs on it and it closed up.'

'I want to see, I want to see,' said the boy, lifting Themis' chiton. 'Oh! It's covered.'

Chloe sobbed suddenly. Themis bent down and picked the boy up. 'Come inside where it's cooler and let me sit down and your mother can take off the bandage. She may have something to help it heal faster.' He raised an eyebrow at his sister.

She nodded, and led the way into the courtyard wiping tears off her chin.

'Is Hipparchos here?' asked Themis.

'He'll be back tomorrow. There's an Assembly today.'

When Canthus had had a look at the disappointingly dry wound and left them, Chloe said, 'What will happen about the farm now?' Themis winced as she soaked yellow and brown crusts from the scar and prodded around it with a firm finger. 'There's no inflammation,' she said.

'I'll have to be there a lot more,' he said. 'There's no one else to deal with it now, is there? Things will have to change,' he added grimly. 'I'm planning to marry this autumn and then my wife can be there full time and maybe I'll be able to get back to painting and sculpting.'

Chloe stopped and looked at him with a half-smile. 'Oh dear. Do I detect a certain reluctance to grow up, my brother?'

Themis sighed. 'I suppose that is part of it,' he said.

Chloe stood up and put her arms around his shoulders from behind. 'Naturally,' she said. Then she came round in front of his chair, took his hand and said, 'And who is the lucky girl?'

'At the moment, I've no idea,' said Themis with a shrug. 'Mama introduced me to two possibilities. They were both cute and from good families, but … all girls seem to do is simper and hide behind their hands. I need someone efficient and fun. Someone I can trust with my thoughts and feelings.'

'They're just shy,' said Chloe. 'But why the hurry? Why not get a matchmaker to find you someone suitable and take a bit of time to get to know her?'

'I promised Diodotos he'd have a nephew by this time next year,' said Themis.

Chloe leveled a cool glance at him. 'Marriage is not just for baby production, you know,' she said.

'Of course it's not!' Themis exploded. 'I'm not a complete idiot, whatever you may think! But a promise is a promise.'

Chloe shrugged and kept quiet as she wrapped up his thigh again with herbs between the layers of fine linen. He didn't even twitch. When she had finished, she stood and looked at him for a moment. Then she said, 'Be patient for a month or so. Things often change as the summer cools and the storms begin.'

Themis let his head fall against the chair-back in frustration. Looking at the ceiling, he said, 'I'll have to try and be patient about a lot of things for a while. I'm ordered back to Epidaurus to build a siege-wall around it. The Epidaureans killed most of the guards at Argos while we were all at Mantinea, scattering like ducks from a bear while our so-perfect golden boy was shitting himself with panic in the mountains.'

Themis found he was on his feet and shouting with Chloe staring at him. He lowered his voice and said, 'We lost Mantinea, two generals, and probably a thousand men, because he wasn't there, and the Eleans he'd pissed off didn't come back and the Athenian reinforcements came too late. So now he's trying to save face by pulverizing Epidaurus in reprisal.'

Themis could hear Chloe's two older boys playing outside, yelling 'Complete idiot! Complete idiot!' at each other.

'Ach, may the gods forgive me,' said Themis. 'You of all people don't deserve to deal with this.'

'We're all in it together,' said Chloe. 'The whole family. Don't forget.'

Themis relaxed his shoulders and gestured at the chair where he'd been sitting. 'I won't. You're right. And thank you for this.' He touched the new bandage. 'I'm sorry.'

'Oh, you men!' said Chloe, tidying her herbs and bandages away. 'So when will your wall be finished?'

'Well, I have to be back for the grape harvest, finished or not,' said Themis. His leg was less painful as he limped out to the cart.

They were driving up to the house in Athens when the door opened and the Skionian stepped out. Frog pulled up with a flourish and jumped down to unload sacks from the farm. Themis caught a glimpse of the smile and the wink that passed between Frog and the girl.

He swallowed hard, patted the herm on the head, and went in to the house where he was now the only master.

Mika was standing in the courtyard. She seemed to have shrunk, but her smile was as broad as ever as she said, 'Welcome home, Master Themis.'

'Thank you, Mika,' he said. 'We brought you some stores.'

Mika's eyes overflowed in spite of the smile. 'You sound just like Master Diodotos when you say that,' she said.

Themis looked around at the courtyard. Inside, he felt contorted, stiff, hollow – deeply and irrevocably changed.

And yet the well and water trough, bench and stools were still the same. The columns still needed repainting. The bunches of grapes on the vine hung, as always in late summer, in clean linen bags to fend off the wasps.

He turned to the shrine and laid the late lavender he'd found by the road in the offering tray. He silently thanked Zeus of the House for its continued existence, and went over to the water trough to wash.

'You're wounded,' said Mika, handing him a cloth to dry on.

'It's healing,' said Themis, shaking drops from his beard and hair. 'Chloe dressed it on our way here. We took my brother's bones to my mother and she said to leave the urn with her until I can paint a better one.'

'I see,' said Mika. She stood up straighter. 'There's cold fish soup in the kitchen and new bread. Just call when you're ready.' And she hurried away.

Frog had brought all the stores in and was standing irresolute by the shrine. Themis gestured a question at him as he toweled his hair dry.

'It's the armour,' said Frog. 'Do you want me to bring in both sets, or will you do it yourself? We've lent Tanu to the livery stables for five days to earn a few obols.'

'You stay with it in the street while I prepare the stands in the andron.'

Melanas and Mikro had spent hours cleaning and polishing both sets of armour. They had been carefully wrapped for their journey from the farm. When they'd unpacked and hung them, Frog and Themis stood back to admire the panoplies, shining and resplendent in their customary corner.

As they rolled up the last lengths of wrapping linen, Themis sighed and said without looking at Frog, 'So have you learned her name, then?'

Frog went on contemplating the armour. 'She says I wouldn't be able to pronounce it, so we agreed on Io. It's short and easy to spell.'

'So she talks now?'

'A little.'

'And writes?'

'How did you guess?' asked Frog.

Themis shrugged. 'It's only my leg that has a hole in it, not my head,' he said, and sat down on a couch. 'And is she pregnant?' he asked.

Frog looked sharply at Themis. 'Would that be a problem?'

Themis relaxed his shoulders. 'Of course not, you imbecile. That would be a great step forward. And we're going to need a few steps forward …'

Frog nodded. Then he asked with a twinkle in his eye, 'What about you? Similar plans?'

Themis stood up again and limped testily into the courtyard. 'Tomorrow I, and you, will be off to Epidaurus for a month or so. When we get back from there, we'll have the grape harvest.' He counted on his fingers. 'While that's going on I'll need to choose a bride so the wedding can be at the winter solstice. Then we have to hope that the Spartans don't take courage from our criminal weakness at Mantinea. If they come raiding in the summer, it'll be just as I'm getting to grips with being a farmer and my wife is swelling with our son.'

'Ah,' said Frog. 'I see. A month … It wouldn't stop your beard growing, would it, if Io and I got married once we're back?'

Themis turned to him and the tension went out of him. 'No,' he said, 'my beard would get yet thicker. You do say some odd things these days.'

'Oh, it's Io's brilliant grasp of Attic Greek,' said Frog with a grin.

Themis put a hand on his arm and dropped his voice. 'But, apart from all the other changes in our lives, there *is* one warning I need to give you.'

'What's that?'

'While I was at Argos, I saw … Xenovia, the priestess – ' he choked.

' … who killed your father?' Frog finished for him, eyes wide in horror.

'Who has it in for our family in general,' Themis managed to go on. 'If it really was her that I saw, she may try again to harm us. Mind you, she's near enough a cripple now, all smashed up down the left side. She hides it with her clothes but it's obvious when she moves.'

'That wouldn't stop her,' said Frog.

Themis shivered. 'So we need to be careful. I didn't tell Mama though, so don't go gossiping about it – at least not till I'm more sure.'

'Right,' said Frog. 'But I should keep an eye open for an old woman who limps and hides her face and casts spells?'

'Something like that.'

'Hmm. Recognizing her among the hundreds of old women in Attica who limp and wear veils and mutter to themselves will be pretty straightforward then,' said Frog.

'Yup!' said Themis with a tired smile. 'Shouldn't be too difficult.'

'Who's it from?' asked David. His accent in English mixed French consonants with American vowels. Suzanne usually found this amusing, but not today.

She swallowed her mouthful of ravioli and said, 'It's not who it's from that's upsetting me. It's why they sent it. I'm pretty sure who told them to investigate my "mental problems" further. And that's what makes me so angry.'

David was sitting back in his yellow plastic canteen chair. It creaked. He was slim, but no lightweight at one metre ninety-eight. 'What does it say?' He sat forward and stretched out his long arm. 'Can I see?'

Suzanne put down her fork and said, 'I'll read it to you.' She opened the envelope again and read, 'From Commonwealth Games England, etcetera etcetera. Dear Miss Short, It has been brought to the attention of the selectors for the athletes to represent England at the Commonwealth Games in Australia in 2018 that, after your serious accident in 2010, you have had mental health problems that are not explicitly described on your trainer's application form. Please would you telephone our offices (number below) to make an appointment to clarify this with our health team before July 31st. Please quote the reference at the top of this letter when calling. Yours sincerely ...'

'So. You are ... disturbed?' asked David with a chuckle. 'This we know. We are all crazy who do these stupid competitions.'

Suzanne laughed. 'Well, it did take a long time for me to recover, and I did spend a lot of time with shrinks. But it doesn't affect my fitness or my ambition now.'

'I am interested in shrinkers,' said David. 'Could they make me smaller so I can jump higher?'

Suzanne looked at him from under her lashes. 'You're laughing at me,' she said.

David's grin widened and he shrugged. 'You. Myself. The world,' he said. 'You may be a little bit maniac, but you make me feel good and so I laugh.'

Suzanne looked at his gleaming, smiling face. He made her feel good, too.

<<<

Chapter 46: duck pies and doubts

(Breeds of Sheep 30)

Themis stood on the top of a half-built tower in the fortifications round the port of Epidaurus. He was directing where the next stones should be placed. The tower was already higher than the wall it guarded, and would have a wide view.

He looked out south and east at the sea and the mountainous coastline as it faded into the hazy distance on his right. Ghost-like in that haze, the volcano of Methana rose out of the blue water, its summit leaking smoke.

There was no wind and the heat was intense. He took off his wide-brimmed hat and shook the sweat out of his hair. It was time to call the mid-day break for food and rest. As he took a breath, he felt a whisper of breeze touch his damp shoulders. He shivered and looked back and down, to the inner side of the wall. A boy was hopping between the spoil heaps and stone-carrying carts. Four masons were trimming a large corner stone in a cloud of chips and dust. Frog was standing stock still beside them, watching the boy run off.

Then Frog turned to look up at Themis. He gestured to him to come down. There was a shocking look of abject grief on his face.

Themis called the break and slid down the ladders.

'What is it?' he shouted as Frog ran towards him. 'What's happened?'

Frog stopped in front of him and handed him a small scroll. 'It's Anthoussa,' he said, his voice cracking. 'She's gone.'

'Gone?!' Themis grabbed the scroll and broke the seal.

Melissa had written, *'My mother died yesterday, giving us another brother. She knew the birth would be dangerous. She said to tell you that the Underworld would be more comfortable for her than here, but she would miss you and her children. She prayed that you would be able, in time, to return to being part of the family. The boy has my father's black eyes and dark hair. I was to tell you this face to face, but I*

Themis sat down on a block of stone. It burned through his chiton, but he hardly noticed. 'But it was a boy who brought it,' he said stupidly.

Frog said, 'He'd been paid by an old woman.' He laid a canvas bag on the stone and sat beside Themis. He handed him a water skin. They took turns to drink in silence. The men around them were noisy as they left their work and walked off to look for shade. Soon they were alone.

'Can you get away?' asked Frog at last.

'It's only four days until I'd have to leave anyway,' said Themis. 'A supply boat goes back tomorrow. We'll be on it.'

They sat on, staring at the half-built tower, the sun scorching their knees.

As the supply boat bumped against the jetty in Piraeus harbour, Themis and Frog jumped off.

'Have you still got money?' Themis asked Frog as they wove their way at a run between the carts and carriers.

'Enough to rent horses,' Frog answered.

'Good. I'm starving. Take the bags. I'll get a couple of pies and meet you at the temple of Zeus the Protector.' Themis set off along the line of stalls. He stopped at his favourite and bought two duck pies. The woman whose stall it was, called after him as she always did, 'Watch out for bones!'

The main street to the temple was at a standstill with traffic, so he took the parallel one. It was almost empty and he could run. He crossed a side street. The next street would bring him back out near the temple.

At that moment, a wagon turned out from it into the road in front of him. He moved towards the wall to be out of its way, but it rushed towards him at a great pace, scattering pedestrians into the shops and against the high walls on either side. He jumped back against the wall, bumping into two other men.

One of the men pushed him into the path of the wagon! Themis dropped the pies but managed to keep his balance well enough to carry on right across the street under the noses of the mules pulling the wagon as it careered past.

Two other men were waiting on that side. A short sword gleamed and Themis turned his headlong rush into a somersault. He was back on his feet before the two men could move. He crashed their heads together, checked that they were unconscious, and ran up the street. One of the men from the other side chased him, knocking people out of his way. The other was already ahead of him, knocking over a melon stall. The melons rolled all over the street and Themis had to dance to avoid them. The two men were closing in on him, trying to trap him between them. He picked up a melon and threw it at the man ahead so hard that it broke against his chest, blinding him with its dark red pulp.

Themis turned to face the man behind him. He saw again the flash of metal. The street went quiet for a moment as people stopped to watch. Then they began to shout, some encouraging Themis, others siding with the two men.

'Good shot!' 'What's he stolen?' 'Spit him till he squeals!'

Themis kept his eye on the knife. He knew the man covered in melon would be angry now, so he wasn't surprised when he felt an arm wrap round his ankles from behind. He twisted round, hitting downwards with his hands held together. He got the man full in his messy face, and kicked out at him as he fell away.

The man with the knife had run in, expecting Themis to fall forwards onto his weapon. It grazed across Themis' left flank. Themis grabbed the hand that held it in his own right hand. With his left, he bent the man's wrist until he screamed and the knife fell into Themis' grasp.

Two horses came pounding into the street. Themis heard Frog call, 'Need a ride?' The knife man was recovering. Themis kicked him hard in the chest, and he bent over, retching.

Themis ran for the empty horse, leapt on and he and Frog skidded into the nearest side street at a canter.

'So what was the point of all that?' said Frog as they reached the comparative quiet of the main road. 'Who were they?'

'Heaven knows,' said Themis. 'It could just have been thieves, taking advantage of the runaway wagon. This knife is foreign, though ...' He held it up, then slipped it into the bag hanging from his saddle.

'Seemed to me like you were supposed to die,' said Frog. 'The poor sods just didn't know that you're Hephaistos' own adopted son.'

Themis laughed shortly, exhilarated by their escape – and the bitterly sweet but forbidden joy that awaited him in Athens. 'Sorry about the pies,' he said. 'Victims of the wagon. And thanks for coming when you did.'

'Heard the yells. And you don't usually take all day to buy pies. You going to report this?'

'Of course!' said Themis angrily. 'We're going to make a great fuss and try and get news of it up on the wall in the Agora in Athens. I wasn't expecting the most cheerful homecoming of my life, but having Xenovia or whoever try to murder me the minute I step off the boat has made me ... ' he clenched his left fist and set his jaw, ' ... extremely unhappy.'

'Thank the gods for that!' said Frog.

That evening, a messenger arrived with a rolled and sealed scroll from the new Archon of the City Watch. It was an official welcome home and mentioned that Nereus had been seen taking on extra slaves lately and that accusations may be imminent. It was signed Lysikles. *'As street assassins at Xenovia's request, perhaps?'* thought Themis.

Now bathed, bandaged and dressed in a clean chiton, he walked to the street where Anthoussa had lived. Outside Agorakritos' house there was a small, quiet crowd. He was let in immediately, and taken through to the empty andron by Skopas, Melissa's brother. Themis could hear a baby crying in the women's rooms. The house smelled of funerary foods and purifying herbs.

'Please, sit, Uncle Themis,' said Skopas. 'Father said I was to tell him as soon as you arrived, so excuse me a moment.'

A slave brought Themis wafers and sour wine. Then he was alone. He could feel Anthoussa's presence. Her body had already been cremated, of course, but he could almost see her soul, slim and lithe as she was before this last pregnancy, her smile of joy at seeing him lighting up the room, her arms outstretched to him. The hollow, gnawing ache of grief had twisted in his gut as he entered the house. But it eased a little now as he drew in air that she had breathed – and that Melissa was breathing.

He found he was smiling, so he reminded himself that Agorakritos might still ban him from the house. The smile faded.

The boy's tired sobs were rhythmical now. A woman was singing a lullaby to him. It sounded like Melissa. She must be here, in the women's rooms. Themis paced restlessly. How could he feel such sorrow and such joy, both at the same time?

The door opened and the man who came into the andron was a different Agorakritos. He was newly clean-shaven, the handsome face pale and lined under the vanished beard. His dark hair had been cut short and was streaked with silver. His whole body seemed hollowed out, and the shadows round his eyes were almost black. He came forward as Themis rose, and stood still in the middle of the room.

He said, 'She did love you, you know.'

'Of course she did,' said Themis. 'And I loved her.'

'That was only too obvious.'

'But I stopped wanting her as a wife long ago,' said Themis.

'When she grew old,' said Agorakritos.

'No,' said Themis. 'When I grew up. She'll never grow old.'

'Not now,' said Agorakritos, and he suddenly bent his head as a spasm shook him.

Themis waited a little, then said, 'Was there something else you wanted to talk to me about?'

Agorakritos looked up and sighed. 'Yes. Come and sit down. She made me promise to ask your advice if Nereus came calling.'

They sat on couches at right angles and Agorakritos said, 'He came the day after she died.'

Themis' skin crawled. 'About Melissa?' he asked, controlling his voice.

'Yes. Melissa has come home, to help with the baby and all the other things her mother did so well and so quietly. I couldn't manage without her just now.'

'Of course not,' said Themis. 'This is where she belongs.'

'Well,' said the older man. 'Nereus came here before the funeral even, and offered me "two efficient and comely" slave women as wet nurses. He said he assumed there would be a lot of changes now and suggested that he give me the slaves as a gift to help me with those changes, while he took Melissa immediately as his wife.'

'What?!' said Themis, leaping to his feet, his fists clenched. Then he shook himself and said, 'Sorry. But that man always seems to say the wrong thing at the wrong time.'

'Exactly. My wife's dead body was still in the house, and the baby was crying. Nothing had been purified yet. What did he think he was doing?'

Themis was appalled. But Anthoussa had wanted him to give an opinion on the situation. He sat down again. 'Just being Nereus,' he said. 'So what did you say?'

'I asked him to give us thirty days to sort things out, and then I would speak to him again.'

'And he agreed?'

'What else could he do? I refused the two slaves and he took them away. But we had to have a wet nurse and some help for Melissa, because the old nurse who'd been taking care of her mother had to leave. So I took on Adrasteia's sister on a temporary basis. My old colleague, Alkamenes, owns her. She had a baby herself a year ago and still has milk.'

'And what advice is it you want from me?' asked Themis. He was now so tense he was almost shaking, digging his nails into his palms. 'You seem to have dealt with Nereus very well.'

Agorakritos stood up and paced up and down. 'But what am I to say in thirty – no twenty-seven – days' time when he comes back? Melissa is adamant that she won't marry him, but I agreed in the spring that she would.'

Themis let out his breath slowly. 'I'm going to mention something that I shall deny if you ever refer to it.'

Agorakritos stopped pacing.

Themis went on, 'I received a message today from someone who is investigating Nereus. The message did not say what exactly they think he's done, but they are preparing to make accusations.'

Agorakritos said, 'Accusations that will stick?'

'If they are brought, I imagine yes.'

'And is it possible that it's Nereus that's holding up my citizenship application, too?' asked the older man.

'That should be easier to find out,' said Themis. 'I'm sure you have the right to ask the Council to show you any official objections.' He was thinking, *Just get on with it, old man! Stop complaining and find out.*

'Really?' Agorakritos sighed. 'So many things I've ignored since Anthoussa fell pregnant this time.' He glanced ruefully at Themis. Then he straightened his back. 'But now I'll see about that. And if he turns out to be a criminal, all the better. I need Melissa at home for as long as possible now.'

'Don't mention this to her just yet,' said Themis. 'I'm not sure of it myself.'

'It's enough that there may be a way out,' said Agorakritos. 'Thanks for letting me know.'

Themis was finding it difficult to sit still. He stood up, hesitated, then said, 'Do you think I could speak to her? I'd like to express my sorrow about her mother.'

'If you wish,' said Agorakritos. He looked into Themis' face for a long, thoughtful moment. Then, his face softening, said, 'Shall I call her now?'

'If she's free,' said Themis. 'Or I can come back later – or tomorrow.'

Agorakritos went out and Themis heard him call Melissa.

When she came in, he wasn't ready for the sudden weakness in his legs and rush of blood to his face and groin. He found he had to sit down again. He was furious with himself and arranged his chiton to hide his erection. He also stopped himself grinning like an idiot and tried to look pleased to see her but sad about Anthoussa, just as a real uncle would.

She had grown a little taller and looked surprised at his sudden collapse onto the couch. Her chiton was old but of fine blue linen. There were stains down the front, probably from her new brother's vomit. Under it, her breasts were firm and fuller than the last time he'd seen her. Her hair was dishevelled but her eyes glowed with welcome and concern. She ran to him and took his hands.

'Oh, Uncle Themis!' she exclaimed. 'You've been wounded and then they tried to kill you in Pireaus. I promise I didn't tell anyone about your being the Merman.'

'Melissa,' he said. His voice was a croak. He cleared his throat and patted the couch next to him. 'I know that,' he said. 'You look so … well … grown up.'

She was suddenly confused, took a half step backwards, and frowned slightly. 'Thank the gods you're safe,' she said formally. She sat on her father's couch. 'Will your wounds take long to heal?' she asked, looking down at her hands.

Themis shifted against the cushions. 'Flesh wounds,' he said. 'Nothing important.' His felt ridiculous suddenly, in the face of her formality.

'Truly?' She looked at him briefly with a bright glance.

'I am so deeply sorry about the death of your mother,' he said. 'You know how much I feel it. I don't have the words.'

She was looking at her hands again. 'I hardly have time now to think about losing her,' she said. There was a pause. Then she said, 'But … you wanted to see me?' and her green eyes challenged him warily.

The force of that look focused his mind. He took a slow breath, leaned his elbows on his knees and looked at her seriously. 'I wanted to talk to you about Nereus,' he said.

Her eyes flashed briefly. Was it anger? But she said calmly, 'I thought that must be it.'

'How do you feel about your situation now?' he asked.

Melissa spoke very quietly, looking him in the eye. 'There is no way I will leave my father until I have found him another wife, or a trustworthy woman to take care of him and the children. We are five children in the family now. Adrasteia can't manage us all, with or without her sister, and the boy needs a new tutor. If Nereus needs a wife so urgently, he can go to a matchmaker. I am under the protection of Artemis and Hera. They both told me that my place is here, at least for a while.'

'They spoke to you?'

'Not clearly. Not like the warning about the harbour. But I know that's what I must do.'

'So your father asked Nereus to be patient.'

'Yes. But I told you, back in the spring before you and Diodotos left, that I knew I'd never marry him.' Her eyes suddenly filled with tears. 'Oh, Uncle Themis, both our families are now without foundation stones.' Her tears spilled down her cheeks and her nose began to run. She used the corner of her chiton to wipe it. 'Sorry,' she murmured.

Themis stood up and took her hand, pulling her up. He held her tight, her cheek against his aching chest, and let the sobs come. What was he crying for? Anthoussa? Diodotos? The impossibility of ever holding her like this again? This last thought set up a reaction.

She must have felt it because she stepped back slowly, wiping her face with the hem of her chiton. She seemed to be short of breath.

When she looked up at him, her sad smile held a glimmer of mischief. 'It's odd it's still there,' she said.

There was no point in pretending he didn't know what she meant. 'Not entirely under my control,' he said ruefully. 'And not appropriate to the moment. My apologies.'

She laughed briefly, shook her head and sat down on a stool a few feet away. 'At Vravrona they told us that some gods encourage fornication after a battle or a death, to replenish the family. We were warned that most men find this impossible to resist.'

Themis sat down on the couch again feeling shocked. He hadn't thought about it like that before. 'Which gods?' he asked.

'Hera. And Demeter. Isn't there something about it in the Mysteries?'

'Not in those terms,' he said thoughtfully. 'Anyway,' he said, looking at her in wonder, 'now that you are such a wise person, have you thought how to prevent Nereus from holding your father to their agreement?'

'He'll probably have to pay him,' she said.

'Do you still manage the finances of your father's sculpture yard? You took over from your mother, didn't you?'

'I did. In the spring. But they got into a terrible mess while I was away and she was … ill. I haven't had time yet to see if we can afford to buy Nereus off.' She stood up. The baby's voice was making itself heard in the women's rooms.

Themis stood up too. 'Tell me, did anyone ever ask you about the business of the "attack" on the triremes?'

'Not directly. Father and his fraternity have met here a couple of times since then and discussed it in my hearing. But no one knows I know anything about it. I promise you, those men who tried to kill you in Piraeus didn't know anything from me.'

'I believe you,' he said. 'They've had their eye on me since I identified some of them for the Archon that day with … er … Melissus.' They both smiled. 'But I didn't expect them to attack the minute I set foot on land … And anyway, they may have been sent by someone completely unconnected.'

'Have they been arrested?'

'Not yet. I only reported it this afternoon.'

'So they could try again?'

'I'm not sure. I've been summoned to see Lysikles, the new Archon of the City Watch, tomorrow. I'll see what he thinks. And shall I say anything to him about you?'

'You can mention that I'm ready to go underground for him if that would be useful – as long as it has nothing to do with Nereus. Meanwhile, I'm fulfilling my daughterly duties,' said Melissa with an ironic smile.

He said, 'So, if there's no other way, I should recommend to your father that he buys out of his agreement with Nereus, then?'

Melissa said, 'Of course. What other way is there?'

'Well, I've heard of fathers allowing prospective husbands to kidnap prospective wives,' said Themis, half seriously.

'Oh, I don't think he'd do that,' said Melissa as she went towards the door. 'Anyway, Nereus wouldn't dare. He wants to remain a general, and that kind of thing doesn't go down well in the City. It only happens in villages, and even then it's just pretend.'

Themis stood up and followed her to the door. 'Shall I come over sometimes for a chat?' he said. The baby bellowed.

'Oh yes!' she replied by the door. 'If you have time.' And she was gone.

'I shouldn't have said that,' thought Themis. 'Eros is an idiot! However she makes me feel, she's never going to be a "proper wife" in the way Diodotos and Father would want. What the fuck am I doing? I must be mad.'

Chapter 47: price list

Suzanne closed her laptop. She had had to do two long, exhausting sessions of typing in the last three days, forcing herself to continue. This one had started around two o'clock in the morning, when she'd woken from an obscure nightmare – her own or Themis'? There'd been a pony ... and a thunder storm ... Anyway, she couldn't sleep again, so decided to write it all down, hoping to stop the flashbacks by confronting them. The towel round her neck was damp with tears. 'I'm not being objective enough,' she said to herself. 'I need to stop feeling as if I'm *him* so often.' She stood up and stretched. 'If I could really talk to him, maybe I wouldn't so much.'

The sun was up and it was time to get out to the training stadium. As she was showering she thought, '*But you do drive me nuts, you know, Themis! Why can't you just accept the business of having "foreign" children and get on with it. Who cares about being "pure" Athenian – or a "proper wife" for that matter. How boring would that be? She'd obviously rather marry you than Nereus. And I know you're totally hooked on her. Your body doesn't react to other women like it does to her. I'm so glad I'm not a man! It's complicated enough fancying someone you hardly know without it making visible bits swell up.*' She turned off the shower. '*And you have grief in common with Melissa. You're trying to be the tough one, hiding how shredded you are. You should let it out more.*'

As she was dressing, a message from Cassie came up on her phone. 'Called them and explained you've been ok for years now, but they still want to see us in August. Seems more like bureaucracy than a threat to your chances. XX'

Suzanne slammed her door and ran down the stairs grinning. She was meeting David to run to the stadium together. '*Just be glad he likes women,*' she thought.

<<<

(Breeds of Sheep 31 – He heard me!)

Themis was last in line at the gym for the wash down. He didn't usually bother, but today he had got so hot he longed for cool water to wash away the sand of the practice pit rather than oiling it off. He nodded to the water slave and showed him three fingers for three jugs of water. Standing under the trickle the slave was pouring, he felt muscles he'd forgotten he had relaxing. He shut his eyes …

And heard the nymph's voice. She was laughing and seemed to be saying his attachment to Melissa was a good thing, and that she, the nymph, was glad she didn't have to deal with erections. Themis laughed and got water in his mouth. He choked and found he was crying and laughing together. He signalled to the water slave to pour all the water at once.

'So,' said Lysikles, new Archon of the City Watch, 'the army is too ashamed to come home yet.' He waved an arm towards two stools.

'Is that what they're saying in the Assembly?' asked Themis, sitting down. They were in a basement room under the Painted Arcade. It was pleasantly cool and quiet, though it smelled of rats. The Archon's hair brushed the ceiling.

'Of course.' He said, and sat down, too. 'You'll see. The Spartans will become more arrogant than ever now. The Argives are going to have a hard time … '

'Alkibiades doesn't seem alarmed,' said Themis, keeping his tone neutral. 'I don't know where he was for the battle, but he turned up at Epidaurus to encourage the wall-building and keep all the late reinforcements busy.'

The Archon shook his head in irritation. 'That man is an expert in arrogance and expedience,' he said. Then he looked at Themis. 'I understand you have inherited the farm from your brother.'

Themis sighed and said, 'It still feels unreal. It seems my next task is overseeing the grape harvest.'

'Of course. I got a report on the Piraeus attack today. There's no mention of these men's identity.'

'They were professionals and worked together, but they didn't speak. Their faces were very pale, from the north somewhere, beyond Thrace, perhaps?'

'So. Sounds like you're being hunted.'

'Maybe. I'm not sure how seriously, though.'

'Why do you say that?' Lysikles looked at him sharply.

'It is not difficult to kill a man if you must,' said Themis. 'So far, my hunters just seem to want to scare me.'

'Let's hope so,' said Lysikles. 'Or perhaps … maybe your luck is being boosted by a guardian deity?'

'Perhaps,' said Themis. After losing his brother and Anthoussa, he was not feeling that the gods favoured him much. Anyway, Lysikles had a reputation for irony. He went on, 'Or maybe I know something they want. Is there any news of the chest in the bay, for instance?'

'It hasn't been found,' said Lysikles. 'They did find a net that's the wrong shape and weight to be a fishing net. It might have been the one the chest was wrapped in. A fisherman caught it on his oar as he was coming in with his catch a month or so ago. But then again, it could be from anywhere, thrown overboard from a passing ship. I'll send you news if I get any. My tablets have a leopard's face on the spine.'

'Thanks,' said Themis. He stood up. 'Did Apollodorus mention a "boy" who gathers information for your department sometimes? One Melissus?'

'A boy who is in fact a girl, engaged to Nereus? Isn't she at Vravrona?'

'Not any more. I have a message for you from her.'

'So she finished there already?' said the Archon.

'Not exactly,' said Themis. 'She came back early and asked me to tell you that she is "fulfilling her daughterly duties" but would be happy to spy for you any time, as long as she doesn't have to marry Nereus to do so.'

'Hm! Nereus is a friend of mine and told me her story.' Lysikles stood up, too, and they walked to the steps up to the door. 'He'll have his work cut out taming that young woman.'

'Not just yet,' said Themis. 'Her mother died, so she's needed at home.'

'Her mother died?' said the Archon. 'Nereus didn't tell me that. Of course she must stay with her father for now.' He opened the door at the top of the steps. 'You leave first. I'll wait a while.'

Themis looked around as he stepped into the busy street. No one seemed to take any notice of his presence, so he set off for home, frustrated that Lysikles probably wouldn't help Apollodorus in his investigations of Nereus' activities. Would they even continue, now that Apollodorus was out of office?

'Where have you been?' asked Themis as Frog appeared in the courtyard. 'I thought you were clearing space in the stable, but Mika says you were out.'

'I was doing a small experiment,' said Frog.

Themis was pacing the colonnade. 'Experiment?'

'Yes. I wanted to see how alert you are to the possibility of being followed.'

Themis stopped to stare at Frog with a frown. 'You were checking up on me – without telling me?'

'Of course. And you didn't see me!' said Frog with a grin.

'No. I didn't,' said Themis. 'Where were you?'

'No matter,' said Frog. 'You know I'm good at being invisible.'

Themis went on pacing. 'Ah…' he murmured with a nod.

'And you need eyes front and back now we're home. *And* your mind on something other than a certain young woman …'

Themis shot a glance at him. 'Watch what you say,' he warned.

'Don't pretend to be angry with me,' said Frog.

Mika came into the courtyard. 'I have a messenger in the kitchen,' she said, 'from Agorakritos' sculpture yard.'

Themis and Frog exchanged looks. Themis said, 'Bring him in.' Mika went back into the kitchen. Themis went on, 'Frog, go and check on the new horse. I'll need the cart this afternoon.'

So he was alone when the messenger came in with a bowed, hooded head and a small scroll in his hand.

'What is it?' asked Themis.

The messenger threw back his hood and grinned. 'Did you really not know it was me?' asked Melissa.

Themis shook his head, caught between anger and pleasure.

'Well,' she went on. 'I brought you a price list for the steles we have in stock. Father wants you, if you agree, to carve one for my mother, and I learned from the slaves that your own mother wants you to make a memorial for Diodotos at the farm.' She handed him the scroll.

Themis' eyes suddenly pricked with tears as he said, 'Thank you, miss business woman. That will be really helpful.'

She looked around for something to sit on in the shade. 'We have to stay busy,' she said. 'It's the only way to deal with the grief once the ceremonies are over.' Her eyes overflowed, the tears making dark lines on the rough fabric of her garment.

Themis sat beside her on the bench.

She sniffed and wiped her nose on her dirty chiton. 'You said you'd come by for a chat,' she said.

'That's not even a day ago,' said Themis, looking at her and smiling through his own tears.

'Feels like years,' said Melissa, blushing and looking down. 'But I probably shouldn't tell you that.'

He wanted to grab her hands and kiss them both. He wanted to tell her to forget all about him as he had to look for a 'suitable wife'. He sat stock still and said, 'Why not?'

'Because,' she said, suddenly vehement, with her jaw set and her eyes narrowed, 'because I don't know what I am to you. Am I a tiresome child, or a desirable female object, or an equal grown up person?' She stood up. 'When I showed you how I was feeling on the way to Vravrona, you said we needed an agreement that would make allowances for "unsuitable behaviour" if necessary. I assume you meant that if I showed you my woman's feelings, I shouldn't trust you to behave properly towards me. And so your "bad behaviour" would become my fault, not yours.' She stood in front of him, arms akimbo.

'And that makes you very angry,' said Themis, taken by surprise.

'Yes! You want to avoid responsibility for your actions – like most people. It's hurtful in someone I've thought of as a friend all my life.'

Themis thought for a moment, looking at the ground. Then he looked up at her and said seriously, 'You're right.' He stood up and walked out into the sunshine. He turned to look at her, standing there in her oversized, scruffy chiton. 'I was thinking of you married to Nereus and that I would have to keep my distance, as I did with your mother all those years ago. I was shocked and appalled by my sudden lust for you, to tell you the truth. After all, as you say, I've known you since you were born.' Melissa looked down at her frayed sandals, so Themis went on, 'I knew seeing you at all when you married him would be harder than anything else in my life. I suppose I just wanted to make it easier for myself.'

'With no thought of how easy it might be for me?' she said, looking him in the eye.

'In my experience,' he said with a smile, ' – my comprehensive and wide-ranging experience – it is not as difficult for women to resist the madness of Eros as it is for men.'

Melissa shook her head. 'There is no way you can make a comparison. You will never be a woman. It's a lot more complicated than it looks.'

Themis sighed. 'Of course,' he said. 'And perhaps you're right and I'm being arrogant. Especially as your feelings are so new to you. So, perhaps we need a … different agreement?'

'I don't think we need an agreement at all,' she said. 'After all, I'm not going to marry Nereus. But I do need you to be my friend. Especially now.' She stepped a little closer and sighed. 'Oh. I have to get back … It's not a happy house.'

The sadness in her eyes made him risk wrapping his arms around her.

She held him tight and made a slight sound as he squeezed her. He breathed in her smell. It was not pleasant, and helped him keep control.

'Huh,' he said. 'This garment could do with a wash.'

She pulled back and laughed. 'If it was clean no one would have been deceived.' She indicated the scroll, lying on the bench. 'I've made you some good offers there,' she said. 'Please come and see us soon.'

Themis had a sudden thought. 'Does your father know you're here?'

'Of course not. I heard him praying at dawn. He may still feel guilty about you, but he'd be disgusted if he knew I came to see you alone – now that I'm a fully grown woman,' she said wryly.

'If he asks, the slaves will tell him, but I won't,' said Themis. 'And I'm glad you came.'

She grinned and pulled the hood up over her hair. 'Me too,' she said, and disappeared into the kitchen again.

Chapter 48: haunted

From half way along the street as he approached the sculpture yard, Themis could hear a flute and drum beats. Agorakritos' voice was shouting orders. He arrived at the gate as a huge block of glistening white marble floated in the air over a large wagon.

'Hold it there! You feeble donkeys!' yelled Agorakritos to the team of loaders. 'Ah, Themistokles! Help them here,' he called, gesturing for Themis to join the sweating slaves and workers and pull on the ropes of the wooden loading scaffold. The foreman called, 'Bring it down like a feather. Delay the final moment! You all know how to do that, don't you?'

The music began again as the laughter died down. Themis slid in beside a hefty young man he knew as Kallimachos, who nodded to him. The lines of men on the ropes took the strain as the shout, 'Lower now!' rang out. The men on the other side of the wagon gradually released their hold. Grunts and shouts of 'tighter' and 'don't let go!' mixed with the creaking of the pulleys, the groaning of the beams, the heartbeat of the drum and the piercing notes of the flute. Themis noticed they had an audience in the street, gawping through the gate. Someone pushed their way through the crowd and came into the yard. It was Melissa.

'My hands are slipping,' growled Kallimachos in Themis' ear. 'Had no time to pick up my gloves.'

'Nearly there,' grunted Themis.

'Slowly, now!' shouted Agorakritos. 'Keep it steady!'

And the great, gleaming block came to rest on the bed of blankets in the well of the wagon.

'Like a leaf on water,' said Kallimachos.

Everyone sighed, then slapped each other on their sweating backs and congratulated the drummer and the flautist.

The scaffolds were pulled away and oxen were brought up to be harnessed to the front of the wagon. They would have a hard pull to get it to the buyer's yard.

'Whose is it?' asked Themis. Kallimachos shook his head to show he didn't know. Melissa stepped up to Themis and whispered, 'Paionios. He drives a hard bargain. Father is a little scared of him.'

Themis and she exchanged knowing smiles. 'Well,' he said, 'I've come to see what kind of bargain I can drive for my piece of stone.'

'Yours?' said Melissa with a frown. Then, 'Oh, of course, you need one for your family as well as the one for us. You're going to be busy …'

Themis nodded. 'I have the dimensions here,' and he opened a small tablet that hung from his belt.

Melissa came close and looked down at it. The scent of her hair filled Themis' head. She said, 'A full hand-span depth – isn't that a bit thick for a stele?'

'True,' said Themis. 'But Mama wants a memorial out at the farm to my father and sister, as well as my brother. So the relief will show them all welcoming Diodotos and Astrapi to Hades, and for that I'll need to include two or three layers, one set of faces carved behind the others.'

'Complex,' said Melissa. 'And this other one is for my mother's stele?'

'Yes. Again there'll be lots of faces as I'm sure your father will want to show all five of his children, with himself and Anthoussa in front of them.'

He could see Melissa was making an effort not to cry, but she was her professional self when she said, 'In that case, you'd better have a quick look at the blocks we've already got here, but you may find we have to order directly from the quarry.'

'Come and show me?' suggested Themis.

The carters had got the wagon ready to leave and there were roars of encouragement to get the oxen moving. Men from the yard helped by pushing the back of the wagon and as it began to move, a cheer went up.

Themis and Melissa slipped into the forest of standing blocks that extended round the back of the office and main sculpting area.

'Business must be good,' said Themis as he noted the scores of blocks and tiles for sale.

'Oh, it's always brisk at this time of year. The sculptors like to have their stones ready to work on in the winter.' Melissa put a hand on a wide piece of particularly crystalline white marble and stroked it. 'I was thinking this one would be good for Mother.'

Themis ran his hands over the face of the narrow block. It was warm from the sun at the top and cool at the bottom. He shut his eyes, with the palms of his hands cupping the top corners. He felt the stone begin to draw the sadness out of him. He looked at Melissa's concerned face and nodded. 'It's a good one,' he said.

'The most expensive of this size,' she said. 'Father likes it, too.'

Themis looked around for a thicker piece of stone, larger altogether, that he could use both as a stele and as one of the four walls of the shrine he was planning for his own family.

Melissa led him to the back fence, where older pieces of stone stood, some upright, some leaning slightly, all streaked by visiting birds, some with weeds growing at their bases.

'What do you think of this?' she asked, running her hand over a piece of ivory-coloured marble, swirling with clouds of the palest grey and pink. 'Long ago, my father wanted to split it but I begged him not to. He teases me that it will never sell, but it was too beautiful to risk breaking.'

Themis had not imagined a stone that was lovely in itself for the memorial. 'I'll be painting the reliefs,' he said, 'and that would hide the beauty of this stone. I'll consider buying it just as one of the other three walls so that its colours are not lost. Haven't you got a plainer block for the sculpture, though?'

Melissa sighed. 'You are probably the only person who knows what I mean about this one,' she said with a smile and gestured with her arm. 'Look around for another for your main piece.'

Themis surveyed the many blocks and slabs. They threw elongated shadows in the early autumn sun. The normal sounds of the yard had started again, the chipping and grinding, the calling and teasing. He realized that they were out of sight of everyone. 'There's something else I'd rather do,' he said quietly.

Melissa looked up at him and suddenly they were kissing and clinging to each other. They lost their balance and slid to the ground in a frenzy of giggles and caresses. Themis knew he had to take charge of this situation, so he forced himself to limit his hands to holding her face and stroking her soft cheeks. She grabbed his long, unbound hair and pulled his face towards her for a kiss.

'Please, please,' he murmured against her lips. 'Please have mercy on me!'

She exploded in giggles and pulled away, her nose wrinkling gleefully. 'Which is merciful?' she asked. 'More or less?'

He was shaking with laughter and held her at arm's length. 'Neither and both,' he gasped. 'Now, sit still here,' and they sat with their backs to a long low block of stone, their sides touching from shoulder to toes.

She pushed against him and he pushed back. 'Stop it,' he said, but turned and gathered her up into his arms again. He sat her across his legs and then held her face in his hands once more.

'I just want to look and look at those eyes,' he said. 'How did you get such beautiful green eyes?'

'From my mother's family,' she said, looking down into his face. 'Just as you got your grey ones from yours.' She pulled a ribbon that had been plaited into her hair. It came out and she gave it to him.

'But your mother's eyes were hazel,' he said as he took it. 'And sometimes they were actually brown.'

Now she twisted his hair in her fingers. With her other hand she traced the line a drop of sweat made as it ran down from his throat to his chest. He shuddered.

Agorakritos' voice suddenly sounded close by. 'Where in Hades are you? Melissa!'

Themis and Melissa tried to jump up, but they became tangled in each other's garments. They were just unwrapping Melissa's long peplos from Themis' leg, when Agorakritos appeared.

'In the name of Athena, what are you doing out the back here?' he asked loudly. 'Stop trying to sell Themis that old chunk of sculptor's bane.' He strode up to them, stopped suddenly and looked them over. 'That *is* what you were doing, isn't it?' he said with heavy irony.

'We were talking about how to use it in the memorial to his family for the farm,' said Melissa. Her cheeks were flushed and Themis' hair was disheveled.

Agorakritos looked at them, his lips pressing hard together. 'Seems I wasn't all that wrong about you, Themistokles, after all. You're a slimy customer. You'd better stay away from my daughter, or I'll happily hand her over to Nereus.' He turned on his heel and strode off.

Melissa gasped and Themis took her hands in his. 'He's right, you know,' he said. 'We need to keep our distance, at least for the moment. He well might make good his deal with Nereus.'

'But he can't!' exclaimed Melissa. 'That would make him look ridiculous. Everyone already knows he's reluctant to honour it.'

'So if I stay away out of respect, you'll just have to badger him all the more until he gets out of it,' he said. 'I'm sure the huge sum I'm going to pay you for these pebbles will help with that!'

She sighed. 'Maybe,' she said. Then she turned to him. 'Is it wrong to be so happy and so sad at the same time?'

'Wrong?' he said. 'I can't see how it's wrong, but it is … bewildering, isn't it?'

She shrugged. 'It feels like I'm a goddess one moment and a lost soul the next – but I never felt so alive in my life.'

On his way home, Themis' bewilderment became too much. He thought he was going to explode with happiness and frustration. He had to allow himself to admit that all he wanted was to make Melissa his own. The nymph was right.

He set off at a run up to the Peripatos, around the Akropolis to the west side, down and up again to the fortress on the Hill of the Muses. The guards there ignored him as he ran up the ladder to the top of the wall and stood for a moment looking down towards the west. Between this high fortress and the sea, the long walls cut the plain into two segments. He never tired of this view. The sky and the sea beyond the curving coast were milky blue in the midday heat, the island of Egina with its pointed mountain floating in the haze.

He was thinking that surely something that felt so right must be possible. After all, Anthoussa would have wanted it and at least in part it fitted in with his promise to Diodotos. And surely Apollodorus would not let him down about Nereus, and Agorakritos would manage to get his citizenship sorted out. Wouldn't they?

Now the tame and prosperous vista began to annoy him. He needed wildness. He took the precipitous cliff path down to the Illisos valley, leaping like a goat. He sprinted across the river on the bridge by the Temple of Artemis, and started up the skirts of Mount Hymettos. He would leave Melissa's ribbon for Zeus in his precinct on the top.

Soon he was above the fields and olive groves, at the edge of the pine forest. There, he passed the Sanctuary of Demeter in a fold in the mountainside. The little valley was choked with dark trees and the small, brightly painted temple glowed among them. He stopped to drink at the spring by the track, a mere trickle after the long dry summer. As he turned away, shaking the water from his hair, he found himself looking into the partly veiled face of an old acolyte standing behind him with a water jar.

The one eye he could see opened wide with shock. It was the searing green eye of the ancient priestess Asterodia who had brought him back from the dead after his fall when he was twelve. Then the cloak was thrown over it and in two surprisingly agile leaps, the woman had vanished into the shadows among the pines across the road.

Themis ran across the road to follow. There was no one under the trees. He stopped to listen. There was no sound of anyone running. There was no path and the only sounds were birds and cicadas and the slight breeze. The trees grew very close together, interlacing their branches, casting shadows as black as night. Had she been a ghost?

He went back and sat down by the spring. Asterodia's ghost? No, it had been more like Xenovia, but surely this woman moved with such alacrity that she had the use of both her legs. So not Xenovia either. Of course, both priestesses came from a large family. Perhaps a cousin or aunt?

Themis sighed and got up. 'I must ask Lysikles if he can find out if Xenovia really is still alive,' he said quietly, partly to himself and partly in case she was listening. 'Her family is powerful. Someone will know.'

Then he remembered how it had felt to have Melissa sitting on his lap. He left the ribbon for Demeter and sang all the way home.

When Themis got back from the gym next morning, Frog called to him from the yard. 'Melanas sent a message.'

Yellow padded over and Themis caressed his ears and said, 'The grapes are shrivelling on the vines?'

'Something like that,' agreed Frog, bringing bread and goats' cheese and figs. 'The phrase was "monkeys' scrotums".'

'Hah!' Themis shook his head. 'I'll go up tomorrow. Maybe I can take the stone from Agorakritos' yard with me. And you too, Yellow, if you want.' The dog rested his chin on Themis' thigh as he sat to eat.

'And a messenger left you this,' said Frog, put a sealed tablet by Themis and went back into the kitchen. A leopard was sketched on the spine.

'Thanks,' Themis grunted. He broke the seal and read as he ate.

'We received this last night,' said the note. 'Suggest you disappear for a bit.' A scrap of tattered papyrus was enclosed, scrawled with irregular letters saying, 'Tell Themistokles three slaves, ex-hunters, are buying their freedom by helping him to Hades within three days.'

'Frog!' called Themis.

Frog put his head out of the kitchen. 'Bad news?' he asked.

Themis shook his head and spoke quietly. 'Not exactly. Looks like *someone* is looking out for me, at least. And it means it's better if I leave today, not tomorrow. But we'll pretend that I'm still here.'

Frog came and stood behind Themis' shoulder and read the tablet and the note, wiping his hands on a cloth. 'Huh. Might be those Piraeus men.'

'That's what I was thinking. And it would be good to get them caught. But it could be someone completely different. Even Agorakritos, come to think of it. He threatened me in the marble yard yesterday.' Themis stood up. 'I'll get my work stuff together, then I want you to come with me to his yard to collect the stone to work on here for Anthoussa's stele and to pay for our own stones. We'll arrange to have them delivered to the farm. We'll say I'll be going there in two or three days to work on them.'

'But in fact you're going now?'

'Probably, though I heard Alkibiades will be in the City soon. I was planning on going to the Assembly when he gives his version of Mantinea, to heckle him. Anyway, while I'm away, I want you and the women to behave as if I'm here all the time.' Themis ran up the stairs to his workroom. 'Tell them to call out to me from time to time, or gossip about my annoying habits – things like that.'

'They'll love that!' said Frog. 'D'you want me to come back here straight away or can I get to the market? Mika needs fish, and some new baskets.'

Themis leant over the rail. 'That'll be fine. I'll come back alone, and then just melt away.'

Chapter 49: hunted

(Breeds of Sheep 32)

Frog nodded and Themis went in to collect his painting and sculpting tools. As he gathered them from the shelves, he dislodged a pile of sketches on papyrus. He bent to gather them up and found himself staring at the face of Xenovia as she had been 15 years ago, before her fall into the gorge.

The hairs on his arms stood up. 'Which god is taunting me?' he thought. 'I was sure I'd thrown that drawing out.' The image reminded him vividly of the half-face he'd seen at the spring, but that face had no eyebrows, and the drawing had prominent, black brows that followed a particularly pleasing curve.

He shook himself, set the picture aside with its face to the wall, and began packing again. The light from the doorway behind him darkened.

'What is it, Frog?' he asked.

There was no answer. Themis turned in alarm.

Melissa's voice was soft. 'Getting packed to leave?' she asked. She was dressed as a woman.

'Yes, I am, though I didn't mean to go for another day or two. And no one's supposed to know, but I've had a message that suggests I disappear immediately.'

'Ah,' said Melissa. 'So it got to you. And you're going so soon?' She had a rueful, teasing expression on her face.

'What got to me?' Themis asked.

'The message I got from a … friend. He'd overheard your name on a crowded street corner and stayed to learn more. I sent his message on to Lysikles. I thought it might refer to the men who attacked you in Piraeus.'

Themis shook his head in wonder. 'All I can say is thank you,' he said, stopping himself from reaching for her. 'But you shouldn't have come here now. We agreed I'd stay away from you anyway, so I'm going tonight for a while, though I don't want you to tell anyone else that.'

'I won't,' she said, 'but it would be nice if you could stay a little longer.'

He put his satchel down on the old couch and took her hands in his. 'I'd have gone tomorrow anyway,' he said. 'I have to see to the vintage. But I'll come by the sculpture yard today, to pay for my stone.'

She reached up and put her arms round his neck. 'How will I deal with it all without you?' she asked.

'As you always have done!' he said. He could feel himself losing resolve as his legs buckled.

She clung to him with her cheek against his chest. 'Don't go,' she whispered. 'Not just yet.'

'You shouldn't be here,' he breathed back, putting his arms around her and pulling her gently to him as he sat down on the couch.

She said loudly, 'I've come with Adrasteia to check your design for our stele.' Then she sat astride his lap and pulled his head down to her breast. His heart was pounding so hard he could hardly hear her voice as she whispered, 'Seeing you is all I think about.'

'Me, too,' he groaned. He kissed her golden skin where her breast began to swell at the edge of her peplos. He raised his head and kissed her neck and her hair. She put one hand under his chin and caressed his bearded cheek with the other. If he'd been standing he would have fallen. He took her whole weight as he lifted her and laid her on the couch.

He looked down at her oval face. Her eyes were shut but her lips were slightly parted and moist. Her chest rose and fell with her irregular breath.

He leant down and kissed her lips gently, blood roaring in his ears. Her mouth did not open as an experienced woman's would, but her lips were hot and soft. An involuntary moan escaped him as he pulled back a little. She opened her eyes and looked up at him in surprise. Those green, almond shaped eyes – so like Xenovia's eyes …

He couldn't breathe.

He pushed further back and jumped up, looking down on her in dismay.

'What's wrong?' she said, sitting up. 'What's wrong?'

He took a step back. '*This* is wrong!' he said. 'This is so wrong. I'm sorry, Melissa. So very, very sorry. But some god … You are … I … I can't do this.' He turned away in confusion and looked down at his shaking hands. How could Xenovia's ghost be in Melissa's eyes? Why was it everywhere he looked today? The picture with its face to the wall seemed to have moved. What did it mean? Was it Xenovia who had hired those slaves to conduct him to Hades? Was some god warning him? Or trying to drive him mad?

He shook his head and took a deep, shuddering breath.

When he turned back to Melissa, she was standing by the couch, her clothes once more neat and her face stony.

She glared at him. He looked back in despair. Before he could speak, she said, 'I don't know who your gods or your daemons are, or which woman you would rather be with, but don't imagine you'll ever get another chance like that with me. And there'll be no more warnings. I might even help them get rid of you!' She turned and ran down the stairs.

Themis strode to the door and watched as she crossed the courtyard to the main door. He saw her appear in the street beyond and walk, her head unveiled and held high, with Adrasteia behind her, running to keep up. They turned the corner and disappeared. He couldn't stop shaking.

'Ready to go?' called Frog.

Themis set off later in the cart with Frog for Agorakritos' sculpture yard. There, he looked around, then went into the office and found the usual clerk. His stomach was full of writhing snakes, but settled a bit as there was no sign of Melissa. He paid the price for the two pieces of stone he was buying for Athmonon. The stone for Anthoussa was ready to take away.

As he came out into the late afternoon sunlight, Agorakritos stepped in front of him. Themis' clenched his hands behind his back.

'She's not here, you know,' said Agorakritos with a snarl, the skin under his growing stubble darkly mottled.

Themis stepped back and stood with his feet apart. He found he was blinking away tears as he said, 'You have every right to be angry. Melissa and I ... thought we had special feelings for each other, but it turns out that ... we are not suited. I have paid for my own family's memorial stones and brought the cart to load with the stone to work for Anthoussa's – '

'No need,' Agorakritos interrupted hoarsely. 'I'll be making the memorial for Anthoussa myself.'

'Ah. I see,' said Themis. 'Well. I've just left the money for both my stones with your man. Can you deliver them to my farm in Athmonon?' he asked. 'I'll pay for their passage when they arrive there.'

'Indeed you will, or they'll come straight back here.'

'Of course,' Themis said, settling the strap of his satchel on his shoulder. 'I'll be following them there in a few days. My regards to your family.'

Agorakritos snorted and went into the office.

Themis and Frog set off conspicuously towards home in the empty cart. They didn't speak. Frog knew nothing of Themis' humiliation and Themis had no intention of telling him. He dropped Frog off to go to the market and wasted no time at home in gathering his saddlebags and himation. He climbed over the back wall into his neighbour's yard and slipped through the slave entrance to that house without anyone noticing him. At a scruffy livery stable near the City gate he hired a passably healthy horse, and set off to find Lysikles.

The Archon was just leaving the council offices as Themis walked up, leading the horse.

'I'm following your instructions,' Themis said quietly. 'This present threat could be from any of three or four sources, but I'm sure we could learn something if I had an officer with me. Could you spare me one?'

Lysikles was in a hurry, but nodded and changed direction to go to the barracks of the Scythian Archers just off the Agora. There he arranged for a man to accompany Themis, then marched off again on his own business.

'Themistokles, son of Kallistos,' said Themis holding out his hand.

'Damon,' said the officer shortly. His grip was like iron, but his grin was cheeky. 'I'll just get a horse. Don't leave without me!'

'We're acting as bait,' said Themis as they took the road north.

'For whom?' asked Damon.

'Three, maybe four, men who've been assigned to rid this world of my presence,' said Themis, with a short laugh. 'That sounds ridiculous, but they could lead us to their employer. And that could be very important.'

'Being bait is just part of the job,' said Damon. 'Any idea where?'

'Somewhere on the way to Athmonon.'

They had to go fairly slowly at first, but once through the city traffic and out among the vineyards beyond, they could canter easily, leaving the carts and pedestrians coughing in their dust.

Not far from the spring near the turn off to Athmonon, Themis' hired horse began to limp. Damon kept watch while he dismounted and examined its feet. It had picked up three sharp little stones in one of its hooves.

'One could be chance, but three, all the same shape and colour?' said Themis quietly.

'Change mounts, then you go on as normal,' said Damon, his eyes suddenly excited as he leapt off his horse. 'I'll walk your horse and keep out of sight till they find you.' He slapped his sword hilt with a wink.

Themis checked his dagger and short sword, then mounted and walked the horse towards the bend that hid the spring from view.

As he got nearer, he could hear raised voices. He checked that Damon was within hailing distance and rounded the bend. A fight seemed to have broken out and one man lay in the dust. Another was strutting around shouting about how he'd been cheated and the sack of wheat was mouldy. There was a sack broken open on the ground near the spring, and it was indeed sprouting and mouldy. It stank, even in the dry heat of midday.

Themis looked down from his horse and asked, 'Have you killed him?'

'Of course not,' raved the aggressor. 'Look, he's moving.'

The man was beginning to moan. 'You should take him to the inn beyond the next turn off,' said Themis, gesturing along the road.

'I have no horse,' said the aggressor. He was small and wiry. He had a staff, but no other weapon that Themis could see. 'You can see what he was trying to sell me. He deserves to suffer.'

'He must have a mule to be carrying sacks like that,' said Themis gesturing to the split grain sack. 'Where is it?'

A third man came out from behind the wall of the spring. He led a tiny donkey on a rope. On its back was a similar sack, intact. The man looked sheepish, as though caught stealing.

'Oh alright,' said Themis dismounting. 'Help me get him onto the horse.'

The man on the ground sat up, swinging a whip towards Themis' ankles.

Themis had his knife in his right hand and his short sword in his left. He leapt in the air and the whip missed. He ran round behind the horse, slotting his dagger into his belt. He grabbed the mane. But as he jumped to mount, one of the men lunged between the horse's dancing legs and grabbed Themis' foot. The horse plunged and whinnied, but the man held on and Themis couldn't free himself enough to make the jump onto its back. He kept hold of the mane and slashed at the hand round his foot with his short sword. He saw blood dripping and felt his foot freed. But a spear was levelled at his chest by the 'cheated' man, who was dancing from foot to foot. His hood had fallen back. The hair was cut very short.

'Now!' shouted Themis, knocking the spear away with his left arm.

Damon appeared with his sword at the spear man's throat.

Themis turned to grab the donkey man's arm as he began to run. The man with the 'injured' head now had a real wound, and was sitting on the ground nursing a savage gash in his forearm.

The scene was being watched with interest by a growing group of passing pedestrians. Damon called out to them, 'This is an official arrest. Unless you are going to help, keep away.'

One man looked around at the others, who began shuffling on along the road. He said, 'Can I be of use?'

Damon nodded and pointed with his chin at the two men Themis was holding. 'Help him get them tied up,' he said.

Themis suddenly thought that this new man might be one of the gang and reluctantly handed him rope to tie up the donkey man. But he did a good job and soon all three men were trussed like ducks, their heads bare, showing the shorn scalps of the newly enslaved.

While the helpful man removed the stones from Themis' horse's hoof, Themis stood over the prisoners as they sat on the ground. 'So who sent you?' he demanded. 'Who was going to pay you if you succeeded?'

The slaves looked sideways at each other but didn't speak.'

Themis stepped up closer. 'You know what they'll do to you once you get into the City. Tell me now and I can save you that.'

One man took a breath to speak, but the man who'd had the whip spat out some words in another language. All three looked down with a slight smile. They weren't afraid of Scythian persuasion, it seemed.

Themis walked away from them and spoke quietly to Damon. 'Looks like they expect to be rescued,' he said. 'Be on your guard on the way back. You'd better take my horse,' said Themis. 'I can get where I'm going from here on foot.' He told Damon which stables he'd got it from and the two men set off back to the City on horseback with the three prisoners tied between them. The tiny donkey, relieved of its sack of useless grain, was almost dancing at the end of its rope from Damon's saddle.

Once onto the road to the farm, Themis set off at a lope. As he ran, he came to the conclusion that the three slaves were probably sent by Nereus, with his connections in the slave market. The Piraeus attack might really have been unplanned, or perhaps at the orders of Xenovia, but this one had a different feel to it. From the expressions on the men's faces and their practiced abilities with everyday weapons, he knew it had been meant to be deadly. And Nereus would be sure of having influence with the City authorities if the assassins looked like betraying him.

He doubted that Agorakritos would have ordered his death, or that he would have had the will or connections to set this up. He briefly wondered about Melissa, and whether she'd meant what she said, but decided probably not, and anyway, there hadn't been time. He swore, quickening his pace and disturbing a row of swallows preparing to leave their summer home in a ruined barn. Their chatter followed him till the next bend.

He arrived at the farm just as the sun set and gave orders for the gates to be barred and the windows shuttered.

>>>

'You go ahead,' panted Suzanne. David was obviously keeping his long legs in check to run beside her. 'I'll see you back at the stadium.'

David sent a grateful smile over his shoulder and pulled ahead. Others were running at their own pace in a long line up the zigzagging road to the Col de la Forclaz. They were to meet at the café at the top and be brought down by minibus. The views were amazing, with the lake gleaming turquoise below and the mountains forested up to the walls of sheer grey rock at their summits. Suzanne had a stitch, so she stopped to breathe and enjoy the sun and the breeze. She took a couple of photos with her phone. '*It's almost nicer without those flocks of birds fluttering everywhere and schools of fish churning up the lake, as they would be in Themis' world,*' she thought. '*The quiet, and these views – feels like real freedom.*'

Two fellow athletes passed her so she set off again. But the slope made her feel far from free. '*More like wading through syrup. But … no pain, no gain,*' she said to herself with a smile. '*Though why I need great thigh muscles is a mystery. I'm not a cyclist.*'

A tractor and trailer piled high with bales of hay was growling up behind her. She kept close to the side of the road. There were wild flowers growing on the verge; big blue daisies on tall stalks and brambles that made a kind of fence along the top of the drop to the next zigzag. The tractor's gears grated behind her, so she stepped off the road into the vegetation to let it pass.

But the vegetation was growing over empty air and she fell through it, tumbling over and over down the slope. She curled into a ball to protect her head from the rocks among the brambles. The noise and pain was phenomenal. Eventually she came to rest on the side of the road below. She stayed rolled in a ball, catching her breath and deciding what hurt most, amazed she was alive.

In the sudden quiet, she could hear voices approaching. The most painful thing was the right side of her lower back. It made it difficult to breathe. She must have hit a rock that gave her a kidney punch. She began to sit up, trying to keep her breathing regular as the pains shot through her.

She opened her eyes just as someone reached her, shouting in French.

She was looking at her legs. The right one had two knees, one in the normal place and then a smaller, sharper one lower down which was bleeding. She looked up at the middle-aged man who was trying to help her up. 'I can't get up,' she said. 'It's broken.'

324

Chapter 50: priorities

<<<

Themis was not surprised when word came next day from Lysikles that the men had been found dead in their cells before any information could be wrung out of them. So he swallowed his frustration and stayed close to the farm, working as hard as a slave himself in the vineyards.

A couple of days later, a tablet arrived from Frog to tell him that his orders about making it look as though he was still there were being followed. It said: '*You swore with the voice of a goat, / When a bone got stuck in your throat. / In your anger you smashed the dish / Which had held the wicked fish. / You called for the healers, while your slaves became squealers. / The neighbours woke up and loudly spoke up / About coming and helping but Yellow was yelping, / So you retired with a croak and a "sorry I spoke".*

'*Since then it's been peaceful, but someone left a little jar of pulverized walnuts mixed with oil on the doorstep. You're going to have to thank them one day … *'

'Did you know that paste made with walnuts and oil will get rid of a fishbone in the throat, Melanas?' Themis asked as they heaved a great wine jar into the cave.

'In my country we ate grass,' panted Melanas. 'The fibres drag the bone into the stomach.'

'Hmm. Well, I'm glad it wasn't the real me that swallowed the bone.'

'This is the last one,' grunted Melanas, settling the forty-ninth jar into the sand under the rack.

'Forty-nine full and one empty,' said Themis. He lifted the torch out of its bracket. The cave was cool and roomy, the racks well-built. 'More than last year. Let's just hope the Spartans don't come for it.'

'And that it stays sweet,' said Melanas. 'This cave's a bit damper than I'd choose.'

Themis ducked out of the entrance into the autumn sunshine. Until now, he hadn't had to consider his next move. The vintage had had to come first. And the constant activity had diverted his grief and anger. But now he'd have to get back to merciless reality. He was torn between going to the city to deal with the matter of marriage, and staying here at the farm to work on the shrine, so avoiding further possible assassination attempts.

News of Alkibiades was infuriating. He was trying to make it sound as though Mantinea had been a victory in spite of the fact that Argos was now in the hands of its oligarch faction, and most of the Peloponnesian cities were going over to the Spartans. More than a hundred Athenians had died and the Agora was boiling with resentments and opposing views.

So the battle really had been a disaster. The world Themis knew seemed doomed to change for the worse. Democracy was under threat. The gods were angry. Men ran around like disturbed ants, trying to appease them.

He stood gazing down at the Attic plain. The sea gleamed silver in the distance. It had rained earlier and now the air was clear enough to see, furthest away to the right, the steep-sided hill that was the acropolis of Korinthos, tiny and pale against the dark mountains of the Peloponnese and the bright blue of the sky. Inlets and spurs set pale mountains against dark blue sea between there and the island of Salamis, which lay like a dragon behind the nearer hill of Aigaleo. From this distance, Athens and Piraeus looked like toy bricks at the mercy of a wilful god's kick into oblivion. Looking left, he could see the road to Athmonon. It was busy today, tiny figures and carts embroidered on a pale ribbon.

He sighed. Melanas was locking the gate into the cave. Together, they untied the ropes that held back the great bush that disguised its entrance. The branches sprang back into place.

'You take the wagon back to the farm,' said Themis. 'I'll follow on foot when I've swept up here.'

Melanas nodded and climbed up onto the wagon seat. The mules were only too ready to get home, and set off down the track at a good pace.

Themis used a bunch of dried grass to brush away the signs of their feet near the cave entrance. Then, on a whim, he went in the other direction, around the flank of the mountain.

Between his land and that of his neighbour there was a small sanctuary to Apollo, beside the shallow rock basin of a spring. It was usually unattended, and as boys, he and Frog and other friends had spent many lazy hours there, playing Persians versus Greeks, splashing in the water or drawing in the dust of its yard. Now, as he approached, he saw it was not deserted. An acolyte was lighting a cauldron by the altar in that same yard.

'Do you have a festival today, then?' Themis asked.

The elderly man looked up at him, nodding slowly. 'Today the god is preparing for winter,' he said.

'I have nothing with me to give him,' said Themis.

'Go in and speak to him,' said the old man. 'If you like what he says you can send something later.'

Themis smiled. 'Thank you,' he said. He washed his hands and face, then stood back to watch the water spill over the edge of the basin and become an oozing stream. It had a strange, slightly bitter taste and was known for its purging properties, so he only rinsed his mouth with it and did not drink. There were times lately when his stomach and guts behaved badly enough without help from the bitter spring.

Inside, the little temple was dark and smelled of its cedar beams and aging thatch. Two torches flared and wavered in brackets on the walls. The statue was also of wood, its complexion dark and archaic, its curls picked out with gold. It stood on a high plinth, the large painted eyes staring steadily down at whomever came in the door. Today it wore a heavily embroidered cloak and a necklace of fresh orchids, cyclamen and herbs. A garland of scarlet and yellow vine leaves adorned the god's hair and was strung across to the lyre in his left hand. An offering bowl at his feet already held figs and loaves.

Themis stood before Apollo and closed his eyes. 'Clarify your question,' he said to himself. Or was that the god who spoke?

'My question is, should I take one of my mother's recommended "nice" Athenian girls as my wife, or should I try to make it up with Melissa? Her father's delay with Nereus is up in two days, but his citizenship is still in question.'

'She will be a difficult wife.' It was a light, lilting voice.

'But Eros has chosen her for me. She and I are alike in many ways. She understands when I have to work, how tired I am when I stop, when I need peace, my kind of jokes.'

'That's because until now she was a child, sometimes even a boy. Now she is a woman and women have different priorities.'

'So would any girl.'

'But you could keep a "nice" girl in order.'

'Hm. And be bored and annoyed by her? Melissa is an artist herself, we feed ideas to each other.'

'But look what has happened since Eros got between you.'

Themis sighed. 'Yes … We've started to … cause each other pain.'

'Why?'

Themis thought about this for a moment. 'Because we have different expectations,' he decided.

'Then you must discuss and accept these. Think carefully about them. Change yourself if necessary. Eros is often wild, wilful, and fickle. But you have tested him now for a month and found him persistent. It is time to visit Melissa's father.'

'And if he refuses? Or if, after all, I really cannot go through with intercourse with her?'

The voice of the god seemed to laugh as it said, 'It appears you are more afraid of that than of the battlefield … but if it happens, your mother has two lovely young maidens panting for your manhood to choose from.'

Themis laughed out loud. 'Apollo, you are outrageous!' he whispered, turning towards the door. A crimson vine leaf drifted down and fell at Themis' feet. He bent and picked it up, laid his hand on his chest in thanks while looking one more time at that familiar, slightly smiling god-face. Now he knew what he wanted, all he had to do was to overcome his own impotence and her total rejection of him. Easy! He went out into the fitful evening sun with a smile on his face.

In the kitchen at the farm, he took a small, lidded jar of honey from the store and half a loaf from under Kalliope's nose, wrapped them in a napkin, and called Mikro.

'Take this with care to Apollo's shrine by the bitter spring,' he said. 'Leave it in the offering bowl at his feet, and tell the attendant it comes from me. He's a new man. I haven't seen him before.'

Mikro nodded and ran off with the little bundle.

'Where is everyone?' Themis asked and picked up the rest of the loaf for himself.

'What a good thing I baked three barley loaves today,' said Kalliope without looking up from stirring a large pot. Then she lifted her chin towards the window and said, 'Arianos saw someone coming on the road from Athens and went to meet them. Melanas is in the barn paying off the last of the workers.'

Themis thought, *Another responsibility I should be dealing with*. He walked across the yard to the barn, but before he could go in, Arianos and a rider came through the farm entrance. The rider was Frog. His chiton was torn and his face and arms blackened and grazed.

'Frog! What's happened?' Themis asked, holding the bridle of the horse.

'There was a fire at the house,' said Frog as he dismounted. 'Someone managed to set fire to the bushes in the yard and it spread through into your mother's salon, and burned part of the staircase.'

'My work room?' asked Themis.

'There's smoke damage, but nothing destroyed there.'

'And Mika and Tanu – and the Skionian?'

Themis handed the horse to Arianos, who led it off to the stables.

'We're all fine. Luckily the well had plenty of water and it began to rain, so we put it out before it reached the stores. Two or three passers-by helped. The first one was that merchant Tryfonos, just back from along trading trip, and later Photios' oldest brother. Tryfonos didn't know whose house it was, but he got wet and dirty and wouldn't take any thanks when the fire was out and they all left.'

Frog stopped by the little shrine to Demeter and put his offering of almonds in the bowl. Then he went over to the water trough and washed his face and arms carefully. Themis stood in the middle of the yard in growing irritation, legs apart and arms folded. Frog turned to him as he dried himself on the cloth Kalliope handed him.

'Of course the whole city will know by now that you weren't there. But all the helpers believed you were there and asked for you. We had done our work too well.' Frog was smiling mischievously.

'Really?' said Themis. 'You let someone set fire to the yard and then can't stop it till it's destroyed half the house, and that's doing well, is it?'

'Yes, we did well,' Frog said calmly but with a frown. 'You see, we'd convinced the outside world that you'd come back and – '

'You said that on the tablet. How had you done that?'

'Someone has got quite good at sounding like you,' said Frog. 'So we set up a little scene in the yard where "you" and I had a ... disagreement. Mika said she heard it from down the street and thought you were really there.'

'Ah. How very clever. You playing both parts, I suppose?' Themis' tone was heavily ironic.

'Actually, no. Io's got quite an ear for voices.'

'And finally a voice of her own?' said Themis.

'She prefers to talk with someone else's voice,' said Frog. 'It can be a bit confusing.'

Themis sighed gustily. 'So. Now we only have half a house.'

'Yes, but we know who did it.' Frog was grinning.

Themis looked at him seriously. 'We do?' He'd been considering whether Melissa was angry enough to lob a torch or two over his wall.

'Tanu saw them throw the torches from the street and rushed in to tell me. He saw which way the arsonists ran off, so he dealt with the fire and I followed the two men back to their lair.'

'And where was that?'

'They ran to an inn just outside the Diochares Gate. Not far away,' said Frog. 'They're in the prison now, but not talking about who sent them. The Warden is waiting for orders.'

'And when did this all happen?'

'This morning.'

Themis called out, 'Arianos! Prepare me a fresh horse!'

Frog said, 'But that's not all.'

Themis deliberately kept his voice calm. 'Go on,' he said.

'Agorakritos has sent Nereus packing.'

Themis' mouth fell open. 'Are you sure?'

Frog nodded happily. 'He had a long conversation with him, it seems, at home. And Nereus left, looking so shocked he could hardly walk.'

'When was this?'

'Yesterday morning.'

'How do you know?'

Frog smiled with delight. 'Melissus came and told me. Before the fire. He ... er ... she had two messages. One was the City Council has finally passed her father's application for citizen's rights and the other was about Nereus. She said she wants you to know, even if you don't want to know.'

Themis shook his head in frustration, grabbing fistfuls of hair. 'I'll never understand women,' he said with his eyes squeezed shut.

'Better not to try,' said Frog, nodding wisely.

Themis forced his horse to gallop back to the city, weaving through the traffic on the road with a big grin on his face. He'd told Frog to go back to the house in Diomea at his own speed and, although he wanted to see Melissa more than he ever remembered, rode straight to the jail himself.

'You again,' sighed the Warden. 'What do you want this time?'

'You're holding two men who set fire to my house,' said Themis. 'I want to talk to them.'

'You'll get little out of them. They've been worked on by the Scythians' persuaders, but nothing much has come of it.'

'What did they say?'

'Oh, a load of prayers that the gods forgive them, and the priestess intercedes for them, and that they don't know anything else.'

Themis caught his breath, then tried to speak calmly. 'The priestess?

Is that a normal reaction to the persuasion?'

'Fairly common, though it's usually a priest.'

'Has anyone asked them specifically which priestess?'

'I doubt it,' said the Warden. 'You know of one who wants your house burned down?' His tone was ironic.

'Possibly,' said Themis seriously. 'Can I see them now?'

The Warden made a 'fancy that' face and called a guard over. He said, 'Show this man the arsonists. They can talk through the hatch, but don't let them out. He's not official.'

The men were in the cell at the end of the corridor, next to where Photios had been. Themis looked through the small hatch in the door. He saw only two men. They were sitting on the floor on opposite sides of the cell. One was slumped down asleep or unconscious.

Themis put his face to the hatch. 'You tried to burn my house down,' he said pleasantly. 'You did this because you were told to by a priestess. If you tell me where to find her, I'll see if I can get you out of here.'

The man who was awake looked up with hope in his battered face. He was shaking, but struggled to his feet and dragged his chains as near to the door as they would go. When he spoke, Themis saw that he was missing two teeth and talking was an effort. 'I don't know where she is. I don't know which priestess. It was a man told us that a great priestess wanted this done. He said it was because the owner of the house had offended Athena. He said she would protect us if we were caught, but that we wouldn't be caught. But we were.'

'What was he like?'

'Tall, black beard, wore grey. Couldn't see his hair. Hat.'

'Not short and twisted?'

'Nah.'

'Why did you agree to do it?'

'We needed the money.'

'For anything special?'

The man leered gap-toothed at Themis. 'When you get a taste for the poppy, nothing else is quite as good.'

'And the poppy is expensive…'

'Yeah. If you have to pay. But this man gave us 20-dose tokens - lots.'

'Tokens? What do they look like?'

'They're shells, flat shells, with numbers scratched on.'

'Where are they?' Themis asked. 'Have you got them here?'

The man hung his head and swung it from side to side. 'The guards found them and broke them up.' The man was sobbing. 'The bastard said we'd get two more shells each when we'd burned the house.'

'Where did you meet this man?' asked Themis.

'Where they caught us. '

'Right,' said Themis. 'That's a help. By the way, you should know that the house was saved. Well, most of it. And I'm not injured or ruined, which I imagine were the objectives. So you wouldn't have got the rest of your tokens anyway. But I'll see if I can find this man. What else can you tell me about him? He wore a hat, and … ?'

The man went over to the other, who hadn't stirred. He kicked him and he groaned. 'Eh! You talked to the priestess' man. What did he look like?'

The man mumbled and shook his head. The man on his feet moved nearer. 'I only saw him as he walked past me. Smelled clean. Talked posh.'

'Good. Well, that's enough for now,' said Themis. He turned to the guard. 'Let's go.'

The man in the cell shouted, 'Eh! You said you'd get us out! Don't just leave us here to rot. Hey! …'

His shouts faded as Themis strode to the outer door. He said to the Warden, 'No more "persuasion". They've told me something that may make things easier for them. They didn't do this on their own and whoever it was that employed them was wearing disguise.'

The Warden shrugged. 'Well … I'll have to clear it with the Archon.'

'That's fine. I'll make it right with Lysikles. I'll be back tomorrow at the latest,' said Themis. 'Be careful they don't escape in the meantime.' He smiled to himself as he walked away. The building had been strengthened since he'd helped Phidias escape. And now he knew for certain whom he had to find, although why she hadn't just arranged for his murder, rather than his kidnap, he couldn't understand. If she was working with Nereus, perhaps he wanted Themis alive so he could humiliate him in public. *I'd better keep Yellow with me more,* Themis thought.

>>>

Chapter 51: reconciled

Suzanne watched David come towards her hospital bed with what she thought of as the slow elegance of a giraffe. She didn't remember anything about being brought there, just a man at the roadside saying he was a physician. She hadn't seen anyone from the training school except its own doctor. Now she was in a ward with three patients, her leg in plaster, crutches leaning against the bedside cupboard, and a delicious meal of wild-mushroom-stuffed peppers on her mobile bed-table. David put down her laptop in its case on the same table.

'Hey,' he said, pulling over a chair from under the window. ''ow is Mademoiselle Trois-Genous et Deux Mondes?'

'Two worlds,' said Suzanne. 'Well, you're the only person I've dared say much to about that. And look at me now. My world is as messed up as Themis'.'

'So you are feeling … how do you say déprimée?'

'Is it depressed?' said Suzanne. 'No, I'm not feeling depressed. I'm feeling stupid.' She touched the laptop. 'Thanks for thinking of bringing this.'

'It's nothing,' said David. 'But you know, you are not stupid. You are clever.'

Suzanne looked at his face. He was serious. 'So in your opinion it's clever to break my leg because I wasn't looking where I was going – just when I have the best chance ever of joining an international athletics team to compete in one of the most important meets of the decade? You. Are. Totally. Mental!'

'It was clever,' he replied calmly, 'because you tell yourself to slow down. You need to rest, choose priorities for your life, retire for a while – and enjoy some more French cooking!' He looked pointedly at her meal.

Suzanne looked into his kind eyes. 'I don't get it,' she said.

He shrugged. 'You do difficult and complicated studies. You train very 'ard to represent your country in your difficult and complicated sport. You live in – or per'aps just imagine, I don't know – a difficult and complicated "other world", which you are spending hours writing about.' He opened his hands and tensed his shoulders. Then he relaxed and smiled. 'This is too much like 'ercules, no?'

Suzanne felt something inside collapse. Her eyes filled with tears. She found she was sobbing.

David leapt up and moved the bed-table back. He rested one hip on the bed and took both her hands in one of his while he took the paper serviette from beside her plate to wipe her eyes.

'Stop it!' said Suzanne, grabbing the serviette. 'It's just the drugs they're giving me.'

'No,' said David quietly. 'You are training 'ard for – what? Five, six years? And now you can't go to Australia. But you know? I believe you in fact don't care. It is not the drugs. It is truth coming out. That's all.'

Suzanne shook her head fervently. 'No, no. I do care. I care a lot! You've got it wrong,' she said.

David smiled and took her hand again. 'Naturally,' he said. 'I know nothing about these things – or about you. I must be wrong.'

Later, in the quiet of the small hours, Suzanne woke smiling. She'd been dreaming. David had lifted her into a boat on a great, still lake. Then he'd presented her with a live fish that leapt out of her hands into the water. It was a beautiful fish with rainbow colours and she'd watched it swim away, feeling happy for it as it enjoyed its freedom.

Now she looked around in the dim hospital ward. One of the other patients was snoring quietly, the others seemed asleep but quiet. She sighed and shut her eyes again. She was surprised she didn't feel more upset. '*It* must *be the drugs,*' she thought sleepily. '*I even feel I could trust David to read a bit of Themis' story. Though I do wonder why he and I see winning so differently.*'

'Because we have different expectations,' Themis' voice said thoughtfully.

'Then you must discuss and accept these,' said another voice, light, masculine, lilting. 'Think carefully about them. Change yourself if necessary. Eros is often wild, wilful, and fickle. But you have tested him now for a month and found him persistent. It is time to visit Melissa's father.'

'And if he refuses?' Themis' voice suddenly cracked as he went on, 'Or if, after all, I really can't manage sex with her?'

Suzanne almost laughed out loud. She whispered to the darkness, 'Oh, come on, Themis! You're more afraid of that than of the battlefield … but if it happens, your mother has two lovely young virgins panting for your manhood to choose from.' She was still smiling as she stretched herself as much as she could and drifted back to sleep.

(Breeds of Sheep 34 – As I was in-putting that last bit, it was really weird writing down when Themis heard my words and thought they came from Apollo. Maybe I should study quantum physics to see if words can hang around in the ether for millennia … just joking, but I felt my arm hairs stand up when I heard my own words said in a voice different to mine. Must ask what they're giving me!)

Themis deliberately took the horse rather than running on foot through the city to Agorakritos' house. There was no sign of his being followed. No strangers approached him. If he was sweating, it wasn't from running.

'We got the message so she's expecting you,' said Skopas as he opened the door and beckoned Themis in. 'They put the fire out?'

'Yes,' said Themis, walking through into the courtyard. 'What happened with Nereus?'

Skopas laughed happily. 'Ha! Dad had been down in the City and just learned that he's to be a full citizen after all. No explanation for the delay. He saw Nereus in the Agora and invited him to come to the workshop. He didn't say anything till he had him in the yard. And then he sent him off with a nettle up his arse! You could hear them right down the street.'

'What did he say?'

'Oh, he just accused Nereus of paying to delay his citizenship, of being a hypocrite and irreligious, of demanding a young girl leave her rightful home and duties. He said Nereus was like Hades stealing away Persephone to the Underworld and using her just for his pleasure. He called curses down from Demeter and Athena and – oh, I don't know, all the gods, just about … '

They were standing in the shade by a great urn. The vine that grew up from it to the roof was turning yellow. Shrivelled leaves danced at their feet in the restless evening breeze.

Melissa came out of the house and stood in the sunlight.

Skopas said, 'Ah, good. I've got to go. See you later, Uncle Themis!'

Melissa had dressed carefully. Her fine, pale blue chiton was belted with a wide sash of green with dark blue tassels. She was wearing a strophion under it, flattening her breasts. Her hair was perfectly dressed in an elaborate series of plaits and ribbons. Her sandals were new. Her face was composed, but her breathing was shallow and fast.

'I understand that no one was hurt in your fire,' she said, the cool hostess.

Themis remembered to breathe. 'Did you get my note?' he asked.

She remained calm. 'The one where you apologized and said your … inadequacy had nothing to do with me? Yes, I got that,' she said.

'But you didn't answer.'

She turned to sit on the bench under the vine, by the door to the andron. She gestured he should sit on the stool set beside it. When he did, she looked at his face closely and her shoulders relaxed, her lips filled out and she smiled ruefully.

'I'm glad I didn't at the time,' she said. 'I was very … confused. I've had time to think since then.'

Themis was surprised to see tears shining in her eyes. He kept his own gaze on the smooth skin over the sweet line of her jaw. A pulse was beating fast in her neck. He couldn't speak.

'You see,' she went on, 'it wasn't just Eros that prompted me to come to you that day.' She looked down. A drop splashed onto her clenched hands in her lap. She rubbed it off on the skirt of her chiton. 'I had a plan.'

Themis frowned. 'Go on.' His voice came out as a whisper.

Melissa wound her fingers together. 'I wanted you to take me so that I wouldn't be a virgin and Nereus wouldn't want me any more. I thought that would solve all my problems.'

Themis looked at her for a moment as if he'd never seen her before. Then he sighed and, reaching forward to take her hand, said, 'May I?'

She didn't withdraw it, so he took it and turned it palm up in his. It was rough from working at the yard and the nails were ragged, but her fingers were long and tapered and trembled slightly. He closed them into a fist and held it closed.

'I didn't think … ,' she began a little breathlessly. She had prepared this speech. 'I didn't realise that, by doing that, I would bring dishonour to my father. Nor that not just Nereus, but others might blacken my name, and that you would perhaps think badly of me yourself. It hadn't occurred to me that my mother would have held back her forgiveness if she'd been alive, or that you and my father would have been enemies for ever.' Her voice rose a little. 'I just wanted the freedom to feel as I do about you and to act as I feel, and not as I … as what is expected.' She spat out the last word. She looked back at his face, breathing fast.

Themis sighed deeply. He squeezed her hand a little, stopping himself from grabbing her and squeezing the rest of her to him. 'And did you think at all about why I stopped it?'

She shrugged a little and looked at him pointedly. 'For all those reasons, surely,' she said.

'For none of those reasons,' said Themis. 'Although they are very good reasons and they should have been uppermost in *my* mind rather than yours.' He returned her hand to her lap and stood up. 'No, I couldn't go through with it that day because I was being haunted. For days I kept seeing things that reminded me of someone. You have a look of her, and I was once besotted with her ...' A look of alarm appeared on Melissa's face. Themis went on with a smile, '... but she is now seriously disabled – and very old!'

Melissa relaxed. 'Oh ... The priestess who fell into the gorge?' she asked.

'Yes,' said Themis. 'She was the most beautiful woman I had ever seen, and I was captivated by that beauty. But she had a withered and evil soul with a deep and obsessive hatred of my father. He had passed her over when he came to marry, so she spent her time trying to destroy his family.'

'And she looked like me?' Her smile was mischievous.

Themis said, 'Mainly her eyes. But green eyes are not uncommon, especially in her far-reaching family.'

Melissa nodded. 'And she's been haunting you?' she asked seriously.

'I've seen her for sure only once and that was near Argos,' he said, 'but I keep thinking I see her. I do know now that she didn't die in that underground river.' He walked a few paces and came back. 'I probably shouldn't tell you this because it doesn't help our situation,' he said quietly looking down on her, 'but when I was holding you and you had your eyes shut, I had given in to Eros. I couldn't resist any more in spite of the reasons you said. Then you opened your eyes, and they seemed to be *her* eyes. When I was a boy of twelve and she was as old as my mother, she had looked at me just once like that ...' He sat down on the stool. 'It was her way of enslaving men, and she enslaved far better men than I am.'

Melissa looked at him thoughtfully for a moment. 'So you thought I was trying to enslave you?'

Themis had to smile. 'By your own confession, you were, weren't you?' he said.

Melissa jumped up. 'You see!' she said, swirling round to shout at him. 'You see! Anything I say, you twist to make me feel ashamed. You are the only thing that makes becoming a woman tolerable to me. You are the only man who, even now that I am a woman, accepts me as a person, and allows that I have opinions and talents of my own. I nearly told you this months ago, but I stopped myself. I was right to!' She turned her back on him. 'Trying to be honest is ... is ... pointless!' She clenched her fists.

He stood up and put his arms around her from behind. 'No,' he said quietly. 'Not pointless. Hard, yes. Scary even, yes. But not pointless.

You are in fact a truly opinionated and talented female person.' Melissa tensed up as though to break free. Themis went on, 'And it's very important that we recognize each other's talents and opinions if we are to marry.' She stayed still but rigid in his arms. 'That was just my way of teasing you,' he said. 'But perhaps it wasn't the best way.'

'No it wasn't,' she said. 'That would only be right if we could trust each other.' Her voice was calm and serious now. Her face was to the urn and the yellowing vine, but every word was directed behind her to Themis. 'Trust each other to never do anything or say anything on purpose, to hurt the other. We must respect each other's freedom to think and speak as we really feel.' She turned in his arms and stepped back, looking directly into his eyes. 'Is that possible with me, Themistokles, son of Kallistos?'

Themis felt as though the gods were watching them, judging his reaction while offering him the world as a gift. His heart sang and his fingers prickled as he took her hands and looked into those dark-fringed, glowing eyes. 'Possible,' he said, 'and necessary, Melissa, daughter of Agorakritos.'

'In that case,' she said with a sigh. 'I promise to keep my eyes shut at the critical moment.'

They collapsed onto the bench in giggles.

The wetnurse appeared with the baby in her arms. He was awake but quiet. Melissa stood up, suddenly business-like, and said, 'Uncle Themis, this is Philomena. She is Adrasteia's sister. Philomena this is Themistokles, … er … my father's friend.'

Philomena bowed her head as best she could in Themis' direction. Then she murmured to Melissa, 'Please, miss, could you hold him while I do some laundry? He's been making messes and now he won't settle.'

Melissa made a smiling but exasperated face at Themis. He stood up.

'I have to leave, anyway,' he said. As Philomena hurried away, he said quietly, 'I have a criminal to find. You could have helped as Melissus. I may have to call on you, even as Melissa. Now that I feel we are friends again.' He examined the baby's face. The boy was looking round the courtyard with wide dark eyes. He had a cock's comb of dark hair that curled like Agorakritos'. 'Hmmm. Clearly not mine,' Themis said with a grin. 'I'll try and come by again in the morning. I'd like to have a word with your father.' He leaned over the restless baby and kissed Melissa's forehead.

Her eyes glowed as she looked up at him. Then she took the child into the house.

Chapter 52: accusations

Themis found the inn not far east of the Diocharus Gate. It was called the Holey Basket. The torches were lit but it only had three customers.

'Yeah, they arrested two men here,' said the innkeeper. His snub nose reminded Themis of a satyr, but a satyr with eggyolk in his beard.

'Were they regular customers?'

'I'd seen them before.'

'Did they have other … friends they'd meet here?'

'Well, let me see … ' The innkeeper was stalling.

Themis made the coins in the purse at his belt clink. 'I mean,' he said, 'was there someone they could have been working with?'

The round eyes above the round nose didn't blink. 'Well, there was a big man with them yesterday. I'd never seen him before. When he'd gone, they seemed happy, and it was like they did a deal with a man who came by soon after – exchanged things I couldn't see. He's a skinny man with a withered leg and he's been here before, with that Sokrates bloke.'

'Really?!' said Themis. 'And do you know the skinny man's name?'

'Nah,' said the innkeeper, raising his eyebrows in a negative gesture.

'Or anything else about him, or the other men?' Themis shook the purse.

The innkeeper shook his head.

Themis selected an obol. 'How long ago was this?' he asked.

'Last night, quite late.'

Themis gave the innkeeper the obol.

The house smelled of smoke and wet wood. Themis ran upstairs to check on his workroom. His drawings and other work were piled in the usual corner. Someone had thrown a blanket over the heap to protect it.

The courtyard had black smears on the walls and on the two columns nearest his mother's salon. The little back yard where the burning torches had landed was a mess. The salon would have to be repainted and the wooden chairs and the floor replaced.

When he reached the kitchen, Themis could see it had no damage a bucket of whitewash wouldn't fix. He said, 'Thank you, Mika, for taking care of my work upstairs. That was quick thinking.'

Mika's wry smile creased her aging cheeks. 'In fact you should punish me,' she said, 'because I went up on the day you left to snoop at your secret painting. Frog wouldn't tell me anything.'

'Hah!' said Themis.

'But the wind was quite strong that day and dust was blowing in. I thought I'd better make sure nothing got damaged with the winter coming. I had a look, but didn't see anything I thought should be secret. You've improved lately, though. I like the pictures of myths and faces, not just designs and measurements. Anyway, I covered everything I could with a blanket.' She held out a bowl of walnuts. 'The food will be ready soon.'

Themis took the bowl and laughed. 'I'm just glad you didn't lose your eyebrows in the fire,' he said.

'It wasn't that bad,' said Mika. 'You can see. It was mainly the plants in the yard and the wooden benches. Mrs Eirini's room needs renewing anyway.'

Frog came in from the stable. 'How were things at the jail?' he asked.

Themis said, 'I got enough to work on, but I might need some help in the next day or two.'

Mika looked up. 'Not tomorrow morning,' she said. 'I need everyone I can get to move the broken pots and benches from the yard. I have a man with a cart coming.'

Themis nodded. 'Of course.'

Mika laughed. 'Not you,' she said. 'You get off to the palaestra. You need the exercise. You've been away. We'll manage.'

Frog's mouth twisted wryly, but he said, 'I can meet you later in the Agora, if that's any help.'

'Thanks.' Themis lifted the bowl in his hand and said, 'Now, *please* bring me some real food, Mika. I'm starving!'

Frog followed Themis to the andron to prepare the couch and table. 'All well at Agorakritos' house?' he asked.

Themis grinned. 'So far so good,' he said. He stretched out on his favourite couch. 'Frog,' he said, 'how do you stop the gods knowing your thoughts?'

'You planning something blasphemous?' asked Frog, plumping a cushion on another couch.

'It's just … there are moments when I'd rather the nymph didn't … er … wasn't present. And she seems to be here almost constantly just lately.' He tapped the middle of his chest.

'Could be embarrassing,' said Frog, pursing his lips. 'Specially if …' He made a lewd gesture.

'Exactly,' said Themis. 'But not only that. There are lots of times I'd rather she wasn't here. It would have been better if she hadn't been with me when Diodotos was killed, but I think now that she was, and it's affected her. Things like that.'

'Well, there'll be no more "things like that",' said Frog, his chin quivering. 'That can only happen once.'

Themis jumped up. 'By all that's sacred, he dumped me right in it, didn't he?' he said, marching up and down, beating his left fist into his other hand. 'Everything's my job now! Farm, finances, all you slaves, producing the next generation. Couldn't he at least have got himself married and had kids before he went off to become a war hero?'

Frog was looking at Themis with wide eyes. 'You'd have ended up with even more responsibilities if he had,' he said pointedly. 'You worried about something specific?'

'No, of course not!' said Themis. 'With all those hefty claims on me, what else could possibly be bothering me?'

'That you think you'll fail,' said Frog quietly.

Themis stopped dead and looked at him. 'Actually, no. I hadn't thought of that. No. What I *am* worried about is that these attacks on me may succeed. I'm worried that I shouldn't be making plans to marry because I may not be here for long.'

Frog laughed. 'Which is exactly what you accused your brother of! Delaying until he died first. You just get on with it. If she, or Nereus or whoever, kills you before you manage it, at least you will have tried.'

Themis nodded and sat down again. 'Ture. So I'd better find her and get the attacks stopped, hadn't I? And I think I know where to start.'

Next morning, after the gym, Themis found Sokrates and his followers sitting on the steps of the South Stoa. He nodded to the master as he joined the outer circle. Sokrates nodded back, but didn't interrupt what he was saying. Themis carefully studied the backs of the nine seated students he could see, but none of them seemed to have a withered leg. Two were the right build but neither was turned towards him. He settled down to listen. A young man at Sokrates' feet was speaking.

'But what you first asked was what is the origin of guilt. We've got sidetracked into forgetting that.'

'Quite right, Rizos,' replied Sokrates. 'Let's re-consider the sources of guilt and its true meaning – and I don't mean the criminal meaning of guilty, I mean the feeling we might get if for instance we tell someone who trusts us a lie. What other circumstances engender guilt?'

'When I find myself in a position where either I must hurt a friend or suffer some dire trouble myself,' said a serious young voice.

'And if that friend were never to learn of this dilemma, would you feel guilt then?' asked Sokrates.

There was quiet for a moment. Then the same voice said thoughtfully, 'Perhaps not.'

'So it is because you have gone against the expectations of this friend and he knows it, that gives guilt its hold over you, is it?'

Again there was a pause. Then a different, harsher voice answered. 'Whether the injured party knows or does not know that he or she has been injured, the guilt is still the same. It can live quietly in the heart for years. If you have kept a secret that might have helped someone out of trouble, or if you are to blame for their misfortune even though they don't know it, in the end, guilt will reach into your every thought and action.'

Sokrates turned to look at the speaker with a kind expression on his ugly face. 'This is guilt that has been left to fester,' he said. 'But surely there are ways to avoid such a dire outcome?'

'The only way then must be death!' The harsh voice suddenly broke and the man began to cough. Themis felt the hairs on his arms rising. He tried to see the man's face but could not without disturbing everyone by standing up.

The other men looked at each other and murmured in alarm. Sokrates gestured for silence with his hands. 'How could death undo the original wrong? And whose death? The wrong-er, or the wronged?'

'Either,' croaked the man, covering his head and face with his himation as he began coughing again. He stood up. 'Forgive me, Sokrates, gentlemen,' he said as he turned to address the students. 'As you can hear, I'm not well, so I must leave now. But I hope to see you again tomorrow.' And he stepped out of the circle of faces and limped down the steps towards Themis.

Shock turned Themis hot then cold. This was not a man, it was Xenovia. How had he not recognized her? He stood up in her path, with no idea what to do with her.

The 'man' froze for an instant. Then, 'No!' he shouted, his voice a kind of bark. 'Not yet! NO!' And he began to run. His shambling gait looked painful but carried him rapidly away towards the crowded alley behind the Stoa. Themis set off to follow him, but tripped on the guy-rope of a stall awning. He fell to one knee, recovered almost immediately, and looked up to see where his quarry was. But the limping 'man' had disappeared into the throng.

Themis leapt up, furious with himself, and ran directly to the Council Offices. The scribe showed him in to Lysikles' office immediately.

'I just saw the woman, the ex-priestess Xenovia,' said Themis. 'She is alive and pretending to be a man. She knows I saw her and ran away behind the South Stoa. She has a limp and always covers half her face with a cloak or hood. She also has a cough at present. You must arrest her. She had another man employ the men who tried to burn my house, but then checked that he had herself.'

Lysikles said, 'I can't have her arrested because she dresses as a man.'

Themis took a breath and spoke more calmly. 'I have a witness that this "man" was behind the employment of the two arsonists who tried to burn my house down.'

'Ah,' said Lysikles, walking towards the door. 'Is there anything else that would make it easier to identify or apprehend her – or him?'

'If your men call either the name Lythaia, or Xenovia, she would react.'

'What was she wearing just now?'

'A dark brown himation over a dirty grey chiton. She kept the himation pulled over her head, so I don't know if there was a skullcap under it. It's the left leg that's withered – and the left arm, but that may not be obvious.'

Lysikles went out and shut the door behind him.

Themis went to the window and stared out at the secluded garden. It was now so obvious it had been Xenovia! He shook himself in frustration.

And where had she gone? He tried to imagine her movements. Where would she go, whom would she ask to shelter her? She must know a lot of people among the petty criminals of the city to be able to find men to do her bidding. Had she been the 'Benefactor'? If so, she must be rich, however she dressed. She was originally from a very wealthy family, but they had disowned her when they learned of her thefts from the temple and her murder of Kallistos. They wanted nothing to do with her, alive or dead. And her mother, Asterodia, had had all mention of her removed from the official lists of the priesthood. If she had money now, it must come from a dubious source.

The door opened and Lysikles came in.

'Keep a record of this,' said Lysikles to his scribe. 'Themistokles, if you want this person arrested, you must make an official accusation to the Council at the Prytaneion as soon as you can. The Officer of the day expects you. He will need any proofs you can give, names of witnesses, and any relevant documents. He will also have to choose a place to hold this person if it indeed turns out to be a woman. My own thought is that we should ask the priests of Apollo to incarcerate her in the cave under the temple by the quarry on Lykavitos. She will have to be tried in a full court of justice at the first opportunity.'

Themis nodded. 'Thank you, Master Lysikles. I shall leave a message as soon as I have made the accusation. Will you be able to get the men in jail for setting my house on fire a pardon?'

'I doubt that. But I can direct the court to be lenient,' said the Archon. 'They might be sold as slaves rather than put in the Samian Shackles.'

'Thanks,' said Themis. 'I gave my word I'd try to get them out of jail and asked the Warden to stop the torture.'

Lysikles grunted assent. Themis nodded his thanks and left.

When he'd made his formal accusation and notified Lysikles' office, he returned to Socrates' gathering to apologize for the disturbance.

'No need to apologize,' said the philosopher. 'She's a woman, of course, one with a chaotic past. And she is, in my opinion, far from being the danger to the City that you may think she is. I hope she is found well.'

Themis didn't stay to disagree and excused himself politely. He made his way to the Dipylon Gate where Frog was waiting for him.

'Any luck?' asked Frog coming to meet him.

'The Scythians and other officers are out looking for Xenovia. But she's very good at disguising herself in spite of her injuries,' said Themis with a sigh. 'Perhaps I can ask Melissa to put the word out among her … acquaintances. But I don't hold out much hope. She'll probably leave Athens now for a while.'

They turned for home and heard Themis' name called. 'Themistokles!' It was Photios, waving a hand with three fingers.

'Time for a snack at the Hungry Bear?' he asked.

Frog went off to buy stores for the kitchen. Themis and Photios settled into a corner under the Bear's awning with a jug of sour cherry cordial and platters of quails' eggs, olives and barley buns. Photios examined Themis' face. 'What's going on?' he asked.

Themis grinned. 'When did you get back?'

'Two days ago. I've been seeing to things at home. My sister had a daughter while we were in the Peloponnese, and my father's been ill.'

'All right now?'

'Fine again. But you have a happy light in your eyes and a grim line to your jaw. You must be missing your brother.'

'Yes, I curse him and I miss him. His dying has meant I have responsibilities I never expected to have and no one to argue with about them. But there is also the prospect of being sure once and for all who's been trying to kidnap me and why.'

'I heard about the fire.'

'And that's the least of it,' said Themis. 'It looks as though the person who ordered that is in fact Xenovia. She seems to have been employing various people to capture me.'

'Capture you? Whatever for?'

'It's like the year of the Olympics all over again,' said Themis. 'Except that year she wanted my whole family dead. But now it seems she's going out of her way to take me alive. What could she possibly want to do that for? If I could catch her, I wouldn't hesitate to have her tried for the murder of Father, however long ago that was.'

'Maybe she wants to apologize?' said Photios, smiling and shrugging.

'Ha ha,' said Themis ironically.

Photios looked up from his platter and asked with his mouth full, 'And the happy light in your eyes?'

'Well, if all continues to go well, it looks like I'll be betrothed to Melissa as soon as I request Agorakritos' permission properly.'

Photios laughed and clapped Themis on the shoulder. 'That's wonderful! What about Anthoussa? What does she say?'

Themis frowned. 'You don't know? She died giving birth to a baby boy just over a month ago.'

'Oh, Themis,' said Photios, suddenly still. 'No. I didn't know. That must have hit you very hard.'

'Both of them within forty days of each other,' said Themis looking down at his hands. 'The gods are getting greedy.'

'That's three reasons for the grim line,' said Photios, tears shining on his cheeks and in his blond beard. 'My dear friend. What can I do?'

Themis shook his head to dislodge his own tears. 'Stop weeping like a woman,' he said with a sad smile. 'It's catching.'

'Then we'd better focus on women,' said Photios with a laugh, using a napkin to wipe away the tears. 'Tell me about Melissa.'

Themis rubbed his bearded chin. 'Ah, yes. Melissa ... She is of course, perfect in many ways. But entirely imperfect in others.'

'You're not making sense,' laughed Photios.

'I know,' said Themis. 'It doesn't make sense to me, either. Until about three months ago she was just a little girl to me. Intelligent and talented, but just a girl – who liked pretending to be a boy.'

'So what happened?'

'Didn't I tell you before we went to Argos, that she and I … er … discovered that … she'd grown up?'

'No. I don't think you did,' said Photios pointedly.

'Well, any contact was impossible then, of course. She was at Vravrona, preparing to become Nereus' wife, as agreed between him and her father.'

'Ah. So Eros was not just acting secretly, but also illicitly?'

'Mmmm.' Themis ate another egg. Would Photios know anything about not being able to go through with the sex act? Probably not. And anyway, he didn't like the idea of explaining why. 'The … attraction was secret only because it *was* illicit,' he went on. 'And it was also volatile. It's had me up and down like a boat in a storm.' He looked up at Photios. 'I thought it would never come to anything and I would spend years moping over an impossibility like I did with her mother when I was a boy. You can imagine how angry I was with myself.'

'What changed?'

'The day before yesterday, Agorakritos terminated his agreement with Nereus and, in Skopas' phrase, sent him off with a nettle up his arse.'

Photios almost spat out his mouthful. He managed to swallow and said, 'The gods be praised. But why?'

'It seems Agorakritos had his citizenship confirmed and so had the confidence to speak. He was angry at the way Nereus behaved over the death of Anthoussa.'

'Arrogance?'

'And no sense of what's appropriate in the circumstances.'

'So Melissa is now the mistress of that household?'

'Yes.'

'And mistress of herself, I imagine. Does she still dress as a boy?'

'When it suits her. I think she misses the freedom, and the street kids she used to spend time with.' Themis sighed. 'Of course, this means she's far from the "right" girl to marry and have children with – more of an Amazon than an Athenian wife . What my mother will say, I daren't think. I shall have to ask Melissa to stop all that and pretend I disapprove.'

'And you don't?'

'Only if it's dangerous … She knows so much about street crime. She has "friends" who seem to protect her, and their connections can be very useful. She heard about plans for an attack on me and sent a warning.'

'Well, she won't be able to disguise herself for long when you get her pregnant,' said Photios with a wink.

'True,' Themis sighed.

>>>

Chapter 53: invalid

(Breeds of Sheep 35 – Themis was thinking about controlling what I see of his life. I wish I could explain to him that it's not my choice what I see through his eyes. It's still like when I was ill immediately after the accident all those years ago – random and unstoppable.

It's possible he may have found a way already, though. There seems to be quite a gap. And certainly there's been a gap in *my* life. I hated leaving David there but Dad put me up till I could get back to Lancaster. It's taken so long to recover, what with the sacroiliac problem as well. I used some of the time to study and some to catch up with this and edit it a bit. I'd fallen behind with it at training camp.)

<<<

'You found her?' asked Themis.

The officer of the City Guard looked down at a tablet in his hand. 'And you are?'

'Themistokles, son of Kallistos, of Diomea.'

The officer nodded. Themis' name was on his list. 'She'd collapsed in the street and is now at the Asklepion precinct under the Akropolis.' The officer pointed with his chin. 'They reckon she's on her way to Hades. Man from her family came to take her home, but she's officially under arrest. He left.' The officer smiled wryly. 'He looked relieved. You related?'

'No,' Themis said emphatically. 'But I need to talk to her.'

'I'll apply for permission now. Usually takes five days.'

'But she could be dead by then!'

'Or not,' said the officer. He noticed the expression on Themis' face. 'I'll push it through earlier if I can,' he said. 'You'll probably need permission from the temple priests and her family, too.'

'Thanks,' said Themis, making a promise-of-money sign with his fingers. 'Do you know what happened to the two men being held as arsonists? They tried to burn down my house, but no one has asked me to give evidence.'

'They've been sentenced to a year in the silver mines. It was either that or have their left hands cut off.'

'They did it for poppy powder, you know,' said Themis.

'They won't get much of that in the mines,' said the officer.

Two days later, a burly young priest led Themis down the central corridor of the newly built, secure clinic for the 'god-possessed', behind the Asklepion under the southern cliffs of the Akropolis. There were two guards at the start of the corridor and one at each door that led off it.

The place smelled partly of sweet herbs and burned incense, partly of vomit. The sounds from behind the doors were disturbing.

When the guard opened the door of Xenovia's room, a woman came out with a basin covered by a stained cloth. The smell was new to Themis and extremely unpleasant.

Xenovia lay on a mattress stuffed with un-spun wool in a hammock slung from the ceiling beams. All the time Themis was there, her breath rasped in her throat and she moaned when she breathed out. Her face was turned away from him so that he saw only the good side. But he was sure she was aware of him. She was closing her eyes as he and the priest came in, pretending to be unconscious. Themis stopped himself striding over to strangle her.

'Xenovia,' he said. His voice bounced off the walls. She seemed to twitch. He relaxed his jaw a little. 'I am Themistokles, son of Kallistos. I won't hurt you, but I want to understand why you hate me and my family so much.' Xenovia's moaning didn't change, but her face twitched again. 'Is it still that my father spurned you and then tried to get you arrested for stealing from the temples? Or are you working with others who hate us, like Nereus or Kallias or someone else, perhaps?'

She didn't move.

Themis spoke to the priest without taking his eyes off her. 'What's wrong with her?'

'She has a fever, her joints have swollen up and are painful. If we touch a swelling she screams.'

'Not the plague? I was in Masalia all the time it was in Athens.'

'No, no,' said the priest. 'The swellings are full of water and pus. We lanced the ones at her knees and ankles by strapping her down. But she hasn't allowed us to relieve the elbows and shoulders.'

'Will she recover?'

'We think not, but we pray for her, and treat her as best we know how.'

Themis turned to look at the priest and sighed. 'It would be a great help,' he said, 'if she were well enough to answer some questions about what she has been trying to achieve and who has been helping her.'

'Obviously,' said the priest. 'And I have been given instructions by the Officers. But so far, I cannot report anything except that now and again she cries out as if in panic.'

'Does she call any names?'

'She seems to feel guilt. "Betrayal" is a word she often says, and "shunned". And yesterday I heard her say something about Athena and planning more punishments. Strange, as well as sacrilegious.' The priest took Themis' arm to guide him towards the door. 'Of course, we all know what she did in the past, the robbing of the statue, the murder of the chief of the temple guards – your father, I believe – after he discovered her calumny. Perhaps it is these things that prey on her mind, and her broken body is not strong enough to resist.'

'You are wise,' said Themis, 'but my family needs to know if there's a curse and if so whether it will continue, even if she dies. She has made many attempts to kidnap me. If it had been to murder me, as in the past, I would know why. But each time, her "operatives" failed to kill me.' He raised his voice so that Xenovia would hear if she were able. 'I need to know why this is. If you don't want me dead, what do you want? And the City Officers wish to hold a trial so that you can answer the accusations against you.' He bent towards the priest and continued more quietly, 'Do *you* know? Has she instructed others to continue to haunt me and my family? Has she been acting alone in this persecution? What is it she's trying to achieve?'

'I know nothing about that. As for her being alone, the only thing I can tell you is that she has a slave who has come twice now, asking whether her mistress has any orders for her.' The priest pushed open the door and they went out into the corridor. The healer woman had returned and went in. The guard closed and bolted the door again.

As they walked out into the courtyard, the priest went on. 'This slave is a clever woman. I overheard her asking Xenovia to indicate where the keys for a cabinet of "powders" were as they had customers clamouring to buy.'

'And did Xenovia answer?' Themis was wondering if she'd been involved with Lethe's Ladder as well as the poppy powder trade.

'She must have heard and understood because she beckoned the girl to lean down to her. The girl left, looking serious but satisfied. And I think I heard her give some coins to the guard.'

'So Xenovia is still involved with charms and drugs,' said Themis. He nodded slowly. 'That must be where her money comes from. I assume the temples do not pay her?'

'All I have been able to ascertain so far is that she spent many months at a shrine near Korinthos three summers ago. She underwent a rigorous series of cleansing rituals and was finally declared to have been forgiven by the gods. From then on she could take part as a junior priestess in various ceremonies, earning a small stipend, but she may not direct any religious activities.'

Themis sighed. 'So, it seems we're not going to learn anything from her after all, nor that the City is going to be able to prosecute her.'

'In the circumstances? No doubt in my mind,' said the young priest.

'Well, thank you, anyway,' said Themis. 'Please make sure I'm informed of any changes.'

As he walked out into the sunshine, he was thinking, '*If only she were a man – young and strong! I'd have dealt with her just like that.*'

And he clicked his fingers. But he was passing the bench where he and Anthoussa had talked before he left with the army to Argos. The memory and his sudden sadness held him imobile for a moment.

'But she wouldn't like me to grieve,' he told himself. He could almost hear her voice. 'Get on with marrying Melissa! There's nothing you can do about Xenovia. She's restrained and can't order any more attacks. So focus on your wedding!' No, it was his own voice, but Anthoussa would have said the same.

He remembered the night he had finally got over his passion for her. He and Photios and other youths were celebrating their release from army training, after two tough years.

They'd begun by visiting Aphrodite's shrine, followed by a night of fornication and wine at the school of the Perfect Cave, run by Magda, a much-respected madam from Egypt. Themis' knowledge of the geography and pleasures of a woman's body changed significantly that night. He smiled to himself, but noticed the nymph's hum.

'I'm going to deliberately think about something else,' he whispered to the air. 'Don't be angry. You wouldn't enjoy it.'

He was expected at Agorakritos' house that evening. The celebrations to mark the sculptor's new citizenship had been muted because of the mourning for Anthoussa. But both were over now and today Themis would request Agorakritos' permission to marry his daughter.

That's when Madam Magda's lessons would come in useful. There was even one he remembered that might help if he had the same problem again. He felt his excitement mounting. He danced a couple of steps as he ran, then a couple more. Frog, who was waiting for him outside the sanctuary of Dionysos, applauded.

'She must have said something good,' said Frog as they loped past the Odeion on the way back to the house.

'Xenovia? No. Nothing at all,' said Themis. 'She's supposedly in a coma, but I'm sure I saw her close her eyes as I went in.'

Frog shook his head and pursed his lips. Themis heard him whisper to himself, 'Where will it all lead?' Out loud Frog said, 'So you're skipping because you're happy? That won't last. Your sister and Hipparchos have arrived. She's preparing a bath and was mending the frayed edge of your best himation when she sent me to get you.' They slowed to a walk.

'Well,' said Themis. 'I just hope she knows the phrases I need to use.'

Frog nodded sagely. 'Hipparchos has them written down. Mrs Chloe wanted to know when are you expected?'

'At Agorakritos' house? I believe that the first sign of dusk is the appropriate time, but perhaps she knows better.'

Frog shrugged. 'When Hipparchos came to ask for her hand from your mother, it was at the time we lit the lamps.'

'Where was I?' asked Themis.

'Building a wall in Methana,' said Frog.

Themis sighed. 'Along with hundreds of others, including my infuriating but lovable brother.' A stab of pain went through his chest.

They walked on in silence.

>>>

It was taken for granted now that Theo was living in the Lancaster house which Suzanne, Natasha and Penny rented. He, Natasha, and Suzanne were eating in companionable silence in the kitchen.

Suzanne was thinking about David, who hadn't left the training camp. He'd been having problems in his home town where locals made life difficult for immigrants, especially black-skinned ones. He'd got a part-time job at the camp so that he could stay on there instead of going back home.

He'd read a bit of the Themis stuff and insisted that it proved she wasn't nuts. So, though the interview at Commonwealth Games England in August had been stressful, she'd had the confidence to press for her name to remain on the list, assuming she was fit enough in time. Though they said that only about fifty per cent of the athletes on that list would be selected in October.

When she'd started trying to train again, she'd found she couldn't keep her balance. And when she drove the car her father gave her for her birthday, driving hurt her lower back more than her leg. David had encouraged her to tell her new trainer at Lancaster.

And *she* had sent Suzanne to the physiotherapists, as it turned out that the flat sacroiliac joint in her pelvis had been displaced by her fall. After X-rays, a really cool physio guy had given her a hard push in the back and right away she stopped needing the walking stick. So now in late September, she could drive and walk without pain unless she got very tired. '*Should be able to train properly again soon,*' she thought for the thousandth time.

Meanwhile, Theo had turned out to be a whizz at making pasta dishes though he spent all the rest of his time on his computers. He had a laptop for his studies and a huge desktop for gaming.

'More?' he asked, standing up from the kitchen table. He went to the cooker and started piling more spaghetti onto his plate.

Suzanne pushed her empty plate away. 'Thanks but no, Theo,' she said. 'It was really good but I have to watch what I eat till I can exercise properly again.'

Natasha got up. 'I'm off to see "Mother!" with Penny. We're meeting at the cinema. We'll see you two later.' And she was gone.

'Wanna play? I've got a great new battle game …' Theo was collecting plates and trying to be a good housemate.

'You go ahead,' said Suzanne. 'Just keep the volume down. I'll clear up here and then do some work.'

As she settled down to write, she found herself talking to Themis.

'It worked, you know,' she said to him silently as she opened her laptop. 'I only get little bits of your life, anyway, and I certainly didn't get the Madam Magda evening. But please don't shut me out completely. Mind you, if you ever go into battle again, I do *not* want to come too … ' Then she gathered her thoughts and spoke under her breath.

'There's something I need to say to you about sex, Themis, something I learned about from my studies. Maybe Madam Magda mentioned it? You have feelings sometimes that worry me … There are times,' she was saying the words carefully in her head, 'when men feel the need to take a woman roughly, to prove their strength, or as a kind of revenge – perhaps for all the

352

times they want sex but can't have it? But that's not the woman's fault. It's how nature works – hormones! So don't blame the woman for that. Be kind.'

The files on the screen opened. She was enjoying writing up Themis' story more these days, with happier things happening to him. And the university doctor had prescribed some mild sleeping pills until she could train properly again, so the nightmares she'd had after watching Diodotos die were fewer.

Later she knocked on Natasha and Theo's door. 'Yeah?' he called.

'You want some coffee or something?' she asked.

'Come on in,' he said. She stood behind him, leaning on his chair. 'I'm the Spartans,' he said, pointing with his chin at the screen. 'Oooops. Not sure I meant to do that. My Archers can't get there in time. Oh well, whatever. I'll just use these guys instead.'

'Situation log updated,' said the desktop. 'Hostile cavalry detected.'

'The enemy's got twice as many men as you …' said Suz, watching the bird's eye view of an ancient battlefield. It looked very real, with trees in the distance throwing shadows and a dried up river meandering away to the left.

'Best thing, then, is to kill the enemy general,' said Theo. 'Oh, shit! All my archers got mown down. That was stupid.'

Suzanne began to feel surreal. There were unmutilated but dead bodies strewn across the screen and tiny jubilant enemy soldiers in the background. There was martial music, too, though Theo had that turned down low. 'How many are dead so far?' she asked, mesmerized, the ground-level battlefield at Mantinea flooding her mind.

Theo was excited. 'Hey, look at that! Their cavalry's chasing my right flank now. Dead? I dunno, maybe a thousand. But hey, there's lots more if I bring these in…' and he spirited a whole new army from behind a hill.

She pummelled his shoulders lightly. 'The Spartans didn't have archers till later! And you can't just do that!' she said. And suddenly she couldn't stop hitting him. 'You just don't get it, do you?' Tears splashed onto his hair. 'That was a real battle with real men, really dying. Bleeding, shitting, screaming, body bits everywhere. No big band music! No extra armies behind a hill!'

Theo stood up and caught her hands. 'Hey, hey. Calm down. What's wrong with you? It's just a game.'

'But it's not a game!' shouted Suzanne. 'It really happened. It still happens – in Syria and places – all the time. How can it be a *game*?' Her knees were buckling even as she was beating his shoulders with her fists.

Theo put his arms around her, picked her up and sat her down on top of Natasha's discarded clothes on the sofa. 'Stop now,' he said, grabbing her flailing hands. He was panicking. 'This isn't you! What've you taken?'

Suzanne pulled her hands free and covered her ears, turning her head from side to side, her eyes tight shut. She was panting and crying. 'All I can hear … is the horses screaming and … the men yelling and ... Oh, god, the stench... How can you imagine it's a game?'

Theo stood back, looking down on her more calmly. 'You've seen the real thing, then, have you?' he said with irony.

Suzanne opened her eyes and stared hard at his wryly smiling face. 'Yes,' she said. 'Yes, I've seen the real thing, and that's just – '

Theo pushed her further to the back of the sofa and sat down beside her. 'How?' he said, his eyes shining. 'How? Tell me about it.'

Suzanne closed her eyes and choked on a sob. 'You don't want to know.'

'But I do,' said Theo. 'What's the secret? Come on lass, you're so mysterious with all your writing and those great long runs you used to do. What do you take? Or is it what you watch? How come you know about real battles?'

'Because I see stuff in my mind,' Suzanne yelled. 'I see stuff I can't believe myself. But it's there and I have to live with it.' She grabbed a cushion and put it over her face. She couldn't stop sobbing. '*Stupid!*' she was thinking. '*Why did I say that? He'll tell everyone I'm mental But I don't care. Cos I am!*'

It sounded like Natasha had come back and was sending Theo away. The cushion was pulled down and a cool hand stroked the hair off her forehead.

'Sit up, hun,' said Natasha. 'Give me a cuddle.' Suzanne found herself hugging Natasha's thin shoulders as if her life depended on it.

'You just need someone to talk to about it all,' Natasha was saying. 'You need to let it out, have someone listen … have a proper chat. Not just texts like with that David, however happy they make you.'

Suzanne nodded against the bony shoulder. 'Mmmm,' she said. 'He makes things seem so easy.'

'Things are easy nowadays,' said Natasha. 'You just have to know who to ask for help and who your friends are.'

Chapter 54: betrothal

(Breeds of Sheep 35 continued – They're all being really kind now. Trying to carry on as if nothing happened. So I'm managing to do the same – so far.)

<<<

'I smell like a perfume shop,' complained Themis, twitching his dark green embroidered himation on his shoulder. He was impatient to get this over with. He'd kept away from seeing Melissa, partly out of respect and partly because he had never felt so unsure of himself. Frog had nailed it when he said, 'You're walking barefoot over hot rocks, aren't you?'

Chloe looked up at the shuttered window of Agorakritos' house as she said, 'Dear brother, you are suitably clean and presentable.' She stroked the head of the herm. 'Mama would be proud of you.'

Hipparchos snorted and laid a sympathetic hand on Themis' forearm.

'With all due respect, brother-in-law, be glad your mother is not here to interfere,' he said. 'The fewer relatives involved in this sort of nonsense the better. Otherwise it could go on for days…'

The door of the house opened and Skopas, carefully dressed and with his hair rolled and garlanded, beckoned them in.

'Welcome to our house,' he said. 'My father will join you in a few moments.' He turned and led the way into the courtyard.

Lamps and torches had been lit. Chairs had been set in a circle. A small table, which held an elaborate set of exquisite antique jugs, stood to one side. The remaining leaves on the vines whispered in the breeze and shone darkly gold in the torchlight, casting swaying shadows across the yard. Chloe made offerings for them all at the house shrine.

A small altar had been placed in the centre of the courtyard, festooned with golden ribbons and wreaths of red and yellow flowers and leaves. A flame flickered in its shallow basin.

Themis hadn't seen Agorakritos since their angry exchange on the day he had left for the farm. A few days ago, he'd sent a note suggesting that he would like to ask for Melissa's hand, if that were acceptable to her father. That was when he'd felt the rocks hottest.

The note had been answered by Agorakritos, suggesting that an official request be made in the usual manner. Gossip via the slaves confirmed that he would accept Themis' suit. Themis wasn't sure whether this would involve Melissa being there herself, and Chloe said that would depend on her father. No mention had been made of any dowry or bride price, but that would surely be discussed.

And so they waited with another two couples in the courtyard, not sure whether they should sit down. They nodded to the strangers and Themis went over to the table to look at the jugs. They were finely painted at the workshop of Polygnotos of Thasos. Like Agorakritos, Polygnotos had been a metic, a 'foreigner'. But before he died, he too had succeeded in gaining Athenian citizenship.

A door opened and Themis turned, his heart thumping. Agorakritos came out, followed by a man and a woman in patterned and bordered robes, with the traditional garlanded headdresses of the goddess Hera's priesthood. A harp player slipped out behind them and stood silently by the wall.

There was no sign of Melissa.

The priestess went over to the altar and threw some powder onto the flame. It flared yellow and white and she and her male companion began a rhythmic chant about the rules of marriage, intercourse and child rearing. The harp player accompanied her.

Themis looked sideways at Hipparchos, who nodded with an 'I'm afraid so' expression. Themis occupied his mind by examining the torchlight on the rich reds and blues of the robes.

After some time, and still chanting, the priestess took Themis' hand and drew him towards the altar. She took up one of the jugs and poured water over his hands into a bowl held by the priest. She took a towel from the table and dried his hands. Her words celebrated the removal of all traces of other women from Themis' mind. At least, he thought that was what they said. The language was traditional and opaque.

At this point the door opened again and Adrasteia came into the light, followed by a young veiled woman. She wore sheer cream linen robes that emphasized rather than hid her curves. Her veil was so fine that Themis could see her nose and eyes through it. From the dangerously mischievous twinkle in them, he knew Melissa was also on the edge of giggles. He looked away, keeping a straight face.

Melissa approached the other side of the altar. The priestess washed her hands, too, intoning words to do with cleansing any thoughts of other men from Melissa's mind, upon pain of dire retribution from Hera.

The priestess dried Melissa's hands, then beckoned Themis and Melissa to stand side by side. Their hands were placed with the fingers laced together and a piece of embroidered linen was wrapped around them and tied with an embroidered ribbon. Themis squeezed Melissa's hand and she squeezed back, but they didn't look at each other. He felt dizzy.

At a last chord of the harp, Agorakritos stepped forward and nodded to Adrasteia to show the priest and priestess out. They bowed politely to each member of both families and left with their harpist.

Agorakritos gestured to the chairs. 'Let's all sit down,' he said in a normal voice. Chloe held a chair for Hipparchos to sit, then went round the circle to sit with the women.

Agorakritos came over to Themis and Melissa and separated their hands. He indicated chairs for them to sit in the men's and women's parts of the circle. Everyone sighed and relaxed a little. Agorakritos went over to the door into the house. 'You can come out now,' he said through it, and a middle-aged woman in a brightly patterned gown came into the light.

'This is my sister, Hermione,' said Agorakritos. 'She has come especially from Paros to be my support at this time of family change.'

Hermione's voice rang out, filling the courtyard. 'Oh, come, little brother,' she cried. 'You know it's just that I'm curious to see this possible nephew. You don't need me to support you, though of course I would if you did.' She came forward and stood, looking up steadily into Themis' face. She said more quietly, 'I also came to tell you, young Themistokles, that you will have me and mine to deal with if you fall down on your duties as a fiancé or a husband in any way.'

Her eyes were black in the half-light, her skin finely lined, and her hairstyle old-fashioned. The line of her brows was dark and straight, and her head was held high and proud. Themis bowed and lowered his eyes in respect. This would be a tougher person to cross than her brother, or than Anthoussa, for whom she was surely the substitute.

Hermione stood back and clapped her hands. 'So, Agorakritos,' she said, 'Do we eat or bargain first?'

'Oh, sit down and behave,' said Agorakritos calmly. 'Themis and I will deal with the bargaining while you all have some refreshments. Introduce yourselves. Oh, and don't forget to pour a libation to Demeter as well as Hera and Zeus of the House.' He gestured to the shrine in the wall, then took Themis by the arm and led him into the andron.

'There's something you should see,' said Agorakritos, waving Themis to a couch. He reached up to the highest of the shelves near the door and turned to Themis. 'As you know,' he said, 'Melissa has often been asked to design embroideries and tapestries. She is involved in the work that began at the Chalkeia festival a few days ago, making next year's peplos for Athena at the Little Panathenaia.'

'Something of an honour,' said Themis, impressed.

Agorakritos went on, 'So you know that she has always done drawings and designs.'

'And has a talent for likenesses and pleasing patterns,' said Themis, wondering where this was going. Was it a ploy to decrease her dowry, as she was capable of making her own money?

Agorakritos handed him a small papyrus. 'Whom do you see here?'

Themis looked at the drawing. The style was Melissa's, not her father's. A naked man, drawn from the side and unaroused, was gently removing the last folds of a fine chiton from a woman. Themis immediately recognized himself. The boar's tooth was on a thong round his neck and the hair was cut short and loose as he preferred. But who was the woman in the drawing? She came up to his shoulder and wore her hair as Anthoussa had done some years ago. The likeness was clear. It was Anthoussa before she lost her figure to her many pregnancies. Themis looked up to see Agorakritos' eyes intent upon his face. He felt sick.

The older man said, 'Can you understand my belief that my wife and you were having an affair? I knew about your infatuation with her when you were a teenager, and I found this drawing the day before I … she … told you to stay away. It had somehow got in among others that Melissus had been making for a group of statues we were bidding for.'

'But how … ? Did you ask him … her about it?' Themis looked back at the drawing.

'No. I replaced it and didn't mention it to her. I believed it proof of Anthoussa's guilt. She denied it, as you know. But have you read the caption? I didn't notice it that day, only later.'

Themis saw that there were words among the stones at the feet of the figures. They said, 'If only … ' Themis' mouth fell open, his heartbeat shaking his whole body. He saw now that the woman was tautly muscled, her breasts small and high. Anthoussa had never been athletic.

He leapt up and turned to Agorakritos, who was saying, 'I finally understood the day before I sent Nereus out of our lives. I saw another drawing of Melissa's, of herself, dressed as if for her wedding. She looked the same as here. So this is not a drawing of my wife with you,' said Agorakritos quietly. 'It's a drawing by Melissa, of Melissa, as she wants to be when she's older. A drawing of a young girl's longing.'

Themis stood shaking his head, tears in his eyes. 'Can that really be true?' he said. 'She has always behaved to me as if she were a boy, even when she had to be a girl.' He looked down again at the couple in the drawing. 'But,' he went on slowly, 'it does explain something else. I got a message from Anthoussa not long after you denied me your home. It said she couldn't explain yet, but that I was not to blame. I must be patient and not lose my love for you.'

'Ah. So either Anthoussa also found the drawing, or Melissa showed it to her, and they agreed to hide Melissa's feelings, perhaps so as not to tempt the gods. So Anthoussa couldn't tell me – or you – and died keeping her secret … I can't imagine what that cost her during her last months. I was not kind.' Agorakritos sighed deeply and shakily. 'I leave it up to you whether you tell Melissa what you know. I did not tell her I intended to show you the drawing.'

Themis was both appalled and elated. Brushing tears from his beard, he said, 'Melissa will always be my friend first and my wife second.'

'Huh. Not so easy,' said the older man grimly. 'Women are not made the same as men. You'll see.'

Themis shrugged with open hands.

'Sit,' said Agorakritos. 'Now we have business.'

They sat down opposite each other. A single lamp burned on a stand behind Agorakritos, so his face was in shadow.

'So tell me, what are you expecting?' he asked.

Themis kept his face serious and focused in spite of his excitement. His future father-in-law was well known for his bargaining skills. He looked at Agorakritos steadily. 'I have been advised to request half of your stake in the quarries on Paros.'

Agorakritos frowned. 'I can't agree to that. I have two sons and three daughters now,' he said. 'It would be irresponsible of me to sign away so much. It would make the share for each of them unworkably small.'

Themis inclined his head. The light was full on his face. 'I don't want any part of the quarries in Paros for myself, but Melissa should inherit her share from you in her own name, as far as the law allows.'

'Of course,' said Agorakritos. 'I have Hermione on my back about that already. Melissa will get a fifth share unless her siblings challenge her. The Parean law doesn't allow for women to inherit, so she would almost certainly lose it if they did.' A slight smile changed the shadowy contours of his face. 'But for yourself? To keep Melissa and any children comfortable?'

'I am curious as to what you would offer,' said Themis, grateful for the formulaic structure of this part of the proceedings. 'I have learned there are facets of your businesses that I didn't know about.'

Agorakritos got up again. He walked a few steps and turned. Now the light was on his face. 'I have interests in Sicily and in Taras in Greater Greece, where there are customers both for my quarried stones and my finished works.' He sat down again. 'I am happy to promise you a share of the proceeds of the business in Taras.'

'And the Athens workshop?' asked Themis.

'That will go to my eldest son, Skopas. It is not particularly profitable except as a source of materials for the foreign trade.'

'Cede me a quarter of the profits,' said Themis, 'and I'll allow Melissa to continue to keep the accounts until her brother is old enough to do so. By then, I hope to have my own business for her to manage.'

Agorakritos took a quick breath.

Themis continued, 'And I understand there's a tract of land under olives north of Elis that was Anthoussa's. Would that be something you could put into Melissa's name now?'

'My sons might object.'

'But would their eldest sister?' said Themis. 'I think not.'

Agorakritos stood up. Themis did, too.

'So,' said the older man, 'a quarter of the profits of the sculpture yard, including its foreign incomes, as accounted for by Melissa until Skopas is twenty five years old, and the Elis olive groves in her name.' His tone indicated the bargaining was over.

'For myself,' said Themis, 'I would ask a new cart and two horses that I may keep after they bring my bride and her effects to my house.'

'Ah,' said Agorakritos, a little taken aback. 'That was to be my own present to Melissa.'

Themis nodded. 'Perhaps the olive groves would stand in its stead?'

Agorakritos looked at Themis thoughtfully. 'I would prefer to cede some of the olive trees to you personally, and have Melissa own her own cart and horses.' He went to the door, then turned. 'She has a history of … disappearing, and I don't want to have to go through the courts against you when you accuse her of stealing your vehicle.'

Themis could see Agorakritos' face clearly now and he was smiling. He seemed again the handsome, energetic Agorakritos of Themis' memories. Themis smiled in return. 'Agreed,' he said. 'Say ten trees?'

Agorakritos inclined his head in acceptance. He stood in the traditional position, hands apart and made the gesture to ward off any jealous gods. 'Are you sure that is all you require, Themistokles? Perhaps you do not drive a hard enough bargain. I may become a demanding father-in-law.'

Themis laughed. He replied in the accepted way so that the Fates were not tempted to destroy his happiness. 'Perhaps I won't prove to be the perfect son-in-law,' he said, offering his hand. Agorakritos took it in his.

'Come!' he said loudly, for others to hear.. 'Let's eat and drink to our long friendship that is now to be kinship.' And he whispered, 'Good luck to you with Melissa as a wife and my sister Hermione as an aunt!'

Chapter 55: advice

There was no moment during the following hour when Themis could even get close to Melissa, let alone talk privately to her. The company enjoyed making this impossible, as tradition demanded. But as Themis' family left the house, music and light following them into the street, Frog stepped up to Themis and pressed a scrap of papyrus into his hand.

Themis stopped and read it in the light of Frog's torch while Chloe and Hipparchos walked on.

'Don't know how or when, but I'll get to see you unofficially in the next day or two. Please don't leave the city till I do.' An exquisitely drawn young sapling leaning over a rock in the wind filled a third of the papyrus.

Themis strode on smiling and put it carefully into his chiton pocket.

As he walked, he planned where to entertain Melissa when she came to see him 'unofficially'. The women's rooms, or his own bedroom? The public deflowering would come later, probably at her house, so that everyone knew the engagement was truly underway. But she obviously wanted what he wanted, which was a chance for some private practice.

He had fallen behind a little when the sack fell over his head. It smelled of crushed mulberry leaves. Voices surrounded him, some calling his name, some making animal sounds, a loud one singing a bawdy song. He recognized Photios' voice and a couple of others from the gym, but there must have been ten or more. A drum beat and at least two flutes played in competition with each other.

'You're deafening me!' Themis roared from inside the sack. 'And disturbing the neighbours.'

'We *are* the neighbours,' someone shouted, as they pushed and pulled him along the street. He was held against a herm for a few moments while a door opened, then the whole party moved into the courtyard of a house, still shouting and singing praises of Themis' prowess in the past and the string of sons to come.

A great knocking roused Themis from a deep sleep. He groaned as he forced an eye to open. It was broad daylight. He was on his own bed. Frog was standing over him.

'Go away,' he said.

'Messenger from Lysikles, Archon of the City Watch,' said Frog.

'Tell him to come back later.' Themis turned over. He noticed he was bandaged tightly between his legs and around his bottom. He sat up. 'What did they do to me?' he asked in surprise.

'Nothing permanent,' said Frog with a frown and a shrug. 'I think you may find some interesting designs drawn on you, though.'

Themis sighed. 'Get me some water, please, Frog. I can't go out into the courtyard like this.'

Frog's serious expression cracked into a grin. 'I've put the messenger into the kitchen with Mika. You can clean up at the well.'

The messenger led Themis to the executive building in the Agora, the round Tholos. There, Lysikles' scribe met him and led him through to Council Office Gamma where he had first met Apollodorus in the spring.

'We have some developments,' said Lysikles. 'We've heard from Hyllos, who is trying to buy his return to the City by being "cooperative". He says he was advised to offer you the wall-painting by a man with a damaged face and a limp. This seems to be confirmed by the priestess Xenovia's ramblings. I'm hoping she'll say something else to lead us to the top man.'

Themis felt his jaw harden. 'How? What did she say?'

Lysikles shrugged. 'Something like "Hyllos agreed to the wall for Themistokles. Couldn't fail" and something about worth every effort.'

'Is there any evidence that it was she who was paying?'

'We've searched her shop and where she was living. Nothing to show she's particularly wealthy, but who knows? She obviously deals in addictive substances, one of which is what Ilarion and Kallias take – we asked them. They get it from her place now that Zotikos has stopped keeping it. Her shop has hundreds of customers. Addicts will pay, even if it kills them. She may be owed thousands.'

'Can I speak to her?' Themis' tight throat made his voice sound strange.

'The doctors say she is not conscious of her surroundings. They have to tie her down sometimes because she thrashes around so much. She attacks herself and her carers with equal violence. They say this is a common phase before death, the purging of a burdened mind.'

'Can she be convicted?'

'Not unless the medical circumstances change. Proofs are beginning to fall into place and a small number of men who may have been connected with her have been arrested. But she herself is too ill to stand trial.'

'What about Nereus?' asked Themis. 'Have you found any proof of his involvement? My arsonists mentioned a man fitting his description.'

'And that of about a third of the citizens of Athens,' said Lysikles dryly. 'So far we can prove nothing against Nereus. We can't even prove a link between him and Xenovia.'

Themis paced the room. Would he ever know for sure what Xenovia's problem with him and his family had been? Was it really still revenge? Or was she a malignant fury released by a god to fulfil some kind of curse? He could almost hear his Uncle Panainos laughing at him for that thought. The gods were personifications of human traits for Panainos – never tangible beings. Would his intangible nymph have an opinion?

He looked up at Lysikles.

'Thank you for the information,' he said. 'Is there anything else?'

'I felt I should warn you that our recorded investigations so far cannot disprove the possibility that you were in fact acting with treasonable intent, and that there are those in the Council that want to bring you to trial.'

'What?!' Themis spun round. 'Even after I risked my life again and again to find out who was behind the attempts on the harbour?' He looked pointedly at Lysikles. 'Who is it that doubts me?'

'General Nereus has a friend or two,' said Lysikles. 'He is known to have been humiliated by your future father-in-law however, so no one takes him very seriously. But you need to know that he is plotting, and he has a following.'

Themis shook his head. 'That's nothing new,' he said. 'I believe Nereus has been plotting against me for some time. I tried to get him to talk to me in the Agora a few days ago, but he's not a man to forgive humiliation, even if it's unintentional. He threatened me, then walked off with his men.'

The Archon stood up and walked towards the door. 'We are writing down what sense we can when Xenovia speaks. You may wish to read through the results?'

Themis nodded. 'That would be helpful,' he said.

'And we are still on the lookout for that evasive chest from under the water in the bay,' added the Archon. 'Meanwhile, I offer you my congratulations on your engagement, though I believe that is the main reason Nereus will continue to harass you.' He held his hands open towards Themis, who bowed and accepted the formal embrace.

'Thank you, Archon Lysikles,' he said. 'Your predecessor was a great help concerning my choice of wife.'

'So I gather,' said the Archon with a dry smile. 'May you both live to make each other happy and become parents many times.'

Androklos the Healer was walking down the steps as Themis approached the Asklepion where Xenovia was held.

'Themistokles!' he called. 'I hear congratulations are in order!'

Themis nodded ruefully. 'No escaping it now,' he said.

They both laughed.

'I was coming to find you,' said Themis. 'Have you got a few moments?'

'Feed me and I'll give you all evening,' said Androklos. 'I've been here since before dawn and I'm ravenous.'

They walked briskly to the nearest tavern.

'So why were you looking for me?' asked Androklos with his mouth full of bream baked in pastry with cheese.

'The official coitus is worrying me,' said Themis. 'Melissa and I reached the moment before the engagement, but I couldn't go through with it, even then. Imagining how everyone will be listening, ready to cheer us on is not helping. Is there something I can use to make sure I can perform?'

'Hmmm,' mused Androklos, chewing. 'Was the problem in your mind or your … er … body?'

'Mind, I suppose,' said Themis. 'Melissa's eyes reminded of someone … dangerous.'

Androklos looked cynical. 'Are you sure that won't happen every time? She's definitely the wrong girl to try and and have a family with if it does.'

'Oh, she's the right girl,' said Themis. 'I can't imagine coitus with anyone else now. But there's another thing … I've never taken a virgin before.'

'Ah. Eros has struck.' Androklos smiled wryly. 'Well, I'll get you something to use in an emergency. But I suggest you try again naturally before dealing with the pressure of family surveillance.'

'And there's something else,' said Themis.

'Mmmm?'

'There's a woman in the new guarded unit behind your hospital who is supposed to be on the first steps to Hades.'

'The priestess who killed your father,' said Androklos. 'I know about her. Interesting case. I wondered if this was about her.'

'Is she really as ill as they say?'

'They say that her body is holding its own in spite of those ghastly old injuries. But she's refusing food, and drink too, when she's conscious. She'll be gone in a week unless she overcomes her mind daemons.'

'Meanwhile, she's delirious and I can't talk to her.'

'No one can. I haven't seen her, but I've heard her at night … shrieks and sobs. And they say Prometheus was tormented!' Androklos pushed his bowl away and wiped his fingers. 'Move on, Themis. She's dead and you're alive. Look forward. Prepare for your wedding! I'll get you that ointment,' he said with a smile. 'Is it a case of no pregnancy, no wedding?'

'Not for me, but there are pressures in the family.'

Androkles laughed. 'So … get to work!' he said, picking up his cup.

Chapter 56: warm rain

Themis glanced down from the trireme as he collected his satchel from his bench. The Row Master had been in a foul mood today and all the rowers had suffered. They rolled their eyes at each other as they prepared to leave the ship. Themis was glad it had been hard. For a few hours he'd been able to stop planning how he'd have sex with Melissa. It was being arranged to happen, effectively in public, at her house by her family. It was, of course, his affianced duty and he was looking forward to it, but also dreading it.

Unusually, Frog was waiting for him on the black mule and leading Parilios. Their shadows came and went as clouds scudded southwards.

'Why have you come to meet me?' Themis asked, running up to him. 'Anything wrong?'

'Just thought you'd be tired,' said Frog. 'You going to get washed?'

Themis made a dash for the water spouts before the other sweating rowers. When he'd sluiced himself from head to foot, Frog handed him a towel and a clean chiton.

'What's this for?' he asked. 'Come on, tell me. I'm supposed to be working with Master Zephus today.'

Frog shrugged. 'And you'll need to be clean,' he said. 'Can't sit among all those other vase artists and stink everyone out.'

'What are you up to?' Themis asked, but Frog had turned and started up a narrow back street. It was one that led to a mountain path to the

City and they often used when hunting or in a hurry. It climbed high onto the flank of Mount Ymittos and attracted very little traffic.

When Frog's mount stumbled, they were above the villages and temples on the lower slopes of the mountain, cantering round the base of a great outcrop of rock called the Lion's Lookout. Frog dismounted. Themis reined in Parilios a stade or so further on.

'You alright?' he called.

'You go on,' Frog called back, holding his mule's hind hoof gingerly. 'I'll catch up – or see you later at the house.'

Themis raised a hand and cantered on. The track looped down into a gulley, thickly wooded with oaks and pine trees. It had rained the previous night, so a narrow stream ran across the road at its lowest point. Parilios slowed at the sweet smell of the water. Themis allowed him to stop and drink. It was a charming, lonely spot. Would he be propositioned by the local water nymph? He was smiling at his superstition when he heard another horse carefully approaching from the opposite direction.

Its rider was dressed for the cooler weather in a long himation and hood. Horse and rider crossed the stream and turned beside Themis without speaking. The two horses drank side by side. Themis' smile widened to a grin. The other rider laid a hand on his arm and threw back her hood.

Melissa was laughing. Themis was too, at her loveliness, and at Frog's machinations. She pushed her loose hair back and kicked her hired horse into a canter up the streambed.

Branches made an arch overhead as they raced, splashing water and scattering stones. Themis pushed Parilios to catch Melissa. He'd just managed to get a hand onto her reins when they burst into a wide glade. The stream made a pool under a low waterfall. The horses skittered to a halt and Melissa leapt off hers onto the short grass.

She began to run towards the ring of trees. Themis was off his mount and after her before she had taken four steps. He grasped her round the waist from behind and pulled her to him. She wriggled to be free.

'Oh, no you don't,' he breathed into her ear as he pulled her back towards their horses.

'Let me go!' she giggled. 'I want to show you something.'

Themis held her tight with one arm and pulled his saddle and blanket off Parilios with the other.

In one smooth movement, he tripped her so that she fell on the blanket, lay down beside her and pinned her down with an arm across her waist.

'What will you show me?' he asked in her ear.

She turned over towards him and slid her arm round his neck. She grabbed his hair and pulled his face towards her. 'Nothing,' she whispered, her lips against his.

'You know this will hurt?' he said.

'But later it will be wonderful.'

'Is that what they told you?' He was arranging their clothes for access.

'Yes. But we practised, too.'

'Right.' The implications of that could wait. He was more than ready. He spat on his hand and smeared her with the saliva. She groaned.

He was rough and she cried out as he broke in. She seemed surprised. When he fell away from her, she was looking confused.

As he caught his breath, lying flat on his back, she stood up. She pulled a cloth from a pocket, then winced as she wiped her crotch. The rag came away bloodstained. He watched with interest, his first virgin.

She looked down at him, her expression bewildered, disappointed. But all she said was, 'I remembered to keep my eyes shut.'

He laughed and sat up. 'So you did. Thank you.'

'But is that all? It was … very quick.'

'That's how to please the gods,' he said.

'Huh!' she said, still bewildered but angry now, too. 'I dare say. The male ones. But I thought I'd feel *something* nice at least, like that day in the rain.'

Themis stood up. 'We can try it again, if you like,' he said, his whole body focusing on a repeat.

'Not now,' she said, shaking her head and looking at him through tears. 'Not if it's like that.' She turned away.

Themis caught her wrist. 'It won't be. I promise. This time it'll be for you, not for me – nor for the gods,' he said quietly. She was taut, ready to run. He took her hand gently, turned it over and stroked her calloused, damp palm. 'Nor to make a child for Diodotos.' He remembered the nymph, and tilted Melissa's face so he could look her straight in the eyes. 'Nor as revenge for all the longing and agony you've put me through. This time, it's for you.' He paused. 'Except … '

Melissa looked alarmed. 'Except what?' she asked, pulling back.

'Except, you'll have to show me how to do what *you* like. Teach me. Tell me what feels good so I know how to please you.' He smiled mischievously. 'Perhaps the practice you mentioned will be a help.'

Melissa grinned. 'Really? You mean you don't know?'

'Madam Magda always said every woman's different, like every kithara. You have to play each one accordingly.'

'Well, I'm certainly not a kithara! And at Vravrona they told us we'd usually have to look after ourselves for the pleasant bit – that most men don't have the patience.' She threw her arms round his neck. 'But as you say you have, you can start here,' she whispered, guiding his hand.

Some time later the breeze began to rise. They slept on and didn't feel the first warm drops of rain. They didn't hear the birds' alarm calls or the slow thud of hooves coming up the little valley until they were quite close. Themis opened his eyes, leapt up, and threw his half of the blanket over Melissa. She was smiling in her sleep. He reached for his knife.

The hooves stopped before the horse broke cover. A voice called quietly, 'You'll catch a chill.'

Themis laughed and called out, 'Go away, Frog. Just for a bit.'

And he went on laughing when Melissa's eyes opened in a wide, green stare. She sat up quickly. 'What?' she cried with a half smile.

Themis spread his hands to the rain, then leant down to help her up. 'We're getting wet – on the outside now,' he said, his grin making his cheeks ache. 'The gods have sent us rain to wash us clean – and give us their blessing.'

Melissa stood up and re-organised her clothes. She was also grinning. 'Rubbish,' she said. 'They're jealous because we have more pleasure than they do. Was that Frog?'

Themis nodded, watching her movements, speechless with wonder. Why had he worried that he wouldn't be able to couple with this girl? She was … 'You are just so perfect,' he said.

Dressed now, she came over to him. She put her arms up around his neck and held him as tight as she could. He lifted her off her feet and swung her round. They were laughing so much they couldn't talk. The rain trickled down their hair and began to come through their clothes. Themis could feel the heat of her body against his chest.

Frog appeared on foot in a felted wool cloak against the rain. He collected up the saddle and blanket and led the two horses downstream into the trees. 'There's a dry cave lower down,' he called. 'I'll be there.'

Xenovia was still alive when Themis called again at the guarded part of the hospital. He could hear her groans, but he was not allowed to enter. An official from the jail sat on a stool by the door.

'She could be gone any time, they say,' he said to Themis.

'So there's no chance of speaking to her?'

'She's not making sense even when she's awake enough to talk,' said the man. 'Nothing's changed.'

Themis thanked him and left, those hollow groans following him as he walked away. *I should be grateful that the gods are punishing her,* he thought. *And I suppose I am, but if we can't ask her, how can we find out what's behind all these attacks on the harbours – and me? Was she working alone, or with Nereus, or someone else? He hasn't answered my invitation to talk, of course. Was it she who employed Menestratus and those others to murder Damianos?* His thoughts were coming with the rhythm of his steps. *And what in Hades was in the chest in the bay? Where is it now? Does she make the Ladder drug or just sell it? Is that how she funded her treachery? Or is she backed by the Spartans, or even the Persians? When she's gone, will it all stop, or is she just one spoke of the wheel?*

He saw Androklos hurrying along the crowded road ahead of him and ran faster to catch him up, relieved at the interruption to his thoughts.

'Two things, Androklos, if you have a moment,' he said as he drew level.

Androklos put his arm round Themis' waist as they strode along. ' I was going to drop by your house and see how well you'd done your duty,' he said, giving Themis a squeeze.

'It went fine,' said Themis. 'Wondered if you'd like the ointment back.'

Androklos looked sideways at Themis with a smile. 'Yes, I'd like it back. And the second thing?'

'I was wondering whether the hospital would object if I put a guard by Xenovia's door to see who comes and goes.'

'Hmmm. It might. We have official guards in that block already.'

'If she dies without explaining what's going on, I need to know who's been taking her orders or helping her out. It could save my own life or others in my family just to know what we might be up against.'

'Oh, I understand that,' said Androklos, stopping at a busy crossroads. 'But you're not the only one – we get requests from the City Security people almost every day and it's just not possible to allow everyone access. Look, I turn here. I'll talk to the chief physician.' He disappeared into the milling crowd in the Street of Tripods with a cheery wave.

>>>

Suzanne closed her laptop with a sigh. She felt a bit shocked, disillusioned. 'How I kept quiet, I don't know,' she whispered to herself. 'Weird and slightly upsetting, feeling it from the man's side. Interesting in a way, though.' She had to smile. '*And once he was sure of himself, he was kind*,' she thought. '*I even had the feeling he knew I was there and was kind of showing off, till he decided to fade me out.*' ' Total exhibitionist!' she said out loud.

Natasha knocked, then poked her head round the door. 'You feeling better today? Who's an exhibitionist?'

'No one you know,' said Suzanne.

'Certainly not you. Famous for secrets, you. Everything bottled up.'

Suzanne sighed. 'Well, I do have one question on my mind I can unbottle,' she said with a wry smile. 'What am I going to do now?'

Natasha shrugged and shook her head. Suzanne went on before she could speak, 'I should be out there training. But with Keir's "interventions" and breaking my leg, I can't believe I have any real chance of getting into the squad for Brisbane. I've always found training easy, and now it's so hard. I have to force myself to start and my results are – well, not exactly encouraging.'

'Hmm. I can't help with that,' said Natasha. 'But I do think you should talk to a professional about your … psychological wellbeing, so to speak. You have quite noisy nightmares, you know. That won't be helping you get physically stronger – and it gives me the creeps, hearing you.'

Suzanne frowned. 'I didn't know I was noisy. You never said.'

'Now I know there's a definite issue,' said Natasha, 'it's worth mentioning. I er, I heard of someone you could talk to. Not a shrink! Promise. A brain man – interested in your – what do you call them? Visions?' Natasha was folding up Suzanne's dirty tracksuit so as not to look her in the eye.

'Who?' Suzanne thought she'd probably met whoever it was seven years ago when her dad was determined to 'cure' her. 'Where?'

'He's called Mr Sears,' said Natasha. 'He's a neurosurgeon in Durham.'

'Bernie's in Durham … But it's miles away.'

'You could drive there. It'll take about two hours and cost ten pounds each way for petrol.' Natasha looked Suzanne in the face. 'We can go together. Soon. I have details. Or you can ask Bernie to go with you, if you'd rather.'

'He'll cost a lot,' said Suzanne, remembering the bills her father had paid.

'First consultation's free,' said Natasha, her head on one side.

<<<

Chapter 57: vigil

Themis found Photios sitting on a folding stool by the cypress tree outside the window of Xenovia's room. They'd made an agreement to watch there rather than inside by the door. Photios had two tablets, one he was writing on and another closed on the ground.

'My turn?' said Themis quietly, sitting down cross-legged on the paving. 'Any news?'

'She's quiet,' said Photios. 'Listen!'

The only sound from the open window above was gentle snoring.

'What's going on?' whispered Themis.

'Your sculptor friend Polykleitos is in there, drawing the good side of her face. They must have found something to give her that makes her sleep more calmly.'

Themis stood and stretched up on his toes to look into the room. Polykleitos had his back to the window. The hammock had been re-slung so that the light fell clearly on Xenovia's sleeping face. The nursing woman sat dozing on a stool by the door. Themis sat down again. 'How did he find her?' he asked.

Photios shook his head. 'No idea,' he said, putting his work into his satchel. 'That's something you can do to pass the time – ask him.'

Themis nodded. Then he said, 'Thank you, Photios, for helping with this. It should only be for a few days.'

'So you said,' said Photios, standing up. 'Well, as far as I could tell, she had no other visitors except the doctors and their assistants today so far.' He handed the tablet from the ground to Themis. 'Here's the list.'

'Thanks again,' said Themis, getting up. 'See you in the morning?'

Photios nodded and walked off, humming to himself.

Themis folded the stool and hid it in a rosemary bush.

The corridor inside the security block was busy. The guard outside Xenovia's room shook his head. 'Can't go in just now,' he said.

'It's you I wanted to talk to,' said Themis. A strong smell of faeces and vomit suddenly surrounded them as the door of the next room opened and an assistant came out with a bucket. Themis covered his nose, but the smell had taken him back to the battlefield and he gagged.

The guard nodded. 'You'll be wanting to know why we let Master Polykleitos in.'

Themis spoke behind his hand. 'I know why he's here. I just

"

wondered whether anyone brought him.'

'The usual slave girl,' said the guard.

'Is she here now?'

'Nope. But I dare say she'll be back tomorrow, same sort of time.'

'Good. Will the priestess last that long?'

'Probably.'

Themis nodded his thanks and went back to his vigil under the window. The sharp smell of the rosemary as he collected his stool cleared the stench of the corridor from his head. He sat under the window and read the list of visitors that Photios had made. They were all staff except for Polykleitos. Photios had obviously missed seeing the slave girl, as she wasn't mentioned.

Themis had brought papyrus and charcoal to while away the time. He thought of Polykleitos inside drawing the lovely features of Xenovia's one-sided face. He would then have to make a mirror image of them for the other side of the face of his Hera.

'I could have given him that old drawing of mine,' Themis thought. *'I suppose I still could.'* He shuddered. Memories of his feelings for Xenovia when he was a boy always made him ashamed. He began work on a scene by a stream where a nymph who looked very like Melissa was removing the armour of a soldier ...

There was movement in the room, so he stood up to see what was happening. Xenovia was awake. The nurse was helping her to drink some water. Polykleitos was standing near the door.

Xenovia said in her cracked voice, 'Enough. Go!' and the nurse withdrew. 'Not you, Master Sculptor,' said Xenovia to Polykleitos. 'The drug is still working. I want to see what you've been drawing.'

Polykleitos walked to beside the hammock. Xenovia looked at the sketches in his hand. 'And you will use this for your Hera?' she asked.

'Yes.'

She moved her head a little as though nodding. 'That will be good. Ironic, but good,' she said. The crackle of her laughter came as a shock to both Themis and Polykleitos. He jumped back from the hammock and glanced at Themis through the aperture of the window.

'Thank you, Sacred Lady,' he said. 'You have been my inspiration.'

'Well, half of me has,' she said. Themis could only see the undamaged side of her as she lay under the window, facing the room.

Polykleitos shook his head. 'You have helped me immeasurably,' he said.

Themis saw her chest rise as she took a deep breath. 'I've done all I can do,' she rasped, 'but it is not enough, it will never be enough. Athena cannot allow him to prosper in her city. Nor will she allow me to live much longer. He is safe for now, yes, but you will see – he must leave or die.' Her head fell sideways in the hammock though her breathing did not stop, grating in her throat like a file on new stone.

Polykleitos looked up at Themis. 'Who's she talking about?' he asked.

Themis shrugged and whispered across her, 'I don't know. They say her mind wanders. How did you know she was here?'

'I asked at her shop. I'm on a short list of people the slave woman was allowed to tell, it seems.'

When Polykleitos left, Themis went back to his drawing. Xenovia slept.

Later, the moon rose. Although it was almost full, he couldn't see well enough to go on drawing. He sat with his back against the wall. It was going to be a long night …

The nymph was saying, ' … things people don't talk about much. I learned a lot, so thank you for not cutting me out. And Xenovia's right about leaving the city. It would be better if you did quite soon. Bad things are coming for the men of Athens.' She reached forward and stroked his beard! He felt his head touch the wall behind him as he lifted his chin and opened his eyes. He wanted to see her, to ask her what and who she was and how she knew the future.

'There you are!' whispered Melissa, her hand still against his cheek. 'You didn't say you'd be out here. I was looking for you inside.' She bent down and held her face against his.

He stood up, lifting her with him. He hugged her tight and kissed her forehead, then allowed her feet to touch the ground. He held her away from him. She was dressed as a boy but her hood was off and her hair was loose down her back. Themis longed to pick it up in both hands and rub his face in it.

But he said sternly, 'Obviously you shouldn't be here.' Then he smiled. 'But I'm very glad you are.'

Melissa laughed silently and held him tight, her cheek against his chest. After a few seconds she looked up at him. 'Our hearts are beating so fast and hard, I can't tell which is which,' she whispered.

Themis looked around the garden in the moonlight. There was a copse of holm oaks near the end wall. He unwound her arms from his waist and nodded in its direction. She looked up at him and her face beamed. She laid a finger on her lips, then walked towards the copse.

Themis looked briefly into the window. Xenovia was groaning quietly

in her sleep, and the nursing woman was dozing on her stool. He
gathered up his satchel and his own stool and followed Melissa.

In the morning, once Photios had taken over and Themis had been
to the gym, he worked at home on the reliefs for the family memorial.
But trying to remember the exact shape of Myrto's nostrils and
Diodotos' chin brought back his grief. So he stopped earlier than
planned and ran to the hospital. Perhaps Melissa would manage to join
him again tonight.

He found Photios under the window as before. He nodded silently to
him, then stepped up to look in. Things were quiet again. But the healer
woman was standing whispering with a slave girl.

Themis turned back to Photios. 'Did you see this girl yesterday?' he
whispered.

Photios looked in at the window. He turned back to Themis shaking
his head, but with an excited expression. 'No,' he said. 'No, I didn't.
But I know her!' He took Themis' arm and they stepped away from the
window.

'How do you know her?' asked Themis.

'You know my father wasn't well lately?'

Themis nodded.

'Well, one of his friends suggested I go to a specific herbalist and get
a particular preparation that would help Father. And it was this girl –
woman, really - who served me.'

'I guess she's the one Polykleitos spoke to,' said Themis. 'She might
be able to explain a few things.' He set off towards the main door, then
turned. 'If you see me with her, join us. I may need you as a witness.'
He ran into the building and along the corridor to the now familiar
door.

It was a different guard from yesterday. 'Can't let you in,' he said.

Themis nodded. 'I know. I'm just waiting for the woman to leave.'

The guard grunted and stood back to attention.

A few minutes later, the door opened and the slave came out. She
walked fast towards the main door at the end of the corridor. Themis
strode behind her, ready to grab a wrist if she began to run, but she
didn't seem to notice him.

Out in the forecourt, he overtook her and stood in front of her. She
stopped and stared up at him against the sun. 'Can you tell me how the
priestess is today?' he asked.

She said, 'Who are you?' But then she seemed to recognize him and her eyes opened wider. 'Why do you want to know?'

Themis stepped to the side so that she could see his face. 'I know she is very ill,' he said, 'but she has been paying people to harass me and my family. I would like to talk to her, to find out why.'

'Well, I don't know anything about that,' said the slave. In this bright light, Themis could see that she was no longer young, perhaps older than he was, although she moved with speed and energy.

'Please tell me your name,' he said.

She made an 'I'm not that stupid' face and turned to leave. He fell into step beside her and Photios appeared by her other side. 'Don't run away,' said Themis. 'We won't hurt you. I just need to ask you one more thing.'

Photios said, 'They call you Popi, don't they? And you're a herbalist at the pharmacy owned by the priestess Xenovia.'

'That's right. I know you,' said Popi to Photios. 'You bought some Cretan dittany from us for your father's bladder complaint some days ago. How is he?' Her light brown eyes were paler than her skin. When she smiled she was attractive.

Photios nodded. 'He's much better. Thanks.'

'So, what do you want to ask?' she said turning to Themis. 'I know nothing about my mistress' other activities apart from the shop.'

'I believe you,' he said, 'But it's very important to me to know who else she is working with.'

Popi stopped for a moment and batted away a fly. 'Go on,' she said.

'Well, many times this year, Xenovia has sent men to either kidnap me or perhaps even kill me. Obviously I've escaped so far. I was wondering if she's arranged for this to continue once she's dead.'

'Are you sure?' Popi looked genuinely shocked. 'This doesn't sound like my mistress, at all.'

'And yet, by her own admission, she has been behind these attacks and possibly much more serious crimes.'

'Well, I can't tell you what I don't know,' said Popi, shrugging in confusion. 'But I'll take better notice of anyone using the shop as a meeting place, or anything else suspicious and let you know.' She looked up at them each in turn. 'Now I really must go. I'm working on a recipe that may help my mistress and I have to measure the time ...'

'Then thank you,' said Photios. 'I'll come by the shop one day soon.'

Popi smiled sadly and hurried away.

'Come on,' said Themis, turning back. 'It's my turn to watch. Show me your list for today.'

Themis was on watch after a long chilly night. Xenovia's condition was the same and his lack of sleep was taking its toll during his working days. He was thinking seriously of giving up the vigil, when he heard an officer of the City Guard talking to the healer woman in the sick room. Themis caught up to him as the guard was leaving the building.

'Good evening, Officer,' he said. 'My name is Themistokles, son of Kallistos. Clearly, the woman Xenovia is still alive. Can you tell me, will the City continue with its prosecution of her?'

'The Council can only wait until she either dies or recovers enough to stand trial,' said the man. 'What is it to you?'

'I am one of the accusers,' said Themis.

'Ah yes. Themistokles. The swimmer.' The officer stopped and turned to him. 'Lysikles did mention that if I saw you I was to tell you that "we can now link her to some of the men we held for the second harbour assault. We still haven't found the missing evidence, but other evidence is growing against her from further enquiries. She seems to have been known by the men who burned the ships. The charges against her will now include treason, as it's obvious she favours the Spartans".'

'Is there any chance she'll recover enough to be tried?'

'The physicians say not. They seem to think she should have died already, as she is eating nothing they give her. And if she dies, the priests of Athena have asked that her body be taken out to sea and disposed of there. Her family don't want her remembered at the temples, it seems.'

Themis was surprised. 'Even if she hasn't been convicted?'

'That's what I've been ordered to arrange.'

'Can I be informed if this happens?'

'I'll mention that in my report.'

Themis stood watching him march off, his mind more conflicted than ever with unanswered questions and frustrated guesses.

'Perhaps I need to do as Androklos said and stop worrying about the past,' he thought as he turned away. *'Xenovia obviously can't or won't tell me if she's been working with Nereus. Melissa's contacts haven't heard any rumours of further attacks from within the City. Nor have my own among the potters and sculptors. Lysikles hasn't asked to see me. All I can do is set the slaves to watch and listen.'* He swore under his breath. Then he grinned and whispered to the dawn, 'But I could get on with getting married!' He broke into a run.

A few days later, Melissa sent Themis the traditional fiancee's invitation to spend an evening at her father's house. As it turned out, this involved a great deal of teasing by Agorakritos and his male family members, and far too much wine. At the end of the evening, Themis was escorted upstairs to the women's rooms, and left outside Melissa's door, with much drunken whispering and banter.

Themis knocked and entered and found Melissa naked in her bed. He lay down beside her and began to stroke her thigh, but the wine sent him to sleep before he could go further.

He woke when she blew in his ear. She had lit a lamp and arranged a bowl in case he was sick. He was not, but he did have to go outside to the latrine. When he got back, she was lying naked on the bed, shivering.

'Get back under the cover,' he said, 'and we can warm each other up.'

Melissa snuggled in under the Thracian wolf skin specially bought for this occasion. 'But you're meant to leap on me and ravage me,' she said through her giggles.

'We've done that already, and now we know it's not our style, is it?' said Themis, gathering her into his arms. 'Just lie still and stop shivering. Are you not sore from last time behind the rosemary bush? We were a bit rough with each other.'

Melissa cuddled up to him. 'A bit, but I was sent a poultice by your sister.' Themis grunted happily. 'Of course,' he said, stroking her back gently and deliberately, and then her buttocks …

Chapter 58: missing

(Breeds of Sheep 38)

'Are you off to the pharmacy again?' asked Themis as he and Photios scraped off after exercise. The weather was windy and rain threatened.

'I like to sit in the tavern opposite and watch Popi's clients come and go. You wouldn't believe who uses her concoctions!' Photios pulled on a fine chiton and took his warm brown himation off the hook. 'But it'll be too cold to sit outside today. Come with me and have some breakfast.'

Wrapped in their cloaks, they sat under the awning until rain drove them inside. They'd seen two generals and a philosopher go into Popi's shop, apart from seven well-dressed slaves and a handful of foreigners.

'All those visitors just in the time it's taken us to eat our meal,' said

Themis thoughtfully.

'We'll see Nikias or Alkibiades next,' joked Photios.

'Not a good enough reason for you to sit here all day.' said Themis.

'Well … not that on its own.' Photios' eyes sparkled. 'Actually, there's a girl. She lives in the large house next to the pharmacy.'

'Ah. Do I know her?'

'She was at Vravrona before Melissa. Her name is Terpsichore. I am working up the courage to meet her.'

'Good luck!' said Themis. 'Look, I have to go …'

'Are you off to see Melissa?'

'Not just now. Her new brother keeps getting chills so she's busy. Also, I find the atmosphere of expectation in that house uncomfortable.'

Photios snorted into his cup. 'Not paying you enough attention, eh?'

'It's not that,' Themis said with a grin. 'Melissa sent for the old nurse they had, but she hasn't appeared, so Melissa's on duty all the time.'

'Didn't you say your mother's coming in to the city for the winter?'

'She's here. That's why I have to go. But she's only staying a few days and she wants to talk to Melissa of course, about the wedding.'

'I can't somehow imagine you as a married man,' said Photios, standing up to walk with Themis.

'Nor I you,' said Themis putting an arm round Photios' shoulders.

'Don't tempt the fates!' said Photios with a laugh. 'There's little likelihood I'll be seen as a good catch.'

A man had arrived at Popi's shop. A woman who looked a little like Popi stepped out into the rain to welcome him. The man had his back to the street, but Themis recognised Tryfonos, the merchant. He and Photios stopped under the awning and watched. The woman was shaking her head.

'But you must know!' said Tryfonos. 'She was Popi's owner! Where have they taken her?'

Themis looked at Photios in alarm. He took a step forward. Photios held him back, but kept his eyes on the scene.

Popi herself appeared as the other woman stepped back into the shop. 'But *I* can help you with anything you need,' Popi was saying, her eyes wide and welcoming and she ushered Tryfonos into the shop. 'There is no need to insist that my mistress makes up your recipe.' The door closed.

'That's Tryfonos!' said Themis. 'He's a customer of Master Zephus. And I owe him thanks for helping stop the fire at my house. But did you hear what he said?'

'Xenovia must make him something very special.' Photios grinned

'But he said she's gone!' said Themis. 'Come with me to see what's happened?'

At the hospital, Xenovia's room was unguarded and empty, the hammock taken down and a bed placed under the window.

Themis went straight to the small office at the entrance to the asylum block. An elderly man was arranging tablets on a shelf.

'What has happened to the priestess Xenovia?' asked Themis.

'Ah. You are not the first to ask that this morning,' said the old man. 'And she was a criminal, they say. So many people interested in a shriveled up, evil old woman …'

'Where is she?'

'They took her away to dispose of,' said the old man. 'They came from Athena's temple. No need to worry about her any more.'

'When did she die?'

'Around midnight, I understand. "They took her away without delay."' The old man chuckled as he turned back to his task, murmuring further lines from a play Themis didn't recognize.

Themis went out again into the rain, shaking his head. 'She's died!' he shouted to Photios, who was waiting under a tree for shelter. 'It seems she died in the night and they took her away and dropped her in the sea! Popi must know about it. And Xenovia's family. I'll just see the director here. Someone must know something!'

But the hospital director was no further help. 'We were asked to hand her over to the priesthood yesterday evening after she had a seizure,' he said. 'I didn't see her myself, but the staff said it was clear she was no longer breathing. So we complied.'

Themis asked, 'Who else has been here since then?'

'That you must ask the staff in the asylum block. No one else has asked to see *me* about this.'

Themis was furious. He left Photios to go home and ran back to the pharmacy, by which time he was wet through. Popi did not look so pleased to see him as she had been to see the wealthier Tryfonos. She shrugged her shoulders at Themis' questions. 'My mistress gave me my instructions. Some time ago she signed the shop and my freedom over to me upon her death. If her body is to be thrown into the sea, I can't stop that.'

'Do you know where it is now?'

'No,' said Popi, shuddering and looking at the floor. 'They took her away – the family took her away.'

'What did Tryfonos want earlier?' Themis asked.

'Tryfonos?' Popi's eyes were wide and round as she stared at him. 'What d'you mean?'

'Tryfonos was here this morning. He seemed angry about Xenovia not being at the hospital.'

'Then you know what he wanted,' said Popi dismissively. She looked exhausted.

Themis said, 'Look, I know this must be hard for you. But what I meant was, why did he want Xenovia herself? Was she making a specific mixture for him?'

'I don't know. I have no record of that. He usually buys one of our standard recipes. And he and the mistress sometimes had a chat. But today he asked about her, bought some of his usual, and went away.'

'Just like that?' said Themis.

Popi nodded wearily.

Themis looked up at the churning grey sky in frustration. 'She can't really be gone! How will I get at the truth now?'

'She is gone,' said Popi. 'It's over. We've all known it was coming for a while now.' She turned away.

A tiny part of Themis was ecstatic that this was true at last. But another part was horrified at the issues Xenovia's death left unresolved. Perhaps, if he could get Nereus to talk to him he would learn something, especially if the general hadn't heard of Xenovia's death yet. He set off to run to Nereus' expensive home in Melite, not far away.

As he ran he formed a strategy in his mind. He'd start by saying it seemed the marine corps of swimmers hadn't had much backing. Would Nereus be prepared, in spite of the unpleasantness with Melissa, to accept Themis' help in advocating such a project? Had steps already be taken to realize this aim? Were there others involved that Themis would know and be able to influence?

He wished he'd brought Frog or Yellow with him. In fact, maybe he should go home and get one or both of them. If Xenovia had been part of his organization, Nereus probably knew already about her death. He stopped in the road, unsure now what to do. A voice called his name.

'Themistokles! Have you come to see me?'

It was Apollodorus. Themis realized he was standing just outside the former Archon's house.

'No, not you,' said Themis. 'At least, I'm pleased to see you, but I was hoping in fact to find General Nereus at home.'

'He's not there at the moment. I saw him walking down to the centre of the City a short time ago.' Apollodorus gestured towards his house. 'Come in and allow me to congratulate you properly on your engagement,' he said. 'You seem to be wet through. Surely you have a few moments … ?'

Themis suddenly remembered his mother was probably at home waiting for him. 'Thank you,' he said.

With his wet cloak dripping by the street door, sweetmeats and wine on the low table, and deep cushions at his back, Themis began to relax. Apollodorus was saying, 'I heard that Agorakritos' citizenship was suddenly passed and that he immediately cancelled his agreement with Nereus concerning Melissa. Did you have anything to do with that?'

'Nothing at all,' said Themis. 'I was as surprised as everyone else.'

'But you put in your suit for her immediately, I hear.'

'Quite soon,' said Themis. 'Not indecently so, I hope. It was almost two months since her mother died.'

Apollodorus smiled. 'Hmm,' he said. 'So why do you need Nereus?'

'Well … I cannot prove what I'm going to tell you,' said Themis, 'but I believe that Nereus ordered my murder on the road. Lysikles sent me a warning and lent me an archer to prevent it. Which we did, and the assassins were arrested, but were themselves killed in jail. Some time later, my house was fired by two men who seem to have been paid to do so by a man who looked like Nereus. I want to learn whether that was really him and if Xenovia, who has now died, was also involved.'

Apollodorus said, 'Has she now? That may be relevant.' He leaned back and looked thoughtfully at Themis. 'I suggest you get your facts together and accuse him to the Council. Face to face, he will just ridicule you. I learned this morning that there's a case being put together against him for fraud in the buying and selling of slaves. Your evidence might be useful.'

Themis stared at the older man. 'Are you sure?'

'That's what I heard.'

'How do you think my evidence could help with that? All it shows is that he has been hounding me ever since I got back from Epidaurus.'

'It it's proven, what it shows is that he's prepared to carry on his vendetta anonymously instead of challenging you directly. The whole city knows he's jealous of you. Someone as underhanded as that should not be a general, even if he is not found guilty of the fraud charges.' Apollodorus stood up. 'It's a shame he can't come out in the open with his personal anger. He's usually such an efficient and energetic citizen.'

'I know he has powerful friends,' said Themis, standing up too. 'I'll do what you say, and try to be patient. But all I really want to do is to challenge him to a boxing match!'

Apollodorus laughed as he led Themis to the door. 'That's natural,' he said, 'especially from you. But keep your rage for the Spartan.'

Themis sighed and took the hand Apollodorus offered. 'Thank you for your advice,' he said. 'Now I must go and meet my mother, who has come into the City to check up on me!'

'Not an easy task,' said the older man waving him off. Themis ran towards home wondering whether Apollodorus meant his own task or his mother's.

Chapter 59: distrust

'Mrs Eirini is up in her rooms with your intended,' said Frog.

'Really?' said Themis. 'Melissa didn't tell me she was coming today.'

'I don't think she was expecting to see your mother,' said Frog. 'She came dressed to undress.' He winked.

Themis shook his head and glared at Frog.

'Don't blame me.' Frog's eyes were innocent. 'Blame … Eros, perhaps? Or Aphrodite.' He ran laughing to the kitchen when Themis raised a comic fist at him.

In the courtyard, Themis could hear the murmur of conversation from the rooms upstairs. He smiled and climbed the stairs, carefully missing the creaky fourth step. He sat at the top, shamelessly listening to his mother and future wife.

Melissa seemed to be disagreeing respectfully, 'And so I must be pregnant! And if I'm pregnant, there'll be no excuse not to marry.'

'Are we sure now that your family is accepted as citizens?' said Eirini.

'My father says the official acceptance ceremony will be in a few days, but in fact he has a signed certificate already.'

'But if the process isn't completed, we could have problems with property and voting rights.' Eirini sounded sceptical and stern. 'And of course, you need to be sure you have had full coitus.'

Melissa exploded with a quiet laugh. 'Oh, I'm sure,' she said.

Themis sat and smiled, shaking his head at his mother's tone.

'And when did you last have menses?'

'It's thirty-five days today.'

'So they *are* late. But you are very young and they may be irregular.'

'They've been on time since I started,' said Melissa more seriously. 'D'you think I might not be pregnant after all?'

'It's possible still. We'll only be really sure when you begin to swell.'

'If I'm not, are you suggesting we postpone the wedding?' Melissa sounded incredulous.

'Usually the groom will not commit himself to marriage until he's sure his fiancée will give him children. You know that from our lessons at Vravrona. And for Themis this year, it seems he feels it's imperative. He made a promise to his brother.'

'I know about the promise,' said Melissa, her tone suddenly deflated. 'I hadn't thought he might choose someone else if I don't conceive.'

Themis thought of interrupting to deny any such plan, but wanted to know what his mother would say, so he kept quiet.

'Well,' Eirini was saying, 'he might stretch the point a little, but he really does have to provide us with an heir soon.' Eirini was now trying to sound patient and kind, but Themis knew that wobble in her voice was not weakness, but the determination to take control.

He ran silently down the stairs and picked up the satchel of chisels he'd left on a bench. He dropped it and the chisels spilled onto the paving with a great clatter.

Eirini's face appeared at the window of the bedroom she now used. 'Ah, Themis!' she called and disappeared. Melissa looked out as Eirini started down the stairs. Themis looked up at her and winked in reassurance, then went forward to greet his mother.

Some days later, looking at a drawing by Melissa of herself weeping because she wasn't pregnant, Themis was shaking his head.

'No, Mama,' he said. 'I had not thought of revoking, as you put it, my engagement to Melissa. At present, that is not an option.' He had invited his mother into the andron and sat opposite her, fondling Yellow's ears. He was surprised at how angry he felt at her suggestion, but was trying not to show it. She had lost so much.

His mother stood up and walked up and down between the couches. 'But you also promised your brother.'

'I did. And Melissa and I've been doing our part to keep that promise, believe me. If Melissa's body is still too young, or she's too tired and grieving for her mother, or the gods have different plans … well, I'm happy to keep trying.' He shrugged and grinned.

'There are of course plenty of other girls.'

'Stop it, Mama!' he said, standing up. 'Give it a little more time. It's still forty days until the winter solstice.'

'But you are ordered to Argos next month. If she doesn't conceive by then, how will you marry this winter?'

'I will be back and we will marry after the solstice as planned,' said Themis. 'If we find that she does not conceive within the first year, I may think again, but just now I can't imagine it.'

'So, we should go on with the wedding preparations?' Eirini was deeply disapproving. 'Would that be wise?'

'Of course we should – and yes, it would!' He sighed, stepped towards his mother and opened his arms. 'It's no good tempting the Fates by talking like this. They're having enough fun with us as it is! We can deal with this as a family.'

Eirini looked up at him, pursing her lips. '*You* will have to deal with it,' she said. 'No one can do it for you.'

Themis had to laugh. He wrapped his arms round his reluctant mother and said, 'How right you are, Mama.'

They walked out into the courtyard, an uneasy peace between them. As Eirini began up the stairs to her room, Frog appeared.

'Just had a message from the pharmacy woman.'

Themis frowned. 'Popi?' he asked.

'Yes. Seems she has something for you from the dead priestess.'

Themis looked up at his mother on the stairs. 'I'd better go and see what it's about,' he said. 'Do you want to come too? Perhaps she'll sell us something to solve our "problem".'

'I'd leave that kind of thing to Chloe if I were you,' said Eirini. 'No need for all the world to know your bed business.'

Themis sighed, shook his head, and led Frog into the kitchen.

'Shall I come with you?' asked Frog. 'It could be a trap.'

Themis nodded. 'Good idea,' he said. The Skionian looked up from the fire bench, her eyes round with apprehension. She, at least, was clearly pregnant now.

>>>

'You know this is pointless,' said Suzanne. 'All they ever want is to cross examine me until they can put a label on what they think I've "got" and then write it up in their professional papers to show how clever they are.'

Bernie pushed the door into the department open. 'Are you really that cynical or just trying to be funny?' she asked.

Suzanne laughed shortly. 'I've learned from experience,' she said.

'Then why did you come?' asked Bernie. 'You've just got cold feet. Not all men are Levites. Some are Samaritans.' She pushed Suzanne up to the reception desk. 'Try,' she whispered. 'Just this once.'

They sat in silence for a while. Bernie took a photo with her phone of a wallchart showing the areas of the brain. Suzanne was flipping over the pages of the National Geographic, but she said, 'You promise not to tell anyone about this – or why we're here?'

'Of course,' said Bernie. 'This is for my own education. I won't be posting it on social media. I've even switched off my location.'

'Miss Short?' said the receptionist. 'Mr Sears is ready for you.'

Suzanne stood up and looked at Bernie's hopeful face. She nodded, gathered her thoughts, then went over to the door and knocked.

'Come in! Come in.'

He stood up behind his desk to greet her. He was tall and rangy with crinkly dark hair and a long, smiling face.

'Please, take a seat there,' he said and moved over to where there were two deep armchairs either side of a low coffee table. On the coffee table there was a pile of books. The top one had a picture of a Greek vase on the front. Suzanne stopped in surprise, then ran her fingers over it as she sat down. The painting was by Makron on a pot by Hieron, like the kylix Themis had in pride of place in the andron. The painting on this one was Helen being taken away by Paris and the gods, but on Themis' it was a symposium.

She thought to herself, '*Careful. Keep each reality separate.*' As Mr Sears sat down in the other chair, she looked around the office. It was modern, light and cheerful – the opposite of the waiting room.

'What would you like me to call you?' asked Mr Sears.

'Suzanne is fine,' said Suzanne. There was a time when she thought this was a trick question, but she'd soon learned it was just routine. She lowered herself into the other armchair.

'You pole vault, I gather,' said Mr Sears.

'Trying to get back in training,' she said. 'I broke my leg in the summer and it looks like I'll miss the Commonwealth Games next year even though I got through the qualifiers.'

'How did you break your leg?'

'By not being careful enough where I stood. I fell down a bank in France.'

'So are you angry with yourself, or with your "other self"?'

Suzanne looked up at his face. His eyes were concerned, blue-grey and kind. She relaxed her shoulders.

'It never occurred to me to be angry with "my other self",' she said. 'He's not really "another self". He's a totally different person. And he had nothing to do with it.'

'He's not antagonistic?'

'Not at all.' Suzanne was confused.

'Many people hear voices that tell them to do things that will harm them or others,' said Mr Sears.

'Oh yes. I've heard of that. But no, that's not what I experience.'

'So, if that is not your problem, how do you think I can help?'

'Well, as you must know from my notes, I started seeing this boy's life in 2010.' Mr Sears nodded. 'Well, he's a man now and I began seeing through his eyes again a few months ago. I keep his mind separate from my own by writing down what happens to him. It's hard sometimes, living in two minds, but I was managing fine until lately. And now I'm failing. I've been disturbing my housemates with noisy nightmares, and I had a bit of a meltdown. They thought I'd taken hard drugs.' Suzanne took a long breath. Mr Sears sat patiently watching her. 'So I read up on what you can do as a surgeon and I thought you might be able to find where in my brain this all happens and tone it down a bit, or make it possible for me to "switch it off". I have no control, you see.'

'What happened that triggered the meltdown?'

Suzanne watched him carefully as she said, 'The battle of Mantinea.' He looked impressed. She went on, 'My man was wounded and his brother was killed. It was … messy … Watching someone play computer war games brought it all back and I couldn't stop my reactions.'

'How do you feel about it now?'

'Honestly? I feel a failure. I feel stupid talking about it.'

'Why do you feel stupid? It must have been a horrendous experience.'

Suzanne stood up and paced the floor. 'That was. Yes. But in general, the whole thing makes me feel stupid. And angry with myself. And …'

'Different from other people,' Mr Sears finished.

'They don't know how to deal with it – *I* don't know how to deal with it! They think I'm lying, or that I'm showing off somehow. I thought maybe you could help.' She looked at him, a challenge in her eyes. 'Can you?'

'Well, I know you're not lying,' he replied mildly. 'I know that from the test results all those years ago. During the few moments when you say you "went back", the scan shows that the activity in your brain followed a completely different pattern from your "normal" brain activity. What I couldn't see is where the source of that activity is in your brain, though I'd be interested to find out. If I knew, I might be able to get rid of him. Would you want me to eradicate him?'

'NO!' Suzanne almost shouted.

He looked down, thinking. Then he said, 'So your problem seems to be that, although what I'll call your conscious mind is able to manage the two lives and keep them separate, your subconscious mind isn't, and you see that as a failure.'

'Yes. So I read up on Post Traumatic Stress Disorder,' Suzanne said. 'It feels a bit like they describe that, though perhaps not as bad. I know it all happened a long time ago, so mostly I can think of it as a kind of movie.'

'Has it occurred to you that you may be creating this man's life yourself?'

'You mean imagining it?'

'Yes.' His smile was very attractive, genuinely kind.

Suzanne sighed. 'Yes. I've thought about that. And I really wish I could believe it. Then I'd feel he was a part of *me*, part of *my* mind, and it wouldn't be so weird, so … what's the word? Inexplicable? And frightening, if I let it.'

'But it doesn't feel like that?'

'No. When it comes, it's too real. Too unpredictable. And full of his memories and references that I can't possibly know.'

'Interesting,' said Mr Sears. 'But hard work? A bit of a burden?'

'Yes. Keeping up with the writing and never being sure whether there'll be more, or when. But I need it, to be clear which is my world and which is his.'

'Quite enlightening, I imagine.' Mr Sears' smile was now a little envious.

Suzanne nodded. 'Mm.' Then she laughed. 'Especially about some things. It's mostly not war.'

'No wonder you don't want to lose him. So I definitely couldn't help with surgery. But you know, if I had that kind of contact with someone from a different time, and of the opposite sex, I would see it as a gift, not a burden.'

Suzanne sat down slowly. 'A gift?'

'Yes. It must be fascinating.'

Suzanne thought for a few moments. 'But it's a gift that feels dangerous, like it could make you crazy. And it marks you as different.'

'But you *are* different. We all are.' Mr Sears shrugged and smiled. 'That's not a bad thing, you know. Think about ways you could use that difference, what you learn from it.' He looked at his watch and went on, 'Do you have a friend you trust to tell if you feel too different, or that you've lost control?'

Suzanne shook her head. 'Not that I trust … enough. No. No.'

'Would you be prepared to talk to a professional counsellor if I recommend one? I know someone in Lancaster who is discreet and kind.'

'Depends on their attitude,' said Suzanne, remembering other mental health professionals in her past. Then she looked at him with bitter resignation. 'So you *do* think I'm ill.'

'No! Not ill. Far from it,' he exclaimed. 'You do seem to see things in stark black and white, as success or failure. And that is making you unhappy. But you're managing your life extraordinarily well, achieving better than most. And this is just another level of extraordinary.'

'You were ages,' said Bernie when Suzanne came out at last. 'And have you been crying?'

Suzanne grinned tearily. 'Yes. Kind of.'

'What did he say? Tell me!' Bernie pulled Suzanne down beside her on the waiting room chairs.

'He's something else, you know,' said Suzanne. 'He said that, from the file, he knows I'm a perfectly "normal" person, but with an extra dimension! He showed me how lucky I am and what opportunities it gives me, even if what I "see" isn't true – like that I'm imagining it. That, in itself, is a kind of power, he says. Oh, and I'm too obsessed with measuring success and failure.'

'He's right there!' said Bernie with a laugh. 'You always have been.'

They stood up and nodded goodbye to the receptionist.

As they walked along the street outside, Bernie said, 'So he couldn't say whether you're imagining it or it's some other weird nameless phenomenon?'

Suzanne laughed. 'I like that – nameless phenomenon. That's what I'll call him now – my nameless phenomenon.' They crossed a busy road, then she went on, 'It is conceivable to you of course that I'm imagining it, and sometimes I can't see what else could explain it, but I really don't think I am. Anyway, Mr Sears says he doesn't need to see me again, operating is pointless, and I can see a counsellor if I want to. And I'm not ill!!! So-o-o-o.' And she did a little twirl on the pavement. 'This trip is being a great success – if I'm allowed to use that word! I feel a different person, and David's arriving tomorrow, *and* I've seen you again!' She put her arm through Bernie's as they walked.

'Come on then!' said Bernie. 'Lunch by the river at my favourite café.'

Chapter 60: bonuses

(Breeds of Sheep 39 – Keeping on with this and thinking how to make something of it – a blog, a book, a script? And trying to get through to Themis to say thank you, because of course he's real – at least to me. But I don't think he notices his 'hum' much these days ...)

Popi's hands were shaking as she handed Themis a battered tablet. 'She must have written this a while ago,' she said. 'I can't believe it ...'

Themis looked at the outside of the tablet. It was quite old, much used, and the drawing of the simple leaf with the veins at right angles that was Xenovia's seal was scratched on the outside. Inside, the writing was not well-formed, impressed deeply into the wax in anger perhaps, or fear. Themis read aloud what it said.

'While I could, I tried. The gods know, I tried to help them involve him. But Themistokles evades them every time. Why doesn't he see that to survive he must join the ones with the real power, not those who are blind to his merits? What a boon he would be to them! The City doesn't appreciate him. And the others will lose patience and kill him if he can't be persuaded. He MUST choose: be rich and powerful beyond his dreams, or be on his way to Hades. As for me, I have done all I can. They will have to find another agent here. I have my own path to follow to Hades.'

There was no signature and no addressee.

Themis looked up at Frog, whose face was sharp with bitterness.

Popi said, 'I found it among the tablets of recipes. I was looking for a particular one and flipped this open to see what it was.' She spread her hands and shook her head. 'I couldn't believe what I read.'

Frog said, 'She taught you to read?'

'I learned from my previous master,' said Popi. 'He had this pharmacy business, with ingredients coming from all over the world. He needed help to keep records.'

'So how did you come to be Xenovia's?' asked Themis.

'She came to work for my master, making the goods. And when he got sick, he sold the whole thing to her, workshop, shop and slaves.'

'When did she join him?'

'About ten years ago. She'd been away and got injured. She stayed hidden, of course, because of her appearance. But she knew a lot of people and had studied herbs and remedies when she was a priestess.' Popi's eyes filled with tears. 'I had no idea she did things like this, too.'

Themis sighed. 'Sadly, it's no surprise to me. But it's a relief to know that her plan was to have me accept working for the enemy, not to be assassinated. Well, Mistress Popi, now you have a fine shop, with an assistant and a good client list. You'll do well.' He lifted the tablet. 'Thanks for this. It must go to the Archon as evidence in her case.'

'Which will be closed now, of course,' said Frog quickly, seeing Popi's look of horror.

Themis nodded. 'This will mean they can close the procedings and, as you said, it's over now.' *'But not for me,'* he thought. *'Not ever for me.'*

Lysikles, Archon of the City Watch, was by the open window to the garden when Themis came in. He was eating a bun that smelled of garlic. Turning, he said with his mouth full, 'Sorry to hurry you, Themistokles, but, as you can see, I'm hurrying myself, too!' He swallowed and came away from the window. 'You missed the Assembly yesterday but it gave me a lot to do. We'll need all the resources we can muster and the help of the gods for our Thracian campaign.'

'They said you have news for me, and I have some for you,' Themis said.

'Right. Well, I gather that the priestess who has been causing us all so much trouble is now finally dead.' The Archon was looking at a scroll laid out on his long table.

'I … Yes,' said Themis. 'The healers say that she had a seizure and died. The temple staff took her away for anonymous burial at sea.'

'Good. You must have heard that Alkibiades' plans for Argos have come to naught?'

'Argos made a treaty with Sparta not long after the battle at Mantinea,' said Themis bitterly.

'Correct. A great blow to our Peloponnesian plans. But our intelligence insists that the Argive democrats will not stay quiet.' The Archon had finished his bun and was rolling the scroll up. 'It looks as though there'll be an uprising and democracy will be restored. However, at present we are not intervening, and indeed are making arrangements to withdraw from the fort at Epidaurus, as well. So there won't be much action in the Peloponnese for Athens this winter.'

'I suppose not,' said Themis, wondering where this was leading.

'The walls from Argos to the sea that Alkibiades so favours will not be built – at least not now – so our generals won't need your expertise there. As I said, they are now concentrating on Thrace and Halkidiki. We need the tribute and the timber from there for our ships.'

'I see,' said Themis. He was being told there would be no work for him from the City for a while. This suited him well, although the income would have been helpful. But the thought of being free to sculpt and spend time with Melissa was much more appealing.

'However, I'm told that work on the temple of Nike on the Akropolis has resumed. Your aging friend Kallikrates has asked if you can be assigned to him again to add to the decorations. Apollodorus, my predecessor, backed up his application and the Archons have provisionally agreed. Does that suit you?'

'Yes,' Themis said quietly. 'That suits me very well. Thank you.' He made a mental note to send his thanks to Apollodorus.

Lysikles stowed the scroll in the honeycomb scroll-holder on the wall and pulled out another. 'Oh, don't thank me,' he said. 'Thank Kallikrates. You'll get the usual fees and bonuses, though they are less than they used to be, of course, because of the fragility of the peace with Sparta. Got to keep the costs down, you know. You said you had some news for me?'

'Yes. I think there's more than one "master traitor" harrassing me and the City. Xenovia was involved, but on the tablet I saw, she called them "them", not "him". Which might explain why their methods are not always synchronised.'

'Hah! Can I see this tablet?'

Themis handed it to him.

'Is this authentic?' asked Lysikles. 'Very helpful, if so. Look, you leave this with me and I'll make sure it's followed up. Meanwhile, if we find there's military engineering work needed, we'll be calling on you.'

'Of course,' said Themis, turning to go.

'Oh, one other thing,' said Lysikles. 'I want you to be aware that there are rumours that Persian spies have been seen at Lavrion near the silver mines and at Pireaus by the commercial docks.'

'There are always Persians among the traders,' said Themis.

'These are men who have been recognized personally. So the threat from the East is as dangerous as the threat from the Spartans. My point is that you should keep that in mind when you talk about any military installations you've been involved in,' said the Archon with emphasis.

Themis was insulted, but answered pleasantly, 'Of course, Archon. I shall guard sensitive information carefully, as always.'

'Thank you, Themistokles,' said Lysikles. 'Farewell, and please report to me anything you hear that might be relevant to the security of the City or blasphemy against the gods.'

Themis bowed slightly, turned smartly and left.

'That man!' he said to Frog as they walked out into the Agora, 'is so brusque he makes me feel like a raw recruit in the army. He didn't say a single thing I didn't already know, and he behaves as if I have no experience and I'm stupid.' He sighed and shrugged. 'Ah, well. What do we need to shop this afternoon?'

'Your mother asked me to remind you that you need to order a new bed for Melissa for after the wedding.'

'Won't she bring her own from her father's house?'

'They will need it for the nurse who will replace Melissa to look after her new brother.' Frog looked sideways at Themis. 'Unless of course you expect Melissa to sleep on the floor at your feet.'

Themis made a mischievous face. 'Other things happen on the floor,' he said. 'Beds are for sleeping comfortably. Yes, we'll get her a bed … '

Chapter 61: wedding

(Breeds of Sheep 40 – Managed to get this down before I forgot it all. Not sure if I've lost Themis for now, but I've gained so much more …)

Themis threw the vase down in frustration. It smashed on the flagstones with a satisfying crash.

'What was that?' called Frog as he came running out of the kitchen.

'I still can't get it right!' said Themis, gritting his teeth. He gestured to a row of five identical pottery vases on a shelf by the kitchen door, each with the same intricate, elegant drawing of a couple and their child, the perfect offering to Hera, goddess of marriage. 'Why do I have such a problem with painting this woman? Babies are usually the most difficult, but these are fine. It's just her I can't get right!'

Frog said, 'Stop thinking of her as Melissa. Just make her any pretty woman. The couple doesn't have to look like you and Melissa. And anyway, you can write her name on it if you think Hera won't know whom you're marrying.'

'Maybe I should offer Hera a sculpture rather than a jar,' said Themis, ignoring the irony.

'Sculptures can't hold walnuts and honey,' said Frog. He picked up one of the surviving rejects. 'And you can sell these, however bad you think they are.' He went back into the kitchen for a broom.

Themis went to the well and filled its basin with water. He washed his hands, then splashed his head and face. He shivered. *But it'll be even colder on the day of the wedding,* he thought. He tied his belt more securely round his himation and went back to his brushes.

Uncle Zephyros came barging through the street door like a wave into a cave mouth. 'Where's the boy?' His voice boomed round the courtyard. 'Where are you, Themistokles? Come and be congratulated!' He stood in the centre of the yard while his skinny slave unwrapped him from his warm woollen cloak.

Eirini leaned out of her window above. 'Welcome, Zephyros,' she called, 'but for the sake of the gods, sit down over there under the columns and let the slaves bring you something to eat. Themis is being bathed by his rowdy friends down at the gymnasium. He'll be back soon.' She withdrew.

Themis was in fact in the sluiceroom beyond the kitchen, being bathed by Frog and Photios. They exploded in silent laughter at his mother's adept diversion of his uncle's attention. Frog was dealing with the delicate matter of cutting and cleaning the naked Themis' toenails.

While Themis frowned and winced, trying to stop Yellow from drinking the washing water, Photios continued his song in a whisper. 'The ways of the goddess never cloy / Her ravishing voice leads to higher joy / Hear her as she breathes in your ear / And licks from your cheek your jubilant tear.'

'Ouch!' exclaimed Themis quietly. 'Do we really have to do this, Frog? I won't be using my feet for the main task today!'

'You might,' said Photios with a smile and a shrug. 'Maybe Aphrodite will suggest something with her ravishing voice that will mean you need clean feet.'

'Oh, please, Photios!' said Themis with a laugh. 'Give it a rest.'

There was a quiet scratch on the back door. Frog opened it to reveal three of Themis' and Photios' friends from the palaestra with Ariphron, Photios' cousin. Frog put a finger to his lips as he let them in.

'Not lost your pretty curls then,' murmured Ariphron, as Themis came out of the tiny sluiceroom to greet them. 'Nor your muscle tone!'

'Hey! How long is it, Ariphron?' said Themis, embracing him.

'Oh, ten years or more.'

'How is Miletus?'

Ariphron wrinkled his nose. 'It's a building site. Dust, wind, drunken builders.' He sighed. 'But it will of course be beautiful, one day.'

There was another commotion in the courtyard. They could hear Hipparchos' voice and the shrill excitement of Chloe's sons.

Eirini seemed to have come downstairs. The young men could hear her re-introducing her family to each other, handing out their wedding garlands, and arranging where they would all sleep. They heard her say 'Chloe, you and your family have a room waiting for you at our friend Lina's house on the corner.'

Themis gestured to his entourage that they needed to make an entrance, so they all poured out into the courtyard as if they'd just arrived, Photios calling for space for the groom and Yellow barking with excitement.

Eirini went on, 'Zephyros, I thought you could stay at the inn by the gate. They expect you around midnight.' She had to shout this last above the hubbub, and fell back with the others under the colonnades.

Themis, his bronze-coloured curls bound back with a gold fillet, his beard combed and oiled, was wearing only his sandals and a light towel, which Ariphron now whipped off. Chloe gasped and turned her back with a laugh, but Eirini contemplated her fine son with her head on one side. Photios had the groom-clothes over his arm. Ariphron had brought scented oil and began to take the lid off its tall, slim jar.

Themis groaned. 'Not perfume, please!' he said. The young men all jeered and closed in on him so that he was obliged to allow them to massage his chest, buttocks and thighs with oil that smelled of cedar, coriander and wild roses.

Melanas, here for the festivities, appeared and rubbed him down again with a rough cloth, and at last Photios could drop the luxurious sky-blue and gold wedding chiton over his head. Then everyone clapped and backed off as he swirled his deep red cloak with the silver border over his shoulder. Even Yellow stood silently in awe.

'The perfect picture of a handsome groom,' said his mother, coming forward with his elaborate garland of rosemary leaves, ribbons and snowdrops, yellow tulips and narcissus.

'I shall have my potters paint vases of this,' said Uncle Zephyros.

'If I don't beat you to it,' said a voice from near the street door. It was Master Zephus, with a slave carrying a magnificent jar. 'Meanwhile, this will have to serve.' He waved the slave forward.

Eirini nodded at Frog to take the vase and place it on a table by the wall. A scene of a traditional procession with chariot, happy couple, attendants, and gods was painted in beautiful detail around its elegant shape. It was full of oil and very heavy.

Themis came over and greeted Master Zephus. 'Thank you, Master,' he said, looking at the vase. 'One of your own! A real privilege. And thank you for coming,' he added. 'You should meet my Uncle Zephyros, as you have complementary interests in fine pottery!'

'Ah!' boomed Zephyros. 'Master Zephus! Your work is known to me. It sells above all else in Taras.' The two men moved into a quiet corner, their heads close together.

'Time you went and made your offerings, my son,' said Eirini. She turned to Themis' friends. 'When that's done, you can all go straight to Agorakritos' house. I'll meet you there.' She and Chloe, with her youngest on her hip and holding Yellow by his rope collar, climbed up the stairs to the women's rooms.

Melanas began to beat the rhythm, Photios and Frog produced flute and lyre. Dancing in a line, they escorted Themis out into the street. As they progressed, the crowd of followers grew. Themis was pulled and pushed as the dance demanded. He was teased as his attendants assessed him as a warrior, a lover and an athlete, agreeing or disagreeing loudly with the words of the songs.

But as they approached the sanctuary of Aphrodite of the Heavens off the Agora, they became less raucous. They all gathered round the altar and Frog handed Themis his offering of incense and honeyed cream. The priestess accepted these on behalf of the goddess and said the regulation prayers begging her to guarantee a happy, harmonious and successful marriage. Themis prayed silently as the official words rose and fell, calling on the goddess and Anthoussa to help him keep her daughter happy. He thought he heard her voice saying, 'She has two personas. Keep them both in mind and you'll be fine.'

They filed into the temple and wondered again at the statue of Aphrodite made by Phidias when he was young. The goddess wore flowers in garlands and sashes over the peacock blue painted robe sculpted as if clinging to her wet body. Her expression and the gesture of one hand made it seem that, at any moment, she would reach down and caress her suppliants. Themis now took from Frog's basket a smoothly polished, green marble lamp, shaped as a phallus between two breasts, his offering to the goddess of erotic love. It was a hundred years old, handed down in his father's family as a wedding present.

He was thinking, '*I'll be back, Aphrodite. Phidias' magic has made you real for me again. If it was you who brought me Melissa, you deserve a few more presents* … ' He saw his friends laughing at his grin, and straightened his face.

They moved on to the Heraion, and there Themis gave Hera the vase he had prepared. He'd followed Frog's advice and now the painting on it of the husband, wife and baby was just of a beautiful but typical family. Master Zephus had bought the other versions. Themis laid the money made in that sale in a woollen purse on the offering shelf. The prayers invoked Hera's help in conceiving and having many healthy children.

Then the drum began to beat again and they all clapped, glad that the serious part was over. The traditional Groom Song rose as they filed out into the street and made for Agorakritos' house, laughing, singing and dancing to the more polite of the standard lyrics.

The rest of the afternoon passed in a blur for Themis. There were the priestesses with their hymns and aromatic smoke as they burned herbs on the altar. There was the priest who sacrificed the ram and burned the gods' portion, making everyone even hungrier.

He only caught glimpses of Melissa in her red and gold patterned gown, with her veil pinned to hair piled high on her head, netted with a glittering snood. Her jewelry, some of which had been Anthoussa's, sparkled and her tooled crimson sandals gleamed. And he was only vaguely aware of the cooking smells, the perfumes, the teasing, the advice, the constant music and congratulations.

Most of the family from both sides were there, as well as friends from the palaestra, from school, from the army, friends of Diodotos, colleagues from the potteries. Themis greeted Kallikrates and even Polykleitos. He must have thanked everyone in the house for coming. But when it came to shaking Apollodorus' hand, he was pulled close by the former Archon, who said in his ear, 'Make sure you can come to the next Assembly in nine days' time. There will be a vote on whether or not to bring Nereus to trial'.

And later, as Themis was turning away from speaking to the indomitable Hermione, Nereus himself appeared in front of him.

'General!' said Themis, clenching his fists behind his back. He went on quietly, 'Have you greeted our host, Agorakritos? I will find him.'

'I won't be staying,' said Nereus loudly, staring unblinking at Themis' face. Voices around them fell quiet. 'I came to warn you, Themistokles.' His tone was so menacing that some of the guests gasped. He went on, 'Stop hounding me with your accusations and preparations for arraignment. They will come to nothing and will cost you dear in the process. And as for your marriage, you will regret this day in ways you cannot imagine. Melissa is a headstrong, deceiving and deceitful girl. She will make your life bitter and corrode your soul. You will wish you were in Hades with your brother.'

Themis was trying so hard to control his anger that he couldn't speak. He looked around for Agorakritos and found that Yellow was standing at attention beside him, bristling and tense, but their host was nowhere to be seen. Then Polykleitos was pushing his way through the crowd. He came up to Nereus and put an arm around his shoulder. 'Come, Nereus, old friend,' he said. 'You have said your piece. Come with me now. Let's go and see who's singing at the Odeion tonight.' He tried to move Nereus towards the door.

Nereus shook him off, giving him a glance of pure disdain. He turned and spat at Themis' feet, then marched through the parted crowd to the street door, followed by a scuttling slave.

Frog had appeared and grabbed Yellow's collar. Now he held out a cup of something to Themis. Polykleitos turned to the company and laughed loudly. He called out, 'You know you're the best when powerful men are jealous of you!' He grabbed the cup from Frog. 'Come, everyone, let us celebrate Themistokles' luck!' and he poured a libation, then drank deeply. The silence broke in a wave of laughter.

Themis murmured to Polykleitos. 'Well done, sir. Thank you.'

Polykleitos was making a disgusted face and looking into the cup. 'What, in the name of the gods above, is this?' he cried.

Frog took the cup gently from his hand. 'It's just water from our bitter spring at the farm,' he said.

Themis felt his shoulders relaxing. 'It's to remind me not to drink too much wine,' he said with a wry smile.

Polykleitos laughed. 'Well, I *need* too much wine to rinse away the taste of Nereus' jealousy – and that acorn juice!'

The meal was laid out with the women at the smaller table and the men at the longer one. Whenever Themis' wine cup was filled, Frog would come with the water jug and dilute it further. The meat was served with the obligatory quince accompaniment, and the cheeses and rare delicacies were beyond counting.

Agorakritos appeared at last and was a cheerful host in spite of Anthoussa's absence. He sang a happy, lilting song wishing the couple a long and fruitful marriage. Themis answered with a song of Sappho's he'd prepared about the perfect bride. He was singing for Melissa, but he couldn't see her face because of her veil, and anyway her women closed in around her. It ended, 'Even the brightest of stars grow dim / When the moon rises, flooding heavenly light across the skies.'

What did stand out clearly in his memory, though, among all the rituals and songs and aromas, and the riot of colour of everyone's best garments, was when Melissa stood up suddenly at her table in her crimson robes, called his name, and lifted the veil away from her face for a moment. He stood, too and play-acted being shot by Eros' arrow, before their attendants could drag each of them back down into their seats with guffaws and cautions.

The feasting gradually slowed down as everyone began picking at the remains during the toasts to Themis' and Melissa's health. Then Agorakritos got up and called his daughter to the centre of the courtyard. She was once more demurely veiled. He beckoned to Themis to join them there. Everyone was quiet.

Agorakritos called out to the starry sky, 'Themistokles son of

Kallistos and Eirini, I give you this girl, Melissa, daughter of mine with Anthoussa daughter of Iasos, in front of witnesses, for the creation of children and the extension of the honour and prosperity of our families.'

Melissa made the regulation bid for freedom by turning back towards the women. Themis grabbed her wrist to appplause and whistles. Themis heard Melissa giggle, though her head was turned away.

He raised his own voice. 'And I accept her. I will care for her and make children with her if the gods are willing.' He pulled her towards him. She resisted, looking away and down. He pulled again and caught her other wrist. He held them both in one hand, lifted her chin with the other and then lifted the veil completely back.

She flung her arms round him with a gleeful laugh.

Then there was dancing and more drinking. The men did their wildest leaps, Ariphron and Themis competed for who could stay upside down longest. The women made their circle dance seem erotic rather than demure and ended up surrounding Melissa so that she had to fight her way out of their 'prison'. The elders, meanwhile, were trying to arrange the procession to set off for Themis' house.

When at last it was ready, thirty torches lit their way and loud, unco-ordinated music accompanied them. Eirini went ahead and Chloe took the hand of her eldest son, Canthus, as he handed out tiny sweet buns full of almond and honey paste from a basket. The older men, including Hipparchos and Uncle Zephyros, and all the young men helped to lift the bride and groom onto the cart Melissa's father had given her, with Skopas driving. Their feet crushed the leaves and flowers of pine, myrtle and ivy, dried lavender and narcissus. Sweet scents rose around them. The guests picked up bundles and boxes, vases and baskets containing Melissa's possessions and joined the line.

The clamour woke the neighbourhood. Windows onto the street lit up. The songs got bawdier as they approached Themis' house.

'Nearly time to loose the shot, nearly time to show what's what.

Nearly time to get your prize, just be careful of the size.'

Themis was holding Melissa's hand. He squeezed it in sympathy, but when he looked at her, she licked her lips and raised her eyebrows at him. He laughed and squeezed harder.

At the house the street door stood open. The herm wore a lopsided garland and a lamp on his phallus. The guests filed into the courtyard behind the happy couple, delivering their bundles and baskets to Frog and Melanas, who stacked them in the corner and under the stairs. The railings were wrapped in coloured linen strips, ivy leaves and ribbons. A table along the back wall held watered wine and cordials, apples, nuts, olives and tiny loaves. The whole yard was lit with a blaze of torches.

The priestess of Hera had been waiting for them. She stood by a temporary altar in the middle of the courtyard. When the guests had all crowded in, she cried out above their noise, 'Sacred Queen and guardian of our families, Mighty Hera, hear me!'

The guests fell quiet and accepted the specially made drinking cups from the slaves, who were hurriedly handing them round. There was a little watered wine in the bottom of each.

'In humble thanks to you, dear Goddess, and with our pleas for a long and fruitful marriage between Themistokles and Melissa, we pour our libations to you,' called the priestess. She nodded at Eirini, who emptied her cup into the basin on the altar and also dropped some coins into a casket standing beside it. The other guests began to file past and do the same, led by Uncle Zephyros.

Once these final rites had been observed, the priestess was given her due and the casket spirited away by Eirini to join the other gifts. Everyone had their cups refilled. The music quickened and noise levels rose and rose.

A movement among the throng began to propel Themis and Melissa towards the bedroom that was once Themis' and Diodotos'. It had a window looking into the courtyard, now shuttered and curtained.

At the door of the bedroom, Melissa whispered in Themis ear and he called out, 'Just a minute. My wife ...' He smiled and repeated with a grin, 'My wife ... wishes to say something.'

He reached into the room and brought out a chair for Melissa to stand on. The guests were making 'this means he's henpecked' faces at each other and sniggering behind their hands. One or two murmured something about Nereus being right.

Themis gave Melissa his hand to help her up onto the chair.

'I just want to say two things,' she said in her clear, confident voice. She waited for the mumbling and giggling to stop. Then she said, 'Women, by tradition, do not speak on this, the most important day in their lives. But I want to thank everyone who helped me prepare for and celebrate this day: my own family, my friends from Vravrona where I learned to be a woman instead of a girl, Themis' family, particularly his mother, and friends. My father has given me a talent for drawing, as well as a generous dowry. My mother, although she left us before this long-awaited, perfect day, gave me life itself. And my husband ... ' She turned to him, ' … has been my best friend for as long as I can remember. So I am the luckiest mortal woman on earth!' Silent faces stared at her in surprise, most smiling or tearful.

'The second thing,' she went on, 'is to beg one last favour from you all.'

No one spoke, though one or two frowned at the flouting of tradition.

Melissa went on, 'I want you all to enjoy the generous hospitality of my mother-in-law and see out this day in song and dance, but to please … leave me and Themis to get on with our main task!' She turned to Themis and threw herself off the chair into his arms.

The explosion of laughter and applause raised the doves to a clattering flight, made Yellow and the local dogs bark, and brought grumbled protest from houses on the other side of the street. Themis nodded to Photios, who had promised to keep guard, put Melissa down and, taking her hand slipped into his bedroom. He stood breathlessly holding her in front of him by the shoulders while his friends, as tradition demanded, battered on the door he'd just closed and Photios and Yellow fended them off.

Themis turned and pulled the two bolts, top and bottom, into place. The battering continued sporadically.

Then he turned to his new wife and whispered, 'Ready?'

She held out her arms to him with sparkling eyes and a wide grin.

As Suzanne dashed into the terminal, the public address system was saying, 'Flight AF1068 from Paris, Charles de Gaulle has now landed.'

She took a deep breath and relaxed. Manchester Airport was in the middle of road alterations and the signage had defeated her. She'd been driving round and round, looking for short term parking, thinking she'd missed David's arrival. Now she had time to choose a place to offer him lunch.

At first they both felt awkward, hardly touching or speaking. They sat and ordered food. Once it had arrived, David leant forward in his chair and said, 'So how is your ancient man? You texted that the, er, shrink gave you courage to – how shall I say? – accept him'.

'Yes. To think of him as a bonus in my life, not a burden. When he came back this year I loved it at first, although it all felt different from before. But later, trying to keep his life separate from mine became more … difficult.' She smiled. 'Now I feel kind of lucky about it. But I'd much rather hear about you. I love listening to your wonky accent.'

'Hah! I 'ope "wonky" is a compliment,' said David with a grin. 'But it's good you feel better with him – a bonus, huh? And 'ow *is* he?'

'Oh, he's fine. More than fine ... very happy.' David was looking at her expectantly with his deep, limpid eyes, so she added, 'Actually, I've been a bit jealous of him lately.' Why did she say Actually? She never said Actually. '*Relax*,' she told herself.

'Why are you jealous?' He pronounced it jeelus. 'Surely, your life is more comfortable than his. World-wide foods, aeroplanes, cell phones, toilets!'

'True. But he has such intense feelings. Of course, I don't enjoy the grief and anger and pain and dirt. But just now he's in love and that makes everything even more vivid for him, even more exciting to be alive.'

'So,' said David. 'Don't be jealous. There's a better solution.'

Suzanne frowned a little. 'Like what?' she said.

David laughed. 'Be in love yourself! You know that I am only here, in this grey, cold country, because I am in love with you. So this is the perfect opportunity for you to be in love with me!'

Suzanne choked on her soup. Some of it landed on David's tee shirt. She jumped up, paper napkin in hand, to clean it off. He stood up, too, unfolding from his chair, using his own napkin to wipe away the worst.

'You are ready, no?' he said.

Suzanne stood still for a moment, gazing up in wonder at this laughing, beautiful, shining man. Her face felt like it would break apart with her smile. She said, 'I am ready, yes!' and stepped into his arms.

EPILOGUE

Popi leaned into the small wooden boat to arrange Xenovia's tightly shrouded body. It lay in the belly of the boat that was beached on the shingle in the dark sea-cave. A lantern cast wavering shadows from the bow. The priests and the Scythian guards were leaving. The rock walls echoed with the slap slap slap of their sandals as they climbed the steps in the tunnel to the top of the cliff and their way back to the city.

Popi had paid fifty drachmas to consign Xenovia to the deep herself. The Milesian, Menestratus, had provided the boat for a further five. He watched as she began loosening the wrapping over the battered face.

'You really tried to keep her alive,' he said, shaking his head with feigned regret. 'Such skills lost …' He bent to push the boat off the shingle beach into the dark water. 'Do you truly believe Poseidon is waiting for her?'

Popi nodded as she loosened the mouth strap that kept the jaw closed. 'You're lucky she taught me how to make that lenitive for your stomach,' she said. She was holding the two gold coins that had been laid on Xenovia's eyes to pay the ferryman to Hades. Menestratus got into the boat and held out a hand to her. 'It's a pity to waste those. One each?'

Popi ignored his hand and climbed in. She sat on the forward thwart, Xenovia's head between her feet. She looked up at him as he began to skull the boat out of the cave. Twin reflections of the lantern flame flickered in his insolent eyes. 'You can have both if you take the boat where I say,' she said.

He raised an eyebrow. 'And if I just throw you out with her?'

Popi suddenly had a wide-bladed knife in her hand. 'You might find it's you in the water, not me,' she said with a slight smile.

The lines round Menestratus' mouth hardened but he went on skulling. As they emerged from the cave into the starlight, Popi opened the lantern and blew out the flame. 'That way,' she said, pointing along the cliff to their left.

The dead woman in the bottom of the boat groaned.

<<<>>>

Dear Reader,

Thank you for reading this book! The story is imagined, of course. Long ago, when I began writing about Themistokles son of Kallistos, it seemed to me that fiction writers were writing only about ancient Greek Gods and Heroes. I wanted to write a story that could possibly happen to you or me at any time, a story that would answer the question, 'What was it *really* like to live in Athens in the 5th century BCE?' This was partly because I had spent more than 20 years of my own life in Athens, 25 centuries later!

The majority of my characters never lived (as far as I know!), and the personalities of those who did are imagined. However, I have tried to keep the story within the factual framework of what we know about 5th century BCE Greece (or Hellas as it was known then, and by the Greeks themselves even now), as well as the realities of life for a student athlete from Cumbria in 2017–18 CE.

However, I found that scholars through the ages have researched and disputed almost every facet of life in Classical Greece. In the words of Tom Holland, in the Preface to his book *Persian Fire*, 'Readers should certainly be warned that many of the details out of which this book's narrative has been constructed are ambiguous and ferociously disputed'. I have kept to what I found that was relevant to my story from primary sources like Herodotus, Pausanias, Thucydides and others, as well as painted vases and carved inscriptions. But I have added unattested details that logically might have existed, such as the girls' school in Vravrona. And I have used modern pronunciation/spelling for most of the names, as explained on page x.

After *The Boy with Two Heads* was published in 2012, the year of the London Olympics, 30th in the modern era, the main characters remained in my mind, insisting on growing up. Eventually, after many years of resistance, I began to record parts of their adult lives. This was before the Covid-19 pandemic that arrived in the UK in 2020.

The resulting Connection Trilogy is made up of *The Boy in Two Minds* (the revised version of the The *Boy with Two Heads*) as Book 1, *The Girl in Two Worlds* as Book 2, and *An Ancient Connection* as Book 3, which is planned for publication in 2022.

Acknowlegments

A special thank you to those who published reviews of *The Boy with Two Heads* (now *The Boy in Two Minds*) all those years ago! (see first page)

Meanwhile, many people have helped and supported me while I wrote *The Girl in Two Worlds*. The following are among them.

Andrew Petch inspired me to begin and encouraged me throughout. He, Sally Brown, Hilary Turnbull, Alexandra Petch, Connie Jensen (who designed the Birkby Books logo), Dimitris Konstantinidis, Christina Steele, and Dolly Daniel, all had various drafts of the manuscript inflicted on them for comment. Caroline Lawrence took an enthusiastic and helpful interest. The British School at Athens gave me access to their library. David and Catherine Landsman, and Costas Joakimides gave me opportunities in Greece for on-site research. The warden at the Argive Heraion provided me with useful information, as did Hara Yiannakaki of the 2012 excavation team at Sparta. Holly Bradshaw (formerly Bleasdale), Olympic pole vault bronze medalist of Tokyo 2020, was an unknowing inspiration. Fliss Watts ironed out some important details. She also painted the original artwork for the cover, which Kate Jensen designed. Brian Donnelly was my mainstay and support at all times, while Katy Donnelly and family kept me in touch with reality.

Thank you all.

Twitter: @JuliaMNewsome, FaceBook: J M Newsome, author
Blog: www.kneadtowrite.blogspot.com

Birkby Books